The Red Ribbon

Also by H.B. Lyle

The Irregular: A Different Class of Spy

H.B. LYLE

The Red Ribbon

Leabharlanna Poiblí Chathair Baile Átha Cliath
Dublin City Public Libraries

HODDER &
STOUGHTON

First published in Great Britain in 2018 by Hodder & Stoughton
An Hachette UK company

I

Copyright © H.B. Lyle 2018

The right of H.B. Lyle to be identified as the Author of the Work
has been asserted by him in accordance with the
Copyright, Designs and Patents Act 1988.

A CIP catalogue record for this title is
available from the British Library

Hardback ISBN 978 1 473 65548 5
eBook ISBN 978 1 473 65546 1

Typeset in Plantin Light by Palimpsest Book Production Ltd, Falkirk, Stirlingshire

Printed and bound in Great Britain by Clays Ltd, Elcograf S.p.A.

Hodder & Stoughton policy is to use papers that are natural, renewable
and recyclable products and made from wood grown in sustainable forests.
The logging and manufacturing processes are expected to conform to the
environmental regulations of the country of origin.

Hodder & Stoughton Ltd
Carmelite House
50 Victoria Embankment
London EC4Y 0DZ

www.hodder.co.uk

For Annalise, R&E

Part 1

I

Millicent tried not to hurry.

No one suspected anything, she was sure. But she tried not to hurry. She flicked on the electric light and looked at her face briefly in the silver platter on the kitchen dresser. It would have to do. No time. She left a small package out for Poppy. No one at the Embassy had ever been mean to her exactly, but she couldn't stay. Not once she'd found out. And there was Harold.

She put her hand to the back door, listened to the cries above for a moment – ecstasy, real and fake. The hinges creaked. She peered along the covered walkway to the back gate, saw no one. It was now or never—

'Evening, Millie,' a voice came out of the darkness, soft and sinister.

She hesitated. 'All right, Big T?'

'Off out?'

'My shift's done. I cleared it with Delphy, check if you like. You?' Millicent's voice trembled.

Big T, or Tommy, scratched his chin. Millicent could hear the stubble bristle. Her eyes grew accustomed to the darkness and she picked out his long, heavily muscled form leaning against a post, as if he was waiting for her. He wore no hat and he stood still, but his shoulders seemed to twitch and ripple under his shirt. After a moment, he cracked his enormous knuckles and replied.

'Me? Came for a snout, didn't I?'

Millicent saw no smokes. She nodded, pulled her handbag close and stepped past him along the walkway. Don't run. Don't hurry.

As she reached the back gate, she heard Big T's muffled voice carrying through the night. 'Mind how you go,' he echoed.

She closed the gate behind her, looked left and right, then headed south to Buckingham Palace Road. Don't hurry. With every step, with each yard she put between herself and the Embassy, her spirits lifted. Never again. The number 11 turned the corner off to her right and she flitted across the road just in time to step onto the plate.

Each advertisement inside offered comfort, normality, a reminder that life existed outside the Embassy. Her eyes flicked along the strips above the windows. DAILY MAIL MILLION SALES. COLEMAN'S MUSTARD. HEINZ 57 VARIETIES. MAKE 1910 SPECIAL WITH WHITE STAR LINES. FOR COUGHS, COLDS AND INFLUENZA, VENO'S LIGHTNING COUGH CURE. She checked and rechecked her bag, jangled the contents. A well-dressed gent in a bowler glared at her sharp. 'Quiet there, girl.'

She cast her eyes down and stopped fidgeting. Only eighteen but she knew more than the old man would ever know. She let the duffer have his moment, then looked up at her reflection in the glass and recognised something there, something she hadn't seen in a long time. Hope.

What she did not do was look out of the back of the bus.

She hadn't had a chance to say her goodbyes, but that could wait. She really only had one anyway, and she could write to Jax at her mum's taxi hut, when she got the chance.

'All change, all change,' the conductor cried as the bus pulled in at Hammersmith. Millicent hoped he was right. He'd promised, her man, dear Harold, her big-tooted lisper. But could it be so easy? Easier than staying at the Embassy, mind.

She set off down Hammersmith Bridge Road, her heart a jumble of nerves and excitement, the Embassy feeling further and further off as she walked. A great sign flapped in the wind: *Polling Booth*, with a large arrow pointing down a side alley. There was a general election on. It took weeks, and wasn't due to end until the middle of February. Not that she'd ever have the chance to vote, nor anyone she knew neither, other than dear Harold.

It grew colder as she approached the river. The traffic had

thinned. A fine sleet drifted in and out of the street lamps. Up ahead, the bridge. Why did they have to meet here? She wished she'd asked Harold.

The lighting on the bridge was even worse than on the road. A high wind rattled the lamps. She could hear the river ripple and swell beneath her. She stopped, listened, and squinted into the night. Was that a cab? Her hand leapt to the small St Christopher usually hanging around her neck on a red ribbon. Then she remembered she'd left it behind.

Suddenly, out of the darkness, a solitary figure appeared on the bridge, walking towards her very quickly, with purpose.

'Harry,' she called, unsure. 'Harold, is that you?'

Wiggins changed caps. He stuffed the flat cap in his pocket and unfolded a sharply peaked tweed number from his inside pocket, all without breaking stride. His right leg swung round in an awkward limp.

The two men in front of him talked loudly, seemingly unaware of their tail. Wiggins kept his eyes fixed on the taller of the two. He wore a straw boater, set at a jaunty angle, and his side whiskers were a shocking red. At almost six foot, thin and angular, he was a Swan matchstick of a man. His companion, more compact, barrel-chested, wore a three-piece tweed suit despite the warm spring day and strutted along the pavement, shoulders back. The pair pushed through the tourists outside the House of Commons. Wiggins kept pace as they moved into the back streets, away from Millbank and the river. It was emptier here, even in the afternoon, and Wiggins hunched his shoulders and slowed down. The two men showed no sign of being noticed. Yet.

Wiggins's boss, Captain Vernon Kell, had briefed him that morning. They sat in the apartment on Victoria Street that served as the office of the Secret Service Bureau's home section. 'The two men are booked to lunch at Scott's. Follow them afterwards,' Kell said.

'What for?'

Kell looked up sharply. 'Because I order you to.' He sighed. 'I will tell you when you need to know. Is that sufficient?'

Wiggins nodded. It was. After the work he'd been doing for the last six months, following someone through the streets of London felt like a godsend of a task. 'What if they split?'

'If they do, you must follow the leader – I'm not sure which it is, so you'll have to make a judgement.' Kell fixed him with a stare. 'But whatever you do, don't stop them – they are probably armed and definitely dangerous.'

Wiggins kept his face hidden by the cap and limped on. The two men turned into a busier street. Watery sunlight bounced off a pub's windows. A jeweller's sign seesawed in the wind. An argument started up ahead, two streetwalkers fighting over scraps. Wiggins flicked his attention away for a second, then pulled his eyes back to his target.

Suddenly, the two men stopped. They pretended to cross the road, then doubled back towards him. Wiggins didn't break stride. As they neared, he dipped his head still further. Both men held their chins up high. He limped past them and half nodded, in recognition of his lower status. The two men barely batted an eye, although it was quite clear to Wiggins that they were deploying counter-surveillance manouevres.

'Hold on a sec, Bernie,' the taller one said in a loud voice. 'My laces.'

Wiggins ducked into a doorway and listened in. Which wasn't hard, as both the tall one and his mate spoke in such booming voices that he could have been in the boozer opposite and still heard.

Bernie turned back to his friend. 'Hurry up, Viv, we're late.'

Wiggins spirited the pebble out of his shoe, changed his hat once more, and waited for the two men to walk back the way they'd come. They set off again, and Wiggins went after them, hidden behind a nanny pushing a huge pram. He tried to collect his thoughts. They were military, certainly: you could tell that by their bearing, the folds in their clothes, and their shoes.

The shorter man, Bernie, scoped the road behind him once more. Again, Wiggins didn't break stride. The two men continued onwards. Wiggins cursed. He hadn't been spotted but they were looking out for him, for *someone*.

Bernie and Viv (Wiggins couldn't think of them in any other way now) reached Victoria Street. The main road buzzed with veering motor cars, buses and fast-stepping government types, messenger boys and tourists staring up at Westminster Cathedral. The two men stopped for a moment. Wiggins walked close behind them now, a tight tail in the crush. He knew what was coming and grinned. This was the most exciting thing he'd done in months.

Captain Vernon Kell, head of the Secret Service Bureau's home division, drummed his fingers on the table and contemplated a glass of milk. He disliked public houses. They never had anything decent to drink, to say nothing of the mixed clientele. The Duke of Cambridge just off Victoria Street was no different.

He sat, as previously arranged, at a table abutting the wooden partition between the lounge bar and the saloon. It was genteel enough on his side of the screen, though the polished oak panels couldn't shut out the noise from the far more raucous saloon. A glass smashed, a loud cheer followed. At three in the afternoon? Kell looked up at the gap between screen and ceiling, as if the void itself might explain the gulf in class.

'Good day, Kelly.'

Kell looked across the table. 'Good day . . . er . . . C?'

'Cunningham. In public.'

'Sorry,' Kell muttered.

Sir Mansfield Cumming sat down opposite with a glass of blood-red port and an air of undiluted subterfuge. He undid the button of his jacket and tried to look relaxed.

'Not drinking?' he said.

'I didn't see a premier cru,' Kell replied.

'Hard to trust a man who doesn't drink,' Cumming said, as if to himself. The two regarded each other in silence for a moment.

Cumming's brow pinched to an angry point above his eagle nose, and his stiff movements showed his age. Their collaboration hadn't been a roaring success so far. In the days when they'd first got the commission – Kell to head a home service, Cumming a foreign one – it had seemed like a grand new beginning, a secret service designed to counter the threat from German spies at home, whilst at the same time seeking information about them abroad. A fully funded, flexible and alert Secret Service Bureau for the twentieth century. It hadn't turned out that way.

They did not get on. Cumming was a high-handed, self-important bore as far as Kell was concerned: obsessed with code names, secret protocols and needless subterfuge. Every time they met, he insisted on being addressed as Cunningham, while he called him Kelly.

Kell sipped his glass of milk. They sat in silence for a moment longer.

'What time do you expect—'

'It's fluid,' Cumming cut him off. 'You can't put a stopwatch in the field.' He hesitated. 'But I myself do happen to have an appointment at around four . . .'

Kell raised an eyebrow. He heard a single tap on the partition by his ear, then a double rap. Cumming didn't notice. Kell put his glass down heavily. 'Well,' he said at last. 'I hope we can be of some help.'

Cumming sniffed.

'I've wondered why you haven't called on us more, to be honest,' Kell went on.

'You mean Agent OO?'

Kell nodded. 'I know that you like to work alone, or at least you don't like to share your plans. But you must understand, while our work is separate, we stand or fall together. If one of us fails, we both fail.'

'I hope you're not telling me how to do my job, Kelly, because if you are—'

'I am not telling you how to do anything,' Kell snapped. 'I am merely pointing out the facts. We are a new service. In the eyes of our masters, we are the sides of the same coin. Our fates are entwined.'

Cumming glared for a moment. 'I don't like your Agent OO, if you must know.'

Kell lifted a hand to interrupt, but Cumming sailed on regardless.

'I simply can't believe he's trustworthy. His deductive tricks were quite diverting when you introduced us. And I'm sure he can fight well enough in a street brawl. But I need intelligence on German military activity on the Continent. I need men whom I can trust in a clinch. Would you really trust Agent OO not to be bought off by the Germans? His low-born type respond to money first, and money always.'

Kell tried to interrupt once more but Cumming waved him away.

'No, no. Gentlemen make the best agents. Men of honour, men of breeding, men of character. This current scenario is the only one when such a man as OO really has any use.'

At that moment, two men of military bearing came into the bar. Cumming stood up and gestured them over. 'Gentlemen,' he said. 'Good afternoon.' Kell rose as Cumming introduced him. 'This is a good friend, Mr Kelly. Kelly, this is . . .'

'Captain Bernard Trench.' The tall man thrust out his hand.

Cumming stammered. 'I-I was rather hoping . . . No matter, this is . . .'

'Lieutenant Vivian Brandon. Delighted I'm sure.'

'Bonfire . . .' Cumming muttered. 'Your code name is Bonfire.'

'Sorry, still getting the hang of it.' Brandon didn't look sorry in the least. They all sat, Brandon and Trench with broad grins written across their faces, every inch young, off-duty military men out for a jolly in town.

Cumming tapped his walking stick on the floor. 'Were you followed?'

'Absolutely. Reggie told us it was a training exercise—'

'Reggie *told* you?' Cumming said, appalled.

'Rather. So we were on the lookout as soon as we left Scott's.'

Cumming shook his head but gestured for Trench to continue. 'We were followed by a woman outside Westminster Abbey. A streetwalker. She trailed us into Millbank. Luckily Viv here spotted her, and we doubled back to make sure. She scuttled off as soon as she saw us.'

'She weren't a streetwalker.' A small shutter in the wooden partition by Kell's shoulder scraped open, and a voice rasped through the hole. 'And she weren't following anyone. She was selling flowers for evensong.' Wiggins glugged at his beer audibly.

'Who the devil's that?' Trench snapped from across the table. 'Show your face!'

'He's the man who followed you from Scott's,' Kell said.

'Damned sneak,' Brandon exclaimed.

'And don't ever try to *look* at your tail – you's just telling them you know you're being followed, giving gen away for nothing.'

Trench turned to Cumming. 'How dare he speak to us this way. I can barely understand a word, to be honest, but I simply refuse to be addressed so.'

'Steady,' Cumming said. 'This was the exercise. It's OO.'

'It's outrageous. He's . . . drinking in a *saloon* bar. A sneak, I tell you. I'm an officer and a gentleman.'

Kell sighed and looked at Cumming. The older man raised his hand to silence Trench and hunched over the table.

'Look here, Kelly, is there anything your man could tell us here and now? Advice?'

'You could ask him yourself – he can hear, you know.'

Cumming pursed his tight lips, glaring at Kell as he spoke. 'Any advice for men in foreign climes?'

'What climes?' Wiggins answered.

Cumming growled. 'Tiaria,' he said at last. 'I can't say more.'

'Do they have the death penalty there?'

'Of course.'

'Then don't send them.'

Brandon slapped his hand on the table. 'This is ridiculous.'

'Come on,' Kell hissed through the screen.

'You's just sending them to the grave,' Wiggins persisted.

Kell rapped the partition with his stick.

Wiggins sighed theatrically. 'Look,' he said, 'these jokers could be in training for months—'

'I say . . .'

'—and still not know their arse from their elbow.'

'Please,' Kell interjected quickly, glancing at Brandon and Trench. He bent to the partition. 'Anything you can say in a few short, preferably non-obscene words. Which might help?'

More glugging. Cumming rattled his glass on the table, impatient. 'How should we get information out? Documents.'

'Does, er, Tiaria have the post?'

'As good as ours, I'm told.'

'Then post it.'

'Oh, this is ridiculous. Should we address it to the Admiralty?' Trench scoffed.

'Post it to a box somewhere else in . . . Tiaria . . . then forward it on later. It's a cutout.'

'Hmm, I see,' Kell nodded.

Wiggins went on. 'But same rules using the post as anything else – keep consistent with the cover.'

'This is stuff and nonsense,' Brandon said. 'I can hardly make out a word the man says.'

'He means,' Kell said slowly, 'that whenever you use the postal system, send another letter at the same time – a letter that is consistent with your cover story.'

'Handwrite one envelope – the neutral – type the other,' Wiggins finished.

Cumming nodded at Kell slowly. 'In case you are being watched.'

'Zackly.'

'Yes, yes, I see. The Ger— er . . . the TRs would search the post and find the handwritten letter, but not the treasure.'

'Is this all really necessary?' Brandon piped in. 'We're due at the Army and Navy stores at four – we need to get our kit.'

'Of course. Thank you, Kelly, for the advice,' Cumming said.

'Much obliged, I'm sure,' Trench added through reed-thin lips.

Kell nodded. No one thanked Wiggins. Cumming got up, as did Brandon and Trench.

'One more thing,' Wiggins echoed through the shutter. 'Bernie and Viv here . . .'

'How does he know our names?' Brandon said, to no one.

'They should play up the couple. Act like that's what they're hiding.'

Brandon turned to Trench. 'What does he mean?' Trench ignored him, but his cheeks had begun to redden. He clenched his fists.

Wiggins carried on. 'Then it will make sense, if they're acting a bit dodge like. I mean, anyone would think these two are au fait, if you get the drift.'

Brandon didn't. Trench, on the other hand, had gone a deep purple. A vein throbbed in his temple. Kell coughed. Cumming stuttered, 'Ah, well, yes. Gentlemen, shall we—'

'Scoundrel!' Trench cried and leapt across the table. He ripped open the shutter, 'How dare he . . .'

Wiggins was gone. All that remained was a foam-licked glass, glistening wet, empty.

Brandon scowled at Kell. 'Keep your . . . *man* . . . away from us.'

Kell pulled on his gloves carefully. 'As you wish,' he said finally and got up. 'But ignore his advice at your peril. He is the finest *man* in the Service. And if you're going where I think you're going, then you'll need every ounce of help you can get. Your lives depend on it. Good day, Cunni— oh, Cumming. Gentlemen.' He planted his hat on his head, tipped it slightly and left the three men standing around the table, confused, outraged and affronted.

Kell turned right out of the pub and crossed the road to an apartment building on Victoria Street. A squadron of pigeons swooped past the bell tower of Westminster Cathedral. Kell watched as one of the birds, unquestionably white despite a mottling of soot, dipped beneath the others and disappeared, alone.

'Any messages, Simpkins?' he called out as he entered the hallway of the fourth-floor flat that served as his office and HQ.

He heard the clerk scrape back his chair, garble something through a stuffed mouth, and then break a teacup. 'Coming, sir.'

Kell turned to his office and pulled the only key from his pocket. He unlocked the door and stepped into the room.

Wiggins sat at Kell's desk, feet up, waiting for his boss.

Kell stopped the curse on his lips and instead, despite his better judgement, couldn't help but say, 'How do you *do* that?'

Wiggins swung his legs to the floor and sprang up. 'What was the point of all that, then?'

Kell said nothing. He took his coat, hat and gloves off carefully, eyeing Wiggins all the time. His agent prowled around the room, picking up objects at random, placing them down, moving on.

'He sending them jokers to Germany?' Wiggins said at last.

'Tiaria, Cumming calls it.'

Wiggins rolled his eyes. Kell sat down at his desk and removed his glasses. 'I understand your frustration.'

'You think them'll track Van Bork?' Wiggins said.

'I doubt they even know he exists.' Kell replaced his glasses. 'Listen. The work you've done here in England is exceptional. Together we've identified a number of potential German spies—'

'Small fry!'

'Who nevertheless will need to be arrested in the event of war. There's Helm in Portsmouth, Leitner in Chatham, Sternberg in Sunderland.' As he reeled off this list, Kell pointed to his elaborate filing system of Roneo cards. 'You found them all.'

'Nobodies,' Wiggins said. 'And we got no proof they *are* spies, only that they might be when the time comes. We's still missing the big wheel.'

This was true. The year before, Wiggins had helped Kell break up a spy ring, a success that had led to the creation of the Secret Service Bureau itself. As head of the home section, Kell had been given the express task of rooting out German spies on British soil. But Wiggins and he had failed to find the German kingpin behind the spies, a man known to them only as 'Van Bork'.

'We've done what we could for the moment,' Kell said. Wiggins had staked out the German Embassy for months, but had found no leads relating to Van Bork. 'Besides,' Kell went on, 'we don't even know what he looks like, no small thanks to you. If you hadn't let our one witness go, we might have had a decent shot.'

Wiggins scowled. Kell didn't know the whole story, but he'd guessed Wiggins had been romantically involved with a Latvian woman who'd turned out to be an agent provocateur working for Van Bork. The woman had fled the country, and Wiggins hadn't lifted a finger to stop her.

'Send me to Germany,' Wiggins said at last. 'I'll find him, I'll find Van Bork.'

'You? Oh yes, I can quite see that. A slovenly dressed gutter-snipe without a word of German, swanning around the salons of Berlin? You can barely speak intelligible English, man, you're a street urchin grown up, not some diplomatic lounge lizard. Sherlock Holmes may have taught you, but we both know you'd stick out like a sore thumb anywhere other than the streets, amongst your own class.'

Wiggins glowered at him. Kell reached for a cigarette and looked away. He fiddled with a match, then ribboned smoke into the air and went on. 'I know you feel guilty about the boy in Woolwich. But you didn't plunge the knife, Van Bork's men did.'

'I'd have a better chance of getting him than Bernie and bloody Viv,' Wiggins replied.

Kell shook his head. 'Firstly, we don't even know if he is *in* Germany. If he sticks to his guns, then I presume he's still oper-ating here at least some of the time. We must wait.'

'For what?'

'He will show himself again, I know it. We have to be ready to recognise him when he does.' Kell stubbed out his smoke and fixed Wiggins with a stare. 'Secondly, it's not our business chasing spies in Germany. We operate here. We leave the foreign stuff to Cumming. If he asks for our help, well then . . .'

'Is that what you brought me back for? Teaching them toffee jokers to wipe their own arses?'

Kell winced. 'I had hopes for a spy school.'

'Them'll never listen to the likes of me.'

Kell nodded slowly. Wiggins had a point. Cumming had made it clear he only wanted agents of impeccable lineage, Oxbridge, Sandhurst types. And they wouldn't listen to Wiggins – a mistake that could cost them their lives. 'As it happens, I did bring you back to London for something else. The King's funeral.'

'The King's dead? No one told me.'

Kell tutted. 'Not yet, but he'll go soon. And we're to help with the security.'

'You asking me to wait around for someone to die?' Wiggins grinned, disbelieving.

The telephone rang, startling them both. 'Simpkins,' Kell called. 'The telephone.'

Wiggins pulled his cap from his pocket. 'I'll be back tomorra. For orders,' he said.

Simpkins scuttled into the room, pausing briefly at the sight of Wiggins. He reached for the telephone and looked up at Kell. 'It might be your wife, sir.'

'I know.'

As the secretary took the call, Wiggins hesitated, a worried look crossing his face. Kell gestured vaguely with his hand and Wiggins strode to the door.

Simpkins gave Kell the message. 'It's the Cabinet Office, sir. Secretary Pears. He wants to see you at once.'

2

'Oi, that's my snag.'

'Says who?

'Says this!' A punch flew.

Wiggins stepped past the two lads as they closed in a violent scuffle. Behind them, a reporter turned away and called for another boy.

He was in the alleyway next to the Cheshire Cheese pub. Wiggins pushed his way through a gaggle of boys who crowded around the entrance like a colony of birds on the edge of a cliff, flitting to and fro nervously.

The place was rammed, printers on one side, pressmen on the other. It was the best pub on Fleet Street, and everyone knew it. Wiggins went into the public bar. It stank of printers' Woodbines, press ringers' pipe smoke and cheap whisky. It stank of ink and sweat and unwashed clothes. It stank of home. After months away, Wiggins savoured London's stale air, the glorious sounds of a City boozer, swearing, joking, spilt beer and no one giving a toss who you were, or why.

He ordered a pint of half-and-half, took a long gulp, then stuck his head into the alley outside. 'A general for a day's tail,' Wiggins called.

Fourteen hands shot up in unison.

''Ere ya are, guv.' 'Experienced, me.' 'I do *MailExpressEvening News*.' 'Liar.'

Wiggins paused as the boys horseshoed around him. Most were aged between twelve and seventeen, Wiggins reckoned; hard to tell exactly because no one had a scrap on them. All bones and baggy trousers. These were the runners on the

lookout for a job, or 'snag'. Employed freelance by the newspapers, they did all sorts (following celebrities, running errands
and the like) that the reporters didn't have time for. Those
pints in the Cheese wouldn't drink themselves.

Wiggins made a show of scanning all the eager faces, the sharp,
bright eyes like mirrors. Then he thrust out his hand, pointing
beyond the crowd around him to a solitary figure who hadn't
moved. 'You'll do,' he said.

The figure, who until that moment had lounged against the
railings, shrugged and the rest dispersed, muttering darkly.

'He don't want it anyway.' 'It's a gyp.' 'Fucking ponce, is he?'

Wiggins waited. The skinny figure, dressed like the other boys
but if possible even slighter, slunk towards him.

'Jax,' Wiggins said quietly.

'I'm Jack here,' she hissed under her breath.

Jax was the daughter of Wiggins's oldest friend, Sal, and they'd
run into each other the year before when Jax had been inadvert-
ently working for a spy ring. Wiggins had helped her out of that
scrape, but she'd kept running – and kept up pretending to be
a boy. He didn't blame her for that.

He finished his pint and was about to say more when a great
commotion swept through the ranks of runners. First one, then
two, then more messengers came hurtling down the alleyway and
barrelled into the Cheese. Moments later, the pub emptied of
reporters. They came bolting out one at a time, screaming for
runners.

'What's up?' Wiggins said.

'King's all in. He's about to snuff it.'

The runners pegged off one by one, despatched westwards by
the inebriated newspaper men – to Clarence House, Buckingham
Palace, Whitehall. The papers needed eyes everywhere, and the
runners were cheaper than dust.

Jax looked on longingly at all this work going begging. 'Oi,
mister, I can do Downing Street,' she called to a harried newsman,
who glanced up at Wiggins.

'He can't,' Wiggins said, resting a hand on her shoulder.

'Ignore him, mister. I'm raring.'

But the reporter had already engaged another boy. Jax slumped back, upset. 'Still gotta work, ain't I?'

'What do you mean *still?*'

'I'm on a missing persons, but it don't pay.'

Wind whipped stray biscuit wrappers and dust in little eddies about them, the alleyway now deserted. Even the clinking glasses and roar of chat from the Cheese had quietened. The King's imminent death was big news.

Wiggins looked closely at Jax's face. He stilled an impulse to brush the tears from her cheek. 'Don't worry, I'll pay you.'

'It's not . . .' She sniffed.

'What missing person? You a consulting detective now?'

'Don't laugh at me.'

Wiggins patted her shoulder. 'Come on, girl, what's up?'

Jax sniffed again. She pulled herself up straighter and began to talk in her proper voice – higher, not quite as barked. 'My mate Millie. Ain't seen her for months – she ain't home neither.'

'She your age, seventeen? A few months, that's nothing.'

She looked at him. 'She would've said. She's disappeared.'

Wiggins cracked his fingers and examined the backs of his hands. Soft. Hadn't been this soft since for ever, now he didn't have to work for a living. Not real work anyway. 'Anything on Peter?'

'Who?'

'Jax. I have been paying you something, remember.'

'I tell ya, I'm on a missing persons. And you paid me 'alf a crown. Once. That's sod all.'

Wiggins took her by both shoulders and fixed her with a glare. 'Where is Peter?'

Jax shrugged. 'I don't know. I tried, but no word, not at Jubilee Street, none of the dives you told me. He's gone.'

'I paid you more than 'alf a crown,' Wiggins said.

She rounded on him. 'Why don'tcha find your precious Rooski yourself?'

'I'm known,' he said. *And I'm dead*, he did not add.

'Why the hell you care, anyway?'

Wiggins glanced down the alleyway. His best friend Bill had been killed the year before by a gang of anarchist terrorists. Wiggins had tracked down one of their number, a Latvian who went by the name of Peter the Painter. He'd been out for revenge, but in the end it was Peter who'd put a bullet in Wiggins's shoulder and left him for dead.

'I never leave a debt unpaid,' he replied. She was too young to know what revenge meant, to understand how much he'd lost and what he was prepared to do to right that wrong. He'd give all he had to pay that debt.

'Bollocks,' Jax said. 'You's just a skank, grown up.'

Wiggins grinned and shook his head. 'I'll buy you an 'alf.'

Back inside the pub, they sat at one of the now free tables and pushed aside a great splay of the latest newspapers. The Cheese had all the papers, up to the moment. After all, Wiggins thought as he placed a drink in front of Jax, that's where the journos got most of their stories – from the other papers.

Wiggins flicked through the first editions of the evenings as Jax rattled on about her missing friend. 'It's just not her, it's not her,' she kept repeating.

Every now and then, Wiggins asked a question, but Jax didn't have much information on her friend. That's how it was when you met people on the streets. There was nothing to tie them down, nothing to pin them.

'Where she from again?' Wiggins said.

'Her ma's in Lambeth. Vere Street or something.'

'Ouch. And you're surprised she scarpered.'

Jax glared at him with such hurt and disappointment that Wiggins put down the paper. 'All right. I'll take a look-see.'

'Would ya?'

'No promises, like.'

'Fanks, Wiggins,' she smiled shyly.

'In return, you's take another nose around out east. For Peter.'

'I'm telling you, he ain't there.'

Wiggins frowned at her, and kept the stare until she shrugged. 'Good,' he said. 'Now hop it.'

She dragged herself from the table. 'If you find Millie . . .'

'I'll tell her to write. Say bollocks to your mum for me.'

Jax sloped towards the door. 'Oi,' Wiggins called out, holding up a large dull shilling between finger and thumb. 'You forgot your general.'

'Good of you to come,' Soapy drawled.

Kell scratched at his beard. He'd known Soapy for years and yet he was never quite sure how genuine anything he said ever was. 'It's not every day I'm summoned to the Cabinet Office,' he replied. 'Simpkins even referred to you as Secretary Pears.'

Soapy glanced up at Kell. 'I didn't realise you had a clerk,' he said, gesturing to the empty chair opposite his desk. 'Pew?'

Kell sat down, slightly uneasy. Soapy was something big in the civil service, and seemed to wield more power with every passing month. He sat in the Cabinet Office like a lazy cat that never quite went to sleep. But he'd rarely summoned Kell in such a way, and they never met at the office.

'Sorry we couldn't meet at the club, old man,' Soapy spoke to Kell's thoughts. 'Bit delicate.' He leaned forward and offered Kell a cigarette from an ebony box on the desk.

They smoked for a moment. Kell waited. Saying too much in Whitehall could get you into trouble.

'Asquith doesn't like you chaps.'

'So you tell me. Often.'

'Hmm. Yes. But he doesn't like the sewage workers either – doesn't stop him, well, yes, ha ha, you get the point.'

'I do,' Kell said.

Soapy stubbed out his smoke. 'And do you know about the latest treaty with Italy?'

Kell shook his head.

'Exactly! There is no treaty. There should have been, we were poised to make a pact, to stand together in the event of war. But the Italian delegation got wind of some rather damaging information and called the whole thing off.'

'What damaging information?'

Soapy looked up sharply. 'I can't go into too much detail, you understand of course. Suffice to say that many in the Cabinet are not too keen on Italians as a race. Some rather disparaging remarks, often of a personal nature, came to be known to the delegation.'

'Good God,' Kell exclaimed. 'A minister leaked this?'

'Not necessarily.' Soapy drew another cigarette, but left it unlit. 'Some of the material appeared in the minutes.'

'The departmental clerks saw it?' Kell did a quick calculation in his head. 'Then it could be any one of a hundred people?'

'Yes.'

'Who stood to benefit from the collapse of the treaty? Cui bono?'

'And now we arrive at the point. The biggest beneficiary was, of course, Germany. Which is where you come in.'

'You want me to investigate? Surely this is a matter for the police, for Special Branch?'

'I hope you're not this obtuse at home. Not with Constance around.' Soapy shook his head. 'Your job is to find German spies, yes? Very well. My job is to protect the Prime Minister, to protect the integrity of the government. We can't have the police investigating ourselves, can we? It would be unseemly and also bad politics. No, we need to do it quietly. Are you with me still?'

Kell nodded.

'You and your special . . . Agent W . . . can look into it.'

'He's a street man, Soap, a foot soldier.' This last made Kell wince, but he couldn't have Wiggins under anyone else's control. Known to his superiors only as Agent W, and to Cumming as Agent OO, Wiggins was still his alone. 'He'd be lost in the governmental.'

Soapy sniffed. 'Well, have him look into the clerks at least. You can look into the Germans. Half of Germany will be over for the King's funeral, whenever that is. Perfect opportunity to do some of the cloak-and-dagger – though none of the dagger, just the cloak.'

'Why can't this go through official channels?'

Soapy lifted his arms in exasperation and got up. He took another cigarette, frowned at Kell, then spoke again. 'The whole point of you chaps, as far as the PM is concerned anyway, is that you're not quite official. So *be* not quite official, and find out how this information got out, there's a good chap.'

Kell hesitated, then got up and put on his hat. As he reached the door, Soapy called out again. 'Oh, and Kell, not a word of this to anyone.'

'But I was heading to Special Branch, to see if they had anything on the clerks.'

Soapy waved his hand dismissively. 'Try to look at their files by all means, but don't tell them why. Good day.'

Good day, indeed. Kell smarted as he made his way across Whitehall towards New Scotland Yard and the offices of the Special Branch. The wide street thrummed with tourists clogging his every step. Motorised lorries coughed out fumes, private motor cars lurched and jagged between food carts, horses and the bright red open-top buses. Fleets of bicycles sped by. Armies of clerks streamed out of the government buildings as the working day ended, queues formed at the bus stops and people bustled and shoved. Anyone of those clerks could be selling information, he suddenly realised, and it could take him months to find out who, even with Wiggins back in London.

The charge sergeant at Scotland Yard directed him up the stairs. Kell walked through the public waiting rooms, barely glancing at the wanted posters that adorned the walls. Ugly 'mugshots' in the American style and crude pencil portraits.

Special Branch operated out of the third floor, most of which was taken up with their operations room. Kell stood in the doorway for a moment. He eyed up the filing cabinets opposite – a repository of all sorts of vital information. Evidence drawers. A great map of London was pinned to the far wall, flanked by chalk boards scored by the marks of old crimes.

'What do you want?' A detective got up and walked towards Kell, in his shirtsleeves, with a five o'clock shadow and dark, hanging brows. Kell could smell his body odour. He came to a halt, half a head taller, five years younger and bristling with hair on the backs of his hands. 'We don't allow visitors.'

'Superintendent Quinn?'

The detective pondered for a second. 'Far corner,' he grunted, and gestured with his head. 'Don't open the other doors,' he hissed.

Kell inclined his head and strode slowly between the desks. By now, everyone in the room was looking at him. No one spoke. Instead, to a man they leaned back in their chairs and drew heavily on cigarettes, sentinel fires lighting his way to Quinn's office. The room reeked of nicotine and sweat and iron. Can't be iron. Kell shook his head. Blood? His eyes flicked to the interview rooms on his right as he walked. Special Branch had a rough reputation, and getting rougher.

Kell reached the far door and pushed it open. 'Superintendent?'

The man behind the desk did not turn. He sat facing away from the door, looking up at the wall behind the desk. Kell followed the man's gaze. The wall was plastered with information. A huge grid, with scribbles, maps and rubber bands connecting names, places, photographs. Kell thought of London: the telegraph wires, train lines, electric connections. Superintendent Quinn had his very own London on the wall, a complex connecting graph of threats, real and imagined, of political unrest, of terrorism. Kell noted some of the headings: *Republicans. Fenians. Anarchists. The Gardstein Gang*, with a question mark.

Kell shifted his gaze to the right. Another great grid, this time headed with the names of each of the Cabinet ministers – including Prime Minister Asquith – as well as all the senior members of the Royal Family. One of Special Branch's roles was to provide personal security and bodyguards, if necessary, to all the major figures of the British state. Kell saw at a glance where everyone was, who was looking after them and where they intended to be the following day.

Kell coughed. 'Sir Patrick?'

The man in the chair finally swivelled around. Sir Patrick Quinn fixed Kell with his lively, dark eyes. He had the bony, raw and hollowed-out look of an aging vulture, with his beaked nose and the faint suggestion of a widow's peak. In his fifties, he looked good on it, Kell had to admit. Quinn took a pull from his pipe, exhaled and broke the silence with his mild, slightly accented Irish brogue. 'Superintendent will do just fine, so it will,' he said at last.

'I need to look in the files.'

'Do you? To avoid any doubt here, I am thinking you mean Special Branch files?'

Kell nodded. He glanced back at the filing cabinets in the large office behind him, and at the three locked cabinets in Quinn's own office.

'Now then, as a country man, I am not used to the ways of you city folk,' Quinn carried on.

'City folk? You've been head of the Branch for the last seven years.' Kell couldn't keep the irritation out of his voice. He never liked dealing with Quinn. Irish. Clever. Not his sort at all.

Quinn grinned. 'And I'm thinking, what would the War Office be wanting with such files, now. Can you tell me that?'

'You know I'm not War Office any more – I'm the Secret Service Bureau.'

'Right you are, right you are. I remember the letterhead now.'

'Letterhead,' Kell said, incredulous. 'We've been in contact for months.'

'There's no need to be getting in all of a lather now, is there?' Quinn twinkled, enjoying himself. 'I've recalled everything. You find the German spies, we arrest them. When you find them,' he added. 'But as you can see, we are a little busy today – what with the King, poor man, and the very important people going hither and thither. It's our job to protect them, you know, as well as deal with the many other threats to the nation. Now, is that all there is? Shall we be saying good day?'

Kell bridled. He knew very well what Special Branch did. And he knew, too, how few spies he'd had arrested. 'I need to see the files,' he said, again.

'You have a letter of authority?'

'It's coming.'

'Ah well, then I think I'll be waiting for that.'

Kell stepped forward, ready to deliver a 'Damn it all, we're on the same side' speech, about how one agency and another must work together to tackle ever-growing threats. He was about to deliver this when his eye snagged on one of the photographs behind Quinn. It was pinned to the wall, beneath a section marked *Mid-level.* The photograph, of five women on the street, had been taken at a distance, probably a surveillance shot. Three of the women had pencil lines drawn from them out to their names. The other two had circles, with question marks drawn next to them. The photograph wasn't in focus, and Kell stood six feet away, but he recognised one of those circled figures only too well.

It was his wife, Constance.

'I . . .' Kell faltered. 'Er, a lot of anarchist gangs up there,' he gestured, trying to recover himself.

Quinn looked up at him. A shadow passed across his face, quizzical. 'There are a lot of dangerous men in the country, sure enough. How do they concern you, I'm wondering?'

'Me? Idle interest. Anyway, yes.' Kell stepped to the door. 'I will do as you suggest, and wait for official permission. For the files, I mean,' he said. 'Good day.'

'Good day to you too, Captain Kell. Or is it the evening now? Have a bonny one, if I may so say. And give my best to your good lady wife.'

'My wife?'

'Indeed. I am a great supporter of the institution of marriage,' Quinn went on. 'I encourage it in all of my detectives.'

Kell held his eyes for a moment, unsure. Then he nodded and walked back to the door. As he reached it, Quinn called out softly, speaking as if to a child so soft and lovely and lilting was his voice. 'Captain. Never come to these offices again, uninvited. Now, you be careful on your way out.'

Wiggins picked his way through the rubbish and the empty bottles collecting at the end of Vere Road, just as the last of the daylight faded. A fine rain fell. A fine rain always fell on Lambeth, at least in Wiggins's experience, and certainly on a street like Vere. New and shiny twenty years ago, it stank of piss and pus now, ten years of neglect, unemployment and gin.

Children clumped here and there, huddling in doorways against the rain. A scrap of a boy peered skywards as Wiggins passed, in a futile effort to spot the sun amid the soot and smoke and despair. A drunk bawled at the far end of the street. Two stray dogs chased each other in a vicious, yapping circle.

The southern side of the road had a row of small tenements, their doors open onto the street, the children threadbare sentinels.

'Looking for Millie's?' he said at the door to number 18.

'Keep looking, ponce,' a small boy of eight or so said as he squatted next to a ragged young girl.

'No one want an ha'penny?'

'Fird floor,' the little girl barked quickly. 'But mind your head, she's steaming.' She held out her hand.

'Ta,' Wiggins said and palmed her the coin.

The girl grasped the money and then proceeded to follow Wiggins up the stairs, a few paces behind. He looked around at her once or twice, her blue eyes never off him. She was dirtier than hell and twice as sharp. 'You ain't no rozzer,' she said at one point.

'You think the rozzers are after Millie?'

'Is that my Millie, is it?' a throaty female voice rasped through an open door.

Wiggins stepped inside. He couldn't help holding his hand to his mouth. If the street smelled bad, this room stank like the pit. Rag-covered beds ran along three walls, while a fireplace stood empty on the fourth, the door in one corner. A few kitchen utensils cluttered a table opposite, and in the centre of the room sat a woman, the owner of the voice, slumped in a wicker chair.

'Millie? My poor Millie, where is she?' the woman said.

Millie's mother, Wiggins guessed, though he couldn't pin her age. He couldn't pin much about anything in the unlit room, other than that in between her legs Millie's mother had a metal bucket – the source of much of the smell. Wiggins hoped it contained sick.

'Where is my poor dear?' the woman wailed again.

Behind him, the little girl whispered, 'She don't give a stuff 'bout Mills. Watch.'

'Me heart is cleft, good sir.'

'It's coming,' the little girl said. 'It's coming.'

'My only breadwinner gone. It's not the money I miss, it's my poor Millie.'

Wiggins coughed. 'I am come to find her, on behalf of a friend.'

The woman heaved in her chair. 'Fank God, sir, fank God. You have delivered me. You are an angel, like my poor gone Millie, an angel of light and the Lord.'

'Do you mind if I look at her stuff,' Wiggins said, pointing at one of the bedrolls, as directed by the little girl.

'Fank you, fank you. Anything to find my poor Millie. I am willing to do you that favour, good sir.' The woman leaned forward, a gin reek wafting off her. 'Although one favour deserves another, don't you think? A shilling, sir, can you spare?'

'There it is,' sighed the little girl.

'Is she ya ma?' Wiggins whispered back.

The little girl nodded.

'Of course, madam,' Wiggins said loudly, 'I will pay for your time. I wouldn't want to impose.'

Under the little girl's direction, Wiggins picked his way through Millie's meagre belongings. A few old clothes, a dried and dead lavender posy, a handkerchief, a tram ticket. The little girl squatted down beside him.

By this time her mother had started singing wildly.

'Last time she came she had new fings on.' The little girl

pushed her hair out of her eyes. Wiggins knew that gesture, one move away from tears.

'What things? Clothes?'

'Scanties. She showed me. Flash 'uns.'

'She had a fella?'

'Not so as I know. Just the scanties.'

Wiggins pocketed the ticket and stood up. 'Thank you, madam,' he said loudly. 'I will do my best.'

She broke off from her song. 'You do that, good sir. For my Millie. And the shilling?'

'I've given it to the nipper here, for safekeeping.'

'That little bitch?' she shouted and raised an empty bottle.

Wiggins and the little girl ducked out of the room and ran down the stairs, giggling as they did so. On the landing, Wiggins stopped and gave her the shilling.

'It's for you. Do what you can.'

'Fanks, mister. I'll snag a pot of gin and water for her, and keep the half for mesel'. And mister. If you find Millie, tell her little Els says wotcha.'

'Wotcha.'

Wiggins took a tram along the Albert Embankment and over into Belgravia. He made a note of all the stops and got out on the edge of the diplomatic district. It made no sense, but it was his only clue.

He walked around the streets in a grid formation, scanning the grand stucco houses, keeping his ears open. Millie's tram ticket had come from a stop between Victoria and Hyde Park Corner – the fare points – so he knew she'd got on somewhere along this road. The idea that she'd been in and around Belgravia seemed far-fetched on the face of it, but it was the only lead he had. That and the expensive underwear.

It took him nearly two hours (including a stop for a swift pint at the nearest boozer), but as it grew late, one road in particular caught his attention. On the face of it, Ranleigh Terrace was similar to the other streets in the area. Huge houses, with big white porches, large gardens, and embassy insignia on every third building. The ones that weren't embassies looked like the kind of society piles that were empty half the time, with the rich owners in the country. The street traffic consequently was either the posh crowd, all top hats and pearls, or else their servants.

Ranleigh Terrace had more cars on it than the other nearby streets. More taxis, more often. It also had the strangest embassy Wiggins had ever seen. Bright light burst from every window, despite the late hour. A huge electric light illuminated the entrance porch and he could make out from the kerbside the lettering above the door: THE EMBASSY OF OLIFA.

It was a rum go all round. He'd never even heard of Olifa, yet they had one of the biggest houses in one of the best areas. Fully electrified, too, and not afraid of showing it. He hurried on, not wanting to attract attention.

At the end of the street, he took a left and then a left again down the mews that ran parallel to the terrace and along the back. It was darker there but Wiggins had no trouble in identifying the Embassy. They had more lights on than all the other houses combined. His boots slid on the cobbles and his stomach rumbled. He suddenly realised he hadn't eaten since lunchtime, other than the three pints at the Cheese plus the extra one around the corner. It made him feel light-headed and a little wobbly. He almost stopped there and then. What the hell was he doing? He was meant to be finding German spies for his day job, and looking for that bastard Peter the Painter when he had the time. But he'd promised Jax. And something told him all was not what it seemed at the Embassy.

A noise sparked him into life once more, a copper walking past the end of the mews. Wiggins slunk back into the shadows, then hustled towards the Embassy's ivy-clad back door. He took a quick glance around, burped and heaved himself up onto the wall.

The Embassy was alive. Cracks of light striped every window. A gramophone gently wheezed and crackled over the night air. Right up to the very highest windows – it was as if even the servants were partying. Wiggins looked along the garden. A covered walkway ran from the back of the house to the door he'd just tried, out onto the mews.

This was like no embassy he'd ever seen. These Olifans must be fun-loving sorts. But where there're fun seekers, there's also darkness. Where there are parties, there are girls. He took tight hold of the ivy, then dropped down into the garden.

He got up and inched out onto the stone paving under the canopy. The ale repeated on him. He knew he shouldn't have had another. Still. He wiped his mouth, then crouched down and loped along the walkway, keeping one eye on the back door and one on the windows above. Suddenly, the bright button of a flaring cigarette appeared by the doorway, and he dodged behind a bush. 'What the fuck am I doing?' he said under his breath.

'Zackly,' someone said behind him.

Wiggins turned, only to be met by a fist, full in the face.

3

MASSIVE EARTHQUAKE IN COSTA RICA – NO BRITONS DEAD.

Kell threw down the newspaper for the third time that morning. Other than the earthquake, the King's bad health filled the news. There was a piece hinting at industrial unrest in the northern factories, and a dry article about the rising cost of bread, as if he cared about another halfpenny on a loaf. He sat at the breakfast table, waiting for his wife to join him. She had already been asleep when he arrived home the night before, and she'd risen before he'd had a chance to confront her.

He practised what he would say. 'Constance, dear, why are you wanted by Special Branch?' was the straightforward approach, but he baulked at that. Or, 'The advances in photography these days are quite remarkable. Only the other day I was . . .'

It was exceedingly awkward to have a suffragist as a wife. They had argued about the cause often, an argument that he somehow never managed to win. It had come to such a pass that they barely talked about anything else – which meant they barely talked about anything. The government was staunchly against the right of women to vote. Even as they pretended to offer one sop or another, Prime Minister Asquith and his key men were all implacably opposed. So Kell had kept Constance's political leanings to himself.

The photograph, however, represented an escalation. He'd always assumed Constance's involvement had been of the genteel variety, with the other Hampstead ladies. Attracting the interest of Special Branch was most troubling, for her, for him, for his career.

That wasn't the only thing that troubled him about his meetings of the day before. Sir Patrick Quinn was more hostile than usual, certainly, and something wasn't quite right about Soapy. Kell had the vague feeling he was being set up for something, but he wasn't sure what. The secret task Soapy had given him smacked of the near impossible, almost as if he wanted him to fail. And if he failed, who better to step into the breach than Sir Patrick Quinn?

Upstairs, he heard Constance upbraid the children, then issue a stream of commands to the staff. His wife was not a quiet woman. Energy swirled around her like a wind-whipped dust devil. Finally, she clattered down the stairs. She did not come into the room, however, and he heard her rummage in the coat stand.

He moved towards the doorway. 'Where are you going?'

'Why do you ask?' She carried on fussing, pulling on an overcoat, checking her umbrella.

'I just . . .'

'Vernon, what is it? Is there something you want me to do?'

Kell couldn't hold his wife's gimlet eye. Instead, he saw the photograph in Quinn's office, the big question mark beside her face, the peacock feather in her hat.

'Do you have more work for me?' she said as she pulled her gloves on. She'd proved an adept assistant the year before, in a trap he'd set with Wiggins. Razor-witted, hyper-observant, unwavering – in another life she could have been one of the finest agents of the Service, though he did not tell her this.

All he said was: 'No, it's not that. It's—'

The telephone burst into life, right by his ear. 'Only, I—'

The bell insisted.

'I have a meeting. Of the Hampstead committee,' she said, gesturing to the door. 'It's very important.'

'About that, I was—'

'Are you going to answer that, or shall I?'

Kell hesitated. Constance looked at him oddly, then swiped the instrument into her hand. 'Hampstead 202,' she said, her foot tapping the floor in irritation. 'Oh, hello, Soapy.'

Constance listened carefully, stood straighter. 'I see. Yes, of course.' She put the horn down carefully and turned to Kell. 'You're to go to the Cabinet Office at once. His illness is over. The King is dead.'

Wiggins opened his eyes. A band of light ran at a diagonal across his vision. Other than that, the room was musty, cold and dark. He felt his right eye, tender, painful. A shiner for sure. He sat up and checked his pockets – watch, change, all still there. Dust caught in his throat and his head pounded. He raised his hand into the darkness and felt first one sharp corner, then a second and a third. He was in a cupboard under the stairs.

The last thing he could remember was a full, fat fist in his face, and the black eye wasn't going to let him forget it in a hurry. He got to his knees and found the door handle. The band of light was the crack of the door. He hesitated, wary, but what was the point? Whoever knocked him out knew he was there – either the door would be locked, or it wouldn't. He pushed it open.

Stepping into a servants' hallway, Wiggins's first thought was escape – through the back door off to his right. But his head turned to the strange noises coming from the kitchen: women talking, laughing, shrieking, punctuated once or twice by a deep bass voice – a voice that had a hitch in it, a vague tickling of familiarity. Wiggins paused. Was it the voice of the man who had punched him? There was something else about that voice, something older chiming in his mind.

''Ere, he's awake!' A small boy dashed past Wiggins and into the kitchen.

A second later, the boy stood in the doorway and looked at Wiggins with pity. 'In 'ere, mister. You deaf?'

Wiggins nodded and followed him.

He was greeted by the strangest kitchen he'd ever seen. He'd expected it to be filled with maids, cooks, valets – the usual attendants of a grand house. But this kitchen was full of women, and not one of them dressed like a servant. Many of them weren't even dressed at all, bar their underthings. The others had bright, frilly dresses, elaborately curled hair, and thigh-high boots. They all wore long gloves, though, and most had long red ribbons tied either to their dresses or around their necks. Wiggins counted fifteen. There was chatter, great steaming cups of tea and the smell of frying bacon.

The small boy looked up at Wiggins expectantly, but none of the women paid him much heed, except one. Dressed a little more soberly than the rest, and a little older – about his own age he guessed, thirty or so. She cast an amused eye over him while sipping her tea. Black curly hair fell over her shoulders and her dark skin glowed. She smiled at him. The dust of last night's make-up cracked.

'What kind of embassy is this?' Wiggins asked her, incredulous.

'A place of sanctuary, communion, safety.' She took a sip of tea. 'A place for people to speak frankly, to reach out in friendship and fellow feeling. My name's Martha and this is the Embassy of Olifa.'

'You're Big T's mate, ain't ya?' The little boy tugged at Wiggins's arm.

He looked down at the boy, then up again to Martha. 'Academy more like.'

She laughed. 'That's old-fashioned slang. This is a high-class establishment, not a street brothel.'

The kitchen door swung open and a huge figure, a man, appeared. He coughed like a foghorn, then stuffed a bacon sandwich into his mouth.

'Tommy?' Wiggins said, amazed.

The big man swallowed. 'Big T to you.'

The bubble of conversation and giggles had stilled on Tommy's entrance, Wiggins noted. Two women shuffled aside to let him sit, not scared exactly but hardly at ease either. Martha glanced back at Wiggins as Tommy sat.

'You're bigger than I remember,' Wiggins said.

'Stronger too.' He took another gargantuan bite out of his doorstep. Someone placed a mug of tea by his right hand. 'Wouldn't smack me in the face now, would ya?'

'Only ever had a good reason, Tommy.'

Tommy grunted. His huge shoulders rippled underneath his shirt, open at the collar. 'Doing your tricks, are ya?'

Wiggins had been looking at Tommy's calloused knuckles, noted the flecks of grey in his close-cut hair, the shaving nick on his chin, the double crease in the nose, his cuffs.

He left off at Tommy's words and said, 'You've been inside. Twice. Here and up north. Took up boxing proper, and worse. Hard times. But you're doing all right now, I see. Off the booze, clean living.'

Tommy held Wiggins's eye. 'Still sucking God's cock, are ya?'

GOD – that's what they sometimes used to call Sherlock Holmes, their old boss. The Grand Old Detective. Wiggins grinned. 'He's long retired.'

Tommy stared at him, then hawked up a globule of spit and pinged it into his empty mug.

'Right, girls.' Martha clapped her hands, sensing the mood. 'Bedtime. Delphy's due any minute, and we wouldn't want to disappoint her.'

'Sorry, ladies,' Wiggins said, catching Martha's eye. 'Me and Tommy—'

'Big T.'

Wiggins smiled. 'Me and *Big T* go way back. And it ain't always sunny.'

Tommy ate the rest of his bacon sandwich with slow, destructive force. The women bustled past him to the door. One of them, young, not more than twenty, twisted her head around for an instant as she left, locking eyes with Wiggins, then away at the floor.

'Come on, Poppy,' someone called. She flicked her hair and was gone. Ghost-pale, thin, she had the drowsy look of someone about to go to bed – unsurprising, given that it was gone eight in the morning and none of them seemed to have slept. All the same, Wiggins remembered her face, remembered the gesture.

'Boy!' Martha chided the small child, who hadn't strayed far from Wiggins all the while. 'Up the stairs.'

'But Martha, can't I—'

'Up.' She clicked her fingers. The boy's head drooped and he shuffled to the door, casting a doleful glance at Wiggins.

'What's your name, nips?' Wiggins asked.

'Boy, course,' he said. His freckled face suddenly split into the widest of grins. 'Ain't no one asked before.'

'Out of the way.' A deep, female voice barrelled into the room, followed by its owner. A woman of fifty, she was smartly dressed with an air of matron about her – as if she was used to doling out medicine to small boys but this was her day off, her Sunday best. 'To bed, Boy.' She bared a set of crooked, yellowed teeth for an instant and the child ran off.

'Morning, Delphy,' Martha said, dipping her head ever so slightly.

'Martha, Tom, we must prepare.' She didn't give Wiggins a second glance. 'The King is dead.'

'Shit,' Tommy said.

Martha sighed. Wiggins looked at the pair of them. It wasn't the reaction he was expecting. Indifference, maybe – he certainly didn't care one way or the other – or else mock solemnity. He felt sure Kell would don black underwear and not say a word for a week. People were funny about the royals. But this? They looked resigned, inconvenienced, put out.

'You know what to do – clear?' Delphy went on.

'Yes, Delphy,' Martha said.

Tommy inclined his head.

Delphy waved her hand in Wiggins's direction. 'And he must go, now.'

Wiggins shot to his feet, but in the hurry he caught his knee on the table leg. He sprawled onto the floor, breaking a cup and saucer.

'Sorry, sorry,' he said.

'Fack sake,' Tommy muttered.

Martha stooped to help Wiggins pick up the shards. She smiled and mouthed 'Don't worry.' Her skin crinkled once more. Wiggins almost reached out to touch the tight curls of her hair falling between them. He straightened up and looked at Delphy.

'Sorry, ma'am.' He replaced his cap and tipped it theatrically.

Delphy gave him such a severe glare, Wiggins wondered if she was going to take a belt to him. Instead, she flicked a hand at Tommy in a shooing gesture. 'Him, out. You, and Martha, in my study. Quick smart, lickety-split.' She turned on her heel and left.

'Out the back,' Tommy said. He wiped the crumbs from his mouth with a hand as big as a rib-eye steak and twice as thick.

Wiggins nodded once more, trying to catch Martha's eye, but her head was turned. He hesitated, then followed Tommy to the back door.

Once outside, Wiggins fell in step beside him. 'You the bounce, then?'

'Keep walking.'

'A knocking shop, Tommy?'

'Ain't Tommy no more. And it ain't no knocking shop either. It's proper.'

'Right.'

'Quality. This is you,' he said, rapping the garden door with his enormous fist.

'Listen, Tom – T.' Wiggins shifted on his feet, looking back at the large house behind them. 'I know we didn't always get on . . .'

'We didn't ever.'

Wiggins nodded. 'But all I need . . . I'm 'ere for a friend.'

'Two, three months ago. Walked out this door. Never came back.'

'That all? You can't have forgotten everything. You was one of our best.'

'I weren't never yours,' Tommy snapped. 'Look, it happens. People come and go in this business. Can't blame 'em. I've gotta go. And so have you.'

Wiggins took his hand out of his pocket and offered it to Tommy. 'Good to see an old face. Not many left, I reckon.'

Tommy looked down at Wiggins's hand and paused. Then he engulfed it in his great paw. 'Only the lucky ones.'

'I'll buy you a pint,' Wiggins said. 'For putting me up.' He touched his tender eye.

Tommy hesitated. 'You were right about the boxing.'

'You don't say?'

'At the Bloodied Axe, Wednesdays.' He unlocked the door and swung it open. Wiggins ducked through, but twisted around to face him again. 'What's all this about the King caulking it?'

Tommy grunted. 'What do I know? He's dead.'

'Nah, I meant, why you so bothered?'

'Business'll go through the roof.'

Wiggins looked askance. 'Cos the King's died?'

'You used to be smart,' Tommy said. 'The funeral. Half of Europe's toffs'll be here, and the rest. It'll be packed. Now fack off.'

'Ta for the shiner.'

Wiggins stepped away from the wall, into the early-morning sunshine. He looked back at the big house, the shuttered windows hiding all those women with their long gloves, their red ribbons and pale faces. Their drowsy, pinked eyes. Then he looked into the palm of his hand, where he held a small, beaded rosary – left on the kitchen floor for him by the pale girl who'd given him the look; retrieved when he'd pretended to fall. There was more to the Embassy of Olifa than met the eye.

'What on earth happened to your eye?'

'It's in mourning.'

Kell glared at him. Wiggins shifted uncomfortably on his feet and turned his face from the window in Kell's office. 'I bumped into an old friend, is all,' he muttered.

'Come with me, I need to buy a gun.'

They left the office in Victoria Street and cut through to St James's Park. As they passed the Underground station, a news van trundled by. A great bundle of papers landed at the news-agent's door, all black borders and KING DIES across the front. An aproned shopkeeper began pasting up replacement news-sheets. Only one story that day.

'I take it you know the King is dead,' Kell said over his shoulder. Wiggins walked a foot or so behind Kell when they were in public, as if he were his servant. 'I know, chief,' Wiggins said, nodding at a newsboy running by. 'It's in the final editions.'

'Don't call me chief.' Kell kept up a fearful pace as they cut through a squadron of pigeons taking off. 'God knows how they got the news so soon. Can't keep anything a secret these days.'

Wiggins looked at the back of his boss's head. Sweat prickled his neck above the collar, his top hat set slightly aslant. His step was jerky, too fast, agitated.

'We must plan for the funeral,' Kell said.

'I'll pick up the flowers.'

Kell rounded on him suddenly. 'Have some respect!' He leaned in, speaking under his breath. 'Do not speak ill of the monarchy in my presence. Ever.'

Wiggins blinked. He'd touched a nerve. Kell straightened his shoulders and they carried on, over the Mall and up towards Soho.

'We have to be ready. Every monarch in Europe will come to the funeral.'

'A small family do, is it?'

Kell stiffened, but continued. 'Which means every spy will no doubt also be in London.'

'You sending me to the Abbey?'

'No, I am not! I will go to the funeral. You will meet me at Paddington when the procession ends, in case there are any leads to follow up. This way.' Kell pointed across Piccadilly Circus towards the small alleyways around Rupert Street. 'A shortcut.'

'You sure?' Wiggins said, uncertain. He knew these alleyways. Kell did not. But his boss pressed on.

Kell glanced back. 'As I mentioned yesterday, you must reconnoitre the procession route.' He then proceeded to mutter the details of the route – already planned in advance, but still most secret – as they swerved off the main street and into Soho. 'Got it?'

Wiggins nodded as they made their way across the edge of a crowd outside an Italian restaurant, Le Solferino. A band of minstrels, in top hats and boaters, capered and cavorted as they played banjo music. Onlookers grinned and giggled, having a grand time. 'Oi, Sambo,' someone in the audience shouted. 'Show us your cock.'

Kell pulled up, surprised, and turned to him. 'This is a public place, man, control yourself.'

A couple of toughs swivelled to look at Kell. 'Hark at him. Fuck off, toffee.' The larger of the two stepped forward, his right arm raised. A flash of metal across his knuckles caught the light.

Wiggins drove his fist into the man's solar plexus, and then swept his ankles from under him with a well-aimed boot. 'Go,' he snapped at Kell, then pointed at the man's mate. 'Not now,' he hissed.

Kell froze in shock. Wiggins pushed him away, eyes on the two toughs all the while. The floored man spat and spluttered, but they did not follow.

'How dare they speak to me like that?'

'This ain't Whitehall,' Wiggins said as he steered Kell through a flurry of leering streetwalkers. 'Them's a pissed-up crowd.'

Kell nodded, shaken.

Wiggins glanced back as they turned into the grandeur of Regent Street. That was London all right. Big shops, bright lighting, fancy motors, top hats, all cheek by jowl with poverty and desperation and violence.

He felt the rosary in his pocket and thought back to the Embassy that morning. An odd set-up. The pale girl, Poppy, and that lingering look; Martha and her heavy bottom lip, the arch in the eyebrow; not to mention the madam running the shop. And strangest of all, Tommy.

Tommy had been a scrap of a boy when Wiggins last saw him, twenty years earlier, when they both worked for Sherlock Holmes as Irregulars.

'Wall-to-wall clicks out there, I'm telling ya.'

Young Tommy poked at the brazier in the disused railway arch at Paddington that doubled as the Irregulars' home. Wiggins and his best friend, Sally, had been running the gang for years by this time, picking up commissions from Sherlock Holmes, as well as odd jobs out of Fleet Street and the occasional click here and there when the wolf was growling.

Just the two of them when they'd started working for Holmes, over the years their number had swelled to around the ten mark, give or take. A ragtag of orphans, street kids and even a Scouse scally abandoned by an uncle, they rubbed along pretty well, with Wiggins as the oldest. All except Tommy. He'd been quiet enough to start with but now, a year or so after joining, he was starting to get mouthy.

'Easy, ain't it,' Tommy went on. 'They's too upset to notice me. Wait outside the prick's place, dip 'em every time.'

'Not in the old man's backyard. You can't steal from his clients. It ain't right.'

'You what?'

Wiggins reset his feet. He had a couple of years on Tommy – fourteen to his twelve or thereabouts – and he had height and weight. But Tommy had a temper – and a hot poker in his hand.

They eyed each other over the brazier. The poker glowed. A few of the younger ones stood around, watching. Wiggins could feel their nerves. In the far corner, his best mate Sally snoozed. At least, she pretended to. 'It ain't right,' he said at last. 'We work for the old man.' He looked around the archway at the dirty faces turned towards him, the urchins – his urchins. 'Sherlock Holmes, he's famous he is, the best detective who ever lived, and we's his eyes and ears. And we don't steal. Not whiles we work for him.'

'You the boss, are ya?'

'I am.'

Tommy spat into the fire, tugged at his shirt. 'Ain't my boss. I dip who I like.'

Wiggins took a step closer. He felt a ripple go through the others, sensed Sal's eyes on him – even though she still pretended to snooze, he knew she was watching. But she couldn't help him now. The Irregulars were a gang like any other; like the pack dogs out Royal Oak way, they followed the leader. And he was the leader. 'You can't stay here, Tommy – not if you're leafing.'

'Piss off.' He turned towards his bed. Wiggins grabbed him by the arm.

In an instant, Tommy swung his free hand around and into Wiggins's face. The blow glanced off his chin. He sidestepped to avoid the second fist, which flew wide.

But Wiggins's foot caught the brazier, splaying sparks and embers across the floor in a great crash. He stumbled to the ground.

Tommy grasped the poker and turned towards him. Wiggins saw Sal leap up and run to put out the flames. The younger ones stared in shock, unable to move.

'I'm earning money, boys.' Tommy looked around at the rest. 'We could earn buckets if we work together, I'm telling ya.'

Wiggins leapt up and in one movement punched him clean in the face, sending him to the floor. Dazed. Wiggins leaned down, picked up the fallen poker and handed it gently to Sal.

'You did your best,' she muttered. The rest of the Irregulars, even the ever-talkative twins, stared, silent and cowed.

Tommy forced himself up and glared. He rubbed his chin, tears welling. 'You fool. It ain't fair and you know it. We live in a shit pit, working for the old man. What for? Just so you can toady up to the "great detective"? I'm getting out.'

'There's the door then.'

Tommy pulled his coat from a cot and slunk away. He turned at the entrance to the archway and flicked Wiggins a defiant V with his fingers. Wiggins scowled. He didn't see anything wrong with working for the old man. At least it was work.

Wiggins's job now, so it seemed, was to accompany his boss to the gun shop.

Kell looked up at the rows of gleaming firearms in Purdey's as Wiggins stood one step behind. A sales clerk oozed his way over to them, lizard-like, pomaded.

'May I help you, sir?'

Kell pointed to a rifle with a peculiar, ornate sight. 'I'll try that one,' he said. The assistant nodded.

Wiggins shook his head slightly at the clerk. Kell turned to him and went on. 'We need to talk about assassination.'

'In a gun shop?' Wiggins said, although he was looking behind Kell at the assistant. He had his hand up to the gun and was looking over. Wiggins used his eyes to nudge him to a rifle three over, and the man nodded his assent.

'Don't be flippant. I am giving you a commission. You complain constantly about working in the provinces, well here's your chance to stay in London. Is this the gun I asked for?'

'Try it, sir.' The assistant bowed his head. 'This is perhaps the perfect weight for you.'

Kell hoisted the gun onto his shoulder.

'You want me to kill someone?' Wiggins hissed.

'I'll take it,' Kell said. 'Have it sent over with fifty rounds to this address.' He then marched out of the shop, Wiggins at his heels.

Back on the street, Kell turned south and continued. 'The Prime Minister fears assassination.'

'Squiffy's got the jitters.'

'He's not scared for himself,' Kell snapped. 'Every major monarch in Europe will be there, presidents, the lot. The *Prime Minister* . . .' Kell glared back at Wiggins as he said this. He wasn't having him refer to the man as Squiffy, for all that Asquith liked a drink. Not in his presence anyway. '. . . He is most concerned about the threat of political assassination.'

A fire engine sped past, its bell clanging, the helmets gleaming in the May sunshine. They were at the corner of Berkeley Square and Kell was swivelling around, looking for a cab.

'The King's funeral will be the political event of the century, everyone will be here.' He glanced at Wiggins as a master would turn to a servant. 'This is why I brought you back. I want you to highlight any weak points on the route. You know the streets better than anyone.'

Wiggins frowned. 'Who'd be taking a pop? Who're they worried about?'

'Anarchist gangs, probably,' Kell said, then hailed a hansom cab. He didn't like the motorised taxis, or their meters. He got in, left the door open and gestured curtly for Wiggins to join him.

'But that's for Special Branch to deal with. Victoria Street!' he shouted at the cabby, then turned to Wiggins. 'We have a far more pressing problem.'

Wiggins's face was still clouded with thought. 'Special Branch, you say? You got access to their files?'

'That's none of your business. None of *our* business. Are you listening to me?'

'Yes, sir, skipper, sir, aye aye, sir.'

'You may think you're amusing but we've got a big problem. There's been a leak in Whitehall. From the Cabinet minutes. And it's down to us to find out who.'

Wiggins shifted in his seat. 'Suspects?'

'The departmental clerks.'

'Blame it on the workers, eh?' Wiggins shook his head. 'Could've been anyone.'

Kell sighed theatrically. 'So you'd rather I sent you to interrogate the Home Secretary?' The cab burst onto Victoria Street and he directed the cabby to the office. 'No. You will discount the clerks, understand – one by one.'

They got out of the cab. 'Ain't it just gossip? What's the big to-do?'

'The big *to-do* is that this leak cost us a valuable treaty. And who knows what other information has gone missing. Lives are in danger. How would you like it if you went into battle and the enemy knew your exact movements, even before you'd made them?'

Wiggins shrugged. 'It could take months.'

'Which is why we'll start immediately,' Kell said, gesturing to the office. 'We'll get you the clerks' details, and you'll be out on the streets tomorrow.'

'Tomorra's Sunday.'

'And?' Kell raised an eyebrow. 'Are you due in church?'

4

'*In nòmine Patris et Filii et Spìritus Sancti.*'

'Amen.'

'*Gràtia Dòmini nostri Jesu Christi, et càritas Dei, et communicàtio Sancti Spìritus sit cum òmnibus vobis.*'

'*Et cum spiritu tuo.*'

The priest went on. Wiggins stood near the back, on the outside aisle, and looked up into the vaulted roof. Incense wafted over the heads of the congregation, catching in his nose.

He ducked his head briefly and sauntered down the aisle. A couple of people turned, but most took no notice. He didn't understand the words, but they sounded both comforting and, somehow, sinister. Like a violent father, familiar yet dangerous. Was his own father a Catholic, he wondered as he took a seat next to a solitary worshipper. The old girls down Marylebone Lane used to say he had the look of the Irish about him. (No one ever said he had the luck.) It didn't matter.

The priest started doling out the body of Christ, or whatever it was they did, and the young woman next to Wiggins pushed past him to take her turn. He looked up at the imagery above the altar. No master, no God. That's what Peter the Painter believed, that's what he'd told him the year before – before Bela, before the bomb, before that bullet in the shoulder.

He was due to meet Jax later that day, up near Petticoat, to see if she'd found out anything about Peter, but something else tugged at his mind, something that Kell had said about the anarchist gangs and the King's funeral. Maybe he needed to go to the police. The young woman he'd sat next to came back down the aisle towards him.

She took her seat and they both knelt down. He handed her back her rosary, dropped for him to find on the floor of the Embassy kitchen.

'Thanks, mister,' she whispered. 'Looking for Millie, ain't ya?' She cast a shy glance at him, her face an ivory white, her movements nervy.

'Poppy?'

'You ain't no rozzer?'

Poppy was young, younger than he'd first thought, barely of age. Wiggins didn't smile at the foolishness of the question. He shook his head gently. 'Asking for a friend.'

She fiddled with the rosary, her head down, avoiding his eyes. Wiggins could feel her agitation. Her legs quivered beneath her long skirt. She was dressed properly, not like the day before at breakfast with the other whores. Every now and then her hand shot up to a red ribbon tied around her neck.

'What do you want to tell me?' he said softly.

'How ya know I wanted to tell you anything?'

Wiggins nodded at the rosary. 'Left that for me, didn't ya? Knew you'd either be here or at St Matthew's. Them's the Catholic shops local.'

She jerked her head. 'Just cos I'm a whore, don't mean I can't be a Catholic. I believe.'

'I know.' Wiggins waited. The other congregants had begun to rise, gathering belongings, staring up at the cross hanging above the altar and at the stained-glass window beyond, doing the old spectacles, testicles, wallet and watch. He couldn't push too hard; she'd scare easy.

Poppy glanced around her. 'She had a Fred.'

'Her boyfriend's named Fred?'

'Nah. That's what we call the sweet ones, Freds.'

'Sweet ones?'

She clasped her hands, distracted again. 'Who are ya? Can you help me?'

Wiggins tensed, unsure. 'What you mean, sweet ones?'

'We're whores. Some of the men get sweet.' She got to her feet suddenly and shivered. 'Millie had a new Fred, that's all I know.'

Wiggins grabbed her wrist, covered by the tight sleeve of her dress. 'Nothing else? A name?'

'They's all Freds,' she said plaintively. 'I gotta go.'

'But—'

'I shouldn't've said nothing.' She reached her hand up to her face. An old woman passed, glancing at them through narrowed eyes. Wiggins took a step back, ducked his head.

'People come and go in this business,' Poppy whispered. 'I just thought you might . . .' Her eyes drifted away and she lost her thread.

'What?'

She sniffed. 'Half the girls end up at the ferry,' she muttered under her breath and then stepped away.

He tried to call her back. 'I'll come again,' he hissed. 'Sundays.' But he wasn't sure if she'd heard.

He watched as the last of the worshippers filtered out of the church. Poppy flitted among them, carried forward like a scrap of rubbish on the river, and then she was gone. He looked up above the altar once more, the stained-glass image of a mother and child. *H, H, get me the bottle. G'arn, son. Another nip won't hurt.*

Wiggins shook the memory away. He didn't cross himself, but turned to the back of the church. At that moment, and only for an instant, he saw her standing at the doors. She'd obviously been watching him, but she ghosted away as soon as their eyes locked. Tall, well dressed, commanding, black curls tumbling from beneath her hat, it was the other woman from the Embassy, the one with the dark skin and arched eyebrow. It was Martha.

'It will be the greatest coming together of royalty the world has ever known. Not even in the days of Charlemagne, nor even Solomon himself, has such regality been visited in one place.'

A silence greeted this. 'Right-ho,' Soapy said after a moment. 'I think we're all here. Including the Home Secretary.' Soapy nodded at Churchill. 'Who has so graciously set the scene. Sir

Edward Henry, Commissioner of Police, will you take us through the details?'

While Wiggins sat in church that Sunday morning, Kell worshipped at a different altar. He stood with his back to the wall, and surveyed the crowded Cabinet briefing room. Although the meeting had been hastily convened, everybody wanted a piece of this operation, wanted to be part of the funeral arrangements. Everyone wore black. Kell was still too junior for a seat at the table. All the big men of the Cabinet, bar the PM, sat with their assistants behind them. The red ribbons binding their ministerial papers provided the only dash of colour in the room. Sir Edward Henry was at one end of the table. Next to him, Sir Patrick Quinn, head of Special Branch.

Quinn had come into the room with Sir Edward. He'd raised an eyebrow in surprise on seeing Kell – he didn't nod so much as look amused, knowing. Every now and then he glanced at Kell with the same half-amused, half-questioning look.

Sir Edward Henry began his briefing. He outlined the proposed route of the funeral procession intended for the following week. The exact details were to be kept secret from the public, for fear of disturbance, in particular the route it would take through the small streets and poor areas around Paddington Station.

'On the day, we will have officers from half the forces in the south of England, as well as the City of London Police,' Sir Edward concluded. 'I anticipate more than a thousand policemen will be in attendance.'

Grey, the Foreign Secretary himself, raised a hand. Kell noted the immaculate collar, his black suit without a hair on it. His cuffs gleamed white. His hair, silver but full, was perfectly trimmed – as if he'd left the barber only minutes ago. He had two aides with him, one sitting and one standing next to Kell, both similarly turned out – perfectly dressed, sleek, pinstriped. Most of the men of Whitehall picked up at least some evidence of dirt or soot, of living in the city, even if it was only a stray feather attached to the sole of their shoe. These men, the men of the FO, floated through the world untouched.

'I think, gentlemen, that we must get to the matter in hand. I have at least thirty-two ambassadors whose nerves are frayed. And once frayed' – Grey said the word as if it were the worst thing imaginable – 'they come to me to have them restored. Security. What are the plans to guarantee the safety of our overseas guests?'

'Quite right,' Sir Edward Henry nodded, cowed. He gestured to Quinn. 'Sir Patrick Quinn of Special Branch, gentlemen.'

Quinn stood up, glancing again at Kell for a second. No sign of nerves, damn him, Kell thought, not even in front of the cream of Whitehall, the de facto government bar Asquith himself. 'Look at that, cool as you like,' the young man from the FO whispered to Kell. An ally.

'My Lords, gentlemen. We have special-protection officers on every member of the Royal Family.' Quinn droned on with the details. Kell's eye wandered back to the young man next to him. Even his handkerchief, a brilliant white against the night-sky black, was monogrammed with *H M-B* in fine golden thread. Too much money in the diplomatic, he thought. Perhaps Constance would talk to him if he had more money – but then she didn't want for money, never even mentioned the stuff. He turned back to Quinn, who was revelling in his time in the sun. Quinn glanced at him again.

Did he know about the photograph? Had he placed Constance at the scene? And what was the bloody scene anyway, where had she been? And with whom?

'You seem very sure of everything, Sir Patrick,' Soapy said. 'You have no fear of assassination?'

'We are confident we know all the main players who could even contemplate such a thing, sir. The Republican Army—'

'You mean the Fenians?'

'Right you are, sir. The Irish Republican Brotherhood won't come to town. It's too sensitive, too much respect for the deceased, you see.'

Churchill grunted. 'That would be a first.'

'What about the anarchists?' Grey asked quietly. 'Some of our friends are very worried about anarchists.'

'Hardly a surprise, sir, most of them being royalty and so on,' Quinn almost twinkled in reply. 'But I believe that even the worst of the anarchos, say the Gardstein Gang, won't put in an appearance. At least, that's our information.'

'The Archduke Franz Ferdinand is coming.'

'It's the kings we have to worry about.'

'And the Tsar.'

Soapy rapped his knuckles on the table. 'Yes, the Tsar. Captain Kell foiled a plot against him last year, I believe,' he said, glancing first at Kell, then at Churchill.

'Did he indeed?' Quinn said, putting his hand to his chin, but maintaining the look of faint amusement. 'I was wondering why . . .'

'We have a watching brief only,' said Kell. He sounded stilted to himself, unsure. Unlike the eloquent, confident Quinn.

Quinn stared at him for a moment too long.

'You were talking about the anarchists?' Soapy prompted.

'Of course, who could be forgetting the anarchos. We have men at all the ports. Any of the anarchos coming in from Paris will be stopped.'

'Very good, Sir Patrick. Now, I'm sure there are many around this table who would be interested to hear your plans for their own security.'

Quinn nodded and went into another of his elaborate speeches. Kell blocked out the words and instead turned his thoughts to his most pressing task: the Whitehall leak. He was convinced that if a mole could be found, he would be among one of the copying clerks. But a very small part of his mind wondered about those sitting around the table, the various Cabinet ministers who had been in attendance when the dangerous remarks about Italy were made.

His eyes kept returning to two men. First was Winston Churchill, late of the Board of Trade, now Home Secretary and surely on his way to even higher office, such was the towering size of his ambition. Was that ambition powerful enough for him to sabotage his own prime minister in his search for the very top job? He'd crossed the floor already in his career; perhaps anything was possible? The second man Kell looked at once more was the Foreign Secretary himself, Sir Edward Grey. He was Asquith's closest rival for the premiership, and had apparently seethed in private when Asquith took over ahead of him in '06. Had the sleek fox set a trap for the PM?

It was no secret that both ministers, along with half the Liberal Party, had been incredibly angry when Asquith called the general election earlier in the year in order to increase his majority, only to fail to gain overall control. The Liberals were still in government but only by virtue of an uneasy coalition with the Irish. It made for a nasty atmosphere in political circles. Could this be enough for Churchill or Grey to upset the applecart?

Kell shook these suspicions from his head. It was preposterous. The Cabinet might be a hotbed of intrigue, monstrous ambition and ruthless personal disloyalty, but neither of these men would turn their backs on England, on the Empire. Churchill was a Harrow boy; Grey had gone to Winchester College.

Quinn had finally finished speaking and Kell pricked up his ears once again.

Soapy shuffled the papers in front of him. 'Thank you *very* much, Sir Patrick. The detail you've gone to is absolutely exhaustive. On that note, I think we can adjourn.'

'Conceited bloody Paddy,' the man from the FO whispered under his breath.

Kell stifled a guffaw.

'Sorry, not a friend of yours, is he?'

'Good God no,' Kell said.

'You didn't look like a policeman.' The pristine young man put out his hand. 'Moseby-Brown, FO.'

'Kell. Intelligence.'

'Glad to see someone's got it.'

'I say,' Kell said under his breath, 'you couldn't help me with something, could you? Very quietly, shall we say?'

Moseby-Brown lifted his eyebrows, a little taken aback. Just then, Grey rose in front of them, collected his ribbon-bound

ministerial papers and inclined his head to the door. Even the
red tape looked ironed, Kell noticed idly. Moseby-Brown removed
an invisible piece of lint from his cuff. 'My lord and master,' he
said. 'Must dash.'

Awfully young for the FO, Kell thought as he watched the
young man sleekly follow in the sleek footsteps of his sleek master.
Still, it was the kind of youth that could be used if he approached
him carefully.

Kell got as far as the door before he was buttonholed by Quinn.
'So, you're an interesting man, Captain Kell, so you are. I never
knew you were involved with the Tsar last year, when Mr Churchill
called the whole thing off.'

'Really?'

'And so, do you have any other secrets you'll need to be telling
me?'

Kell paused. Despite the hubbub of the room, committee men
exiting around them, Quinn only had eyes for him.

'I'm not in the business of keeping secrets from colleagues.'

'Is that so? There was me thinking that was your very business.'

'Need I remind you that it was you who refused me access to
your files. If anyone's holding secrets around here, Sir Patrick,
it's you.'

Quinn nodded to himself. 'That's a point, that's definitely a
point,' he said, though he showed no signs of agreement.
'Sometimes we don't know that we know.'

At that point Sir Edward Henry bellowed for Quinn, and Kell
made good his escape.

Wiggins pulled his cap low and pretended to be asleep. It never
made sense to catch a copper's eye, least of all when you were
actually in a police station.

He sat on a hard bench in the hallway of New Scotland Yard
and waited. A desk sergeant stared at him across the empty room
and glowered. Wiggins could hear his disapproval, the tuts and
sighs, the unspent aggression.

'How long?' Wiggins said at last, unable to contain himself.

The sergeant leaned forward over the front desk. 'Who knows?' he said, pleased to disappoint. 'Special Branch are very important people. It could be days. In fact, why don't you just—'

At that moment, the doors that led to the staircase swung open and an ape of a man in plain clothes came out. 'This him?' he said to the sergeant.

'It is.'

The ape pointed at Wiggins. 'What do you want?'

Wiggins stood up and glanced at the sergeant. The ape nodded and the sergeant stepped away from the desk. 'I got gen, ain't I?'

'On what?'

'Who are you?'

'Do you want me to lock you up? Spill or hop it.'

Wiggins leaned close. 'I knows of an anarchist plot. To attack the King's funeral, sure as eggs.'

'Really?' The detective patted himself for a smoke, supremely uninterested. 'How much you charging for this?'

'Bint I've been seeing. Her mates. Straight up. Body by the name of Peter the Painter?'

The detective paused, the cigarette between his lips unlit.

Twenty minutes later, Wiggins sat in a grimy, windowless interview room opposite the ape detective and another man. 'Say that again,' the ape demanded.

Wiggins repeated himself to the other detective, a pale man with jet-black hair and dirt under his fingernails. 'I thought Gardstein was in Paris,' the ape muttered.

'They know the route of the procession and all,' Wiggins added.

'What?' The ape slapped his hand on the table. 'Wait there,' he cried and pulled the other man out of the room.

Ten minutes later, the ape came back. 'Stand up,' he ordered. 'There, four feet from the table. Don't speak unless the chief asks you to; don't swear; don't slouch; and don't fucking lie, understand?'

Wiggins tipped his cap.

The ape stepped to the wall and then an altogether different man came in. With his long nose, widow's peak and unmistakable air of command, the man – the 'chief' – stepped to the free chair, sat down and crossed his legs. He looked Wiggins up and down, raised his eyebrows at the ape, then said: 'Now, Detective Jackson here is telling me you know things you should not know; he is telling me you know people you should not know; and he is telling me it does not sound right.'

'Is that a question?' Wiggins shot a glance at the ape Jackson.

'Ah, I see, you're by way of a card. The wit of the native Londoner. I'm thinking it would be a shame to crush that. Tell me, what roads does the funeral procession take from Hyde Park to Paddington?'

Wiggins rapped out the answer, as given to him by Kell the day before. The chief – Wiggins recognised him from one of Kell's newspapers as Sir Patrick Quinn, head of Special Branch – nodded slowly. 'How did you come by this information?'

'Overheard. I'm seeing a Rooski bird, ain't I? Drinking with her down the 'Chapel, off Jubilee Street. She's tight with a bloke named Peter. Some's call him the Painter.' Wiggins watched Quinn's reaction closely. Quinn crossed his legs again, examined his fingernails and finally fixed Wiggins with a stare. 'What's the girl's name?'

Wiggins hesitated. 'Bela,' he said at last. It was the first time he'd said her name in months, and still it hurt. 'But she ain't important.'

Quinn swatted an invisible fly. 'Why are you here?'

'They's up to no good. I'm a patriot, me, always have been.'

Quinn thought for a moment. He pulled a watch from his waistcoat. 'You will meet Detective Jackson tomorrow at eleven in the morning – I am trusting you will be waking up in time for that – whereby you will furnish him with all the information you have on Peter the Painter and any gang he's working with.'

'I've told you all I knows.'

'But you've not told us all the information you will be finding out tonight, understand?'

Wiggins nodded.

'If Detective Jackson is satisfied with the information you provide, then he may, at his own discretion, reward you in a financial manner. Yes?'

Wiggins nodded once more.

Quinn got up then, without any further acknowledgement. He shot a look at Jackson and was gone.

Jackson marched Wiggins out of the interview room and down a small, dark staircase. He pushed Wiggins through a narrow exit and out into a side street around the back of New Scotland Yard.

Wiggins straightened his cap and ambled off towards Charing Cross Station. He bought a return ticket at the crowded office on the concourse – busy even though it was Sunday. London never sleeps, he thought with a smile. Drinkers spilled from the station pub in the corner and Wiggins almost checked his stride. But he pushed on – their beer was rank. Instead, he got on the first train south. He walked through the carriages to the front of the train as it trundled over the river.

As the train slowed into one of the platforms at Waterloo Junction, he quickly moved into the final carriage. It was a smallish but very busy station, with four platforms set across two double sets of tracks. He hurried past the people collecting in the corridor and reached the final doors. He checked his watch, then as whistles burst the air and the engine let off a great gust of steam, he opened the door on the other side from the platform. He dropped down onto the gravel, obscured by the whirls and gusts of steam and smoke.

In one swift movement, he stepped across to the train on the other platform. The wheels squealed and ground as it started to move off. He clambered up onto the side of a second-class carriage, calmly opened the door and stepped inside. A small boy in shorts and a cricket cap stood in the area at the end of the carriage and stared at him, mouth agape.

'Maintenance,' Wiggins said. 'Hobbs is your man.'

The boy ran off, startled. Wiggins glanced back through the window in the door as the train accelerated towards Charing

Cross. As he did so, he caught sight, for an instant, of the bewildered Special Branch detective who had tailed him from Scotland Yard standing in the other train, head swivelling as he searched in vain for Wiggins.

Wiggins got off the train at Charing Cross and hopped on the number 11 bus down the Strand, energised by the whole exchange at Scotland Yard. He had no intention of giving them any more information, of meeting Detective Jackson the next day. He *had* no information, of course. He hadn't seen Peter in almost a year.

What Special Branch had told him, on the other hand, was notable. It had been a risk for Wiggins to go in there, but he'd found out a number of things. One, Peter had probably been in Paris, which suggested why Jax couldn't find him in the East End. Two, there was a very real chance that Peter was back in London. Certainly, the police took the idea seriously. Sir Patrick Quinn wouldn't interview any Tom, Dick or Harry off the street. This suspicion had been confirmed when Wiggins realised they'd sent a detective to follow him.

Peter was in London, Wiggins could feel it. And he wouldn't put it past him to try something at the funeral, though he'd lay long odds that it wouldn't be Peter himself plunging the knife or holding the bomb or firing the fatal shot. Peter would slide into the background and let someone else take a bullet for his revolutionary beliefs. The detective had mentioned the name Gardstein; perhaps he was Peter's latest patsy.

Wiggins swung off the bus at Liverpool Street and went to find Jax, his energy renewed.

'Up there, on the corner,' Jax pointed, although she had her back turned.

'Show me,' Wiggins said.

'Not now,' she said. 'You can see it, there, just round the corner, 'bove the market.'

Wiggins gripped her shoulder. 'Show me.' He'd met Jax just by the station and was eager to get on.

They'd walked up to the edge of Petticoat Lane Market, busier than Piccadilly Circus on a Sunday afternoon. A soapbox orator tried to shout above the din: 'Throw out the evil alien, send 'em back to Russia, to Afreeka, to the hellfire pit they came from. Our island is too small.' Market traders called out their wares: 'Three candles a penny, get 'em before they're lit'; 'Bagel, bagel, bagel!' Wiggins and Jax moved through the crowd. 'Mind out there, love,' a woman cried as she captained a pram like an icebreaker. Chestnuts spat and crackled in a brazier, a sweet, burnt, smoky smell wafting through the throng. The market stalls burst with clothes, live chickens, pots and pans, shoes, hooky fags, knock-off silver plate and sweetheart trinkets, with racks of hats, with purple slabs of meat, flies abuzz, and hot cider and cold ice cream in tubs on wheels and fruits fresh in from the docks, tea from Assam, sugar from Jamaica, Colchester oysters, Nottingham lace, Bermondsey bourbon biscuits, china from Stoke and sad, wilting flowers nicked the day before from down Columbia Road Market, second-hand, the florist-thief swore.

Wiggins hadn't yet told Jax about Millie. He wanted to get all she knew on Peter first. One thing you learned living on the streets, and one thing you certainly learned working for Sherlock Holmes: knowledge was worth something, you didn't give it away for nothing. Not even the great detective did that, unless there were extenuating circumstances. You said what you knew when you had to. Jax had obviously gone to the same school. Which is why he found himself having to almost drag her through the market.

'I tell ya, I sees them blokes go in once, after a powwow up at Jubilee Street. It ain't nuffin', I'm telling ya. Let me go, ya nonce, else I'll scream for the rozzers.'

'No you won't,' Wiggins said, and she didn't. She was doing her utmost not to attract attention.

They entered a small yard, just off the market, with high walls and a low stench. 'In there.' She pointed at one of the four doors. 'Last Tuesday night, two of them came back.'

'Russians?'

'Can we go now?'

But Wiggins was already knocking on the door. No answer. The door was locked, but it had a flimsy, old-fashioned latch lock, which he fiddled open in a trice. 'Wiggins,' Jax hissed, her head buried into her chest. 'We gotta go.'

Wiggins stepped through the door, without anxiety. He knew it would be empty. From what he remembered of Peter's mob, they never stayed anywhere long. The door opened into a single room, which ran into a smaller, windowless anteroom. He sat down on the only chair and cast his eyes around. Jax slunk in behind him.

'Told ya,' she said.

'Shut it.' He got on his knees and thrust his hands out onto the floor. Slowly he examined in between the floorboards with his long, thin fingers. He picked up a few scraps of litter, then leapt up and ran his hands across the walls. Apart from the chair, the only furniture was two bedrolls and a piss bucket, which Wiggins all but ignored. Finally, he turned the chair upside down and examined the underside of the seat.

'Christ alive, anyone would fink you were Sherlock Holmes himself.'

Wiggins shot her a foul look, thrust the litter in his pocket and nodded.

Again, Jax pulled her cap down low and walked behind Wiggins, as if in his shadow. They went back into the market. 'So tells me about Millie,' she muttered. 'Ya promised.'

Before he could answer, a commotion broke out behind them.

'Gotcha, ya facking thief!'

Jax leapt away, whippet fast, but a huge arm swung through the crowd and caught her by the collar. She squealed as she was dragged away.

'Oi!' Wiggins ran after them, towards a butcher's cart.

'Fack off out of it.' The enormous butcher glared at Wiggins. He held Jax hard by the collar in one gigantic fist, while with the other he scrabbled on his bench of tools. 'Sid, where's the facking cleaver?' he cried.

Wiggins hesitated. If anything, the butcher's mate, Sid, was even bigger than his boss. The butcher grasped the cleaver and pulled Jax over to the block with his other hand.

'What ya doing?' Wiggins said. 'Ya can't just—'

'This 'un's a facking leaf, and I'm gonna cut 'is facking hand off.'

Jax stared wide-eyed at him, her head bent low, her wrist clamped to the wooden block. Wiggins stepped forward and placed a hand on the butcher's side. 'Come on, mate,' he said.

'Ya want some and all?' He held the cleaver above his head, murder in his eyes. 'Sid, get Frankie and Mueller – now.'

Wiggins patted him once more. 'Easy, easy. You wouldn't want the cops coming down here, would ya?'

'This ain't cop town. Now sling it.'

'Look, what's he owe?' Wiggins said, tapping his pockets.

The butcher looked at him quizzically. He was breathing hard with anger and adrenaline, but he still had an eye for cash. Jax squirmed again but the enormous fist held firm. 'He's lifted all sorts from here. Steaks, chops, bangers, you name it. And it ain't just me. He's lifted from half the stalls on the Lane.'

'This do?' Wiggins pulled out a pound note and straightened it between his hands in front of him. 'All yours,' he said. ''Less you wait for the others.'

The butcher frowned, licked his lips and glanced up the market in the direction of the disappearing Sid. 'Fack it.' He tossed the cleaver aside and grasped the note.

Wiggins yanked Jax away into the crowd. 'Move it.'

'Where you get a quid from?' she muttered.

'Aargh!' From behind them, the butcher howled.

'Run!'

The two of them nipped between the last stalls at the top of the market, ducked under the arch onto Liverpool Street and jumped a bus as it rattled past.

Wiggins pushed Jax into the main compartment. 'I'm paying this time,' he said. He glanced back to see the butcher and Sid burst onto the road, heads swivelling.

'You lifted it from his money belt, didn'tcha?' Jax said. 'Paid 'im off with his own cash.'

They both laughed, the same high-pitched gurgle descending into giggles and splutters. A matron sitting in front of them turned and frowned. Wiggins tipped his cap. 'No wonder you didn't want to go there,' he said once they'd stopped laughing.

Jax shook her head. The bus trundled south towards the river. 'What about Millie?'

'Did she have any identifying marks?'

'Wot, like your big hooter?'

'You know what she did, don't ya?'

'All I know is she's gone.' Jax looked out of the window as they went over London Bridge, the river thick with traffic right down to the high masts of the big ships out east. She pulled a small trinket from around her neck. 'She wears one like this. Got 'em together, down Petticoat last year.'

'Lifted?'

'Wot you think?'

Wiggins examined the small cross and icon. A St Christopher. 'You gone soft?' he said, handing it back.

'Nah, it's just . . . He stands up for waifs, don't he?'

'You're no waif.'

Jax tucked the icon back into her shirt. 'I just want to know where she is. You promised.'

'I'll have another look,' he said. He *had* promised. But after that first conversation with Tommy and the one with Poppy, he guessed she'd gone off with her Fred. Who wouldn't flee a job like that? Jax looked so hopeful, big blue eyes staring back at him, he didn't have the heart to tell her just yet, and he didn't know for sure. He put his hand on her shoulder lightly, a promise renewed.

The two of them got off the bus at Borough and walked over to Sal's tea hut, just south of Waterloo. Jax's mum, and Wiggins's oldest friend, ran it for cabbies. Open even on a Sunday, every day, all year. The taxis never stopped so neither did she.

Jax hesitated at the door. 'I can't keep looking for this Peter bloke, not unless you pay me. I gotta get back running.'

Wiggins nodded.

'Mum needs the blunt coming in. We're brassick. Always. And don't say nothing about what happened up the Lane – she don't like thieving.'

'Times change.' He smiled. 'You've gotta work when you can. I'll come back when I can pay. I's a bit skint myself.' He pushed open the door to the hut. 'And I just gave up the last quid I nicked. Bought your hand, if you've forgotten.'

'Whose hand?'

'Wotcha, Sal,' Wiggins said. 'Jax was just helping me with my enquiries.'

'All right, my girl,' Sal said. 'You look like you've seen a ghost.'

'Her own. Don't ask.'

'Leave off, Ma.' Jax went straight for the loaf of bread on the sideboard at the far end. Sal held up a teacup and Wiggins nodded. The sole customer saluted with his free hand and blew thick black pipe smoke at the yellowed ceiling.

'Well?' Sal said. A couple of cabbies bustled in, hallooing. They took seats and glanced at Wiggins without curiosity. Sal got up and served them, two times tea, two times bread and butter and one slice of lemon, special like.

With the moment to himself, Wiggins pulled from his pocket the sweet wrappers he'd found in the deserted room off Petticoat Lane. He wet his finger and tasted each of the wrappers in turn. Three mint imperials and one lemon sherbert. It wasn't enough. Peter was addicted to the sweets, but four wrappers wouldn't stand up in court. Not that he was planning to go to court.

'Where you been?' Sal plumped down again.

'Up north, for work. And no, I can't tell you what it is, however many times you ask.'

She pursed her lips. 'Suit yourself.' She got up again and began busying herself in the kitchen area.

Wiggins went after her. They'd known each other for over twenty years; they'd grown up together on the streets. She was his first friend – she'd saved him. And now Bill was dead and buried she was once again the closest thing to his best friend. But when he'd joined the army, a rift had been created that had never really healed. He'd bumped into her the year before, but since then had seen her daughter Jax as much as her. Sometimes he'd look at Sal's fat, chipmunk cheeks and see the girl he used to know, see the girl he'd shared everything with, his fears, his hopes, his last penny pie. But she wasn't that girl any more, and he wasn't a kid.

He stood beside her at the tea urn. 'Here, never guess who I saw the other day? Tommy.'

Sal glanced sideways at him. 'He showed up again, after you left.' She poured water into the urn and said nothing more.

Wiggins waited, looked carefully at her face, then broke into a grin. 'Ya didn't.'

'He'd grown up. He was bigger.'

'Please tell me ya didn't.'

She looked at him for a moment, full in the face. A ginger curl fell over one eye, her cheeks still freckled. 'Nah, I didn't,' she said at last. 'Not that it's any of your biznay.' They both smiled, perhaps for different reasons.

5

'I thought this was your business?' Kell said in exasperation.

'I can't find anything that's not there, can I?' Wiggins replied. 'And I've only been at it a week. *And* I'm on my tod.'

'You've had more than a week. But enough of the excuses. Have you even managed to eliminate any of the clerks from the enquiry?'

Wiggins sighed. 'Arbuckle. Ministry of Works.'

Kell loosened his collar. 'And?' It was three days until the King's funeral, and they'd made no progress on finding the leak.

'Lives in Camberwell, drinks an 'alf over the odds but not more. Wife loves him. Kids don't. Smells.'

'How is that relevant?'

'If he's on the take, then he don't spend the money, is all.'

'Next.'

'Bevington in the Admiralty, Bryce in Labour.' Wiggins reeled off the mundane details he'd picked up from following these government clerks, rooting around in their lives.

'So nothing?' Kell said at last.

'I've only just started.'

The telephone jangled into life, startling them both. Kell grasped the horn himself. 'Kell,' he said, before Simpkins could answer.

'Glad you can get something right,' Soapy's voice crackled down the line. 'Have you got any information?'

'Not yet.' He held the receiver close, so Wiggins couldn't hear. 'It's early days.'

'Early days!' Soapy's agitation almost jumped out of the phone. 'Things have got worse, and if you don't do something about it quick smart we're all out of a job.'

'How?'

'Last night. A minor bash at the FO, diplo bigwigs, you know the drill. A scratch of soup then port and brandy till midnight. PM turns up, German ambassador there, all faux friendship.'

'And . . . ?'

'They know the route of the procession.'

'The German ambassador?'

'One of his staff. Let it slip casually, bragging, probably. The PM's livid,' Soapy went on. 'Can't tell the King, of course.'

'The King's dead.'

'The new one.'

Kell looked over at Wiggins, who sat with his head down, apparently oblivious. 'Sure it's the sneak? Most of the route is common sense. There are only so many ways to get from Whitehall to Paddington.'

'Of course it's a bally leak. We've advertised a different one – only the members of the committee know the real one, with all the details. You were in the room, we *know* everyone who knew.' Soapy paused and breathed in.

This was the worst of it for Soapy, Kell understood: that it was one of the chaps, one of the twenty or so people in the committee room, who had told someone else. It broke all the ethics they had known since school. There was a sneak, a snitch, a mole, a blabber. It was unforgivable.

'Are you still there, Kell?'

'I'm still here.'

'Why? Get out, man, find out who's behind this.' He hung up.

Kell looked at the receiver for a moment, then replaced it carefully. 'Who's next on the list?'

'Carter, chief clerk at the Foreign Office.'

Kell thought of the committee room, who had been there: Foreign Office, Home Office, War Office, Admiralty, Cabinet Office and police. 'You can scrub most of the names on your list,' he said at last.

'You're joking?'

'Look into Carter as planned, then the chief clerks at Home, War and Admiralty.' Kell couldn't quite bring himself to send Wiggins after the ministers. Not yet.

Wiggins hesitated. 'It's your money,' he said and got up.

'And don't forget,' Kell called across the room.

'Forget what?'

'The funeral, noon. You're to meet me at Paddington.'

'How could I forget Paddington?' Wiggins said, and was gone.

Wiggins stepped across the hallway of the apartment and had made it to the front door when he felt a hand on his arm.

'What-ho! Got a letter for you.' Simpkins, the clerk, held out a small envelope.

'For me? Addressed here?'

'I know, bit odd.'

'Ta.' Wiggins took the letter and examined it. 'No postmark?'

'Simpkins!' Kell called from his office, and the clerk hurried away.

Wiggins opened the envelope. A first-class rail ticket fluttered to the floor. The envelope was otherwise empty. He examined the inside of the envelope, and then the writing once more. His name – WIGGINS – and the address were written in capitals. He sniffed the envelope, then turned his attention to the ticket, which came with a compartment reservation for the 0918 from Marylebone the following morning. He hesitated, then thrust the ticket into his pocket and set off for Islington.

Hilldrop Crescent was a pleasant, tree-lined street in a respectable part of Islington. Number 43 sat on the right-hand side of a three-house terrace. Four storeys high, single-fronted, it was an unremarkable building in an unremarkable street. It was also the home of Archibald Carter, chief clerk to the Foreign Office, a civil servant of over twenty years' standing. Wiggins had spent most of the afternoon asking around discreetly – local tradesmen, at various pubs and the like. Now he was posing as a canvasser on the street. He'd filched a magazine from the stall on Holloway

Road and was knocking on doors asking for personal advertisements. People were remarkably open to conversation, Wiggins found, especially if you asked them about their neighbours.

He tapped up the steps at number 39, two down from Carter's but in the same terrace. A middle-aged man opened the door a few inches. 'Can I help you?' He peered at Wiggins through thick, round glasses, much like a mole might peer at daylight.

'It's more a question of whether I can help you. Do you advertise? I see you're a medical man?'

The man shrunk back. 'How did you know?'

From deep inside the house a woman bawled, 'Hawley! Who the hell is that?'

The man glanced back. 'No one, dear,' he said, a slight American twang to his voice.

'Hawley, get back in here!'

Wiggins tried a different tack. 'You've had building work done, I see.'

The man, Hawley, twitched. 'No.'

'But the flagstones – replaced recently?' Wiggins asked, gesturing to the front of the house.

'Hawley!'

'I must go,' Hawley quivered. 'I have no need for advertisements. Good day.' He squeezed the door shut before Wiggins could say another word.

Wiggins walked down the steps to the pavement and looked back at the house and the recently disturbed flagstones beneath the ground-floor window. He considered the rarity of a medical man *not* interested in advertising his wares and recalled the bead of sweat on Hawley's brow, despite the cool evening air. Someone bustled past him on the road, breaking the thought.

A tall, thin man of sixty turned up the steps to number 43. Well-pressed frock coat, bulging briefcase, air of self-importance – Wiggins guessed this was Archibald Carter, home from work, a suspicion confirmed when he heard someone bellow from behind the front door, 'Archie!'

He hesitated. Something about the last house, Hawley and the shouting woman, had unsettled him. His mind was filling with loose threads: Peter at large in London; Millie missing; things amiss at the Embassy; and this tiny mole in the haystack of Whitehall. He shook his head, reset his features into those of an ingratiating canvasser, and rang the bell at number 43. It never hurt to look a suspect in the eye.

'Good evening?' Archibald Carter answered the door himself, as Wiggins had hoped, for he'd only just gone in. 'Can I help you?'

Wiggins opened his mouth to speak but before he could do so a huge bear of a man pushed past Carter and grabbed him around the neck. 'He'll do,' he cried, and dragged Wiggins into the house.

The next morning, Constance Kell said goodbye to the children in the nursery of her Hampstead home and went downstairs. She went straight to the hatstand and gathered up her coat, hat, umbrella and handbag.

'Not hungry?' Kell said, standing at the door to the breakfast room.

She shook her head.

'I wanted to say . . . er . . . the King's funeral – I'm to be part of the security detail. I won't be able to attend with you.'

'I wasn't going to go.' She heaved on her coat.

'Busy?'

'Hmm?' She adjusted her hat, a wide-brimmed red felt affair with a peacock feather arcing into the air.

'Now, are you busy?'

She stopped and looked at her husband. 'Coffee morning, for veterans, in Chalk Farm. Meeting the ladies.'

'Right.'

'Must dash.'

She walked quickly to Hampstead Underground station and caught the train south. She did not get out at Chalk Farm. Instead, she went on to Euston, where she changed lines and finally alighted at Marylebone Station.

Constance pushed against the tide of late morning commuters bustling out of the station, and looked at the departure board above the platform entrances. *No copying please. Thank you* ran across the top of the board in freshly painted white. She smiled at the stationmaster and hurried to her train.

The first-class compartment she had reserved was empty. She went out into the corridor and looked up and down, then thrust her head out of the nearby window. A cascade of closing doors reverberated up the train. There was no sign on the platform either. She checked her wristwatch in irritation, then went back to sit down.

She slid open the compartment door. 'Morning, Mrs Kell,' Wiggins said. He sat by the window.

'Good day, Mr Wiggins,' she said in the crispest of tones. 'I'm so glad you could come. You got my message, I see, and the ticket.'

Wiggins nodded. 'A woman's writing, a woman's scent on the letter. You's the only woman who could possibly have known I'd be at that address. So here I am.'

Constance grinned. For all Wiggins's low birth and shabby attire – he looked like he slept on the streets – she did enjoy speaking with clever people. She took a seat opposite. 'I need your advice,' she said.

'You didn't have to do the old cloak-and-dagger, ma'am.'

A whistle sounded. She looked out onto the platform as the train clanked into action. A *rap-rap-rap* of closing doors. Packages, people, smoke, steam drifting across the expanse of the double platform as a newly arrived train disgorged a riot of commuters tearing off into the city. Finally, their own train picked up speed and she turned her eyes to Wiggins.

'I'd rather my husband didn't know we met.'

Wiggins shifted in his seat and wouldn't meet her eye.

'Mr Wiggins, what *is* the matter?'

'I don't like leaving London.' He nodded out of the window.

'Tosh. We haven't even made Dollis Hill. We'll be back at Marylebone in no time. Now, out with it.'

'I can't, against the chief, I mean, I don't . . .' He fumbled to a halt.

'Come on,' Constance commanded.

Wiggins breathed in. A half-built terrace sped by. 'I can't help ya cuckold the chief. It ain't right.'

Constance stared sharply at him for a moment. Then she burst out laughing. 'You think I intend to cuckold Vernon?'

'You want to know some tricks, right? Some of the old duck and dive. That's why we're here.'

Constance laughed again. 'Isn't that just like a man,' she said at last, dabbing her eyes with a handkerchief. 'To think that's all we care about. Vernon always said that women were your blind spot.' She straightened her shoulders, held her hands together and looked at him steady once more. 'You are right insofar as I want some advice. But I would never be, er, unfaithful to Vernon. Ever. Understand?'

Wiggins shrugged. 'What you want to know?'

'I want to know how to avoid surveillance,' she said simply.

~~~

January the first, 1910, five months or so before meeting Wiggins in the train carriage, Constance went to her usual meeting, the rallying cry for the Society for Women's Suffrage, in Hampstead. Women spoke – fine women. Constance sat in the front row and listened. She clapped. And inwardly she tried to pinpoint the differences between these speeches, these promises, and the ones made on the very same stage twelve months previously. The task was beyond her.

'Excuse me,' a high-pitched voice rang out from the audience. 'I rather think you're talking a lot of old rot.'

'I beg your pardon?' The speaker peered down into the crowd. Constance turned to see a young woman, a few rows behind her, standing up and for some reason holding her hat firmly to her head.

'I said, I slightly think you're talking a lot of old rot.'

Constance stifled a laugh. The girl cut a rather comical figure, cheeks growing redder by the minute, but she stood defiant.

'Here in Hampstead there is a proper way of doing things,' the speaker replied.

'But gosh, that's my point,' the girl went on, hand still clamped to her hat. 'We've been doing things the proper way for years and we've got more than halfway to a big fat nothing.'

A great intake of breath greeted this outburst. 'We should be rebelling, bringing society to a halt – something, anything.' The young woman looked around her in exasperation.

'Take your seat there, miss,' someone called amid murmurs of disapproval.

The old matron at the lectern frowned. 'The cause is just, but it is fragile. We have a long road to travel, and risking anything rash could set us back a generation.' She addressed her remarks first to the young woman, but then she hailed the rest. 'Sisters, join me in song.'

Constance arched her head backwards. The young woman sat down, her face flushed.

> *Shout, shout up with your song!*
> *Cry with the wind for the dawn is breaking.*
> *March, march, swing you along . . .*

Afterwards, as the assembled ladies rose and headed for the door, chatting, Constance shifted towards the young woman.

'You spoke very well,' she said.

The woman turned to her, bright as a small bird. 'Do you really think so? I think I came across as a bit of a duffer.'

'No, not at all. You were jolly passionate, that's all.'

'Well, I am rather. I'm not sorry I said it. Not in a million years. Do you mind?' She handed Constance a huge carpetbag, then slung another one over her shoulder. 'Thanks ever so,' she said, taking back the bag and swinging it on to her other shoulder.

'Would you like a hand?' Constance said.

The girl – Constance guessed she was twenty – turned out to be called Dinah. 'But don't offer me supper, everyone does!'

They stepped out onto the High Street, Constance carrying one of the huge bags. 'Dinah . . . ?'

'Just Dinah. My second name's my father's and that doesn't count, does it? You?'

'Constance,' she replied. And then, 'Just Constance,' with a smile.

Dinah beamed. Her high cheekbones shone pink in the January bite, her hair fell about her face and her eyes danced.

She twisted wildly as a cab jerked down the hill towards Belsize Park. 'Halloo,' she cried, waving her free hand like a quayside sweetheart seeing off a beau. The motorised taxi shuddered to a halt. Dinah opened the door herself, threw in her carpetbag, then turned to Constance for the other one.

'Thanks ever so,' she said. 'I feel like a beast of burden some-times.'

'Surely not.'

'An ass!' She laughed, then put one foot into the cab.

Constance thrust out her hand and touched Dinah on the arm. She'd shocked herself by the gesture, but recovered. 'Do you take tea?' she said.

Dinah looked at her for a moment, one foot on the tailboard of the taxi. 'You mean like a real lady, calling in the morning, sending in my card?' She sounded surprised, but also faintly amused, as if the suggestion were quaint.

'Sorry,' Constance said. 'Silly of me.'

'No, no, not *that*,' Dinah replied, still smiling. 'Of course, I absolutely adore tea.'

'Now you're fibbing.' They stared at each other for a moment.

'You want a lift, miss?' the cabby barked. 'There's plenty of others that do.'

'We're on the meter,' Dinah hollered at him, then turned back to Constance. 'What a grump. New Year's Day, too.'

'Happy New Year,' Constance said.

Dinah got into the cab, shut the door and then leaned out of the window. 'I like Lyons,' she said as the cab juddered into action.

'I beg your pardon?'

'Lyons!' Dinah bellowed as the taxi drove off. 'The Corner House. Thursday at three.'

Constance looked after the taxi as it slipped into the traffic down Rosslyn Hill. She was breathing hot and fast, and her breath bent tight curlicues into the cold air.

The following Thursday, Constance gazed out across a sea of diners. Lyons' Corner House was immense. Like the dining rooms of ocean-going liners stacked on top of each other. She'd tried the two floors below and now she stood at the door of the second-floor tearoom, alone. The building sang with the calls of the waitresses, an army of primly dressed women bustling to and fro. Yet for all the staff, Constance consistently failed to get anyone's attention.

They were moving too fast, smiling too briskly. She wasn't used to it at all. The kind of tearooms and restaurants she normally frequented, the staff would stand to attention when she came in, would even know her name. But this place was entirely different. She was one among many, and if she didn't feel well served, no matter, for another diner would take her place in a moment.

Finally, a livid-red scarf rose from the throng. 'Over here,' Dinah hallooed, bright as a beacon amongst the winter greys.

Constance reached the table, only to discover that there were five or six other young women crammed around it. Dinah embraced her. 'So lovely to see you,' she said. 'Everyone, this is Constance.' She then pointed to each of the women in turn, as if counting. Constance failed to catch all the names, but she heard the final ones. 'Pru, Tansy, Abernathy – don't ask – and Nobbs.'

The women looked up and nodded, but their conversation did not stop. 'Awfully chilly, isn't it?' Dinah said. 'Let me get you some tea.'

'No, I insist,' Constance said, glancing around for a waitress.

'Never a Gladys when you need one,' the woman next to her, Nobbs, drawled.

'I beg your pardon?' Constance said, but no one heard. She glanced at Dinah. 'I rather thought, we'd . . . I mean, you and I . . .?'

'Over here,' Dinah hailed a waitress, then bumbled and fussed over the order. Her hair fell loose over her face when she laughed, wild and unkempt. It was useless for Constance to get her attention again while the tea and cakes were in progress. She sipped her drink and listened. Everyone seemed to be talking at once. It was like a play in which all the characters onstage were given lines, but kept pre-empting their own cues.

'Squiffy'll never see reason, of course. Did you know he has a terrible pash on a friend of mine? Years younger.'

'Does not!'

'Does too,' said the informant, Nobbs. 'Well, all right, she's not a friend of mine, but she's a friend of a friend. School chums. Chap I know works in the Treasury reckons it's true.'

'You don't know anyone from the Treasury,' Abernathy snorted.

'My brother does,' Nobbs responded.

They all laughed at this, apart from Tansy. A woman of twenty or so, with a severe fringe and a faraway look, she sat opposite Constance and had said little. But as the laughter died down she said, almost to herself, 'Acid.'

'What was that?' Constance asked, but she was ignored.

'Are you all right?' Dinah whispered in Constance's ear as Abernathy launched into a diatribe.

'Absolutely,' Constance said. 'Though I do feel very old.'

'Nonsense,' Dinah retorted. 'You can't be more than thirty.'

Constance smiled. It was either charm or naivety on Dinah's part, but it felt nice either way. 'Is this a regular tea date? You and your friends.'

'Wouldn't call it a tea date, dear,' Nobbs said.

'I hate dates,' Tansy put in.

'Although we are regulars, if you know what I mean,' Abernathy said.

'Too sweet.'

Constance caught Abernathy's eye at last. 'No, I have no idea what you mean,' she said.

Abernathy glanced at Dinah, who nodded brightly. 'We are an offshoot of the hot bloods,' she said.

'So you are suffragettes, not suffragists?' Constance asked, astonished.

'Fairyland's the place to learn, I'd say,' said Tansy, who was again ignored.

Dinah giggled. 'Of course we're suffragettes, silly. That's why I invited you, don't you see?'

'She *says* suffragettes,' Abernathy plucked at a half-eaten sandwich, 'but it's more than that.'

'How so?'

Abernathy suddenly ripped apart the sandwich and looked up at her. 'Because we act.'

Churchill was right. It was the greatest meeting of royalty the world had ever seen. May the twentieth, 1910, the funeral of Edward VII, King of the United Kingdom and the British Dominions, Emperor of India. Kell reckoned there were nine crowned heads in attendance – not counting the one in the coffin – as well as numerous dukes, archdukes, duchesses and presidents.

As per Soapy's directions, he'd placed himself amongst the foreign delegations in the funeral procession. He walked slowly through the serried ranks of mourners as the procession went up Whitehall and turned towards the park. The tall plane trees of the Mall dappled the road in front of him. Black-clad crowds lined both sides of the street. The only sounds breaking the silence were the clinking of the sabres and the rattling of tack from the horses and carriages behind. Birds suddenly burst from the trees above him.

His glance drifted out into the crowds once more, and his heart gave a lurch. Constance would not be there. Her blithe refusal to attend had shocked him, even though they couldn't go together. The gulf between them was ever widening. He must act, he thought as they trudged into Park Lane. But what should he do? He felt impotent in the face of her commitment to women's suffrage.

Indecision and impotence had also characterised his approach to finding the Whitehall leak. Wiggins had yet to report back from his investigation into the clerk Carter. Had yet to report back at all, in fact, since Tuesday. He was due to meet Kell at Paddington when the procession got there, and maybe he'd have good news. In the meantime, and rather forlornly, Kell had positioned himself amongst the German delegation. He reasoned that if he couldn't identify the mole from the inside, he might still have a chance of discovering who had received the stolen information.

His eye snagged on a tall, heavy-jawed officer called Count Effenberg, who strode at the head of the German delegation, looking this way and that like a conquering general. Kell recognised him from a party the year before, but had no way of knowing if he was involved in espionage. They'd set a tail on him at the time, but it had thrown up nothing untoward. He could be Van Bork or a nobody. As they turned northwards out of the park, Kell noticed for the first time the man next to Effenberg, walking almost in his shadow.

He hadn't seen him before, but he stood out in such a throng for his very ordinariness. On the street, in Whitehall even, you wouldn't have noticed him. Smartly dressed, yes, but sober, low-key, ordinary, plump, balding. But in such an entourage, where every second man wore feathers and a bucket on his head, the ordinary man stood out.

They continued to walk on, behind the long line of more important people, behind the most important coffin in Europe. Kell dropped back a little, so that he could see Effenberg and the bald, fat man talk. As he did so, Kell noticed the heavy hang of the bald man's coat pocket. A gun.

The procession was up Edgware Road by this time, winding its way through the smaller streets just to the south and east of Paddington Station. Most of the mourners, including the foreign delegations, were due to see off the casket at Paddington and then disperse. Only close family (in other words, half the royalty of the world) and the crème de la crème would board the trains for Windsor. Kell was due to be on one of them, as a rather high-class 'minder'.

He'd ordered Wiggins to meet him at the station as an extra pair of eyes. He guessed that the balding, armed man by Effenberg was probably the delegation's security guard, but he'd get Wiggins to follow him nevertheless. He had nothing else to go on.

All he needed now was for Wiggins to turn up on time.

Wiggins sat at a high window just off Praed Street, close to Paddington Station. He watched from this sniper's nest of a spot as the crowds formed over the morning of the funeral. The previous week, when not chasing after Kell's list of clerks, he'd reconnoitred the route and reported back. If anyone was going to try anything, Wiggins reckoned this would be the spot – where the procession turned off Edgware Road and into the tighter lanes around the station. He had the perfect view.

'Want another cup of cha, lad?'

'Ta,' Wiggins said. 'Black.'

He was in the sitting room of Symes, an aged librarian he'd known for years. Symes nodded his startlingly bald head and disappeared through the door.

They had met when Wiggins was a kid. The librarian, then in middle age, had consulted Sherlock Holmes about thefts from the Reading Room at the British Museum, where he worked. Suspicion had fallen upon Symes, the only northerner on the staff. Holmes, convinced of his innocence but also somewhat bored by the simplicity of the case, had provided Wiggins to watch the real culprit. Wiggins had proved himself adept, and brave, and Symes had kept his job. He'd been forever grateful, and had procured Wiggins a reader's card for the Reading Room in perpetuity.

As soon as he'd been told the route of the procession, Wiggins knew that Symes's place would be the perfect lookout. He looked down into the street as the crowds swelled. So much money, so much expense – the coppers must have spent a grand on Brasso alone, their buttons shone so bright. The poor, meanwhile, his people, had been systematically scrubbed from the picture. Coppers had cleared at least three dosshouses on the route the day before, and the down-and-outs had been shipped out east for the day.

No sign of Peter. Wiggins strained his eyes. Futile, he knew, but there was always a chance. Symes clattered back into the room, muttering to himself. 'What are you reading, lad?' he said, handing Wiggins the tea.

'Not much.'

'Won't do, lad, won't do. Come to the RR next week, I'll have something for you.'

Wiggins nodded, eyes cast on the street.

Symes joined him at the window. 'You say they're worried about assassinations, lad? Anarchists?'

'Something like that,' Wiggins said. He scalded his tongue on the latest cup of tea. 'Ah!'

'Get a lot of anarchists down the RR, mind,' Symes went on. 'Leftists, revolutionaries. Ivans, I call 'em. All false names and bad breath.'

'Why's that then?' Wiggins said, but something caught his attention in the crowd. A familiar hat cutting through the throng.

'Marx, of course. They all come to see where he worked.'

'Who's he?' Wiggins asked absently. The hat bobbed out of view, then reappeared a moment later.

'Karl Marx. It's all about capital, lad, capitalists exploiting the workers. I can understand that. You only have to go down pit to see that. But religion is the opium of the people? Alienation?'

'Alien what?' Wiggins said, but he looked down at his watch, only half interested in the answer. The old man had been droning on and he'd missed the half of it.

The familiar hat had moved again, Wiggins noted with alarm. Its wearer seemed to have met some friends. From further away, around the corner, he could feel the procession nearing.

Symes wouldn't shut up. 'His idea is that we're all working too hard for the rich, who cream off the profits for themselves.'

'And what does this Marx want us to do about it?'

'Throw off the chains, lad, throw off the chains.'

Wiggins nodded and turned back to the window. A flash in

the crowd – the person under the hat had joined with a gaggle of other people. Wiggins could see them pushing through the crush in an effort to get to the front in time for the coffin. It was only because he had such a high vantage point that Wiggins could see they were acting together. And he could see that they needed to be stopped.

'I've got to go.' He swiped his cap from the mantelpiece, nodded a quick goodbye to the bemused Symes, and took one final look-see out of the window. The group with the matching hats had now massed at the corner, ready to strike.

Ready for disaster.

6

Constance had avoided her husband on the day of the funeral for a reason.

She went alone to the procession, but then met up with the girls near Paddington. It was the one place they could really get close to the coffin. The women all wore wide-brimmed felt hats with a peacock feather in the band, so as to be able to see each other in the throng. Constance kept her eyes on Dinah. Her thick, golden-red hair squeezed out at the back in a bun that bobbed crazily as she walked. The crowd was thin enough at the edges that they could walk abreast, but once they approached the route of the funeral procession itself, they had to go single file.

There were policemen everywhere. She could see lines of constables at the station, and inspectors too. A big burly constable with ruddy cheeks and a cider-drinker's nose caught her eye. My word, she thought, he wasn't even in a Met uniform. They've drafted policemen from all over the country for this.

She pulled at her heavy dress. Each of the girls had stuffed flags around their bodies, ready to rip clear through special slits at the moment of truth. At least, she hoped that was all the other girls had on them. It was an ingenious construction, designed by Nobbs, but on such a hot day it was more uncomfortable than even a corset. Sweat trickled down her back. Her arms itched. The street smelled of blocked drains, horse dung and too many people crammed together. It was difficult for a woman of her class not to sweat on a hot day, given a respectable wardrobe, but when you had five yards of heavy cotton flags wrapped around your midriff, it was impossible.

Dinah glanced back at her. Abernathy pushed ahead. The crush closed about them. It was time. Constance checked the ripcord on her dress, looked up again.

Abernathy neared the front of the cordon. Constance hesitated, unsure.

Out of the crowd, a hand gripped her arm. 'Not here,' Wiggins hissed. 'They'll kill ya.'

Constance stared at him, struck dumb by his sudden appearance.

'It'll be a lynching,' he urged under his breath, fear in his eyes. 'They'll have ya!'

She regained herself in an instant, and in one swoop she fainted into his arms. 'Give me room, here. Lady's swooned. A swoon, make way!' Wiggins hollered. She felt his hands cradle her head and shoulder as he continued to shout.

Soon she heard the trills and gasps of her companions. 'Fell like a ninepin, so she did, miss,' Wiggins said. 'Seen it in the army, the heat, the crowds.' Constance stayed limp as he placed her gently on the pavement. He whispered in her ear, 'Diamond,' then she felt his hands no more.

She fluttered her eyes open. Four faces looked down on her. Dinah, worried eyes as large as saucers, knelt at her head; Nobbs crouched on the other side, holding her pulse; Tansy and another girl stood further back.

'We've missed it,' Nobbs said as she timed Constance's pulse.

'Are you all right?' Dinah took her other hand.

Constance smiled. A pang of guilt clutched her for a moment. 'Quite all right, thank you. I don't know what came over me.'

'The whole thing's a washout,' Nobbs said. 'The coffin's gone past.'

Constance groaned. 'I'm so sorry,' she said, pushing herself upright. 'What awful luck.' Although she noted that Nobbs and Dinah – and, indeed, the others – didn't look that displeased to be thwarted. It was one thing to talk about invading the King's funeral procession with banners; it was quite another to do it. And, she suddenly realised with a piercing insight, Wiggins was right. They could very well have been killed. Thank God for Wiggins.

Only Abernathy looked annoyed. She pushed between Tansy and the other girl, arms at her hips, brow deeply furrowed. 'Oh God,' she scowled, 'you're not preggers, are you?'

The following Sunday morning, a casual bystander might have observed Wiggins at prayer, kneeling, eyes down, following the priest's every word. The same bystander might have nodded sagely and assumed Wiggins to be of Italian or Irish descent, given his thick black hair and the fact that the church was a Catholic one.

Wiggins did not pray. He *was* thinking religious thoughts, though. Or rather, as he shifted his weight on his knees, he was remembering the few times he'd gone to church as a child. His mother suffered from bouts of religion much like others got the fever. A week or two here, a whole month of churchgoing there, followed by long stretches of determined faithlessness. It was only much later, when she was long dead and he was into double figures, that he realised she had been going to church for the money. She hadn't been gripped by any new-found fervour, seen the light three times a year; she'd been after any poor relief that was going – and the churches (whatever flavour they were) didn't hand out money to non-believers.

The priest carried on in Latin, but Wiggins thought of the phrases from those desultory church visits of his youth. Our Father, who art in heaven. Our Father? Sherlock Holmes was the closest thing he'd had to a father, hallowed be his name. Wiggins crossed himself at the joke. The Irregulars used to call him GOD sometimes – the great old detective – although always with a snigger, taking the piss, and never to his face. It didn't do to question God.

Wiggins flicked his eyes up to the gilt candlestick by his head. It was polished to a high shine and afforded him a clear view of everybody coming into the church. Small, indistinct figures at a distance, but clear enough for Wiggins to recognise people he knew once they were close.

The woman walking towards him now, bent and squashed in

the convex reflection, was not the woman he hoped to see. And yet, for all that, he felt a twinge of anticipation in him that he wasn't quite expecting.

She walked at a stately pace and her long dress kissed the flagstones with every swing of her hips. Wiggins kept his head bowed, although something told him that she'd already seen him. She walked past, crossed herself quickly and sat down two rows in front. The hem of her dress spilled into the aisle.

Wiggins spent the rest of the service staring at the back of her bare neck. She'd stuffed her tight black curls under her hat, leaving her brown skin to offset the white calico of her collar. He looked around twice more, but there was no sign of Poppy. Martha was the only whore at the church that morning. At least, the only one he recognised.

The service ended and he waited for Martha to get up. She smiled and inclined her head towards him as she went past. He followed her down the aisle.

'I never had you down as a Catholic, I must be honest,' she said as they exited the church. 'An Irish mama?'

'His works is mysterious,' Wiggins said at last.

A ghost of a smile played across Martha's lips. 'Are you here to walk me home?'

Wiggins bowed, then held his hand out to the pavement. They walked in silence for a moment. Wiggins noted her fine, long-sleeved dress, lace gloves, and a small carry bag adorned with a red ribbon. She smelled of spices and lemon and expensive soap. Despite her job, she smelled of sophistication.

'I'm not what you want.'

'Who.'

'Martha's my name, in case you've forgotten.'

'You French?'

'*Une petite partie de moi. La bonne partie.*'

Wiggins looked at her blankly.

'My mama had a French daddy, I think, and we spoke some of the lingo back in Leone.'

Wiggins couldn't place her accent. She said Leone like it was home, but there was London in there too. Docks London, posh London, Frenchie. All sorts.

Her skin was barely brown at all in the sunlight. Wiggins shot glances at her as they walked, and tried not to look at her bust. For all that she was wearing respectable, Sunday-best clothes, he found her distracting. She strode with her back very straight, her eyes forward and alive, her shoulders square: she was not afraid of anything, least of all embarrassment. Wiggins straightened up beside her.

'Let the heart of those who seek the Lord rejoice,' Martha said after a moment.

'You what?' Wiggins glanced at her quickly.

She smiled back, fine teeth, big eyes, pinprick irises.

'I know who you came for,' she said. 'I saw your little romance last week with Poppy, but she ain't praying today.'

'I came for Millie.'

'Millie?' Martha slowed for a second, in surprise. 'Like a young filly, do you? I had you pinned different.'

'It ain't like that,' Wiggins said, half angry, half embarrassed. He turned his face away. 'I'm trying to find her – for someone else,' he said after a moment.

'People come and go in this business.'

'That's what Tommy said.'

Martha rubbed her gloved hands together in silence. He remembered seeing her bare arms in the Embassy kitchen the week before. The cigar burn marks on her wrists, like she'd been owned, once, or still was somehow.

'This business,' she said, as if talking to his thoughts and not his words. 'I've been a whore for fifteen years. My mama couldn't afford for me to do anything else. And you want to leave it every day, whatever anyone tells you. Since I was fifteen.'

Wiggins didn't look at her. A hurdy-gurdy player trundled past them in the other direction, silent.

Martha went on. 'And I see girls leave every day too.' She pulled at the ribbon on her bag. 'In one way or 'nother. Millie's just gone. We all go sometime. The ferry takes us, every one.'

They stopped on a corner, Ranleigh Terrace – and the Embassy – the next right. By mutual, unstated agreement, they hesitated. 'Don't be too hard on Big T,' she said suddenly. 'What would you do?'

Wiggins nodded thoughtfully. His mind caught on something she'd said. 'He boxes, he said. In a boozer. What was it again?'

'The Bloodied Axe, I think. Down Lambeth.'

Wiggins already knew the answer. He wanted Tommy to know he knew, and Martha would surely tell him. He tipped his cap. 'Much obliged, ma'am,' he said, with exaggerated politeness.

Martha curtsied in return. *'Enchantée.'* She paused, looked towards Ranleigh Terrace, then back at him. 'We do walk out – with fellas – sometimes, you know.'

Wiggins hesitated. 'I'm spoken for,' he said at last.

She tilted her head and smiled. She knew a lie when she heard one. 'Good luck trying to find Millie, for your *friend.'* She turned and went, then, her body swinging and moving beneath the respectable dress in a quite unrespectable way.

'Where the hell were you?'

'Been here since nine,' Wiggins protested. He rose from behind Kell's desk.

Kell scowled. 'I meant at Paddington! On Friday. It's Monday morning and now you decide to show up?' He strode around his desk, too angry to even bother asking Wiggins how he'd got into the office again.

He swiped the cigarette box from his desk and slumped into his chair. 'Well?'

Wiggins wandered aimlessly away from him. He gestured at a map on the wall. 'Held up,' he said. 'Thousands out there. Why *you* late?'

Kell fixed his agent with a glare and smoked in silence. He didn't want to admit it, but he was glad to see Wiggins – at least he was alive. He didn't want to admit why he'd been so late either.

He'd just come from another chastening meeting with Soapy,

who was most disappointed that no progress had been made on discovering the leak. 'We've eliminated some of the clerks,' Kell said weakly.

Soapy raised an eyebrow. 'And another thing,' he said. 'Special Branch apprehended an armed German national leaving the funeral.'

'Was he a spy?' Kell said, aghast, thinking of the balding German he'd last seen with Effenberg.

'Well, no, actually, he was a security guard. But at least they are doing *something*. You've got nowhere.'

Kell had left the Cabinet Office with Soapy's final, softly delivered salvo ringing in his ears. 'Quinn's very keen to take your department over, you know. Nothing's been decided, but I'd have a think, all the same. About what else you might like to do. Good day, old man, and best to Constance.'

Good day, indeed, Kell thought as he glared at Wiggins over the desk. He finished his cigarette, pulled another one from the box in front of him and tried to gather his thoughts.

'Would you go back to being a debt collector?' Kell asked at last.

'You what?'

'If I dispensed with your services. Is that what you'd do? I doubt the army would take you back.'

Wiggins sat down in the chair opposite. 'What you on about? I missed a meet by, what, minutes?'

'That missed meeting may have just cost me my job!' Kell snapped.

Wiggins leaned back, surprised.

Kell took a long drag from his smoke. He disliked losing his temper. 'Why did you not meet me?'

'I told you. Held up.' Wiggins shifted in his seat and cast his eyes down. Kell tapped his hand on the table. His agent wasn't going to tell him. That was reason enough to sack him there and then. But Wiggins was all he had, other than a clerk and a working relationship with the chief constables around the country. Special

Branch obviously wanted him out of business, and Soapy's support was as slippery as his name suggested. He'd stick up for you as long as the room was on your side.

Wiggins was all he had, Kell thought again. He unlocked his desk drawer, keeping his eyes on his now silent agent.

'I do not appreciate evasiveness,' Kell said coolly. 'What I said was true, though. Your failure at Paddington has highlighted the difficulty of our position. We may both be out of a job come Friday.'

'You tugging me?'

Kell shook his head slightly. 'Special Branch want to take over.'

'If we had their gilt, we'd be—'

Kell put his hand up. He'd had enough of Wiggins's pert bravado. 'Shush. Listen. We ran up a lot of credit last year with LeQuin and Woolwich. But that won't stretch for ever. We need results. We need to find the leak, otherwise this whole dandy exercise will come to an end. I'll be sent back to pushing pens in the War Office, and you? Well, you'll have to go back to where you came from – not something either of us wants to dwell on, I'm sure.'

Wiggins glowered at him, but Kell went on regardless. 'What about Carter, at the FO?'

To Kell's surprise, a smile flickered across Wiggins's face. 'Archie? He's straight as, no trouble.'

'Archie?'

'We got to talking, over a game of cards. His brother dragged me into his house to make up a four. Top blokes, the Carters. And Archie ain't leaking no gen to anyone, straight up. He's honest. Not so sure about his neighbours, mind.'

'Oh?'

'Thirty-nine Hilldrop Crescent. Get one of your copper mates to have a look-see.'

'As if I have nothing better to do,' Kell muttered as he drew a piece of paper from his desk. 'I think it's time we forgot about the clerks,' he said.

'At last.'

'Here is a list of the men who attended the Committee for Imperial Defence, all of whom knew certain information that then found its way into the hands of a German diplomat within days. One of them must have said something to someone.'

Kell handed Wiggins the paper and watched while his agent scanned down the list. For all the desperate straits the department was in, it gave Kell a tiny tickle of pleasure to see a flash of incomprehension cross Wiggins's face. Kell knew politics. Wiggins did not. He had that over him, at least.

'Know these geezers, do you?' Wiggins said, tossing the list onto the desk.

'I do.'

'Want me to turn 'em over?'

'I hardly think that's appropriate.' Kell leaned back in his chair. 'We must tread carefully.'

'Careful and quick, and more than ten men to follow? That my job, is it?'

Kell ignored the note of petulance. 'Why did you say follow?'

'What else we gonna do? We got to tail 'em one by one, see what comes up in the wash.'

Kell nodded slowly. 'I'll get Simpkins to draw up a list of addresses. Come back this afternoon – it shouldn't take him too long. We'll decide then who to prioritise. Not a word of this, understand.'

'Who am I going tell, the King?'

Wiggins got up and moved to the door.

Kell hesitated. 'Don't you want to take this copy?' he said, uncertain. After all, the list contained many high men of state and their direct assistants, important people. He didn't want it to get out that he was investigating them. He didn't even *want* to investigate them, so horrified would he be if any of them were guilty. But he had no choice.

'In here.' Wiggins tapped his temple. 'Besides, you've got 'alf the Cabinet there. I'm not likely to forget the Foreign Secretary, am I?' Wiggins pushed out of the door.

Blast the man, Kell thought again. Is there nothing he doesn't know? Still, there was no better man in London than Wiggins at following people. He'd been doing it all his life. Kell swivelled in his chair, suddenly caught by an interesting idea. Perhaps he could put Wiggins on his wife. The morality might be questionable, but at least he'd know what she was up to, and – he argued to himself – it was all for her own protection. She'd gone out earlier than him on the day of the funeral and now she hardly gave him a second glance. He had barely exchanged a word with her for weeks.

It was just possible, he thought, that Wiggins could hold the key to the enigma that was his wife.

Wiggins stepped out of Kell's building on Victoria Street and turned west. He didn't like lying to Kell, but he couldn't land Constance in it. Kell was right; he was being evasive. The alternative, however, was to tell him he'd missed their rendezvous because his wife had been about to enact a very dangerous and illegal suffragette protest. He knew enough about Englishmen to know that, for all their manners and the yes sir, no sirs, when they were crowded together – be it at the football or on strike or at a hanging – they were one word or action away from a mob. Constance would have been lucky to survive.

Not something that Constance would want Kell knowing, though, Wiggins felt sure. He had some sympathy for her and her cause. Most of the women he knew were smarter than the men in their lives – why shouldn't that extend to politics?

He took a left into a short alleyway. Great painted advertisements lined the walls on either side: JOLLY'S SANDWICHES. YORK HAM HERE. FRY'S. WOODBINES FOR YOUR HEALTH. He came out onto Horseferry Road, lifted a bottle from a passing milk cart, gulped half of it down and then placed it next to a hunched beggar huddling in a shop doorway.

'Wot do I want wiv that!' the elderly beggar cried.

'It'll make the brandy go longer,' Wiggins winked as he passed the man a couple of pennies. 'Don't go spending that on anything useful.'

Wiggins dodged the carts and taxis that clogged the road – business returning to normal after the King's funeral – and headed towards the magistrates' court.

It was something Martha had said that kept going through his mind, Martha and Poppy: *We all go sometime. The ferry takes us, every one.* What ferry? he'd wondered. The boatmen on the Thames called death 'the ferry cross the sticks', but it was something else that snagged. Close by Kell's office, and not more than a mile away from the Embassy itself, stood Horseferry Road Magistrates' Court. Beneath it, the mortuary dealing with the river deaths of West London: the Ferry.

He looked up at the legend above the door, then ducked around the side of the building and down the stairs.

An attendant sat with his feet up on a desk, cleaning his nails with a nasty, medical-looking spike. He barely glanced up as Wiggins came in. 'We're busy,' he said.

'An enquiry is all.'

'All enquiries must go through the coroner.' The attendant spoke through his nose and didn't look at him. 'I am not at liberty to discuss details with anyone off the street.'

Wiggins examined the attendant, noted the flashy tie, saw a reflection in the man's shoes. Cigar ash littered the desk. Wiggins kept his voice level. 'I need to look at who's come in this week. And any personal effects unclaimed this year.'

The attendant shook his head. 'Do you want me to call one of the constables? It won't take a moment – we have our own cells.'

'Save me the bother,' Wiggins grunted.

The attendant looked up sharply. His weasel eyes narrowed. 'What's that s'posed to mean,' he said. Not quite as hoity-toity as he appeared.

'Knocking off body parts cheap still a crime, ain't it? Teeth. Hair. How much are marrows going for down Limehouse these days?'

'I don't know what you're talking about,' he blustered.

'Coppers will,' Wiggins said, simply.

The attendant sat up straight in his chair, shot his arms out and breathed in deeply. 'If you'll excuse me, sir, I must avail myself of the facilities. I will be no more than *ten* minutes. Please do not look at any of the cadavers stored down there, and I especially warn you to steer clear of the tray of unclaimed effects. Which is just to the right there. And here is the list of admissions over the last few months.' He tapped a leather-bound ledger with his hand. 'I trust you'll be gone by the time I get back?'

'I'll be gone,' Wiggins said.

Wiggins flicked through the ledger quickly. Then he turned his attention to the drawer of unclaimed items. Necklaces, lockets, purses, wallets – no cash, of course, except foreign coins, the attendant and his chums saw to that – cheap rings, a wooden leg, false teeth, fishing tackle, a hook, a cigarette case, damp and soiled visiting cards: the flotsam and jetsam of life, so important on the living but in the hands of the dead nothing more than junk. Then he saw it.

Nestled in a box of twisted metal trinkets, a small St Christopher, an exact match for the one Jax had shown him only days ago. A bedraggled red ribbon ran through a small ring at the top of the figure. Wiggins swept it into his pocket and glanced back at the exit.

Bodies on trestle tables lined the cavernous chamber, fifteen or sixteen of them, covered mostly with sheets. Millie couldn't be among them, Wiggins knew. If she'd died when she'd disappeared, her body would have been buried long ago – and in an unmarked grave, too, for the unclaimed items belonged to those who couldn't be identified. He didn't even know what she looked like, other than Jax's description, but he felt compelled to look at the cadavers.

The room smelled something rotten. Not like the dead he'd seen at Ladysmith, turned rank in the heat, feasted on by flies as big as your fist. This smell felt worse, unnatural. The tang of dead flesh was in the air, but mixed with carbolic and lime, too. This was a room seeped in semi-sanitised mortality.

Wiggins paced down the line, dipping his head into the faces of the dead. Of the women, two were old, one was pregnant and the other was a young child.

At the far end, deep into the bowels of the dark, brick archway, somewhere under the courtroom, stood the last trestle table. The mains light didn't penetrate this far and he swiped a hissing gas lamp from the side. He slowed his pace when he saw the feet – small, shapely, a young woman's. Wiggins took a deep breath, reached down with his free hand and pulled back the sheet.

Poppy stared up at him, paler than she ever was in life. She would go to church no more.

7

Fucking Tommy. Fucking Martha. Fucking Delphy. Fucking whores. Fucking fucking fucking.

Wiggins raged as he strode across the Thames at Vauxhall Bridge and headed to Sal's cab hut. He raged at the Embassy and all who worked there; he raged at the high-and-mighty punters; he raged at a world where young girls like Millie and Poppy had to sell themselves to make a living; and most of all, he raged at himself. Poor, pale Poppy would never have died if it weren't for him. He knew that like he knew the streets.

He didn't know what had killed her, though. There was no obvious wound, and she wasn't bloated from drowning, though she looked all bleached out, like she'd been in the river. She wasn't strangled either, as far as he could tell.

What he did know, however, was that she was seen talking to him, and now she could talk no more.

'Watch it!' Sal called, as Wiggins crashed through the door of the hut.

'Jax about?'

'Where else she gonna be, Buck House?'

Jax was out the back of the hut, sluicing out the bins. She straightened up when she noticed him, and threw down the last of the bins hurriedly.

'Not at the Cheese?'

'Well deduced, Mr Holmes.' She saw the seriousness in his face and said, 'Someone's got to help me ma. I'm going back up later.'

Wiggins nodded. He pulled out the small St Christopher. 'Found this.'

She swiped it from him, then took out her own. 'It's hers, I know it. See, zackly the same.' She held both of them up in front of him.

'What's the red ribbon mean?' he said.

'Dunno. Where is she? Where'd you get it?'

Wiggins hesitated. 'In the bone house, down Horseferry Road.'

'She's dead?'

'Didn't see no body,' Wiggins said slowly. He didn't look at Jax as he went on. 'Don't mean much. She left work, few months ago – walked out one night. No one's seen her since.' The implication was clear. What he didn't want to do was tell Jax about Poppy.

'Wot you mean, work?'

'It's an academy, Jax. She worked in a whorehouse. Up west it is, dead posh.'

'Posh!' Jax cried. She put her hand to her mouth and breathed heavily for a moment.

Wiggins let the news settle. 'Why didn't you tell me she was on the game?'

'I didn't know,' Jax said. 'I thought maybe. But you wouldn't have bothered, would you? No one cares.'

Wiggins opened his mouth to respond, stung. But maybe she had a point. Not about him caring, but who goes after missing whores? It's the old story. He looked out into the traffic filtering towards Waterloo. Straggly pigeons pecked and fluttered aside as best they could. A horse neighed right by them, one of the waiting cabs.

Eventually, Jax said, 'You didn't see no body?'

'Nah.'

'Then there's a chance.'

'I didn't see nothing in the ledger, neither, that said it was her like. A couple of possibles, nothing certain. Did she look old for her age?'

'No,' Jax said quickly. 'At least, she didn't when I last saw her. But you mean there's a hope?'

Wiggins frowned. He was still stunned by Poppy's death, her pale face staring up at him. The Embassy wasn't a nice place. But cold hard reason, the old boss's favourite kind, said: 'There's a hope.'

He dodged back into the hut. Wiggins watched as Sal took tea to a couple of customers. She shared a thin joke with them, then walked back to him with questions in her eyes.

'What you want with Jax now?'

'Leave it, Sal.'

'You's jumping about like a jack-in-the-box, Wiggo. You need to calm down. Twenty-five years later, and you're still running.'

'And you're still making tea.'

Sal stepped back, surprised. By this time, more cabbies were coming in the door. The pre-rush-hour rush. She turned away, hurt. Wiggins stood for a moment, hating himself. Her hands, red raw, scalded many times, nails bitten to the quick, flitted between the cups and urns and hastily sawn hunks of bread.

He left quietly out of the front door. Jax was waiting for him.

'Ain't no body?' she repeated.

'Ain't no body. But don't go to the Embassy, Jax, whatever you do. It's a dark place.'

She didn't reply, didn't even move. Finally, he added, 'I'll sort it. I promise.'

He set out west, his stride fast and angry. He looked at his watch, looked up at the sky. He was due in Victoria Street to see Kell, get the addresses, start the surveillance on the high and mighty of the land. But as he walked, his mind jumped faster and faster, and he almost broke into a run. His temper was up. He'd go to Hampstead later, catch Kell at home, but now there was somewhere he absolutely needed to be; something he absolutely needed to say; and someone he absolutely needed to batter.

'I need information, Kell, eyes and ears. We have many dangers ranged against us.'

'Were you thinking of any dangers in particular, sir?'

The Home Secretary, Winston Churchill, stopped pacing and glared at Kell. That afternoon, after Wiggins had gone to Horseferry Road, Kell had been summoned by Churchill for a private audience. He strode about his huge corner office like a prime-minister-in-waiting. Big windows cast a late-afternoon glow. Kell couldn't help wondering how it was that such a vain, objectionable man could continue to ascend the slippery pole of politics.

Churchill stabbed his smoking cigarette in Kell's direction. 'The country is about to descend into turmoil. The death of a monarch always unsettles people. Anarchists, alien terrorists. Trade unions. The Irish. Indians – have you not heard of Madan Lal? And Women. This vote business is turning nasty.'

'So you need me to keep watch on immigrants, trade unions, the Irish, the Indians, and women?'

'Don't forget the Germans, the Russians and the French.'

Kell frowned. 'What about Special Branch?'

'Special Branch aren't to be trusted. At least, not always.'

'But my remit, sir, is very tight. I am to find German spies. My resources, too, are limited.' Kell shifted his eyes. He was expecting Wiggins back in the office any moment, and he was going to commission him to look for German spies amongst the very ranks of people like Churchill and his closest aides. This was not something he would share with the man in front of him.

Churchill stubbed out his smoke. 'You are *my* man now. I haven't forgotten about Agent W, that business with the Tsar last year. Capital work.'

'But, sir—'

'Pish-pash, I don't expect you to take over from Special Branch. Sir Patrick Quinn will get on with it in his own way – though why we entrust the branch to an Irishman, I'll never know. I need all the resources I can get my hands on. And that means you. You and Agent W.'

Kell blinked. It was never easy to contradict Churchill, and almost impossible now that he was Home Secretary. 'But we work to Haldane in the War Office. I am army. The chain of command.'

'Chains restrict, chains limit, chains imprison. We will not be shackled, eh, Kell?'

Kell sighed, not sure about that 'we'. Churchill suddenly smiled. A gruesome surprise. He gestured to a forest of spirit bottles on a side table. 'Whisky,' he said. Kell thought for a moment he was offering him a drink and was about to accept until he noticed Churchill's outstretched hand. Damn the man. Kell poured them both a drink, handed one to Churchill and waited for him to continue.

'I want you – or your agent, W – to go wherever I put you. I am the Home Secretary. I must know more than anyone, more than Quinn, more than Haldane, more than the Admiralty. Understand?'

'Of course, but my—'

'Oh, carry on with the spy hunting, of course. I shan't call on you every day. I do have the police on my side. But the country is fermenting, Kell, the people are boiling up, in the mines, in the factories, in the dockyards. I can feel it. This summer could be very bad indeed. And what I need W for is the specialist jobs, inside the inside, my man and my man alone. You must tell no one of this.'

'And if I . . .' Kell ventured the thought; dared to think but not quite to say, *disagree?*

'I wouldn't finish that sentence if I were you.' Churchill smiled again, and swirled the last of his Scotch. 'Very good. I will contact you with a mission soon. Sláinte!'

Kell hurried back to the office, only to find that Wiggins had not yet returned. Simpkins handed in a sheet of paper with the addresses of the top ministers of the Committee and, more importantly, their close aides. It wasn't that easy to find out where people lived and Simpkins had been to the records of three government departments already. No one trusted Kell, and he had no authority to demand any records at all – as Quinn had been so pleased to tell him.

He glanced back with longing at his new filing system. He had more accurate, up-to-date and comprehensive data on most of the Germans living in the country than he did on half the people in government. Yet, and this was something his masters had only just realised, the greatest danger came from your closest confidants.

He leaned back in his seat and lit a cigarette. The first plume rose to the ceiling, curling and disappearing into the air. Was this task he'd been set doomed to fail? Was that the point, in fact? Had Soapy and Quinn set him the trap – to discover a mole that didn't exist? Soapy had almost said as much. And yet, Soapy was agitated by the leaking of information. Kell had checked – the Italian treaty really had fallen through at the last minute.

And what was he to make of Churchill's intervention?

The clock struck five. No sign of Wiggins. This unreliability was beginning to grate. Wiggins was living up to his class, or living down to it, more like. Kell looked at the list once more. Could Wiggins really help? His agent's increasingly long absences, his drinking, his surly mien – and if not surly, downright insolent (Kell refused, even in his own mind, to use the term 'cheeky') – made him almost impossible to deal with. Yet he had no one else.

More to the point, without Wiggins, Kell wouldn't be in a position to do Churchill's bidding. As he sat there and smoked, he started to suspect it might only be Churchill who stood between him and one of the newfangled labour exchanges. *Army captain. Seeking employment. Work history: classified.*

At six o'clock, Kell shouted for Simpkins.

'Any calls?'

Simpkins came running into the office. 'The telephone also rings in here, sir,' he said, looking confused. 'And I've been out most of the afternoon.'

'That's a no, then? No message from my wife?'

'No.'

'Very good. You can go. Sharp tomorrow, mind. We need this

list complete.' He tapped his hand on the desk. As soon as
Simpkins closed the door, he slumped back into his seat, then
picked up the telephone himself.

'Hampstead 202.'

Kell waited for the exchange to put him through. Churchill's
interference was vexatious. Working for such a man would be
intolerable. It was as if Churchill viewed the creation of a
secret service as an excuse to spy on the whole country – or
rather, to spy on whomever was causing the most trouble at
the time, be it trade unionists, Indian independence fighters
or women. Kell had assumed that his job, the job of any secret
service, was to battle against agents of enemy powers, not your
own people. And yet now even the suffragettes were on
Churchill's list. Special Branch's photograph of Constance
flashed into his mind. Her hat, unmistakable. He thrust the
thought aside.

No answer from her on the telephone.

He looked down again at the list and suddenly realised that
one of them might also be called an 'enemy within'. But was it
actually he who was being naive in not casting his inward glance
wider, deeper even? Was his only use, in fact, to turn the government's most secret eye onto its subjects while being the holding
place for its darkest secrets, to do the deeds and think the thoughts
no one else could?

A thin voice crackled through on the line. 'There's no answer,
sir. Nobody's home.'

Wiggins pushed through the big doors of the Bloodied Axe and
strode confidently to the stairway beside the bar. He nodded at
the barman, like a regular, and took the stairs two at a time before
the muscled barsmith could even make a comment.

He opened the door at the top of the stairs and entered another
world.

The Becket down Old Kent Road was the famous boxing pub
south of the river. Wiggins had been in there a few times, for a
drink and the occasional barney. But the Axe was a different

kettle altogether. The Becket was pure Queensberry Rules, straight up and down, strike with the flat. A gentleman could have fought in the Becket, save for the fact that he'd have to go down the Old Kent Road. The Axe wasn't quite so cosy. They boxed proper at times, and any decent fighter could find a spar soon enough. But they also fought hard and dirty too, and Wiggins remembered the rumours – that some prize fights at the Axe ended in more than just a knockout.

For all that, upstairs at the Axe looked like any boxing gym, with posed pictures on the walls, a bag, skipping ropes, and an array of muscly lumps limbering up. Early-evening sunlight threw diagonals from the high windows; sweat glistened off naked torsos. And the place stank of unwashed shirts and liniment. The room was dominated by a raised boxing ring at one end. And the ring itself was dominated by one man: Tommy.

He prowled the sprung surface like an oversized cat circling a mouse. The opponent in question bobbed and weaved, with some sharp foot movements. Tommy moved, graceful, slow, unconcerned – because he didn't need to be fast. He angled his head out of one, two, three shots, stepped back, then suddenly a jab jackhammered out of nowhere and the blubber ball tumbled to the deck.

Tommy turned away, rolled his shoulders and looked about him, hungry-eyed.

'I need a word,' Wiggins called from the centre of the gym. 'Tommy!' he added angrily. People turned, someone stopped skipping. All looked up at the ring.

Tommy spat into the corner bucket, straightened up. 'I ain't Tommy no more,' he said. 'And this is where I do my talking.' He pointed to the canvas beneath his feet.

Wiggins hesitated. Then he nodded and began taking off his jacket with exaggerated care. A ferret of a man appeared at his elbow, took hold of the jacket and then grasped Wiggins's hands.

''E's a big fella, but slow.'

The man had a deep-brown bald scalp, leathered by decades of sun. 'Navy?' Wiggins asked.

'Merchant,' the old man said, massaging Wiggins's hands. 'Seen fights on half the ships of the fleet.'

He held up Wiggins's left hand close to his face, then began winding white tape around it. 'Not hard, T – he's amateur,' the man shouted across the ring to Tommy.

'He can handle himself, Bulldog, don't worry 'bout him,' Tommy grunted.

'Bulldog?' Wiggins whispered.

'I could fight, once. Now, concen – he's a nasty bastard, so lamp him for me.'

'Hurry up, Bulldog, this ain't no nursery,' Tommy said.

Bulldog finished taping, held both hands together and stared straight into Wiggins's eyes. 'He's big enough for two of you, but he's slow 'n' all.' He slipped the light gloves onto Wiggins's hands and bashed them together.

Wiggins clambered into the ring as Bulldog continued to whisper, 'Get him on the inside, son, the inside.'

'Wot?' Wiggins hissed back.

'Folks is feart of getting close to T, but it's the only way, son, on the inside—'

'Fack off out of it, Bulldog, I'm getting bored,' Tommy boomed from the far corner.

Wiggins looked up. Tommy rose, massive and close, even though he was on the other side of the ring.

Bulldog slunk back without a word, leaving Wiggins alone. 'No ref?' he said.

'Frightened you ain't got the old man to run to?' Tommy said. Then, 'The lads'll call it.'

Wiggins glanced around. A small crowd had gathered about the ring, in fact everyone in the gym had stopped to watch. Even the little busboy poked his head through the bottom rung, eager for the fight.

Tommy waited in the ring, monumental, slicked with sweat from his last bout, his muscles visibly moving as he eyed Wiggins's approach.

Wiggins shuffled from one foot to the other, trying to trick his body back into good habits.

'Why you have to kill her, Tommy?' Wiggins said through his gloves.

'I ain't killed no one. You here to fight or what?'

Wiggins ducked forward, threw a speculative jab, then bounced away. Tommy grinned. 'That all you got?'

'I see her once,' Wiggins said again, circling. 'Next time I see her, she's down the Ferry.' He breathed heavily, and he felt the heat rising in his face. Tommy was a big man and Wiggins hadn't had a rumble in over a year. He'd got slow and lazy. And soft. But it wasn't just the exertion, it was the anger. Tommy hadn't even flinched when he'd mentioned Poppy's death. Like she was just another whore, dead by twenty.

Wiggins stepped inside, feinted a right hook and – 'Oof!'

Next thing he knew, Bulldog was squeezing cold water over his face as his head rested on the canvas. In the background, he could hear the men around the ring chanting, shouting almost. 'TWO, THREE, FOUR . . .'

'I thought you said he was slow?'

'I said he was slow, not stupid.'

'FIVE, SIX . . .'

'Don't walk into 'em.'

Wiggins got to one knee and shook his head.

'SEVEN . . .'

'You move like a cat, son, make it count.'

'EIGHT, NINE . . .'

Wiggins straightened and held up his gloves to the onlookers. This provoked a great cheer and laughter. 'He's a boy, ain't he?' someone shouted. 'Fink he'll give Young Joseph a run.' More laughter. Wiggins sensed they still wanted to see blood – his blood – but that they weren't all for Tommy either. They liked their own, but they liked a trier too.

He ducked in close to Tommy, swayed inside a jab, then under a hook and away, out of range. 'Why she die, Tommy?' he gasped. 'What you hiding?'

Tommy unleashed a swinging right hook. Wiggins jerked his head back and the punch slid off his cheek. 'I should be asking you,' he grunted. 'She's sound as a pound till you show up, now she's gone.' He lumbered forward and pinged a body shot into Wiggins's side.

Wiggins skipped away, but the punch hurt. 'Keep moving, keep moving,' he whispered to himself. 'I never pegged you a killer,' Wiggins went on. 'A pimp, yes.'

Tommy roared. Wiggins feinted left, then right, and landed a straight right to Tommy's neck. The big man staggered. The onlookers cheered. Tommy wheeled round to face him, his face like thunder. 'Ain't no pimp, ain't no killer. And I ain't no toff's lackey neither.'

Suddenly he was in Wiggins's face. A barrage of punches, lefts, rights, to the body, the arms. Wiggins ducked, weaved, sprang away once more. From the corner, he could hear Bulldog wheezing, 'Inside, son, inside.'

Wiggins looked up. Tommy came at him again. This time, instead of stepping away, Wiggins ducked inside the right lead, feigned a body punch, then caught Tommy's chin flush with a left uppercut. Tommy wobbled, eyes blank. Wiggins leaned in, shocked by the clarity of his punch. As he did so, Tommy grabbed his shirt collar with his left glove.

The two men tumbled across the ring, Tommy going backwards, Wiggins caught in the fall. As they went down, Tommy swung his free fist around. The last thing Wiggins heard was Bulldog shouting above the hubbub, 'NO!' and then he heard no more.

'Facking rabbit. Facking cheat.'

Wiggins opened his eyes. He coughed violently. The foul reek of smelling salts filled his nose. Above him, Bulldog waving them in his face like he was poking a fire, muttering to himself, 'Facking rabbit, facking cheat.'

'Rabbit?' Wiggins said, pushing the vial away from his nose. 'What the hell is that, anyway?'

'Volatile Sal,' Bulldog said, looking at the vial.

'I meant "rabbit",' Wiggins replied, holding on to Bulldog as he got up on one knee.

'Punched you round the back of the head, didn't 'e – facking cheat. You all right?'

Wiggins felt his ribs, his jaw, the back of his head. All right wasn't the term that sprang to mind. 'I'll live,' he said.

'You sure?'

Tommy stood above them, pulling on his jacket. He held himself tall, legs apart, every inch a winner, although Wiggins noted the purpling bump above his left eye. Not quite such a big man now.

'I'll live longer than Poppy, any roads.' Wiggins spat.

Tommy shook his head, straightened his arms. 'Whores die every day,' he said, simply. 'And so do nosy fucking bastards.'

'That right?'

'Stay away from me, stay away from the Embassy.' He clambered out of the ring and began striding to the door.

'Two years on the streets, and that's it?' Wiggins called after him. 'We saved ya.'

He stopped but did not turn. 'Why do you think I let you get up?' Then he relaxed his shoulders, turned and offered more softly, 'I've put a pin behind the bar for ya, have a drink or two on me. But ya can't come back, Wiggins. Not this time.' He nodded, and was gone.

'Let you get up, my arse,' Bulldog muttered as he hauled Wiggins upright. 'You had 'im beat, son. Or would do, once you got in shape.'

'What do you mean?'

'You's flabby. Slow. But you still move like a cat.'

'Well,' Wiggins said at last. 'This cat needs his milk.'

'I'm not sure we should be discussing this on the telephone.'

'Cripes, what do you mean?' Dinah's giggles crackled down the line.

'Such *activities*.'

'But we were just talking about it at tea! Don't be such a sourpuss. Abernathy and Nobbs will come too, we could . . .'

Constance grinned despite herself. She listened as Dinah's enthusiasm fizzed off the telephone like electricity.

'There's so much more to be done, silly,' Dinah went on. 'This bill.'

'The Conciliation Bill.'

'Is that what it's called? How funny. Anyway, it needs to pass, but that's only the beginning. We must push push push, and you need to help!'

'I still have my work with the Hampstead ladies.'

'Boring.'

'Vital,' Constance said. She worried that if she didn't turn up at the Hampstead meetings, they would do absolutely nothing at all – bar a few very polite letters to their local Member of Parliament. (An MP who, ironically, had no need to listen to their complaints because they didn't have a vote.)

Her loyalty to the ladies of Hampstead wasn't her only concern. A note of caution chimed deep within her. She knew people were being followed by the police, and Special Branch, in particular, were becoming ever more interested in the movement.

She also hadn't forgotten that she lived with the head of the Secret Service.

'Perhaps we could meet for tea,' Constance said. 'The two of us?'

'Abernathy will be green not to see you.'

'I wonder whether Abernathy is quite good company for you, my dear, and Nobbs, for that matter.'

'Goose,' Dinah chided. 'You sound like my mother. Look, it will be just chopsticks if you could come.'

'Chopsticks?' Constance laughed.

'The Japanese,' Dinah cried, 'eat with them!'

The front door opened behind Constance. She swung round to find her husband looking at her. 'I must go,' she said.

'Tea tomorrow?'

'Tomorrow.' She put the phone down.

Kell took off his coat and hat. The silence blossomed.

'Another committee meeting,' Constance said at last. The line, the lie, died on her lips.

Kell avoided her eye. As he swept past her into the drawing room, he muttered, 'I hadn't realised they were putting on revues now.'

She followed him into the drawing room. Her mind screamed at her to say nothing; she felt guilt tingle through her like a mineral cure. But she couldn't keep quiet. 'You think it a great joke, do you? Universal suffrage?'

'I wasn't the one laughing,' he said, measuring out a large brandy. He didn't offer her one. 'I haven't had the best of days,' he went on. 'And I really don't want to talk about who can and cannot vote.'

'Is that all you can say? Rank dismissal.' She heard the anger in her voice.

He heard it too, and peered at her for a moment before taking another gulp. 'Must we, now? I . . .' he faltered.

'Always jam tomorrow, eh? Well, I've had enough,' she said, sweeping out of the room. As she ascended the stairs, she felt her anger subside almost as quickly as it had come; she felt the shame, too. Not the shame of her position – she was right about the vote, of course – but her anger shamed her, for it was not caused by righteous indignation. It was caused by her desire to keep Dinah a secret.

Had Wiggins taught her too much already? Was it ever possible to unlearn the knowledge of deceit, once it was acquired? She often thanked God for Wiggins, but perhaps she should thank the devil.

Across town, south of the river, Wiggins had his own devil to deal with – and he'd spent the night chasing it to the bottom of the glass.

'Is there more left on the pin?' he called to the Axe's wary barkeeper.

The barman sloshed another pint. 'That's it.' He leaned in

close over the beer. 'And that's all ya'll ever get here, pal,' the Scotsman growled. 'Big T was particular on that point. Drink ya pin, an' oot.'

Wiggins nodded, took a swig and wiped his mouth clean. The pub had emptied. Old Bulldog had had a drink with him – 'Tonic, with a dash of the bitters, anyfink more and yous lose your edge' – but otherwise he'd drunk through Tommy's pin steadily. A surprising amount, too, Wiggins reflected. Prostitution must pay.

It didn't pay for Poppy, though. He reckoned Millie was dead too, for all Jax's hopes. But it was Poppy's body that stuck in his head: the pale face paler, in the Ferry, most like because of him. He pulled hard at the pint glass. The Embassy was rotten; something there was wrong, although he still couldn't quite place Tommy as a killer.

'Gonna give me 'nother for the road, Jock,' he called out.

The barman scowled. Reluctantly, he poured a rank-smelling gin into a small glass and pushed it along the bar.

'That's it, pal – for the shiner.'

Wiggins held up the drink, and forced a crooked grin. He was drunk, and that was the only thing about his day – his life – that he liked. Poppy dead, because of him; Jax's Millie, missing and him powerless; and Peter, Peter the Painter at large, alive, eating sweets, enjoying life while poor, dead Bill rotted in the ground of Abney Park. The gin scorched his throat on the way down. 'Ain't that illegal?' he gasped.

The Scot shrugged. Wiggins pushed up from the stool. His legs almost buckled with the shock. He was even more drunk than he thought.

Outside, the traffic had thinned and the lighting in Lambeth was poor. He leaned against the side of the pub for a second. A far-off voice shouted in the gloom, at a woman, a child, Wiggins couldn't make it out. He remembered that he needed to report to Kell, that he'd missed a meeting once more. A dog started barking. The shadows shifted. A door closed.

Wiggins whirled around, alerted, but slowed by the drink. He peered into the darkness. Shapes drifted in and out of view. He closed his eyes, swayed against a wall and wished the visions away – for all he saw, in that dark Lambeth alleyway, was Peter the Painter, gun levelled at him once more.

The shadows shifted and he saw not Peter but Bela, his one-time lover, her harlequin face a shadow all of its own. A gas lamp popped somewhere off to his right, shattering the illusion. Bela, not only his lover but Peter's boss, had gone. She'd flown the country. His love, the one woman he thought of as his own, the woman who'd betrayed him.

He shook any thought of her out of his mind. Peter lingered; he was a malign needle in London, the biggest haystack in the world. Wiggins had no way to trace him. Except— He brought his head up in a moment of clarity.

The first attacker came at him clear enough, but as Wiggins raised his arms in defence, pain exploded in the back of his head. He toppled forward, stunned. The first man caught him and smothered his mouth and nose with a stinking rag.

Wiggins felt the power go from his muscles. He kicked uselessly, then gave in to the choking fumes. It doesn't taste as bad as the gin, Wiggins thought, as he fell into oblivion.

Part 2

8

Kell kept his distance. He hoped his target wouldn't take a cab. She walked down Rosslyn Hill, seemingly without a care in the world. Lime trees swished pleasingly in the wind, leaf shadows dappled the road, even the exhaust fumes wisped away and up into the sky rather than clogging up the road. Kell tried to keep Wiggins's instructions in mind: the hat; no sudden movements; be prepared to walk past your target. Act natural.

Acting natural wasn't that easy when you had a costumer's beard chafing at your chin, and dark glasses that made everything purple. And it wasn't so easy when you were following someone you knew.

The woman didn't pause as they reached the shops of Belsize Park. She quickened her pace as they approached the Underground station. Kell hurried after her, unsure whether or not to risk his disguise in the lift. A slight crush at the gate allowed him to get close, but at the last his nerve failed him – instead of joining her in the huge lift, he dodged left down the stairs. Two hundred and nineteen of them, according to the sign. Kell wasn't counting as he took them two at a time, desperate to get to the platform before the lift arrived. He heard the mechanism clanking and straining as he raced.

Finally he clattered onto the platform, out of breath and sweating. A moment later, he heard the hiss of the lift doors and then the clicking of heels in the walkway. He skulked behind a cigarette vending machine, and waited for the passengers to filter down onto the platform.

First a couple came onto the southbound platform, then three men, and lastly an elderly man stooping over a cane. No sign of the woman. A rumbling roar grew in the distance: the arrival of the northbound train. Kell hustled across the platform, surprised that she'd be taking the train north rather than into London. He stepped onto the northbound platform into the torrent of hot air, then came the pulsing roar, and finally the train burst from the tunnel.

She was nowhere to be seen. Doors opened, passengers spilled out of the train and began walking past him to the exit. Kell whipped his head around. Confused, confounded and worried.

Not only had he failed to track his wife's movements, it was now clear to him that she knew she was being followed, and she knew how to evade a tail.

He boarded the next train south. His wife, who had seemed so unaware, so jaunty on her walk through Hampstead, had obviously stayed in the lift and ascended to the ticket hall while he was waiting on the platform.

There could, of course, be an innocent explanation – a dropped parasol, a mislaid handkerchief. But Constance wasn't the kind of woman to drop a parasol, or mislay anything – at least, not by accident. Where had she picked up such tricks? The train rocked and rattled.

He needed Wiggins more than ever, although he doubted his agent would agree to follow Constance. He had a strange awkwardness about women, Kell had noticed, and – for all his rough-and-ready ways, his horribly shabby dress sense and his quite frankly appalling language – an unusual sense of delicacy. He guessed Wiggins would baulk at the job.

Kell rubbed his eyes, stung by tobacco smoke, and got out at Embankment station. He stood in a lift much like the one Constance had used to evade him and thought more on Wiggins. His agent almost certainly wouldn't advise him to follow her. Indeed, if pressed for advice (something Kell imagined Wiggins would be loath to do in the area of women), Kell guessed the advice would be to talk to her. As if talking to anyone you loved was easy. He could never even talk to his mother.

Standing by a cab at Paddington Station, twenty-odd years

previously, was the last time he had tried. Porters heaved his trunk down from the four-wheeler, as the horse whinnied and neighed in the bustle and hustle of that great gateway to the west. Or, in Kell's case, Eton College. He looked at his mother, who fussed and harried the men as they pulled and tugged at his supplies. He wanted to say something, something with a heart and stamina that would stay with them both; he wanted to say he loved her; he wanted to say, *Don't leave me, don't send me away, I love you, I need you.* He wanted to say all this. Instead, he said, 'Leave them be, Mother, they know what they're doing.'

She turned to him, and for a moment he thought she might voice a feeling like his own, something that spoke to the little child within his thirteen-year-old frame. 'All grown up,' she said and nodded. He stood straighter and lifted his chin, ignored the painful pinch of the collar, like his father would have done, in the manner he thought his mother would expect.

A gang of street urchins ran past, wild, free, hanging off each other like monkeys, laughing. It was only later, much later, that he realised she'd wanted him to deny it, at least for a moment; she'd wanted him to step into a hug, to touch him one last time as a child. But he'd missed his cue, and that hug never came.

Eton had made him a man, he thought bitterly as he strode down the north bank of the river and into Parliament Square. A man who could not talk to his wife, let alone his children; even when he suspected, indeed was convinced, that she was having an affair. There could be no other explanation. The stolen words on the telephone, her laughter, her flushed face. And, most damning of all, the lies. Or one lie in particular. Three weeks previously – the day after he'd last seen Wiggins – he had detoured from his usual route home and sat outside at Marinello's. Hampstead community hall stood opposite, the scene of Constance's many meetings. She did not go in with the other ladies at the appointed time. She did not leave with them afterwards. Later that night, he had asked her how the meeting went. She spoke of it. She lied. He knew.

As he entered Victoria Street, Kell suddenly felt eyes upon him. Was he being followed? A man in a heavy overcoat, despite the summer heat, had been with him since the river. He didn't twist or turn, instead he thought again: what would Wiggins do? He went into the Duke of Cambridge and ordered the best Scotch they had. It wasn't yet ten, but there were a few shift workers already setting about pints of porter, and no one gave Kell a second glance. He kept his eye on the door, but no one followed him in. He drank the whisky anyway.

Twenty minutes later, now convinced he was starting at shadows, he walked the final few hundred yards to his office. He made his way up the stairs, breathing the smell of the Scotch in and out with every step. At the door he waited a moment, then pushed in and offered Simpkins a breezy 'Good day' without stopping. He hoped that this time, as he opened his office door, Wiggins would be waiting for him, smug smile spread across his face like a sated cat.

No Wiggins.

Instead, Simpkins coughed behind him. 'A letter, messengered over direct from Cabinet Office this morning. Would you like a glass of water, sir?'

Kell took the letter, waved the offer away and sat at his desk. As he opened the envelope, a scrap of paper fluttered to the floor. He looked at the letter first, for he recognised the hand-writing at once – all sharp lines, jumpy and erratic. Soapy, on Cabinet letterhead.

Dear Captain Kell . . . Not a good start. Too formal. Means he's writing with the possibility that someone higher up the chain, someone with the power to fire both of them, might read the note at some point. *Apropos* – apropos, what a pompous ass – *our meeting of the 23rd ult. I write to enquire of progress in the matter of internal government security. Please report forthwith.*

Yours etc. etc.

Tobias Etienne Gerard Marchmont Pears MBE

Kell frowned and leaned down to pick up the scrap. On this, scrawled in a much messier, rushed hand, it simply said: *Without a breakthrough on this, you're all in, old man. Best Soap.*

There it was in black and white. The threat, not of ruin exactly, but of total abject failure, humiliation in the Service, embarrassment.

He called out to his clerk, 'Here, did you sign for this letter?'

'Of course, sir. You always said—'

'Very good,' Kell said, indicating the opposite. He waved Simpkins away once more and eyed the drinks cabinet in the far corner of the room. Not yet eleven.

Eventually, he cleared the blotting paper, took a half-written sheet of paper from his desk and began writing. Not, however, to Soapy.

At the top of the page, it read: *Report on Insurgency in the Rhondda Valley coalfields, prepared for the Honourable Winston Churchill, Home Secretary. Classified.*

He continued:

As of June 16th, there is no evidence that the miners of Rhondda have any intention to stray outside the bounds of industrial action as detailed in the public utterances of their trade union. While there is a rumbling of discontent around payment restructuring . . .

Kell put down his pen. Churchill had requested the report almost immediately after their meeting the month before, convinced that the Welsh miners were about to pose a significant threat to what he so pompously referred to as National Security. Kell had heard mutterings in the club about various sites of industrial unrest throughout the country. Churchill's fears of insurrection may not have been so overblown after all. The worst of it for Kell, though, was that Churchill had specifically requested that Wiggins be placed undercover at one of the pits in Wales and Kell had reluctantly agreed.

He took a new piece of paper and began again.

There is 'no chance of the Taffs kicking off this year. A march, a barney, but they'll do what the union bosses say'. These are the words of Agent W, who returned to London earlier this month with said report, including some more detailed particulars about the leaders of the dissent and their lack of support.

Kell put the pen down again, aghast at how easily the lies came. Churchill had asked for Wiggins to be deployed precisely two days after Wiggins had disappeared. Kell had taken the commission – it was hard to say no to Churchill – and now he was in a hole. He had no way of finding out about industrial relations in Tonypandy, other than from the press reports (notoriously biased, of course, given that all the local papers were owned by the same people who owned the mines). On the other hand, he couldn't very well tell Churchill that Wiggins had disappeared. To do so would risk revealing his own uselessness in such a matter, just when Kell suspected that it was only Churchill keeping him in a job at all.

He could only hope that Churchill was keeping the 'Wiggins reports' to himself, rather than sharing them with his inner circle. Churchill wasn't a details man, and it would be quite a stroke of bad luck if he noticed anything amiss.

Kell's hunt for the mole was also grinding to a halt without Wiggins. In his absence, Kell didn't feel able to take on the task of tailing the assistants of all the Cabinet ministers in attendance at the meeting – for one thing, he was known by sight to half of them. Instead, he'd been going over masses of government papers looking for anything that stood out, sets of data that didn't quite match. And what he had discovered didn't make pleasant reading.

For while so far he'd found no clue as to the identity of the mole, he was convinced he'd uncovered even more evidence of information leaks, dating back to the beginning of the year. A naval review of the fleet in Plymouth had had to be aborted when a pleasure cruiser happened upon it. The pleasure boat had had a number of foreign tourists aboard, including Germans. This wasn't deemed suspicious at the time, just bad luck. But had it been luck?

In April, a long-gestating plan by the Colonial Office to solidify relations with the locals on the southern edge of Lake Tanganyika had proved a failure when it was discovered that a German rubber company had already given them all jobs.

Kell had found three or four of these odd little reverses; things that hadn't gone smoothly. There was never anything large enough, though, to suggest that someone had blabbed. None of these instances had been marked down as a failure of security; Soapy knew nothing about them. And yet, in one way or another, Germany seemed to be the beneficiary every time. Kell sensed the hand of Van Bork.

He got up and poured himself a glass of whisky, and thought again about the Committee for Imperial Defence. Perhaps this was Van Bork's mistake, his one false move. Soapy had only found out that the Germans knew about the route because of a stray diplomatic boast; a mistake, in other words. There were so few people in that committee room. It *had* to be one of them.

This didn't disguise the fact that he still had no idea who had leaked the information, nor any evidence that could convict anyone of such a crime. The irony wasn't lost on him that after almost a year of not finding any important German spies, when there was evidence of a very real spy operation at the highest levels of government, his department might be wound up for being ineffectual.

The whisky slipped down easily. And with it, a far more unpalatable thought: was he being threatened with the sack precisely because he was getting closer? Did it run that deep?

His head ached. He put his hand to the bridge of his nose and squeezed his eyes shut in an effort to dull the pain. Where the hell was Wiggins?

~~

Wiggins opened his eyes. At least, he thought he opened his eyes. He lay flat on his back. His head hammered. He felt a lurch in his stomach. But he could see nothing. It was as dark as death and twice as cold. *Clunk. Clunk. Clunk.* A metallic sound echoed around him.

He drew his hand up to his face, invisible in the blackness. A great white mist filled his mind. He remembered coming out of the Bloodied Axe, he remembered twisting around, and then the blow, the poisonous vapour. Then nothing. The floor lurched beneath him once again. Bile rose in his throat, an acrid stench

– had he been drugged? His mouth was as dry as the Band of Hope on Sundays, and his head swam.

The floor pitched and yawed beneath him. He sat up and shivered. Took a few quick breaths. The cold air pinched his lungs. This was the coldest place he'd ever been. His mind was catching up with his body, then stalling. He tried to get up but could only reach one knee. He was weak, he couldn't think straight, his head was mush, his muscles jelly and he realised – with the kind of clarity that comes in the midst of a maelstrom, the quiet heart of the storm engulfing his mind and body – that if he didn't get out in the next ten minutes, he would die.

He got on all fours and with both hands began feeling in front of him. The floor was icy wet metal, with a strange, granulated dust. What felt like metal shelves lined first one wall, then the second and the third. His breath was failing him, the cold pinching at his chest. He crawled around to the final wall. His hand caught on the first rung of a ladder. His limbs shook and he couldn't find his bearings in the pitch black. But he had to climb.

As he rose, he neared the clanking sound. His hand slipped, his jaw shook with the cold, but he climbed on. Finally, his hand touched a hatch. Feeling to the side, he found the source of the clanking – an iron spike tied to a hook on the wall. He took as deep a breath as he could, jammed his left arm between the top rung of the ladder and the side of the wall, and grasped the spike in his hand. The room lurched again and Wiggins's feet slipped.

He held on, gathered his footing and swung the spike against the hatch. *Bang! Bang! Bang!*

Nothing. 'Help!' he croaked. All rasp, no power. 'Help,' he screamed. He brought the spike crashing against the hatch, once, twice, three times.

He tipped his head back, closed his eyes and screamed into the darkness again – this time a scream from the depths of his hollow belly, a rage, a final song. Of all the places to die . . . He'd bled on the veldt, in the dirt- and shit-encrusted alleys of the Jago; he'd had Rijkard's cleaver at his neck, Peter's bullet in his shoulder in Holborn . . . Of all the places: a cold, pitch-black hellhole, God knew where. He screamed again, surprising himself with the sound, the pain. Of all he'd left undone, unsaid; poor, dead Bill still unavenged, Peter free and easy; Millie missing, Poppy dead.

And Bela. Bela, Bela . . .

His hand sagged on the ladder, his head swung back. The pain seeped from his body. All he could see was her and all he could feel, now, as his life ended, was a strange, bitter relief. It flooded through him as she smiled, her oval face, the birthmark splashed across it. Bela. She reached out her hand for him, opened her mouth . . .

'*Hallo, daar?*'

'*Hallo, daar,*' someone shouted again, muffled.

The hatch creaked. Wiggins barely registered the noise but his eyes fluttered open, waiting, wanting it to end.

His vision filled with first a brightly lit slither, then bleaching out. He blinked. Bearded angels ringed the view.

He closed his eyes once more, spent. All he heard, as hands reached down to grab him, was an astonished voice cry, '*Verstekeling!*'

Strange, thought Wiggins as he passed out – always thought the God fella would speak English.

~~~

In the weeks following the near disaster at the funeral procession, Constance Kell became more careful than ever. When out on the streets, she routinely doubled back; when getting on the Tube she would take the lift, then reascend; and when entering a cab, she would inform the driver a general direction ('South!') and then be specific only when the car was well on its way. These were all tricks picked up from Wiggins.

'Molinari's, just off Soho Square!' she called to the cab driver as they sped out of Belsize Park.

'Now you tell me,' he muttered.

She'd felt someone following her once or twice, though she'd nothing definite to say one way or the other. She took particular care whenever she went to see Dinah and her girls. Their conversations, ever since the failure at the procession, had begun to get dangerous.

It wasn't that she disapproved of more aggressive action – she could see the need, indeed she fed off Dinah's energy and enthusiasm. Taking the fight to the streets, forcing the powers of the state into reaction was what she wanted; not the dreary recitation of albeit reasonable arguments to rooms full of other women. The whole problem was that the government and the state – their opposition – were not being rational, they were not listening to reason. And so, as Abernathy and Dinah argued, something more had to be done.

No, the problem for Constance was the risk.

She arrived at Molinari's coffee house to find Abernathy holding court to four or five young women, including Nobbs, Dinah and Tansy.

'Constance!' Dinah cried, and pulled out a seat.

Abernathy ignored her and continued, 'We should do something about the post.'

What followed was an urgent discussion about how best to disrupt the postal system. Constance looked at the young women as they calmly discussed various acts of vandalism as if they were planning a garden party. A far cry from the Hampstead ladies. It felt both immature and electrifying at the same time. Their confidence, their bounce. Constance tried to remember whether she had ever had so much – before the children, perhaps? Eventually, the women settled on the use of acid thrown directly into post boxes.

'I know someone at Imperial College,' Nobbs said. 'Used to be a student. Supporter. We could get some there.'

'But shouldn't we take precautions?' Constance said at last.

The women all trilled with laughter. She went on. 'Isn't it dangerous? I mean, the police. Surely Special Branch?'

'Special Branch know nothing about us,' Abernathy said. 'Unless *you've* told them.'

'That's settled,' Nobbs said.

Constance looked around her as each of the women got up

and headed for the door, as if by prearrangement. 'Will you, now?' Constance said. Abernathy looked down her nose at her, and turned to the door without uttering a word. 'Take precautions, I mean.'

The other girls went with Abernathy and only Dinah stopped to say goodbye. 'Don't worry,' she said.

Constance followed her out onto the pavement. Dinah smiled and whispered, 'And don't be too hard on Abernathy. Her cousin did something unspeakable to her last summer. Now she can't have children or anything like that.'

'What?' Constance said, appalled.

Dinah pulled a sad smile. 'You know how it is. Boys rollicking around these country houses in the long vacation. Experimenting, so her papa said.'

Constance shook her head, and looked up. Abernathy and the other women waited for Dinah at the corner of Dean Street and Soho Square.

'But do help us with the post boxes. And come to Golden Square – you must!' she said and sped off.

'What on earth's in Golden Square?'

'Jew-jew Sue,' Dinah shouted. Or at least, that's what it sounded like to Constance.

Who on earth was Jew-jew Sue?

Kell paced up and down the drawing room, cigarette at his lips. Every now and then he stopped at the drinks cabinet for a nip. He'd spent the rest of the day writing up Wiggins's (fictitious) reports for Churchill, as well as being side-tracked by naval reports. Some duffer in naval intelligence seemed to think the Germans were in regular cahoots with a small fleet of Chinese junks, of all things.

His mood was ragged. He couldn't shake the worm of suspicion from his thoughts. Grey, Churchill, Soapy, one of their assistants? How would he ever know? Was he nothing without Wiggins?

'Vernon! Are you quite all right?' Constance stood at the door, back from Molinari's, breaking his train of thought. She wafted her hand across her nose. 'It's like Euston Station in here,' she went on as she moved to the big sash window and pulled it open with a great yank.

'I beg your pardon?'

'What's wrong?'

'What's wrong? What's wrong, you ask? I tell you what's wrong. After securing the intelligence coup of the century last year, my department is now the laughing stock of Whitehall. I anticipate that in the next few days we will be wound up, subsumed under the guardianship of that popinjay Quinn if we are to survive at all. Soapy doesn't speak up for me, Quinn and Special Branch are rampant, and I will be out of a job in a matter of days. Churchill's good will is about to run out, so I can't even do his sneaking for him, especially when he finds out about Wiggins. I will have failed, totally and utterly failed, and I am not yet forty years old. Soapy himself said I'm done. That's what's wrong. My backside's to the fire and I'm burning.' He drew breath at last.

It was the first time he'd managed more than a sentence to Constance in months. He looked up at her again, at the point between her eyes, the soft dark crinkle that had been there ever since the birth of their first child. He wanted to say something more, something with a heart that would last, but he was gripped by indecision, and said nothing.

Constance hesitated, shifted weight onto her heels, but did not step towards him. Instead, she said, 'Where is Mr Wiggins?'

Kell looked away, suddenly embarrassed. 'Gone. For weeks.'

'Gone where?'

'Why are you asking?' he said.

'It doesn't matter,' she muttered and began pulling at her hat.

She'd made a mistake, asking about Wiggins. But before she had to face it, the doorbell rang. Kell waited a second longer, until the bell rang again. This time he went into the hallway and returned holding a piece of paper.

'A telegram,' he said. 'It's about Wiggins.'

9

His dying mother, wrists blood-streaked. Run, H, run. The game's up,
Bill shouted, blood pumping from a hole in his cheek, the game's up. She
was right, she was right. Poppy leaping off the slab, the ferry's got me,
the ferry.

The fever had broken. Wiggins woke up in a small sickbay. A
porthole sealed shut, a medicine cabinet, and three posters
warning of the dangers of VD in three different languages.

A cabin boy poked his head around the door, left a pan of
water and nodded. He then used a series of elaborate hand signals
to indicate, at least in Wiggins's mind, where he might find first
the head and then the deck.

Half an hour later, Wiggins stood at the rail. His mind felt as
clear as the broad, black ocean. The ship still pitched and yawed,
but less so than the last couple of days. He didn't know much
about the sea, other than his passage to South Africa and back
for the Boer War – with a sun-drenched stopover on the Rock
of Gibraltar – but this looked like a standard cargo steamer to
him. Or rather, a standard steamer adapted with new technology.
It had a huge funnel streaming out smoke like a pit fire, and a
small crane was fastened to the deck, set between great webbed
caskets. A refrigerated cargo hold squatted in the centre of the
deck. He'd walked past it on his way up from the cabin – a giant
metal case, fitted into the hold. Now, with the breeze stiffening
his hair, he could spot crewmen here and there, but no one paid
him a second glance.

The cabin boy must have alerted the captain, for not much
later the boy came scuttling along the rail and indicated mutely
once more for Wiggins to follow. The boy took him to a cabin

door and turned to go. Wiggins caught his wrist. 'How long have I been out?' he said.

The boy held up three fingers.

'Three days?'

The boy nodded, and ran off.

Wiggins knocked and went in.

'I am captain. Bobrowski.' He looked up at Wiggins. 'Why you stowaway?' he barked.

'I didn't,' Wiggins said. He stood in the doorway of a small and tidy cabin while the bearded Bobrowski made an elaborate play of lighting his pipe.

'I'd hardly lock myself in a fridge, would I?' The captain looked a question. Wiggins went on. 'The refrigerator. I wouldn't kill myself.'

The captain nodded thoughtfully. 'We have stowaways. Desperate.'

'How many stowaway *from* London?' Wiggins asked.

Bobrowski stared ahead for a moment, then gave a brisk nod. Who would fly the world's biggest magnet? Who would fly the honey pot?

'You work?' He struck a match and put it to the bowl of his pipe.

'You pay?' Wiggins said.

'Passage. Cape Town.'

Wiggins shook his head. 'That ain't gonna fly.'

'What?'

'You got to drop me off at a cablehead. I've got to get back to London.'

Bobrowski frowned. 'Cape Town,' he said, closing a logbook in front of him.

Wiggins paused and scratched his new beard. 'I believe you when you say you had nothing to do with me being in there. I truly do. But I ain't so sure you're allowed to be running guns. Not once you've docked in London.'

Captain Bobrowski stood up, astonished. 'No guns.' He shook his head.

'Not now. But there have been. And there will be again, less I'm more doolally than I think.'

The captain jutted his chin and picked up his pipe again. 'Many men disappear overboard. The sea is bad.'

'Not that bad,' Wiggins said. He dipped his head slightly and waited. The captain, for his part, refilled his pipe. For a moment, Wiggins questioned his own judgement – perhaps this man, this leathery, gimlet-eyed sea captain, was a killer after all. Perhaps he'd taken the cash to stow and dump Wiggins's body in the sea anyway – perhaps he'd misread his mark?

'Canaries,' said the skipper at last. 'Report to second mate for deck duties.' He waved his hand in dismissal.

Wiggins tapped his forehead. 'Aye aye,' he said and turned to the door. When he reached it, he twisted back for one last word. 'Why was it on?'

'Hmm?'

'The refrigeration unit was empty. So why was it on?'

Bobrowski nodded an acknowledgement. 'I don't know. Accident maybe. One of the crew with fat fingers.'

'Fat chance,' Wiggins grunted as he left.

He'd taken a risk putting it to Bobrowski like that – let me off, or I'll blab. But for all that he ran guns, Bobrowski wasn't a killer. Wiggins had deduced the fact that he was a gunrunner from three key pieces of information. The metal flaked residue on the fridge floor, some of which had stayed on his fingers, came from small shells; the fridge floor, which he'd crawled over in his desperation, also had concealed panels. This was confirmed when he compared the size of the fridge unit externally with its internal size. There was a secret compartment underneath.

For all this, Wiggins had guessed that Bobrowski didn't wish him any real harm, otherwise he'd already be dead. And he wasn't asking for the world, he was asking for a lift.

The boy had taken him down to the crew's quarters, where he'd been given a free berth with five other men – all of whom stank of sweat, fish and cheap rum. He took a quick nip from a likely-looking lad, and then went up in front of the second mate.

First he cleaned the head, then hauled up cargo, swept the

hold, and tore his hands to shreds. The physical work, though, showed Wiggins that he was seriously out of a good condition. He'd spent too long lolling about the industrial towns of England looking for spies who didn't exist, drinking Kell's money and getting fat. But Peter wasn't getting bored and fat; he was making bombs, oiling Mausers and eyeing up another score. Tommy wasn't getting fat neither, and nor were his girls, those poor girls.

Most of the crew didn't speak English, but welcomed him well enough. Tots of rum and vodka, an appreciative grunt here and there, Wiggins knew the drill. What he didn't know was who on the crew switched him on – who, in fact, had colluded in putting him on the ship in the first place. It was too neat, too hard to dump a man on someone else's boat: whoever'd picked him up and drugged him outside the Axe, had taken him to this ship – the SS *Patna* – and someone knew.

The second night out of the sickbay, the man introduced himself. Or rather, Wiggins woke up with a blade at his neck and heavy breathing in his ear.

Wiggins kept his eyes closed. The blade quivered. The breathing quickened, but Wiggins did not move. Neither did the knife.

He drew his hand up slowly, as if in his sleep. The blade quivered. The blow did not fall.

Wiggins opened his eyes and grasped his attacker by the wrist. A crewman named Armand crouched over him, holding the knife. He tried to pull himself clear but Wiggins held on. Wiggins shot out his other hand from the bunk and grabbed Armand by the balls.

Armand struggled, in silence, but Wiggins slowly turned the knife outwards. Their muscles shook with the effort, but, bit by bit, Wiggins moved the point towards Armand.

Suddenly, the sailor's fight went out of him. Wiggins could see the faint glimmer in his eyes, all round and white and full of fear. He squeezed harder and harder on Armand's wrist, on his balls. The others in the room slept, the ship creaked, and Wiggins squeezed on.

'I'll tell Big T you missed me,' he hissed.

The brute flinched at the name. 'No English,' he whispered.

Armand released the knife. Wiggins kept hold of Armand's balls. He tightened his grip. 'You try anything like this again, I'll kill you. Understand. Dead.' Armand's eyes grew bigger in the meagre light and Wiggins squeezed on. 'Understand?' Armand tried to nod.

Eventually, Wiggins released him. The wretch scuttled off. Wiggins had got a name. Tommy. Big T, Tom, whatever he wanted to call himself. He should have guessed it – Tommy had never put his hand in his pocket for anyone. There'd been way too much on the pin; he shouldn't have drunk it all. But then Tommy knew he would, knew he'd stumble out of the Axe drunker than a judge.

What Wiggins didn't know was why he was in a ship halfway to Africa rather than lying dead in a Lambeth gutter.

The *Patna* pulled into Santa Cruz on Tenerife more than two weeks later, the delay caused by engine trouble. Wiggins went up to see Bobrowski one last time.

'Thank you,' he said after knocking his way into the cabin.

The captain shrugged. 'I have no choice. We need to fix the engines. And at least now we have oranges.'

'I ain't never met a Polish sailor before.'

'Poles make the best sailors in the world,' Bobrowski said with melancholy pride. 'Because we can't go home.'

Wiggins nodded. 'Armand's a wrong 'un, just so you know.'

Bobrowski cricked his neck. 'Welcome to the sea,' he said. 'Your pay.' He pushed a couple of coins across the table. Wiggins reached down, but Bobrowski put his hand over them for a moment. 'You say nothing? No guns.'

Wiggins grinned. 'All I saw was oranges.'

Wiggins reached the quay and took off his coat. Salt wind whipped his hair, his beard tasted briny. He rolled up his shirtsleeves, held his face to the sun for a glorious moment, and then went in search of the telegraph office and somewhere to change the coins Bobrowski had given him.

The post office stood just off the main road leading from the quay, and Wiggins was relieved to find it opening again for the afternoon. He telegraphed Kell with as few words as possible. The operator indicated that any reply might not reach him until tomorrow. After a deal of hand signals, Wiggins procured directions to a dosshouse where he put down a penny for a bed. He then found a sleepy café where old square men drank brightly coloured drinks from inch-high glasses. Wiggins ordered one for himself, showed the barman his change and was astonished at the lowness of the price. The spirit bit his throat, all acid and fruit and fire. He sat down and ordered another.

'"Tenerife. Home? W."' Kell read it out, then handed it to Constance.

'What's he doing in Tenerife?' she said. 'The sly dog.'

'I must go back to the office at once.' Kell stepped into the hall.

'Why?'

He came back into the drawing room. 'Don't you understand? He's my only hope. Without him . . .' Kell shrugged and turned to go.

'But Vernon,' Constance said, 'I can help—'

He clattered down the hallway and out through the front door, oblivious. He didn't hear her last line. She didn't even mean to say it. But somewhere deep within herself, the offer echoed. She wanted to help him, despite their enmity, their distance, their political disagreements. Perhaps it was the shame that, while her husband had so uncharacteristically unburdened himself about his worries and his work, all she had wanted to know was the whereabouts of Wiggins, for her own ends.

She began extracting the pins from her hat. The thing was, her ends were just. If Vernon couldn't see that, perhaps he didn't deserve her help after all.

GO TO OFFICES OF MAWSON AND SWAIN. SAY MY NAME. K.

Wiggins read the telegram the next morning, through the kind of hangover that felt like home. Hard, heavy and comforting. He walked through the streets until he found Mawson and Swain. FINE WINES, said the peeling paint above the door.

A dark-haired clerk looked Wiggins up and down like he was one of the street dogs that sloped and barked and snarled down the shady alleyways of Santa Cruz. But soon enough Mawson himself appeared, florid and already sweaty. He didn't care to have the likes of Wiggins in his office either, but obliged never-theless.

'Here's some local currency. And we have you a berth in steerage on the SS *Friendship*, which will take you to Tilbury in the next few days. K expressly ordered that you have a shave, by the way, hence the currency.'

'He did, did he?' Wiggins said, pulling at his chin.

'Now, I believe that's everything.'

Wiggins nodded. On his way out, he caught sight of his reflec-tion in a fine, ornate mirror. He looked like an apeman.

He took a turn around the port and was delighted to discover that the old square men of the night before still stood or sat at bars, drinking the same brightly coloured spirits from the same inch-high glasses, even though it wasn't yet ten. Better than rashers and a doorstep any day.

Wiggins ambled along the quayside, aping the lope of a gentleman of leisure, dreaming the far-off dream of money. Not the crinkle of pesetas in his pocket, but real money, the kind that meant you didn't have to worry about where you slept or what you ate or who you had to be nice to; you didn't have to worry about turning your ankle, you didn't have to worry about getting ill; the kind of money that meant your friends – Jax – didn't lose people to a life on their back.

'Hey, you there,' someone shouted at him from above.

Wiggins looked up. A man, bearded like himself, leaned over the gunnels of a scuffed sailing ship and waved at him.

'I say, are you English?' the man asked.

'London,' Wiggins said.

'Army?'

'Gunners.'

'Fought the Boer?'

'Until the biltong bled.'

'Good show. Earn a shilling? Gangplank's there, we don't stand on ceremony.'

Wiggins clambered up the gangplank and onto the deck. The man, a great hulking chap with sunburn and a broad grin, introduced himself: 'Oates.' He thrust out his hand.

'Titus!' Wiggins couldn't help himself. The memory flashed into his head of a newspaper report in the Boer War: Titus Oates, a hero of the veldt.

'I say, you're a sharp one. I would say call me Captain, but not on this ship. I'm likely to splice the hawse, cut the mainsplice, and send us all into a hurricane,' Oates joked.

He set Wiggins to work rearranging the ship's stores and loading more supplies from the quay. Despite the hot weather, the ship was packed with cold-weather clothes, lanterns, scientific equipment and mountains of tinned food. He found himself enjoying it. The hard labour on the *Patna* had got him into some sort of shape. He could feel his muscles working again like they used to. The snap was coming back.

At lunchtime, Oates brought him a hunk of bread and cheese and a jerrycan of brackish water. 'You're a handy chap and no mistake,' he said. 'Thought this lot would take you the day.'

'I ain't no stranger to work, sir. If there's a drink at the end of the day, leastways.'

Oates laughed. 'Yes, indeed. Good job the skipper's not aboard. I tell you what, if you bring up the rest of the kit from the quay, there's another shilling in it for you.'

'And another drink?'

Oates came back for him later that day, clapping, 'Well done, very well done. Here you go.' He handed him the two shillings. 'Don't have any of the local stuff, I'm afraid.'

'This'll do,' Wiggins said.

'Don't fancy coming along with us, do you?' Oates said, only half joking. 'We could always do with good men.'

'Where you going?'

'To tell you the truth, we're going to the South Pole.'

'You've got to be up the pole.'

Oates laughed again. 'Ha! Perhaps you're right. Well, goodbye. And enjoy that drink.'

Wiggins raised a hand in acknowledgement and strode down the gangplank. As he walked away, he idly glanced at the name painted on the ship's hull: *Terra Nova*.

Kell strode to the Underground station at Hampstead. His heart was lighter now that Wiggins was on his way back to London. He shuddered to think what had taken him to the Canaries in the first place, but over a telegraph wire was hardly the place to find out. At least he could put Wiggins back on to the leak, and they might finally make some progress before his job went up in smoke. As he entered Flask Walk, he realised he'd forgotten his briefcase. He turned back.

The only progress he had made was his recruitment of a source in the Foreign Office. He had done so without consulting Wiggins, or anyone else, but the source had been able to furnish him with some useful titbits. He reasoned that if the Germans were trying to recruit from inside the diplomatic service, then so should he. The idea of creating a network of information and informants over one's own people was not something that had been discussed by anyone Kell knew, but he realised that if he was going to adequately protect his position in future, the more he knew about everyone, the better.

He rounded the corner into his road at pace and suddenly saw a privet hedge rustle.

Then he saw a hand.

'You there!' he shouted, surprising himself.

A man shot out of the bushes in a blur. His head down, he barrelled into Kell.

Kell crashed to the pavement, winded. He scrabbled to his feet, but the man, now hatless, hared around the corner in a swirl of dust. Kell pushed to his feet and picked up the attacker's cap.

It had all happened so quickly. He tried to describe the man to himself: a heavy chin, broad-shouldered, dressed in a black suit.

He crossed the road to his house, sat on the front step and applied Wiggins's methods.

The cap was dirty and well worn, but of reasonable quality. From Arding and Hobbs, Battersea, according to the label. Grease stains marked the inside lip, and a few black hairs clung to the lining. He tossed it aside and got up.

He castigated himself for ignoring Wiggins's most basic piece of advice when it came to evading a tail: 'Don't let him know you know he's there. Act natural, act normal. Lose him by accident.' Kell had let on – had shouted it out in the street. He yanked open his front door in annoyance, then snatched his briefcase from the hallway. He regained the street without bothering to call out to Constance. He didn't want her to see him like this, tie askew, trousers and coat dusted, a sheen of sweat on his brow. He didn't want her to see him scared either.

The other thing Wiggins would have done, on losing a tail, was follow the man himself. It was not enough to know that you were being followed, you had to know *why*.

Kell hurried to Hampstead station, replaying in his mind all the mistakes he'd made. This last question was the one that really meant something. His breathing had slowed by the time he reached the platform and he felt settled enough to light another cigarette.

Who could be following him, and why? He tried again to build a picture in his mind of the man in the bushes. He'd meant him no harm, that was for sure – the violence of pushing Kell to the ground had merely been a means of escape. And he was probably working for someone else. The train clattered into the station and he pulled out another smoke for the journey. Was it a three-cigar problem? Sherlock Holmes had advised him once – in addition to advising him to hire Wiggins – that the smoking of a pipe was the greatest aid to thought invented by Man. Kell could never stand a pipe.

A twenty-five minute journey in a London Underground train carriage, however, was as good as bathing in tobacco smoke. By the time Kell got out, his mind was clearer on the matter. For one thing, a man who could afford to pay someone else to tail him was a man who had significant funds at his disposal. Or a government department.

Rather than walking towards his office in Victoria Street, he turned his sights to Whitehall.

'You want to what?' Archibald Carter repeated, all semblance of official calm gone.

'To see the Foreign Secretary, at once,' Kell also repeated in turn. 'It is not an unusual request, is it?'

Carter shook his aged head, as if in disbelief that this man in front of him, walking in off the street, would think it possible to gain an audience with the Foreign Secretary, Grey himself.

'It's an issue of national security,' Kell said at last, hating himself for aping the pompous Churchill. Still, the phrase seemed to impress something on the clerk, for he disappeared down the corridor, head still shaking.

He returned thirty minutes later. 'You can have five minutes.'

Kell floated through the magnificence of the Foreign Office. Past the heavy gilt frames, the majestic paintings, the sculptures, the Chinese vases, the antiquities from every corner of the globe, the Persian rugs beneath his feet, the deep red wallpaper. Stepping into the FO was like stepping into a dream, a world put together of all the best and most expensive things the five continents could provide. It didn't feel like the civil service at all.

Sir Edward Grey sat at his huge oak desk, and – unusually for a Cabinet minister – actually appeared to be working. He didn't look up as Kell came in, but continued writing. 'What's this I hear of national security?' he said. 'I hear of it everywhere now, but I've no idea what it means.' He finally put down his pen and glanced up at Kell.

'I apologise for the dramatic phrasing, Foreign Secretary. I'm not sure I quite know what it means either.'

'It sounds like an excuse to do something of which one might be ashamed.'

'Foreign Secretary.' Kell dipped his head slightly.

Grey sighed. 'Go on, then.'

Kell hesitated. He would have liked to trust Grey implicitly, to give him all he had. But then what use would a secret service be – at home or abroad – if it couldn't keep secrets? And – that small, burrowing worm of doubt in his head – he still hadn't cleared Grey of guilt either: this sleek fox in front of him might be on the hunt for the Prime Minister after all.

Nevertheless, Kell gave a precis of some of the problems involving the leak, in particular that something had come from the Committee meeting itself.

Grey listened, the lines in his frown growing ever deeper. 'But why come to me?' he said at last.

Kell told him. Told him the reasons why, the reasons he'd found so compelling on his Underground journey that morning. The edited version. He cast all this in language that suggested the Foreign Office might contain the leak, not that the Foreign Secretary himself might be implicated. He eyed Grey carefully as he spoke, looking for anything suspicious.

Grey glared back in silent outrage. But Kell held his stare, stood upright, still in good Sandhurst fashion, four steps from the desk. Someone knocked on the door and came in.

'Not now, Gorot,' Grey snapped.

The underling did an elegant and swift U-turn. Kell kept his eyes front. The interruption had done the trick, though. Grey's flash of anger had subsided.

'Very well,' he said. 'I don't approve, you understand, and I am sure you are entirely mistaken. But if you must follow the ball of wool to its end, then you must. Good day.'

As Kell left the building, he bumped shoulders with a young man coming in.

'I do beg your pardon,' Kell said, staring at the man. 'My fault entirely.'

'Think nothing of it.' The sleek fellow, clothes creased like razors, nodded absently.

'I say, haven't we met before?' Kell said, as government flunkeys passed to and fro.

'I don't think so. Would you mind, I—'

'Wasn't it at the embassy?'

The young man looked up sharply and glanced down the street. Kell leaned in and whispered, 'It's all right, Moseby-Brown, no one suspects us.'

'It's just I . . .' Moseby-Brown hesitated, then spoke in an undertone. 'I thought we should never meet at the office. That was what we agreed.'

'Let's walk,' Kell said. 'I'll keep up the charade. Play along.' He then spoke much more loudly. 'No, it wasn't the embassy, you work alongside the Foreign Secretary. We stood next to each other at the Committee for Imperial Defence.'

'Ah yes,' the young man fell into step beside him and joined in. 'You are intelligence?'

'In a manner of speaking.' They'd arrived on Whitehall itself and Kell fixed Moseby-Brown with a stare. 'That'll do,' he said. 'We've maintained your cover. Now, you had better come for a quick livener and tell me everything you know.'

Moseby-Brown nodded and Kell smiled. Bumping into his source at the FO was good news in two ways – he could go for a drink without it occasioning comment, and more importantly, it meant he didn't have to go to the office.

'Have you seen today's *Times*?'

'Sybella's great-uncle used to own it.'

'Shut up, Nobbs,' Abernathy said. 'This speech from Asquith. Says we're all hysterics and troublemakers, says we haven't a leg to stand on. It makes my blood boil.'

The four women stood in a loose circle in the middle of a windswept Golden Square. A few sad trees bent in protest while furtive figures scuttled by. It was at the respectable end of Soho. But it was still Soho. Constance, a late arrival, hovered slightly back from the circle. Abernathy, battered straw hat pulled tight against the wind, held court. Dinah, Nobbs and the ethereal Tansy listened attentively as Abernathy swept her eyes from one to the other and back again.

'It's not as if they've even got a majority,' Abernathy went on. 'Propped up in Parliament by the Irish, clinging on to power like croissant-munching French aristos.'

Dinah snorted.

Abernathy glared at them, resting at last on Constance. 'The movement's going nowhere,' she finished.

'Oh, don't be such a *student*.' Constance could restrain herself no more. 'If Asquith – the Prime Minister, remember – is forced to make such comment, and if it is reported in *The Times*, then it's hardly going nowhere. Nowhere would be silence.'

Abernathy looked away, chastened or contemptuous, Constance wasn't sure. She believed what she said, of course, but a part of her felt Abernathy did have a point. She'd been marching for years, had attended Lord knew how many meetings, and the vote seemed as distant as ever.

'Here she is,' Dinah suddenly cried, waving both hands wildly above her head. A tall, thin woman swept over, toting an umbrella like a lance. She engulfed Dinah in a tight hug, then they all turned to the west side of the square. 'Now we can start,' Dinah grinned, without bothering to introduce the stranger.

'At last,' Abernathy said. 'All this lecturing is *soo* tiring.'

'My friend Dorothea says St Hilda's is a total bust. They still don't graduate you.'

'I didn't mean that kind of lecturing,' Abernathy said, glaring at Constance.

Dinah, arm in arm with her new friend, twisted around to the group. 'Mustn't be late.'

'Why are we here anyway, if not to attend a talk?' Constance said.

'A talk?'

They'd reached a big green door. Dinah reached up to the doorknob. 'I thought we were to hear Jew-jew Sue,' Constance went on.

Dinah's laugh was so loud and hearty that passers-by turned

to look. 'Not Jew-jew Sue,' she whispered, still giggling. 'Ju-jitsu.'

Far off, over the dark grey Thames, through the Sussex Downs where an aging detective tends his bees, along the chopping Channel and out out out into the Bay of Biscay, the SS *Friendship* cuts a jaunty dash.

When first he comes aboard, Wiggins is delighted with Kell's choice of passage. The berth is small but clean, the ship is well run, and it weighs anchor last thing at night – leaving Wiggins to tumble aboard with a bellyful of Canaries wine and a sunburnt face, thinking good, kind thoughts of his far-off boss. A toff to be sure, but he sees a fellow right.

It is not until the first full day at sea that Wiggins's ordeal is completely clear to him. No bar? What about the galley?

Dry.

Dry?

The ship is Quaker-owned; *Friendship* is the hint. Not a drop of alcohol on board. A whole Quaker line, in fact – the import-export of chocolate, and the ingredients to make it. There's a hunk of sweet black chocolate with every meal, but for Wiggins this journey has turned into hell on sea. He doesn't want to dream the dreams of a sober man.

Kell flicked through the pencil-written messages pinned next to his home telephone in the hallway. All had been left by Constance in her slapdash scrawl.

Soapy called. Please get back to him as soon as possible.

Soapy again.

Office. Simpkins for you.

Is this now the role of wife? To answer the telephone for you.

Soapy once more. He really is the most tiresome bore. Seemed annoyed.

Simpkins.

Now I'm starting to wonder where you are.

Where are you?

Kell swiped the messages from the stand and exited the house again, having only been there for a few minutes.

He looked both ways on the pavement, checked the corner, then hurried on towards Hampstead. Without breaking stride, he slipped into the Flask, nodded conspiratorially to the barman and stepped through into a back room where, remarkably, they had recently installed a telephone.

'Simpkins, it's me,' he whispered into the horn.

'Thank God, sir. I've been trying to reach you.'

'I know.'

'Well, actually, sir, Secretary Pears has been trying to reach you. He has telegrammed, government-messengered, telephone-called, written, and this morning . . . well . . .'

'Yes, in your own time, Simpkins,' Kell said. Simpkins had always been afraid of Soapy.

'He came in person, to the office, sir, looking for you.'

Kell hesitated. He knew Soapy was exasperated, but getting him to leave the Cabinet Office was something else, a different order of annoyance altogether. Especially in the height of summer. It probably meant the sack.

'He rather threatened me with the chop, sir, if I'm honest with you.'

'Threatened *you*?'

'Well, the department.'

The news was clear enough – Soapy was intent on his destruction.

'Anything on that other matter I asked you to look into, at the FO?'

'As a matter of fact, some documents just came in from the Land Registry that are rather interesting.'

'Send them to the house. No, wait. Have them held for me at the club.'

'But, sir, what about my job?'

'Don't worry about that now. Is there anything else?'

'A flash telegram came in from the Continent this morning.'

'My God, man, why didn't you say? Read it at once.'

Kell heard the crackle and jag on the line, like the sound of a piece of paper being screwed up in one's ear. Simpkins's reedy voice finally came back on the line. 'It's marked "Most Secret", sir. Should I really, over the—'

'Just read the damn thing,' Kell urged.

'"FAO Mr Kelly, United Importers" – are we sure it's for you, sir?'

'Simpkins, just read it out. '

'It says: "Send bananas to Bremen. C."'

Kell put the phone down. He got up, then stepped back into the bar. He glanced at the publican, nodded and got a small Scotch in return, which he downed in one.

He looked up at the flags and memorabilia that dotted the aged pub, crowded out now by the advertisements. YOUNG'S BITTER. GUINNESS STOUT. TOLLEMACHE'S ALE. Legends of a history not yet lived. He took out his watch and wound it up, a ritual he always savoured. Then he stepped back behind the bar to the telephone once more.

Before picking up the horn, he wrote Soapy a short note. The future of the Service, the whole Secret Service Bureau, hung in the balance and he wasn't going to go down without a fight.

Then he made three calls, culminating in one back to Simpkins. He then walked through the bar, this time ignoring the drink poured for him by the obliging publican. Instead, he turned his sights back home, for his sternest task yet.

He had to talk to Constance.

'By the powers vested in me by the Port of London Authority—'

'Port of London?'

'—I hereby arrest you.'

'You ain't even a real copper.'

Wiggins tried to sidestep the two policemen, a sergeant and a gorilla of a constable. 'What's the charge, eh? 'Ere, get your hands off me.'

The gorilla punched Wiggins so hard in the stomach that he winded him. 'That real enough for you? In the cells, now.'

And so ended Wiggins's homecoming, at the passenger terminal of Tilbury Docks. He was dragged across the expanse of the quay, the shocked Quakers eyeing him askance.

Thirty minutes later, he sat at a plain table, in a plain, window-less room, staring at the steamy swirls coming off a plain cup of plain tea.

'Tea?'

'It's that or a smack in the mouth,' said a hatless copper as he withdrew from the table.

'Tea it is. And they say manners is a dying art.'

The policeman drew his upper lip back in an ugly sneer. 'Manners is wasted on the likes of you.' He turned towards the door.

'No use kicking against the prick, eh?' The policeman paused. Wiggins held his hands on the table. He watched as the copper's fists flexed. The broad, black-clad shoulders rolled for a moment, then the policeman opened the door, closed it and turned the key.

Wiggins called after him, 'Let me know the charge. When you're ready, like.' Then he blew on his tea and waited.

Two hours later, the door swung open and in walked Captain Vernon Kell, resplendent in full travelling suit, with a peaked cap to boot. 'Did they mistreat you?' Kell asked sharply, glancing at the copper who stood in the doorway.

'They're rozzers, what do you think?'

'Yes, well, sorry about that.'

'You didn't have to arrest me.'

'We sail in an hour. I couldn't guarantee that you wouldn't – how shall I say it – decamp to the nearest public house.'

'Zackly.' Wiggins got up and marched to the door. The policeman stepped aside at a nod from Kell.

'No time for the saloon. We must get aboard.'

'I ain't going nowhere. You put me on the slowest boat known to man, stopping at every bleeding port from here to kingdom come, and not the sniff of a drink. It's August, and no booze?'

'Now listen . . .' Kell said. They stopped outside the police station.

Wiggins rounded on him. 'No, you listen. You stuff me on that bloody Quaker line and what I is now is thirsty. And then I've got business to attend to back in the Smoke, and *then* I'll come help you.'

'Good evening, Mr Wiggins.' An amused, upper-class, familiarly crisp woman's voice stopped him from further protestation. He turned.

Constance, also dressed in fine travelling garb, peered at him from under the wide brim of a straw hat. 'I trust you holidayed well?'

'Holiday? What the hell's going on?' he said, glancing first at Kell and then back again.

'I must say, Wiggins,' Constance went on. 'Your complexion is positively peachy. You look as if you haven't had a drink in weeks.'

'I haven't had a drink in weeks. Ask him.' He punched a thumb in Kell's direction.

'Enough of the pleasantries,' Kell snapped. 'Need I remind you that I am your employer, I pay your wages, I set the terms. That's how this works.'

Wiggins bristled.

'It's so instructive to see the Secret Service at work,' Constance interjected. 'It really does remind one of the necessity for keeping women out of such roles; we are too emotional, too hysterical, too indiscreet. We would be forever bawling at each other on public thoroughfares.'

The three boarded the boat to Amsterdam soon afterwards, Kell and Constance heading up to first class, Wiggins in the bowels of third.

At dinner, Constance pleaded indisposition and left the dining room early. Kell glanced up as she left, but didn't go after her. She took a turn around the first-class deck. Far out across the Channel, she could see the faintest yellow dots, the electric lights on the ports and islands of northern France and Belgium. Soon the whole world would be alight, aflame with electrification, and never again would one be able to disappear into the black night.

She ventured down to the lower decks, to second class and then finally to third. Sure enough, leaning against the rail, facing out to sea away from her, bottle by his side, she found him.

'Evening, Mrs Kell,' he said, without turning.

'Mr Wiggins.' She joined him at the rail and gazed out into the blackness. The whirr of the engines was louder here, and the *swish-swash* of the water on the hull felt faster, more hurried. 'Do you mind?'

He shrugged. 'What's going on with the chief?' he said suddenly.

Constance stiffened. She hadn't expected that at all.

'Wiv the booze and that,' Wiggins went on. 'He looks like he's drinking more than me.'

'I really don't think . . . well . . .' she trailed off. She'd been about to give him the haughty double barrels, the 'How dare you talk about my husband like that . . .' But the truth was, she hadn't noticed, and the embarrassment silenced her.

Wiggins took another swig from his bottle, wiped his lips and turned to her. 'Why are you here?' he said, breathing rum into the space between them.

The light was low and she couldn't read his expression. She knew Wiggins, though, and knew he'd spot a lie. 'Because he asked for my help.'

Wiggins nodded slowly. 'How's the old ducking and diving?'

'We still don't have the vote, if that's what you mean.'

'Would it make any difference?'

'Of course – politics matters. Politics is everything. Women must stand together, we must defeat our oppressors, we have nothing to lose but our chains.'

Through the shadows, she saw Wiggins raise the bottle in something like a salute. 'I'll take your word for it, ma'am.' He took a big gulp, wiped his mouth and then went on. 'Here's hoping my tips came in handy.'

'I wouldn't hurt him, that's not what this is about,' she said. 'I would never hurt him.'

Wiggins nodded again and looked out to sea.

She walked back to the stairwell but then stopped, thought for a moment and turned to him.

'And what are you doing, Mr Wiggins? Why are *you* here?'

'Remember, we are on holiday,' Kell said as they entered the splendid red-brick palace that was Amsterdam's central station.

'Does that count for me, too?' Wiggins muttered.

'You've just been on holiday – for months it seems.'

'I've told you, it weren't a holiday.'

Kell waved away the protests. 'Get a porter. We're on the eleven eighteen to Bremen.'

Wiggins disappeared into the throng and Kell turned to Constance. 'Thank you once again, my dear, for coming.'

'Are you going to tell me why I'm here? Why *we* are?' she said, adjusting her hat.

Kell looked at her as she did so. The bustle around them faded, and all he could see was her beauty, unhurried, secure. He almost put his hand out to touch her. Instead, he waited until she looked directly at him. 'If I had come alone, or with Wiggins even, it would have been suspicious. Together, we at least look as if we're touring.'

A brief shadow crossed Constance's face as he talked, but she quickly stifled a yawn and replied, 'Oh, I know I'm *cover* – that's what we wives do so well, isn't it? Provide the decoration on the arm.' She sighed. 'Cover for what, though, Vernon?'

''Ere's a go,' Wiggins said as he appeared through the crowd with a porter. 'This lot speak better English than me.'

'Sir?' the porter said, pitching up his cart beside them.

Kell barked at him in Dutch, astonishing Wiggins. The porter stowed the bags and trotted off. 'There a lingo you don't know?'

'Oh, he has no trouble with languages,' Constance said. 'He is very good at how to say things. What to say, that's the problem.'

Kell paused. He looked between the two of them, sharp as knives. Only the great detective himself could hold a candle to these two. 'I will tell you everything,' he said at last. Any thoughts of keeping the bulk of the mission to himself melted under their twin glares. 'Once we've made the compartment. Wiggins, you are in third, but you had best come and join us when we are underway. I can brief you both then.'

Wiggins nodded curtly. Constance pulled on her gloves. 'That's all very well, Vernon, but how on earth am I meant to pretend we are holidaying in *Bremen*? Oh good day, *mein herr*, we're just here to admire your country's heavy industry. Yes, that's right, and the industrial shipping. And fishing. Or maybe we are fanatics of the Hanseatic League? North Sea birdwatchers? What's our cover story?'

'I'm sure you'll find a way.'

'Come in,' Kell called.

Wiggins hesitated at the door to the first-class compartment. He'd walked through the packed train, batted away the attentions of three separate ticket inspectors and was now going to be briefed on yet another mission for Kell.

The long days of enforced sobriety on that benighted Quaker ship had revealed a number of things to him, not least how much he needed to be in London. He'd worked out a way that would help him track down Peter, for one thing, and he was determined to sort out Tommy once and for all.

But it was Vernon Kell who paid the bills. Wiggins rested his hand on the door a moment longer. Constance had asked him why he was here – and was this his answer, money? Certainly, it was the best pay he'd ever had or was ever likely to get. Trying to find two-bob spies around the ports and factories of Britain wasn't the worst thing to do for such a wage, although it was as boring as biscuits.

He rubbed his hand on the highly polished walnut panel of the door, and thought of all those street kids he knew long ago; he thought of poor missing Millie and her little sister in her Lambeth shit pit; he thought of all the lives left unlived for want of a shilling, and he wondered if he should really be working, fighting, for the people who lived their lives behind walnut panels and spoke of King and Empire. What had the Empire ever done for him and his?

An inspector appeared at the far end of the carriage. Wiggins glanced up, then entered the compartment.

Constance sat by the window, her back perfectly straight, her head turned out to the landscape. Nail-thin trees whipped past.

He sensed the silence that had been in the room, unbroken until he entered. A beast of a silence, a monster; he could almost smell it. Kell sat opposite Constance at the window, but somehow as if on another train. He gestured for Wiggins to sit at the far end of the bench seat. The sleeping berths had not yet been made up.

'Mrs Kell and I are posing as holidaymakers. You are my man,' Kell said finally. 'We are going to Bremen.'

'I know that,' Wiggins said.

'I believe everyone in Holland knows that,' Constance added. 'You seem so keen to announce it to all and sundry.'

'It's *cover.*'

'It's *pantomime*. Act naturally, we have every right to be here.'

'She's right,' Wiggins nodded.

'Although,' Constance went on, 'why we are here is a different matter entirely. I would so like to know. Last-minute dashes to Germany are, of course, very charming, but I do have engagements back in London.'

'We're on a rescue mission,' Kell said finally.

'Oh Christ,' Wiggins said. 'Don't tell me.'

'I had a telegram from my opposite half in the foreign section,' Kell went on. 'Cunningham, or C.'

'You mean Mansfield Cumming,' Constance said.

'I knew it,' Wiggins muttered to himself.

'How did you know his name?' Kell asked Constance, surprised.

'Go on, Vernon, your Secret Service Bureau isn't as secret as all that.'

Kell glowered. 'Cumming, yes, if you must. He has sponsored a mission into Germany. Two Marines.'

'Bernie and Viv,' Wiggins interjected. 'I knew it.'

Constance looked between the two men. Kell relented, again glaring at Wiggins. 'Captain Bernard Trench and Lieutenant Vivian Brandon, Royal Marines.'

'What's the gen?'

'They are gathering information on German naval fortifications. But apparently the mission is going awry. Cumming was so concerned with the last report that he's come out to Germany.'

'Then why are we here?'

'Cumming himself is in trouble. He's not really equipped for field work. He doesn't even speak German. I fear his arrest daily. He sent a distress signal from Bremen. We are to find him first.'

Wiggins blew out his cheeks. 'But what are we doing? I thought we was domestic only?'

'And I thought we were going on holiday,' Constance added.

Kell looked at them both, took a breath, and told the truth. 'It's all up. The Bureau, my job, your job. We are almost certain to be dismantled. Transferred into the functions of Special Branch, if my guess is correct. If Cumming is arrested, captured by the German police, anything like that, then it's curtains for us all without another word. Our whole future depends on this.'

'*Your* future,' Wiggins grunted.

'You think Special Branch would give you a job? Would pay you what we pay you? Or do you think you'd find yourself back debt collecting for Leach?'

Wiggins didn't reply.

'But conversely,' Constance mused, 'if you – we – make a success of this mission, then the threat to the Service might abate?'

'My interest is primarily the safety of Cumming and his men, of course. But . . .' he shook his head softly '. . . it wouldn't hurt.'

'Does Soapy know you're here?'

'Of course not. We are unofficial. Totally unofficial.'

A silence settled once more, though unlike the one that greeted Wiggins when he first got into the carriage. Constance nodded thoughtfully, looked at her husband for a moment longer, then picked up her guidebook. The train rattled rhythmically, lulling them all for a moment, each in a world of their own. The smell of fresh coffee came wafting down the carriage.

Wiggins got up. 'Better get back in my place,' he said. 'Wouldn't want to be caught in the wrong class.'

'No,' Kell said. 'No, that wouldn't do at all.

~~~

Dear Dinah

I am so sorry that I didn't turn up at the latest meeting in Hampstead. I feel especially rotten, since I had urged you so ardently to attend. I hope the night wasn't a total chore.

I should explain . . .

Constance flung down the pen in exasperation. How could she explain? What would she say? *Oh, so sorry, Dinah, I couldn't make the meeting that I insisted you come to because I am on a secret mission deep inside Germany to rescue two spying Royal Marines, neither of whom, I am given to understand, are suffragettes themselves . . .*

She stood up from the writing desk and took a turn around their grand hotel room. Kell had taken one of the better suites, as befitted a couple on holiday. It had three sets of high windows, a dark wooden circular table and an elegant settee.

Relations with Dinah and her gang had rather deteriorated, and they wouldn't be helped by her no-show of the night before. Constance picked up the half-written letter, shook her head sadly and rolled it into a taper. She leaned up to one of the oil lamps and set the paper alight. It burned and blackened in her hand, before she tossed it into the unmade grate.

Standing on her bare feet, Constance stepped into the middle of the room, thrust out her hands and bent her legs.

'Is she the friend?' the tall stranger whispered to Dinah, as the group walked up the stairs at Golden Square. They'd pushed through the green door and were heading up to 'ju-jitsu', though Constance still had no idea what this meant.

'Shh,' Dinah giggled to the stranger.

'She's so *old.*'

Dinah batted the stranger and threw a nervous glance at Constance. 'At last,' she cried. Constance pretended not to have heard.

The women walked into a large, first-floor room with sun-flooded windows and a long mirror. Constance's heart dropped still further. She had hated dance classes as a child – pointless, inelegant posturing presided over by a succession of cruel-boned ancient Mesdames. It looked as though Dinah had decided to inflict that schoolgirl humiliation on them all once more.

'Ladies, line up, please.' Constance was startled out of her reverie. A sharp, aristocratic voice rang out across the studio.

A small woman appeared from the corner behind them. She was barely five foot tall and she wore a loose-fitting dress and no shoes. She bounced out in front of them like a dancer, all lithe power, physical poise and unstated but obvious strength. 'Don't slouch!' she cried.

Constance and Dinah's gang gathered in a line. A few more filed in behind them, all women, mostly young. Constance glanced in the big mirror and noticed that she was definitely the oldest, apart from the teacher.

'Welcome,' the teacher said. 'My name is Edith Garrud. When we are in this room, in session, you may call me sensei. Now, straighten your shoulders. You may have breasts but that is no reason not to walk tall.' She smiled surprisingly. 'I know I am not tall, but I feel tall, I feel strong, and that starts with your posture. Who here is wearing a heeled boot or shoe?'

Most of the hands went up.

'Off! There is a bench there. In fact, all shoes off. If you can't stand on your own two feet, what use are you in the battle? Eh? In future, everyone must come in pumps.'

The women scattered to the walls to unlace their boots. Constance squeezed next to Dinah. 'What is this?' she whispered.

But Dinah had bent her head away, towards the woman next to her, the stranger.

'Up!' Edith cried. Constance scrambled into position, unused to taking orders but strangely compelled by the pint-sized mistress of the studio.

'Ju-jitsu is about balance and harmony. With yourself, with your body and with those around you. It is about using others' strength against them, it is about exploiting their own power and using it to your own ends. It is about defence. You!' She thrust out her arm at Constance. 'Here!'

Constance stepped forward.

'Spread your legs wider, put your bottom out. Don't be shy. Shyness is the bane of our sex, shyness holds us back from debate, from politics, from equality. Thrust your bottom out, bend your legs. That's better, yes, yes. Well done. Now, attack me!'

Constance held the stance, then she bent and slowly pushed first one arm then the other in front of her. She held the pose, and looked in the costume mirror of the hotel room. Not *that* old, she thought, though she couldn't shake the sound of Dinah's giggle. Was she embarrassing herself? Should the radical arm of the movement be for the young only, for the childless? She twisted around slowly on one foot, then thrust her right arm out in a fist, keeping the other fist tucked into her ribs.

Pleasure flowed through her, despite her sombre mood. She had stood in Edith's ju-jitsu class like Saul on the road to Damascus, reborn. The pleasure of using her body, of stretching, of feeling its power, and the thought that with more instruction, and constant practice, she should never again fear physical attack, gave her hope that fear of force, that one sphere of male superiority she'd always bowed to, might become a thing of the past.

She flexed, twisted slowly and breathed. Looked at herself once more in the mirror. She would not give in – to middle age, to the hotheads, to anyone. She would rescue Dinah from the rash radicals, she thought, as she described a wide, scything arc with her right hand, just as they were here to rescue Brandon and Trench. She would describe, too, a new way to fight the fight, she would take the young women with her, she would—

'What an earth are you doing?' Kell cried from the door.

She straightened immediately and turned to see her husband, with two astonished men behind him.

'Good evening, gentlemen,' she said, smoothing down her skirts with as much grace as possible. 'Do come in.'

'You will excuse my wife,' Kell muttered. 'She is . . . unusual.' He gestured to the table. 'Constance, may I introduce Sir Mansfield Cum—'

'Cunningham,' Cumming growled. He barely met her eye as he limped towards the table.

'Cunningham indeed, and this is – what shall I call you?'

'H2O.' The man stepped forward to take her hand. He brushed his lips across it in one well-practised move. '*Enchanté*, et cetera. I must say, Kell, you didn't warn me of your wife's beauty.'

'There wasn't time.' Kell pulled up a chair for himself at the table.

'Of course,' H2O said, though his eyes lingered for a moment on Constance. He was younger than her, she thought, but not by much. Thirtyish at the outside, and he wore his light summer suit perfectly. He shimmered with long-limbed elegance as he flicked a cigarette into his mouth. 'Is there anything to drink?' he said, swinging a chair between Kell and Cumming. He had an air of informality about him, something of the New World.

'Let's get down to business,' Kell said. 'We don't have much time.'

'Quite right,' H2O said. 'We shall have a snifter once we've settled on the plan.'

'Plan?' Constance sat on the settee.

Kell looked over at her, glanced at Cumming and sighed. 'H2O is our naval intelligence's man in Berlin,' he said.

'Part-time,' H2O chimed in. 'Newspaper man is the day job, for Uncle Sam's rags. Help out the mother country when I can.' He slung one arm over the back of his chair and pushed tight smoke rings into the air above him. They bent and stretched and broke like signals in the sky.

Cumming glared at Kell angrily. 'I must insist on code names, Kelly.'

'There's not much point calling me Kelly, is there? My wife does know my name.'

'We should get to business,' H2O said. 'Give us all the gory details, if you would Cumm— if you would, C.'

'Hold on,' Constance said. 'Shouldn't we call Wiggins?'

'Your man?' H2O said, surprised.

Constance noticed Kell nod, then turn his head away slightly, in an embarrassed gesture she knew well.

'He's rather more than that,' she said with indignation. 'I shall ring for him at once.' She stood up and pressed a large buzzer. 'He's not just our man, he's the sharpest agent in the Service.'

I I

The sharpest agent in the Service was in position below stairs, at the servants' long kitchen table, eyeing with glee the second half of his second stein of north German lager. He licked his foamy lips. 'That is mint,' he said to no one in particular.

A large bell clanged, and the porter on duty – a sallow redhead with a pale moustache – pointed at Wiggins. '*Sie oben.*'

Wiggins nodded slowly and downed the last of his stein. He breathed out and said to the porter, 'That is knock-down honest the best pint I've ever had.'

The porter shook his head sadly, seemingly uncomprehending. 'British,' he said.

He walked through the hotel. Stacks of trunks, suitcases and hatboxes labelled *New York* and *Baltimore* dotted the large lobby; great throngs of well-heeled and excited patrons buzzed to and fro, two-deep at the bar, and the hotel restaurant clattered and sang and steamed from six in the morning until eleven at night. But this was a German crowd and they weren't staying at Hillman's in order to see Bremen. It was a transatlantic steamer port, and they were all due to board ships to the United States.

Wiggins wandered down a long, wide corridor and tried not to think too much about America, and who might now be living there. He tried not to think of Bela at all. He knocked at Kell's door and went in. Only Constance looked pleased to see him. She sat on the settee and smiled at him. Kell sat at the table with Mansfield Cumming, the crusty toff who ran the foreign arm of the Service and who, apparently, they were in the process of saving. A third man stood at the window. He leaned against the frame, looking out, and pulled languidly at a cigarette.

'Ah, here's the help. Now we can begin.'

Constance nodded at the man almost imperceptibly, but Wiggins caught it. 'Sorry, gents,' he said and winked at her. 'Doing a bit of the old recon.'

'Really,' H_2O said as he strode to the table. 'I'm sure that's most interesting.'

'Sorry, Mr Bywater,' Wiggins said.

Bywater stopped for a moment, surprised.

'How do you know his name?' Cumming asked angrily.

'What else?' Constance said with glee.

'I'm not used to dealing with Yankees, though I reckon you's English-born. Newspaper man? Drinker.'

'How dare you!' Cumming said.

'That's a compliment. Good nerves. Sea lover. Enough?' He looked at Constance, who nodded in reply.

Bywater sat down. He looked hard at Wiggins, glanced at Constance and then at Kell.

'Neat tricks,' he said. 'Let me know how it's done sometime.'

'The situation is this.' Cumming had been itching to start. He glared at Bywater, who had half turned to include Wiggins in the conversation. 'Two of my agents, Counterscarp and Bonfire—'

'Oh, there's no need for that,' Kell said. 'We all know the two men you speak of are called Brandon and Trench. Calling them by any other name will only confuse us.'

Cumming pouted. 'Very well. Earlier this summer, Brandon and Trench sailed to Holland. Under the cover of a walking tour of the northern German, Dutch and Danish coasts they have been trying to collect information on German naval positions. They are amateurs, and although Royal Marines, are not on the active service list at present.'

'Are they trained?' Bywater asked.

'Barely,' Kell said.

'Madness,' Bywater muttered.

'Plucky amateurs!' Constance exclaimed from the settee. 'It's

as if they read that Childers novel, *The Riddle of the Sands*, and
thought they'd join in the fun.'

Cumming coughed into his fist. 'Yes, well, I wouldn't like to,
you know – inspiration comes from many sources.'

Constance stifled a cry of triumph.

'Can't you control your wife, Kell?' Cumming rasped under
his breath.

'No,' Kell said.

'Let's keep on point, shall we? I'm due back in Berlin and then
Dresden post-haste. I do have a job, even if the rest of your mob
is amateur.' Bywater cast a glance at Wiggins.

Cumming went on. 'They have travelled along the coast from
Holland, gathering data – sketches of fortifications, maps, notes
and the like. I was to reach them at Thomas Cook's in Hamburg
and they were to post updates back to me. The updates have
stopped.'

'What have they been doing with their reports?' Kell said.

'Posting them to me, at an address in Holland.'

'No misdirection, no secondary address?'

Cumming shook his head.

'We told you,' Wiggins said, appalled. 'A cutout address in the
same country, a handwritten letter with the treasure.' He shook
his head.

Bywater raised an eyebrow. 'Good idea,' he acknowledged. 'But
we don't know they're blown yet.'

'How fly are the coppers?' Wiggins asked. 'Would they put the
gen back in the post, keep us off the scent?'

Bywater nodded thoughtfully. 'Crafty. Local police, no chance.
But some of the naval intelligence chaps might just be up to that
– although it is very un-German.'

'Been nabbed then?'

'If so, it must be very recent. They'd surely publicise it otherwise.'

'What will happen to them if they are arrested?' Constance
asked.

'Hanged!' Cumming butted in, eager to break up the conversation between Wiggins and Bywater, who'd clearly reached some kind of understanding.

Bywater waved his cigarette vaguely in Cumming's direction. 'I'm not so sure. The fact that they are serving army officers could save them. Honour, et cetera. I doubt if I or – ' he nodded at Wiggins ' – your man here would be so lucky. As civilians, we'd be branded spies. *Geheimagenten.*'

'Much more importantly,' Cumming bellowed, 'His Majesty's Government, His Majesty himself, would be severely embarrassed were anyone to be arrested. We must spare the new King this, in his months of mourning.'

Wiggins puffed out his cheeks, ready for the smart reply – like swinging at the end of a German rope was a price worth paying to save the King's blushes. He was about to say this, when he caught Constance's raised eyebrow. At least the room wasn't full of idiots.

He'd known men in the army, most of the officers in fact, who'd happily lay down their lives just to make sure the colonel-in-chief of the regiment (normally some syphilitic rake of a minor royal) could hold his head up high at the next Aldershot parade.

Kell tapped the table. 'Let's get back to the point, Cumming. What were you planning to do by coming here, and how can we help?'

'If you must know, Kelly – Kell – I didn't expect you to come quite so quickly and be, er, so well equipped.' He looked up at Wiggins slightly hopelessly, as if he wanted to upbraid the man for being so low-born but didn't quite have it in him. 'If Brandon and Trench are on schedule, they should be in Emden any day now, primarily with the aim of reconnoitring the naval base at Borkum.'

'Borkum? It's as tight as a drum,' Bywater said. 'These blundering amateurs could ruin everything. I supplied you with what I could.'

'It wasn't enough,' Cumming said. 'Brandon and Trench are to make photographs, full sketches, dimensions and, if possible, the signals.'

'Not a hope, old man,' Bywater muttered. 'About the signals book anyway.'

'They are going to do their British best,' Cumming huffed. 'We are the greatest nation the world has ever known, and these men will represent us accordingly.'

'And what were you going to do?' Constance asked from the settee.

Cumming ignored her, until Kell pushed him. 'That is rather the point. What are you planning to do?'

'Look here, Kell, this really should be a conversation between us three here. Your wife, I accept, is good cover. But surely Agent W is for the rough and tumble. We three should plan – we three are in it.'

'I rather think we're all in it,' Bywater drawled. 'Thanks to you.'

After a moment's silence, Cumming went on. 'Very well. I hope they are still in Emden. I plan to intercept them there, to relieve them of any of the important documents they have on them—'

'If they ain't been caught already,' Wiggins interjected.

Cumming ignored the interruption. 'And thence order them to abandon the scheme. To sail home, while I take the train back to Holland.'

A long silence greeted this. Eventually, Bywater walked to the window and pulled out a smoke. Kell glanced at Wiggins, then back to Cumming.

'Do you think you are up to it?' Kell said at last.

'Ain't being funny,' Wiggins added, 'but you stick out like a vicar in an whorehou—'

'He means,' Kell said quickly, 'that you rather look like a British officer.'

'And some!'

'I have a false beard.'

Wiggins would have laughed, if it weren't so serious. It was all right for Kell and Cumming, they'd be treated like officers and gentlemen. But if Bywater was right – and judging by the cut of the man, Wiggins guessed he was usually right – then it was the two of them liable for the chop if things went south.

He liked pressmen, generally. They were easy with the drink, easy with their paper's money and not too bothered about those in authority. They weren't too bothered about the truth neither, but at least they were honest about that. And not much else, except a deadline. But then, trust was overrated. What you needed to depend on in a person was that they'd behave according to their lights.

'I wonder if that's wise,' Kell said to Cumming. 'It's probable you're already being watched.'

'We're all being watched,' Constance said lightly.

They all stared at her, even the dismissive Cumming. She turned the page of a book on her lap, unconcerned.

'What was that, dear?'

'The porter who took our bags at the station earlier today. I saw him this evening in the hotel lobby. Dressed very well-to-do.'

'Coincidence?' Kell asked.

'Not a chance, I'm afraid,' Bywater said. 'Porters' wages wouldn't get you through the door here, let alone pukka duds.' He tapped out a cigarette and idly offered one to Wiggins, who declined. Still, Wiggins thought, you're the first toff I know that's ever offered. He tipped his head.

'All this means,' Cumming said, 'is that you, the Kells and your man here are being watched. I am still in the clear.'

'After visiting this hotel room?' Kell said. 'No, Mrs Kell is right. We're all under the magnifying glass now.'

Constance nodded to herself as Kell was speaking. Wiggins noted the jut of her shoulders, though, away from her husband; she didn't meet his eye, even when he referred to her as Mrs Kell.

All was not right in the house of Kell. Ever since he'd given Constance a few tips – how to spot and avoid a tail, most notably – he'd been troubled by the act. It seemed like treachery; for all Constance claimed she wasn't doing the dirty, Wiggins wasn't so sure. He could never quite read women, but she held something secret in her heart, from her husband and possibly even from herself. He closed his eyes as Kell chattered on, persuading

Cumming to reconsider, and thought of the last woman he'd misread.

'You disagree, Agent W?' Bywater said.

'Sorry, miles away.'

'Lager can do that to a man,' Bywater replied and turned to look out of the window once more.

Kell ignored them both. 'Bywater – or whatever your name is – you seriously think that Mrs Kell and I may be above suspicion?'

'Almost certainly. They would have had you followed as a matter of course, given your military connection. But the fact that Mrs Kell is here too is – how shall I put it? – perfect,' he said, smiling at her.

'Thank you,' she said.

'For the Germans simply would not believe, not in a thousand years, that a British officer and gentleman such as yourself would ever bring a woman – his wife indeed – on any kind of a mission, let alone a clandestine one.'

Constance's smile faded.

'They wouldn't think you had it in you, Captain Kell, if I'm totally honest. They wouldn't think you such a brute.'

'So you are congratulating my husband on his dishonour, are you, Mr Bywater?'

'It is a stroke of genius, Mrs Kell. As long as you are by his side, Captain Kell is above suspicion.'

'That don't follow for you, though, does it?' Wiggins said. 'Nor him, neither.' He nudged his head at Cumming.

'No, it does not. Not now we've met.'

'We carry on,' Wiggins said, thinking fast. He pointed at Cumming. 'You's got to run the dodge. Out westward, look like you're scouting, but fast train out of here.' To Bywater he said, 'You, back to Berlin.'

'But I am here to help,' Bywater said.

'And you can. Get back to Berlin. Again, act fly, but turn out true. You's got a job, ain't ya? Go back to it.'

Kell nodded slowly. 'That's exactly what I was thinking. Only rather more clearly. We cannot risk Bywater, not now.'

The implication was clear: Bywater was twice the man, and certainly many times the agent, that either Bernie or Viv was. If push came to shove, rather the buffoons in chokey than anyone with a brain and legs.

'They might tail you both, but odds are, if yous are right – ' he looked at Bywater ' – they won't take too much trouble over the Kells on their 'ols.'

Bywater considered for a moment. 'It's the only way,' he said at last. 'It will give you a chance to get there and take them out of the field. As for cover, Emden and Borkum have some decent birdwatching.'

'Praise be,' Constance said.

'Quite, but if you take the kit it will help.'

'I had always assumed . . .' Constance went on. She seemed to be the only one enjoying herself, ' . . . that spying was a matter of *infiltration*. The poor fellow in Woolwich, for example. But now I see we are playing a quite different game. We are about to perform an *exfiltration*.'

'Tommy rot,' Cumming muttered.

'Perhaps we should give it a code word?' She twinkled. 'An exfil?'

Kell looked at her, his expression difficult to read. 'I hope we never have to do one again,' he said. 'Whatever it's called.'

'If you're too shy, why don't I do it alone?' Constance said. 'It seems I have the best cover of all.'

Wiggins stifled a laugh. Cumming shot up out of his chair. He took a deep breath, then nodded at Kell and Bywater. 'Gentlemen, I really should retire. It is late, and I must prepare for the morrow. Mrs Kell.' He bowed vaguely in her direction, glanced at Wiggins, then went to the door.

The others muttered their goodnights. Wiggins said nothing.

With his hand on the doorknob, Cumming turned back to the room. 'Captain Kell, I must say the thought, the very idea of a woman going alone on such a mission is, well, it is outrageous. Indeed, if you proceed with such a venture I might have to inform our masters back in London. I am sure no one in Whitehall would approve and it might very well end your involvement in the Service. It is shocking.'

Before Kell could protest, Constance stood up and replied for herself. 'Please accept my apologies, sir. It was my idea of a silly joke. For one thing, Brandon and Trench are strangers, so why would they follow me?'

'I'd wager two red-blooded Royal Marines would follow you anywhere, Mrs Kell,' Bywater said under his breath.

'Not if you knew Bernie and Viv,' Wiggins muttered in reply.

Constance went on. 'In any case, I am quite aware that a woman such as myself travelling alone in northern Germany is far more likely to cause comment and consternation than even an army of English gentlemen and officers, however eccentrically dressed.'

'Madam.' Cumming bowed. 'Forgive me. I am not in the mood for levity. Kell, we will meet at breakfast to enact your plan? Very good.'

The old man pulled open the door stiffly and limped out into the dim corridor. Kell called after him, 'Yes, thank you, Cunningham. Sleep well.'

A silence fell on the room, Wiggins and Bywater still standing, Constance back on the settee, and Kell at the table, hands spread wide.

'Oh come on,' Kell said eventually. 'He's not that bad.'

The laughter came all the louder for the wait.

'Is that with or without the false beard?' Constance said.

Bywater pipped his eye. 'He's even got a swordstick in his room!'

'Tell me he ain't? Please.' Wiggins laughed again.

Kell rapped the table and looked around at the three grinning faces. 'He's brave enough to travel hundreds of miles into Germany to rescue his men,' he said. 'Risking his own life. How many commanding officers can you say that of? Eh, Wiggins? In the Boer War, how many did you know?'

'None,' Wiggins answered after a moment. Kell was right. Mansfield Cumming had stuck his neck out. For all he lacked the chops for the job in the field, he didn't lack the balls.

'For God's sake sit down, and let's hammer out the details.'

And so they did, Wiggins, Kell and Bywater around the table, Constance still on the settee. 'An exfil,' she said, when they were done. 'Wouldn't it be nice in real life to know that if you ever were to get into a pickle, if things weren't going quite as you planned, some clever, determined people would swoop in and carry you away back home, back to where it's safe again?'

No one, not even Kell, demurred.

Kell woke with a start. He thrust his hand across the bed on instinct, but Constance was gone. The bathroom door stood ajar. Morning light filtered around the edges of the curtain.

'Constance,' he called into the empty room. Nothing.

She'd gone to bed immediately on the others leaving the night before, and they'd barely exchanged a word. The silence between them, established in London over the preceding months, had slowly solidified into a monstrosity, a beast of such size that it filled every room in which they were – be it the drawing room in Hampstead, their extravagant hotel room, or even the cabin on the ship over. The cause of it, as always, was suffrage. It was a silence now so profound that it covered even a Special Branch surveillance photograph. Why was Quinn interested? How could Kell even ask that of his wife? Was she having an affair? He began to get dressed.

All he knew for certain was that she had become adept at avoiding his attempts to follow her, whether for political or romantic reasons, he didn't know. She was also disconcertingly good at the mechanics of espionage. It was irritating, impressive and – in the midst of the current mission – indispensable. (The dark corollary to this thought, of course, was that he hadn't a hope in hell of discovering anything about her other life, what she did when she evaded him, what she knew of his life – anything.)

It wasn't yet seven, but he reasoned his wife and possibly Cumming were already at breakfast. He pulled open the door, only to be met by Constance and Bywater. They barged past him into the room. Constance had a heavy wodge of clothes over one arm, and a hatbox in the other hand.

'Ring for W,' Bywater said. 'Quick.'

'What's the matter?' Kell asked, as Constance pushed hard on the buzzer.

'Cumming has gone,' Bywater said. 'Lit out last night, milk train, so the night boy told me.'

'You think he is scuttling home?' Kell said hopefully.

Bywater confirmed Kell's fears. 'Not a chance.'

'If Brandon and Trench weren't in trouble before, they are now,' Constance said, brushing a flake of pastry from her face. 'If our journey here was anything to go by, every train inspector from here to Borkum will issue reports up the line. They won't have a hope.'

This was a disaster. Kell looked between the two of them. If Cumming got himself arrested, then that really was the end of the Service. There would be no way to survive the embarrassment, and Kell, hanging by a thread as it was, would be brought down too. For while their departments and their work were nominally separate, they still constituted the Secret Service Bureau, it was still a new idea, it still had very few results. If one of those results was a spectacular failure with the foreign chief – the chief no less! – being arrested and imprisoned on German soil, then the whole enterprise would be over.

A sudden rap at the door startled them all.

Kell looked at the other two, then called out, '*Eingeben*. Enter.'

Wiggins sauntered in, holding half a bratwurst. 'First the beer, now the bangers. Why we fighting these people again?'

Kell nodded at Bywater, who explained what had happened to Cumming.

'We go after him,' Wiggins said, once he'd heard the news.

'We have to,' Kell replied. 'But how?'

Wiggins looked at Bywater, at Constance. He slung the last of his sausage into the empty fire grate, while the three of them waited. 'Stick with the plan. The big man back to Berlin or Dresden or wherever it is. Too valuable to lose now.'

Kell nodded as Wiggins went on. 'Run the dodge, like we said, yeah?'

Bywater examined his fingernails. 'I'll start straight away. I think I've already made my man. A nasty-looking fellow, skulking around the lobby. I'll take him to the *bahnhof*. I've got an empty suitcase in the left luggage. I can fake a drop. It'll send them loopy for hours.'

'Meantime, we go to Emden and Borkum,' Kell said, curtly. 'I shall pack.'

'I already took the liberty,' Constance said. 'And here, I've got you and Wiggins new jackets, German-tailored. Less conspicuous.'

'How on earth . . . ?'

'I ordered them from the concierge yesterday, just in case we needed to blend in. You want to be a spy, you learn how to shop.'

He stared at her, open-mouthed.

'And now I will try on my new *damenhut*.'

Kell gazed after his wife as she went into the bathroom. 'A pleasure,' Bywater said, breaking the reverie. They shook hands. 'I'd better go.'

Wiggins saw Bywater to the door.

'By the way,' Bywater said, 'how did you know all that stuff about me? Come on now, no sauce.'

Wiggins grinned. 'Your name's on your luggage, course I knew it. Or rather, you's only the third guest staying with an English name, so I guessed.'

'You saw it coming up in the service elevator. I get it.' Bywater nodded. 'The rest?'

'Newsprint on your fingers. Notepad in your trouser pocket. You ain't no printer, so newsman.'

'And the American thing? Is my accent that noticeable?'

'A twang. But it's how you carry yourself that's the tell.'

'What do you mean?'

'Like you *don't* have a poker up your arse.'

Bywater laughed, and held out his hand like an equal. 'Brush up on your German. I fancy we may work together again one day.'

'You think there'll be war?'

'There is always war, sooner or later.' And with that he was gone.

The three took an express train to Emden. Wiggins looked every inch the part in his new German-tailored jacket, dark brown with a wide collar. He'd beamed when Constance presented him with it, almost pathetically, Kell thought. 'Can I keep it?' he even said.

Constance sat opposite them, her head in the little red Baedeker guide. She brandished it theatrically at every ticket inspection, and engaged the inspectors – who entered after each station – in her schoolgirl German. Wiggins dozed.

Kell wondered to himself whether there was any way to put Constance on the Bureau's payroll. It would go against all the rules of decency and military order; it would almost certainly be disapproved of by Soapy, by Churchill, by anyone, in fact, who happened to find out. But he could give her a code name, like the ones so favoured by Cumming, and he could keep her anonymous. Most importantly, it might mean he could control her. On that happy thought, Kell nodded his head to the *click-clack* rhythm of the train and soon joined Wiggins in sleep.

'Oof.' A sharp pain in his shin caused him to open his eyes. Constance, whose sturdy boot had delivered the blow, glared at him.

'Wake up! We are nearly at Emden.'

Wiggins stretched; Kell adjusted his glasses as she went on: 'This train connects directly to the ferry for Borkum. And it was the first express of the day, so we have every chance of catching him.'

'A ferry,' Wiggins cried. 'Christ, if it's an island, we are fu—'

'Going to attend a festival,' Constance interrupted, with a faint smile. 'And yes, Mr Wiggins, it is an island. But we are in luck. Today and for the rest of the evening there is a festival of summer lights.'

'What does that mean?' Kell asked.

'It means that ferries will be going until late in the night.'

'That's if we find Cumming and the other two. How do we even know they are there?' Kell had woken up in gloomy mood. The cosy idea that Constance could ever come under the umbrella of the Service was nothing more than a dream.

'I've been thinking about that,' she said. 'We're agreed that every policeman, stationmaster and blind beggar between here and Holland could spot Cumming for what he is – even in the false beard? All we need to do is ask at the station and the ferry port.'

'That'll put us in the frame and all,' Wiggins said. 'Three English, chasing another English.' He shook his head, unconvinced.

'Why do you think I bought us German clothes? Once we get there, we can pretend to be German.'

Wiggins remained unconvinced.

'Vernon speaks German like a native. *Better* than a native,' Constance said.

She picked up her hat. 'You can claim to be a doctor of the mind – the Herr Freud of Hanover or some such. Cumming is your patient. Perhaps you are of the Vienna school? Yes, that's it, you are a mind doctor, and Cumming is under the delusion that he is a British Army officer, when actually he's a carpet-maker from Krakow, name of Pumpernickel.'

'Steady on,' Wiggins said.

'He's not dangerous,' Constance warmed to the task, 'but you must recover him forthwith, and you've brought your wife as nurse, and a mute orderly from your private asylum in Hamburg.'

It didn't take long to confirm that Cumming had indeed passed through the station directly to the ferry port at Borkum. A talkative ticket clerk proved most useful, Kell playing up his part as the stern psychologist in his flawless German.

'Oh yes, I know the man. Mad, you say? Makes sense. He had the most peculiar beard. He was so British – remarkable what the brain can do. You're a mind doctor, you say. I have this dream, on and on, once a week, about my mother-in-law. It's most disconcerting. Do you have a moment?'

Alas, the ferry to Borkum was due.

Wiggins looked down at his watch, the Doctor's old battered hunter, complete with the bullet mark. Peter's bullet. He stood at the rail of the steamboat, two steps behind Dr von Kell and his nurse wife, as the three of them gazed out onto Borkum harbour.

The sky was a pink blue-black wonder, with faint wisps of cotton cloud hanging like freshly laundered handkerchiefs. 'Dark soon,' he muttered.

Kell looked back at him and said, 'Mute, remember.'

Borkum town was alight, its red-brick houses cheek by jowl with clapperboard huts and beach godowns, the festival in full swing. Beer tents, a carousel, funfair stalls, and the jostle and hustle and jolly high spirits of Hampstead Heath on a spring bank holiday. Mechanical music competed for attention with the great oompah bands. The smell of grilled bratwurst hung in the air. Wiggins followed Kell as he cut through the crowd, wishing they could stop for a feed – and a stein.

But Kell, with Constance on his arm, moved swiftly, like a Herr Doktor on a mission.

'This must be the place,' Kell said.

They'd reached a hotel on the beachfront, a terrace restaurant running to the beach, and the hotel building across the road, KOHLER'S STRAND HOTEL picked out in English above the door.

'Second in the book.' Wiggins nodded. That was the rule he'd suggested to Kell and Cumming months before. In an unfamiliar town an agent should stay in the second-named establishment in the Baedeker guidebook. That was how Kell had known to find Cumming at Hillman's in Bremen.

A party of raucous pensioners in bath chairs had set up camp in one corner of the terrace and were in the midst of a heated debate. Kell and Constance went into the hotel, still acting the medical couple, while Wiggins took up station leaning against the hotel wall.

The Kells came out moments later. 'Let's take a walk,' Kell said. He and Constance then ambled off, Wiggins two steps behind.

'They are here,' Kell whispered. 'Cumming got that right, he tracked them down. The old Frau reckons they've gone cycling, the three of them.'

'You didn't give your name?' Wiggins rasped.

'Do you seriously suppose I'd check into a hotel without false papers?' Kell said icily. 'We are down as Mr Peter Huggins and wife.'

'Huggins?' Constance cried. 'Thank you so much. What's my first name, Ethelbertha?'

Kell looked at her for a moment. 'No, you are Constance. You are always Constance.'

She waved him away. 'Enough of this nonsense,' she said. 'We need to act. I presume Cumming has gone with them on some schoolboy escapade or other.'

'That would make the most sense – *sense*?! We have to assume it's the naval base, on the east of the island. There's no other reason to be here. From what Bywater told me, there's only one road out of town, two miles or so, then a barbed-wire perimeter.'

'We've got to stop them,' Constance said. 'Cumming is a walking diplomatic incident.'

Cymbals crashed as another of the oompah bands went by. Smiling, shining faces jollied past. Wiggins almost filched a wallet, so lax and unaware were these German holidaymakers. Best not.

'Me and the chief will go after 'em,' Wiggins said at last. 'Or the old man, anyway.'

'You should go back to the room, dear,' Kell said.

'Like a good little wife?'

'Like a leaf,' Wiggins said.

She turned to him, questioning. He explained. 'Take a butcher's at their room – see what Bernie and Viv have left for the coppers.'

'How?'

Wiggins ripped a hatpin from her head in a sudden, violent

movement. He bent one end. 'Anticlockwise until the first click, real slow, then reverse until the shift. Got it?'

She nodded. Her eyes sparkled in the gaslight. Kell pursed his lips. 'Be careful, my dear.'

'And don't take anything that could put us in the shi—'

'Yes, Wiggins,' Constance broke in. 'I quite understand.'

She always did.

They walked back the way they came, past Kohler's Strand Hotel, where they dropped Constance off, and then onwards through the raucous pensioners in their bath chairs.

'What's their problem?' Wiggins said to Kell when they were out of earshot.

'Eh? Oh. They are arguing about who has the best machine.'

It took three-quarters of an hour of steady walking. Wiggins insisted they walk parallel to the road, through the light brush.

Up ahead, a high wooden sentry post loomed like a shadow on a shadow against the black sky. Wiggins crouched down. He whispered, pointing, 'There's the wire. Which way?'

'If they still have any sense of naval intelligence left at all, then they'll want information on the guns facing west, placements, poundage, et cetera. Though heaven knows what they expect to find in this light.'

Together, they dodged down the left-hand side of the road and began jogging alongside the wire. Sure enough, a few hundred yards from the sentry post – hidden by a large patch of scrub – Wiggins found a hole in the fence. Kell would have missed it, but Wiggins saw everything. He tapped Kell on the arm.

'Ready?'

Kell hesitated. 'I should go in alone. Bywater was right. If I'm arrested it will most likely be prison. You are a private citizen, it could well be the rope.'

'Ain't no time to be a hero,' Wiggins said curtly. Then he squatted down and slithered through the gap in the fence, leaving Kell to follow.

The going underfoot was easy, short, coastal grass, and with

Wiggins in the lead they made quick time. They kept the fort to their right. It sat monstrous against the night sky, an unlit silhouette. Ahead of them, Kell could just make out a trio of gun placements, the huge canons jutting out to sea. Tangled scrub ran from their position along and under the gun turrets, almost the perfect place to take photographs – were one there in broad daylight.

He was just beginning to think he and Wiggins had made a terrible mistake, that of course Brandon, Trench and Cumming wouldn't be foolhardy enough to attempt such a futile task as sketching and photographing naval bases in the middle of the night, when, from deep in the bushes, they heard the unmistakable sounds of an argument. In English.

'Curtain up at the Alhambra,' Wiggins whispered.

Kell crept forwards, behind Wiggins, approaching silent and wary. The voices suddenly grew in intensity. 'I must have my go!'

A figure burst from the other side of the bush. Kell could just make him out as the man stopped stock-still and held a box on his hip with one hand, while he thrust his other hand high in the air.

'Christ,' Wiggins hissed.

Light cascaded from the man's fist, a burning torrent that bubbled and then disappeared. It was Brandon, lit up like a beacon. 'A bloody flash,' Wiggins cried.

All hell broke loose. Out of nowhere, a searchlight beam swooped onto Brandon. He dropped his camera, and thrust his hands into the air. A second beam swirled amidst the shouts and cries of the German sentries.

Kell stood startled for a second, until Trench broke from the scrub and ran past him. The thickset Marine disappeared into the night.

Cumming stumbled out of the bushes, brandishing his sword-stick. Wiggins tripped him up, then dragged him back into the shadows.

'Let me at my sword – my sword,' Cumming rasped.

'Shut it, you old fool,' Wiggins whispered. 'Gi' us a hand, sir.'

Together, Kell and Wiggins manhandled Cumming into the night, following in the footsteps of Trench. Kell glanced around.

Brandon was ringed by three or four German sentries, illuminated on two sides. He held his hands up, still, while the soldiers jabbed long rifles at him. As yet, no pursuit.

Together they pushed Cumming back through the hole in the fence and frogmarched him out into the darkness. The old man was breathing hard, too hard to speak, and his limp was exaggerated.

No one said anything for a good twenty minutes, until it became apparent that the sentries had not seen them.

'A fucking flash!' Wiggins grunted. By this time he had his neck under Cumming's left arm, while Kell supported the right.

'I didn't . . . it didn't . . .' Cumming's voice faded.

'They are going to connect the dots soon. Even if they don't know about Trench yet, they'll follow Brandon's hotel booking.'

'And they'll speak to the Frau at Borkum,' Wiggins spat.

'You'll be a wanted man soon,' Kell said to Cumming, who hung heavier and heavier on their shoulders.

'We have to get the ferry, sir, else we're roasted,' Wiggins said.

As they limped towards Borkum town, they began to hear a soft, high voice singing. Someone was on the road ahead of them.

'Constance,' Kell trilled, his heart pounding. And not just with the effort of carrying Cumming, nor with the excitement of the evening. There was nothing in his life that had ever sounded as sweet and soft as that song.

She stopped. 'I am on the road. It is perfectly safe.'

He and Wiggins hauled Cumming up onto the raised road. The clouds shifted and a moonbeam cast his wife in a striking pose, hat ajaunt, shoulders square and hands on some sort of machine in front of her.

'What's that?' he asked.

'A bath chair!' Wiggins whistled in admiration.

'When a young man came barrelling into the hotel muttering in English, I guessed it was either Trench or Brandon and something had gone awry,' she said to Kell as Wiggins helped Cumming into the bath chair. 'I remembered our friend here's leg wasn't quite at its best, so I thought I would take a saunter along the road to see if I could help.'

'They have Brandon. But, my dear, you are . . .' Kell struggled for the word.

'A bloody marvel, ma'am,' Wiggins said as he roughly stuffed the blankets around Cumming, right up to his neck. The old man seemed beyond protest, and Wiggins pushed him back down the road. 'Where you get this?' he said over his shoulder.

'Those pensioners. By the time I went to see them, they really were very drunk. And they showed a surprising interest in a woman who bent down.'

'Enough,' Kell said. Constance's appearance had reinvigorated his mind, and he was starting to see a way clear. Reading dusty naval reports was not always a waste of time. 'We must get to the ferry,' he went on. 'This chair is perfect cover. Cumming, play it straight. You are a mental patient, name of Pumpernickel. And I will only speak to you in German from now on.'

'What about Trench?' Constance said.

'Trench can go hang.'

12

A cheerful rabble crowded the ferry quay at Borkum. Wiggins pushed Cumming through the throng. Kell had plied him with the contents of a flask, and now the old man snuffled and snored, chin resting on his chest.

'This way, my dear,' Kell said in German to Constance. He looked back and gestured Wiggins on.

'The bag?' Constance asked, also in German, more quietly. She had rested her head on his shoulder. Kell knew it was part of the act, feigning tiredness so as not to attract any undue attention, completing the picture. Yet for all he knew it was an act designed to establish that they were married in the eyes of the onlooking officials, for all he knew it was for show, he couldn't stop the surge of physical pleasure it gave him to have her so close once more.

Kell shook his head. 'We'll leave the bag.'

'*Guten abend.*' He handed the tickets to the seaman at the foot of the boarding gangway. He thanked Constance's quick thinking at Emden, buying three spare tickets for the way back, just in case. He stood at the plank and waved to Wiggins, pointing to the wide, promenade foredeck. 'On the deck, he needs the air,' he said, again in German. Wiggins nodded.

Kell and Constance then followed them aboard. Wiggins wheeled the bath chair past the lifeboat and out onto the wide pleasure deck. It was a warm night. Wiggins placed them in such a position that they had an easy view of the boarding plank, were one of them to lean forward, though anyone coming onto the boat would not immediately see them.

Wiggins sat behind Cumming, with one hand on the bath chair, like a good, solid attendant. A reek of booze came off the two of them, though Kell chose to think most of it came from Cumming. There was a long way to go if they were going to get clear, and he didn't want Wiggins drunk.

Constance and he sat a row back, on a wooden bench. He found a blanket from under the bath chair and handed it to her. '*Danke, liebe,*' she said. With her basic German and Wiggins's non-existent language skills, the three of them did not think it safe to converse on the ferry. The deck filled up. Drinking songs burst out from young men; families huddled together, cradling small, sleeping children; old couples held hands.

Wiggins twisted around in his seat, and Kell saw his shoulders tense. A commotion rose from the quay beneath them, and the band stopped mid-tune. Kell stood up to see for himself.

Brandon.

Five policemen came marching through the quayside crowd. The leader, a six-foot titan, strode ahead of them, while Brandon – hands in front of him, head hung low – walked in between the other four. A loud hum rose from the onlookers, and several of the drunken young men on board flitted to the rail, eager for the show.

Kell went for a better look. A police inspector led Brandon up the gangplank. Kell strolled towards them as they came aboard. 'In there,' the inspector barked. 'Guard him with your life,' he added in a loud voice, enjoying the attention.

Kell glanced through the door. Brandon sat on one of the benches, flanked by policemen, and began writing in his notebook. Too many police to overcome, Kell thought, and far too risky with Constance and Cumming in tow.

He pulled his hat lower and turned to go, but walked slap bang into a man bounding up the gangplank. 'Ah, excuse me,' Kell said in German, keeping his head low.

'Mind where you're going, can't you,' the man replied, in English, as he strode off without a second glance. It was Trench!

Kell instinctively made to stop him, but it was too late. He looked on, horrified, as Trench walked into the large cabin where Brandon and the police were, and sat down opposite. As cool a bird as you might meet, or the world's biggest fool, Kell couldn't be sure. Trench had no travelling bag with him, just a satchel. Kell hesitated. Behind him, the rail swung shut. They pulled away from the quay. A great cheer went up from the revellers still on shore.

Kell turned away. His thoughts now were on saving Cumming, Wiggins and Constance.

Wiggins rested one hand on Cumming's bath chair and breathed in the last of the slivovitz vapour. The old man had settled down into a deep, shivering sleep, and judging from the look Kell gave them when he came back, there was nothing to be done for Brandon.

Around them, the high spirits of departure had dampened down. A gaggle of young men still boozed at the rail, although their conversation had become quieter, more intense. Some passengers dozed. One of the students played a penny whistle, piercing over the whirr of the steam engines. A faint ditty, it reminded Wiggins of the folk songs some of the Irish used to play in the Strand Union; a bone-shop jig, they'd called it, though none of the grown-ups had the energy to dance. He closed his eyes. That was the joke – a bone-shop jig was played last thing at night, to send you off to the Old Man in the sky. Most of them hoped they'd wake up in the morning. Some of them didn't.

A tap on his shoulder. 'Hans,' Kell said loudly, and pointed. 'Emden.'

Wiggins shook his head awake. Passengers congregated at the rail to look on as the port terminal came into view, startlingly bright with a string of electric lights running along the quay. Cumming stirred too. Wiggins glanced back at Kell, then leaned forward and whispered into Cumming's ear, 'Stay asleep. Or I'll kill you.'

Constance and Kell got up and went to the rail themselves, and Wiggins risked joining them. Not only was the port lit up, but by the terminal point stood a phalanx of police, with two police cars at the waterside.

'For Brandon?' Kell whispered.

'Or for us?' Constance asked.

'Or 'im?' Wiggins nodded his head back to the bath chair.

The ferry juddered into position by the two cars. Wiggins glanced along the rail. 'Yous take 'im,' he hissed. 'I'll run a dodge. We'll meet at the motor garage we saw on the way in, down the side road.'

'Why there?'

'We will steal a motor car.' Constance said this under her breath, but Wiggins couldn't miss the glee.

He ran back to the bath chair and scrabbled underneath. As he did so, Cumming whispered, 'Leave me. Save yourselves.'

'I ain't a gentleman, but I ain't scum neither.'

He pulled Cumming's stick from the chair and hurried along the seaward side of the boat. He scooted around the back and came up to the land side of the ferry just as the gangplank swung down to the quay. There was chatter and excitement as Brandon and his police escort appeared at the top of the plank, the inspector making a great show of going first.

Wiggins crouched under the lifeboat. In its shade, shielded from both the seamen and the passengers, he took the sword from the swordstick's sheath. Twenty feet long by five, the lifeboat hung off the side of the ferry rather than needing to be lowered. And it was held in place by rope, not cable.

Working as fast as he could, he sawed through two of the guy ropes, leaving a small twine intact at each end. Up to his right, he heard the first of the passengers clambering down the gangplank. He pulled himself into the swinging boat itself, teetering against the weakened ropes. Then he glanced back at the quay. The waiting police closed around Brandon as he and his escort arrived on shore, but two more had stayed to watch as the rest of the passengers disembarked. He took the sword to the final, large rope that fixed the lighter to an iron stanchion and began sawing.

A shout rang out from the quay, and another, and sounds of a scuffle. A bottle broke. Wiggins didn't flinch. He sawed through the final strands of the rope and tossed the sword aside.

The lifeboat tilted, swung and then – with Wiggins crouched inside, holding on – plummeted to the quay.

It landed at an angle, like a perfectly sighted Congreve shell, prow first, into the windscreen of the stationary police car. Wiggins was thrown clear. He caught his shoulder hard, but managed to roll away into the cargo stacks.

On the deck, with Cumming in the bath chair and Constance on his arm, Kell waited. The police at the gangway questioned everyone disembarking, clearly trying to establish whether or not they were German. He whispered to Constance in his superb French, 'I've put some marks in your handbag. Stand behind Cumming and myself now, act separately. If we are stopped, you go ahead. Take the first train to Rotterdam. You will not be arrested.'

She hissed back, '*Non*—'

Just then, Kell saw a plain-clothes man in a felt hat approach the policeman on the gangplank. He flashed a piece of paper. 'Naval intelligence. There is no need for this,' the man in the felt hat said. 'We already know who we are looking for.'

'But, the inspector . . . I must—'

'I said, there's no need—'

CRASH!

The crowd turned as one to see the lifeboat sticking up from the front of the police car. The police on the gangway shouted out, and ran towards their stricken steed.

Many of the passengers followed, while the rest streamed from the ferry, unimpeded by officialdom. Kell glanced at the man in the felt hat – German naval intelligence – but he simply stepped aside and let the passengers past.

'Oh I say, he *is* clever,' Constance murmured as they reached the quay and walked off among the rest of the travellers. 'I hope he hasn't hurt himself.'

'Not Wiggins,' Kell replied out of the corner of his mouth. 'He always lands on his feet.'

Wiggins pulled his cap low and joined the returning passengers as they walked back into Emden town. It was easy enough to blend in amongst the long shadows. The pools of electric lights didn't spill into the side streets and soon enough he was almost ready to join the Kells at the rendezvous. But he had one last task.

He slipped into step behind one of the ferry passengers as they walked into town, unnoticed. He waited until they were out of earshot from anyone, and said in a low voice:

'You've got to come wiv us.'

The man, Captain Bernard Trench, turned around angrily. He peered through the gloom. 'It's you!' he said. 'How dare you speak to me.'

'Come, now. Else you're kippered.'

'The police know nothing of me,' he said. 'I will go back to my hotel. I'm sure they'll let Vivian go in the morning. We will claim a misunderstanding.'

Wiggins reached forward and took Trench's collar. 'Now,' he said.

Trench angrily pushed his arm aside. 'Touch me again, and I'll knock you down. I will not take orders from the likes of you, and I will not wish you goodnight.' He turned on his heel and marched away into the darkness.

Wiggins sighed. You don't tell people twice. He looped through the backstreets until he found himself in the side road by the garage. Only the far lights of the main seafront illuminated the road, but he caught the shape of the bath chair first, jutting out between two cars.

As he neared, he heard Cumming grumbling incoherently. Kell and Constance manhandled the old man into one of the cars, a grand machine with a huge engine and an open top.

'He ain't coming,' Wiggins hissed. 'Where's the crank?'

Kell handed him the crank without saying a word and got into the passenger seat, with Constance and Cumming in the back.

Wiggins bent down and wound the starter. The engine caught at the second attempt. Wiggins raced around to the driver's seat, released the brake and they were away.

'Trench will be discovered,' Kell said. 'They knew already. About him and Brandon.'

Wiggins shot him an alarmed glance. 'The leak?'

'Probably. In any case, we don't have long. As soon as the police collate reports from the hotel and the station, they'll realise there are more of us.'

'Westward Ho!' Constance said.

'No.' Kell put his hand on the wheel. 'Straight on. We head east.'

'Ain't it a spit to Holland? What's the dodge?'

'We won't be able to get there in time,' Kell said, looking up at the stars and pointing along the road. 'Have you got the Baedeker?' He stretched back to get it from Constance. 'It's got a map.'

'Are you sure?' she asked. 'That means going deeper into Germany.'

'I did do geography at school,' Kell said, squinting at the map in the darkness. 'Remarkably.'

'Sarcasm isn't very attractive in a person.'

Wiggins rolled the car out of town onto a deserted road and then cranked up the accelerator, eastward. As they cleared the last of the lighting, and the road was plunged into utter darkness, they heard the church bells ring out furiously.

'The hue and cry all right,' Wiggins said.

'Blasted Trench,' Kell said, then added, 'Open her out. We must get to the Weser before sunrise.'

'Then what?'

'We must hope it is the Year of the Rat.'

The car handled like a dream, despite the harum-scarum pace. They pushed on hard through the night, stray villages punching by in seconds. Even so, it wasn't until the dawn light began pricking the horizon ahead that the sea came into view.

'Where we going?' Wiggins said at last.

No one had said much after leaving Emden. Cumming had slumped back to a disturbed and shivery slumber. 'I hope it's not far,' Constance said from the back seat. 'I fear our passenger is somewhat the worse for wear, and my stomach positively aches for sustenance.'

Kell steadied himself with the windscreen, and stood up. 'There should be a coastal road north before we get to Wilhelmshaven.'

'Wilhelmshaven? Isn't that a naval base?' she replied.

'One of the biggest,' Kell said.

'Otherwise known as the lion's den.'

Kell sat down and glanced back at Constance. 'We have one chance,' he said. 'It won't be comfortable and it won't be pretty. I urge you again, my dear – we can drop you somewhere. I'm convinced that you'll be able to get a train to Rotterdam without difficulty.'

'What, and miss the fun?'

For the second time that night, Kell was struck silent by a show of loyalty. First Wiggins at the wire on Borkum, and now Constance. He nodded. 'Left there,' he said. 'Slow.'

They skirted the edges of Wilhelmshaven and reached a secluded road that ran along from the northernmost tip of the port. A watery pink light stripped the far horizon. As Wiggins slowed, he looked out across the black-grey sea and across to a far, far shore. 'It's a river mouth, the Weser,' Kell said, and then: 'There!'

Up ahead, pitched up on a thin spindle of a pier out into the sea, were three small and low-slung sailing ships. 'Stop here,' Kell said. 'Wiggins, with me. Constance, make sure Cumming doesn't wake up.'

'But—'

'These people won't like you. You're bad luck.'

'Because?'

'You're a woman,' he said.

'What the hell are them, then?' Wiggins asked, as he and Kell walked down to the pier.

'Junks,' he said. 'Chinese vessels. These will carry low-level contraband mostly.'

'This close to the navy?'

'Who do you think their biggest clients are?'

As they picked their way to the pier, Wiggins regarded the junks. They didn't look like the kind of shipshape rig you'd see out of Chatham or Portsmouth. In fact, they looked like they'd been patched together from the scraps in Petticoat Lane. The nearest one had a sharp prow and three masts, with the central mast an impossible spike high up into the sky. Sails hung like rags and smoke drifted up from a brazier on the deck.

Kell marched up to the first ship. A straggly lascar appeared on deck, wary.

Suddenly, Kell rapped out a violent burst of language.

The Chinese watchman growled but stepped back, surprised. He replied.

Once again, Kell spoke in a loud and forceful stream, quite unlike his usual self. The lascar bowed slightly and disappeared below deck.

'What the—?' Wiggins couldn't say more, flabbergasted.

'River Chinese,' Kell said calmly. 'I served in China for years.'

'But . . .'

At that moment, an older man came on deck, sporting a lungi, a patchy beard and a bare, hairless chest. He shrugged on a loose top, yawned, spat and barked something at Kell.

Kell launched another volley of Chinese at the man, who Wiggins guessed was the captain. The transformation in the captain as Kell spoke was remarkable. At first bored and dismissive, he soon ducked his head lower and lower.

'Get the others.' Kell turned to Wiggins. 'We set sail in twenty minutes.'

Five minutes later, Wiggins returned with Cumming holding his arm and Constance trailing behind. Kell was on deck, with the captain hanging on his every word. Constance didn't blink an eye.

'You knew he could speak that?' Wiggins said.

'He's my husband. Now, Vernon, firstly – is there breakfast? And do we have our own cabin?'

The cabin was the hold, and the four of them squeezed in between cargo bundles. A heady smell hung over them.

'You know, it doesn't smell nearly as bad in here as I thought,' Constance said, sleepily. They lay down, four abreast, with the bundles crammed in on either side. 'And my hunger seems to have gone.'

'Go on, sir, how'd you get the lift?' Wiggins asked, a drowsy edge to his voice.

'I served in China – against the Boxers.'

'Yeah, that explains the language. But that skipper, he's scared. What you say to him?'

'I made some acquaintances while there – locals, you understand? The fact that I spoke the language rather marked me out in that respect. Anyway, during that conflict we had to make friends with some types who we might otherwise have, well, disapproved of.'

'Come on, Vernon, get to the point,' Constance said dreamily.

'Well, I happened to do some work with – or alongside – a certain Chao Lan.'

'That a bird or a bloke?' Wiggins said.

'Or a typhoon?' Constance giggled along.

'He was the foremost triad leader in southern China.'

'Ooh, scary,' Wiggins said. Then: 'What's a triad?'

He and Constance stifled their laughter once more. Even Kell found himself grinning into the darkness. 'Huge criminal gangs,' he said. 'Vast networks of smugglers, prostitution, extortion, murder.'

'Hold up. You telling me you just threatened 'em with murder?'

'Not quite. But they know I have very powerful friends. In any case, we will pay for our passage handsomely.'

Wiggins slumped back into his place, lying next to the comatose Cumming. Kell stared at the wooden deck above. The boat, now out at sea, rocked and yawed violently, but Kell felt calm, peaceful almost.

'You know,' Constance said at his shoulder, 'no one's asked me what I found in the hotel rooms at Borkum.' She held up a small pamphlet, just visible in the light of the swinging lantern. 'My German's not all that *gut*, but it looks like a sketch of the naval positions.'

'Is that right?' Wiggins said.

'Vernon, this could save your precious Service – if nothing else, it shows some intelligence.'

'I believe it could,' he said, and laughed. 'Whitehall could do with some intelligence,' he added.

Constance stuffed the papers back into the front of her dress and shifted position. 'Such a pleasant smell,' she said.

'Ain't it,' Wiggins muttered.

'Wiggins,' Constance called softly over her husband's prone body. 'Tell me again, why are you here?'

'Why?' Wiggins said. 'Well, my best mate was binned by a gang of Latvian anarchists, and ever since, I've tried to bring 'em down. Body by the name of Peter the Painter.'

'A decorator? How odd, or an artist?'

'A killer.'

'I hope you do this in your spare time,' Kell said, as if it were the greatest joke. And then, in a wondering tone, 'Is this why you were late for the funeral?'

Wiggins smiled to himself. 'I was wiv friends, ain't that right, Mrs Kell?'

No one seemed to mind, or even to react very quickly to, what anyone said. Another silence settled over them as the boat jagged and leapt in the wind.

'I thought you were going to say you were a patriot,' Constance said. 'Your reason for joining up.'

Kell and Wiggins laughed again, as if Constance had landed a great joke. She joined in after a moment, then yawned.

'What *is* that smell? It's very, very pleasant,' she said at last.

The ship slewed violently, then righted itself. 'Some sort of flower? Poppies?' Constance said after a moment, as if to herself, almost asleep.

'No, no . . .' Kell drifted off, his head too heavy to lift.

Wiggins felt his muscles slacken, his eyelids droop. 'It ain't poppies,' he said, his voice a soporific whisper. 'It's opium.'

13

'Where the bally hell have you been?'

Kell sat down and beckoned to the elderly waiter. 'A double whisky and soda, and a cheroot.'

'Make that two,' Soapy said. 'Out with it, man. I've been trying to lay a hand on you for weeks. I've seen more of the new King than you. And what the devil's wrong with your eyes? You look as if you've been swimming in a gin bath.'

Kell relaxed into the chair. As soon as they arrived back in England, he'd sent Wiggins to the office and Constance home to Hampstead. Kell had rushed straight to see Soapy, whom he'd found in the Bengal Lounge of their club. He knew that his chance of surviving in the job depended on honesty, relied on speed, and trusted to delicacy – the delicacy of unstated blackmail.

'Glad to hear you've been hobnobbing with royalty,' Kell said. 'I trust we're in safe hands?'

'Of course,' Soapy said shortly. 'But what of you?'

Kell lit the cheroot and explained what had happened: Cumming's ill-advised rescue mission, the night in Borkum, the arrest, the scrap of useful information, and the escape. 'The arrest will be in the German papers by tomorrow, and here by the next day,' he said finally. 'I thought I'd better give you a warning. And an explanation.'

Soapy whistled. 'Thank you. The warning will be most helpful.'

'You didn't know anything about Brandon and Trench's mission to Germany? Beforehand, I mean?' Kell asked, offhand.

Soapy drew on his smoke and ignored the question. 'You got some useful intelligence, you say? That's important.'

Kell hailed the waiter once more. 'Could I have some biscuits, please? And cheese, and perhaps a salad. And maybe a chop?'

'Hungry, are you? Funny you should say chop, though,' Soapy said. 'We were about to cut you off, old man. Quinn's champing at the bit.'

'You don't have to be in intelligence to know that.'

'Right you are. You may be a soldier, but you've picked up the civil servant's strongest weapon – delay!'

'Not an issue any more, though, is it?' Kell said as he tucked into his food. 'You can't fire me now.'

'Why not?'

Kell considered for a moment. 'You can hardly sack the head of the Bureau in response to a failed mission to Germany, when that very mission is meant to be unofficial. It's as good as claiming that Brandon and Trench were there under orders.'

'It needn't be made public.'

Kell picked up his glass. 'Word gets about, Soapy, you know that.' There was the threat. Kell held Soapy's eye a touch longer than necessary. If they fired him, word would get about – Kell would make sure of that, and Soapy knew it.

'Ha!' Soapy said, and broke the stare. 'There's no need for anything unpleasant – not just yet, anyway. The PM's got other things on his mind.'

'Oh?' Kell mumbled. A deeply veined Stilton had arrived, with a splay of Bath Olivers. He fell on them without hesitation.

Soapy looked at him curiously for a moment, pulled at his cheroot and continued. 'We're nearly into September. Parliament's due back soon, and it looks as if there'll be another election. Can't have the bally Irish propping up the government for long. Coalition never works, not with this hoo-ha in the Lords to boot. I'll just talk, shall I? No need to nod – seems as if you haven't eaten in a week.

'As you know, there's been rather a lot of trouble in the country this summer, and it's only getting worse. Not only are the Commons and the Lords at loggerheads, but the industrial unrest is quite unsettling. And it's growing. That's not to mention these wretched suffragettes.' Soapy paused and idly examined his half-smoked cheroot to let the thought sink in. 'Yes, I rather think Quinn and Special Branch may have too much on their plate just now to start chasing Germans after all. Still, you've got to keep up your end of the bargain, Kell, the PM won't forget about this leak for ever. Have you any news?'

Kell dabbed at his mouth with a napkin. The one fact he'd omitted to tell Soapy about the escapade in Germany was the conversation he'd heard between the German naval intelligence officer and the policeman that they *already knew* to look for Brandon and Trench. In other words, for all their incompetence, the two Marines had almost certainly been betrayed into the bargain. Cumming had been too feverish to make much sense after the boat journey, but Kell planned to get out of him exactly who had known of the mission beforehand. It was yet more evidence of a hidden hand at work, Van Bork's hand, stretching into the heart of Whitehall and plucking out its innermost secrets. The fact that Brandon and Trench were so maladroit had disguised the betrayal, but betrayal there must have been.

He folded the napkin neatly. 'The net is tightening,' Kell said at last. 'It will take some time, but the list of suspects is shrinking. We will find our man, whoever he is. I promise you.' He freighted this last sentence with as much gravity as possible. After all, Soapy himself wasn't above suspicion. He wasn't Caesar's wife.

'Very good,' Soapy replied airily. He never quite said what he meant, but it was clear enough that the Bureau had been given another chance, at least in the short term. What was less clear was what he, or Quinn for that matter, knew about Constance. Probably more than him, Kell thought with a bitter pang.

Soapy looked at his watch. 'This Brandon and Trench business won't reach the papers until tomorrow, you say?'

'In Germany. Here, two days at least.'

'Good. I won't have to convene the Committee until tomorrow. Care for another?' he said.

Kell shook his head. 'The office . . . I should go.'

'Jolly good. Listen, can you get us a German spy to play with?

Tit for tat, as it were? Someone to arrest when this news hits the papers. I fancy a couple of the chaps in the Committee – the *politicians*, you understand – might request that. A counterblast.'

'There is no one important.'

'No one at all?'

Kell stood up and dusted the cheese crumbs from his trousers. He couldn't quite remember how it had happened that Soapy had become his de facto boss, that reporting lines of the Secret Service now ran somehow – seemingly without anyone writing it down or making the decision – straight to Number Ten itself, via the oleaginous, disaffected form of his old school chum, Tobias Etienne Gerard Marchmont Pears. Still fagging for him, twenty-odd years later. Then as now, Soapy's commands were always lightly dropped, but miss them at your peril.

'We'll make an arrest,' he said at last. 'Once the news breaks.'

'Just so.' Soapy raised his glass. 'You know, funny thing about your business. Success is always secret, no slaps on the back, medals or notices in *The Times*. But failure? Failure is writ large across the world. Good luck, old bean. And give my best to Constance.'

'Helm,' Wiggins said as soon as Kell got back to the office. 'Portsmouth.'

'He's hardly a big wheel, is he? I doubt he's a spy at all.'

'There ain't no obvious spies! But pick up Helm. He's been sketching Portsmouth for months.'

'Get down there tomorrow, take the train.'

'Nah, get the cops to do it. You go down there.'

'I think that opium may have gone to your head. You do realise I am still the chief of this operation?'

Wiggins sighed heavily. He'd been waiting in the office for Kell since they'd returned to London earlier that day. He sat in the swivel chair opposite the desk and patiently explained: 'You should get the credit. I'm secret, ain't I?'

'Too busy with finding Peter the Painter for yourself, is that it?' Kell snapped, although he could see the truth in what Wiggins said.

Wiggins shook his head. 'Gotta find digs, ain't I? Recover from me German holidays.'

'I suspect it's best if we don't mention that again. Cumming, by the way, intends to pay you ten pounds from his special dispensation fund. When he recovers. He has gone to bed.'

Wiggins whistled.

'I think you've finally won him over. Although he's most annoyed about losing his swordstick.'

'A tenner, eh?' Wiggins said. 'I didn't pick him as a spender.'

Kell shuffled his papers in an attempt to reassert his authority. 'I will go to Portsmouth tomorrow and set Helm's arrest in train. It is the best course of action. You, on the other hand, must get back to our main job. We need to find this leak.'

'Gi' us a chance. I cleared Carter, didn't I, and the other clerks.'

'I suspect our friends Bernie and Viv were betrayed too.'

Wiggins leaned forward in his chair, alert. 'That must tighten the circle. Who the old man tell?'

'I don't know yet, but I'm assuming Foreign Office, Admiralty, possibly War.'

'It rules out the cops, though, don't it?'

'Yes, I think it does. In the meantime, I've got a list here of the ministers and their key assistants, with home addresses. You were meant to pick this up a while ago, remember? But instead, you decided to take a holiday to the Canaries.'

'I've already told you, that weren't my idea.'

'We need to get to this immediately.'

'Can't I at least have a sandwich first?'

Kell opened a letter on his desk, ignoring Wiggins's entreaty. It was from Churchill. 'And I have orders here from the Home Office with which you'll need to help me. Yes, yes.'

'No time for a beer?'

Kell looked up from the papers. Wiggins was a mess. His hair lay tangled about his face, stubble smudged his chin and his eyes peered at him, pink and watery. He even had a rip in his collar.

'Very well. Report back here on Monday.'

Kell looked down again, but Wiggins hadn't moved. 'What is it now?'

'I need cash, for a scratcher.'

Kell tutted, but pulled out some change.

'I'll pay you back when I gets me tenner,' Wiggins added, wearily.

A thought suddenly struck Kell. It was Wiggins's opium-fuelled honesty – the admission that his goal was to track down some East End anarchist – that made him speak. Honesty among spies. 'This Peter fellow? You're not going to get into any trouble, are you?'

'Nah.' Wiggins pocketed the money, then wandered to the door. 'I'm going to the Library.'

~~~

'Ain't no moolah coming in, least not what I can see. Two weeks. None of the girls come out neither, 'cept the brownie. She been out one or two. The boss's missus?'

'I doubt it,' said Wiggins. 'Go on.'

Jax cleared her throat and went on. 'The big ugly 'un . . .'

'Tommy.'

''E goes down the Bloodied Axe, once, twice a week.'

'What else?' Wiggins stepped back from the window and turned to Jax.

Since getting back to London from Germany, he'd taken a small room at the top of the White Feathers, a corner pub with a view to one end of Ranleigh Terrace. It was the closest place he could find to the Embassy. It didn't have a line of sight to the big brothel, but it was as near as Wiggins could afford. From his high window, he could see any comings and goings south of the brothel. Once he'd found the billet – none too hard as he'd offered twopence above market for a fleapit with a leak in the roof – he'd set Jax to do a long-term recon while he put in the hours for Kell.

'It's a bust. She ain't in there, is she?' Jax said.

'We don't know where Millie is. But something's going on in there, Jax, and they know more than they's letting on.'

'Wot you ain't telling me? Why you care?'

Wiggins looked out of the window again, down into the street. He watched as a dray horse pulled a cartload of beer barrels away. Steam rose off the horse in the autumn twilight. Someone called out from below, a pub argument breaking out. A glass smashed.

He couldn't get Poppy out of his head. Dead, because of him. But what did she know? He could walk away, of course, let Tommy think he'd killed him. But that weren't right, not when she was lying in a pauper's grave because of him. He paid his debts, and he owed her.

But that wasn't the only debt he owed. He owed Bill too, even if he was a dead man. He owed Bill justice, and he would pay that debt; he would find Peter the Painter if he had to turn over the whole of London and beyond. He would find him, and he would pay him out.

Ever since he'd got back from Germany, though, Kell had sent him about town following government bigwigs. It was slow work, for most of the men on Kell's list were far above him socially. He'd had to make friends with the servants, ask around and observe from a distance. Kell had baulked at his offer to break into the houses and root around their personal effects. This meant that so far they'd turned up very little. Wiggins was on his own, furthermore, and consequently it was almost impossible to mount adequate surveillance on more than one person at a time. Still, he'd reasoned, he'd do the work and take his wages – the rest was Kell's concern.

Jax stood up and idly paced the room. She tugged at Wiggins's small pile of clothes, kicked the bed leg, then peeled off a thin strip of sagging wallpaper. She glanced at a half-empty bottle of gin, then up at Wiggins.

'Helps me sleep,' Wiggins explained. Not that he'd been sleeping much recently. The opium vapours had put him to sleep on the Chinese junk, but ever since dark dragons had invaded his dreams. And they breathed out blood.

He took hold of Jax's wrist. 'I'll find out what happened to Millie, I promise. Now, what about Tommy – he go anywhere else than the Axe?'

Jax hesitated. 'I don't know.' She pulled her arm free and stepped away.

'Jax,' Wiggins said. 'Spill.'

'First time I followed him, I lost him. Up Victoria.'

'How did you lose him?'

'It was busy. I came back here. Then a coupla hours later, so did he – with an 'eavy bag on his shoulder, like.'

'And the second time?'

'He goes back up Vicky, but he takes a bus. Doesn't get out there but goes up Hyde Park Corner, then drops the bus and picks another one going the other way. Then he takes a cab, so I lost him.'

'Bastard,' Wiggins said. 'He made you.'

'He didn't make me.'

'Believe me, he made you. He was taught by the best.'

'Who that?'

'Me.' Wiggins shook his head. 'You can't come back here. *Never* come back here, understand?'

'But—'

'Let's go,' Wiggins said, taking her by the shoulder. He surprised himself by the vehemence of his words. But the thought of Tommy on Jax's tracks scared him. He didn't want another death on his conscience, and certainly not Jax's.

She swore blue as they trundled down the backstairs and out into a side street. 'Get off me, you ape,' she cried.

'Shut it. Move.' He near pushed her along the pavement as they walked in the opposite direction from the Embassy.

She calmed down after a while. Wiggins breathed a little easier as they broke out onto the main road and into the traffic. 'You giving me the old heave-ho? I ditched running for you. I'll be brassick.'

'I've got another job for you.'

'Wot's the pay?'

'Don't you want to know what the job is?'

Wiggins stopped at a street stall and ordered scaffold and pole for two. They watched as an enormous, red-faced man flipped fried fish and potatoes into a fold of newspaper.

Vinegar reeked off them. Wiggins passed a packet to Jax, then popped a chip into his mouth.

'I'll pay you a fiver if you find Peter the Painter before me.'

'Again? You're cracked, you are. I ain't never gonna find him, that's daylight robbery that is, a fiver. It could be a year's work, least. Is there a sub?'

Wiggins grinned. 'A pound down.'

'Done.'

Jax ran off to bunk a train soon after. Wiggins hoisted himself onto the back of a passing tram, like the old days, but instead of hanging off the back, he clambered into the door and nodded at the conductor. 'I should fine you,' he said.

'Where's the fun in that?' He held out his fare.

He picked up a discarded newspaper and scanned the headlines. Strikes in Liverpool. Suffragette vandalism. Naval build-up. Nothing about anarchists, no terrorist incidents, no clues as to where Peter and his gang might be hiding – and Wiggins was taking the longest of long shots on that hunt.

Only one item really took his eye. In the case of the captured British Marines, Brandon and Trench, new evidence had come to light. Under interrogation, Brandon had given the German authorities permission to open his post held in Holland, which revealed a further tranche of incriminating documents. This had led to a search of Captain Trench's hotel room in Emden, which led to the discovery of more hidden photographs, sketches and the like – all hidden under Trench's bed. The report concluded with a rather tart comment about the lack of common sense shown by the two officers, and compared it unfavourably with the so far honourable restraint shown by the German authorities.

Wiggins left the paper on the tram at Tottenham Court Road, and walked towards the British Museum. Poor Bernie and Viv, he thought with a smile, what greater shame than to be deemed worse than a German. Anything but that.

'Quick!'

Clunk. Clunk. Clunk.

'I can't,' Dinah giggled. The large front window of Boots the Chemist remained unbroken.

'Come on, you two,' Abernathy cried from further up Regent Street.

Dinah turned to Constance, her round face poking out from a swaddling of clothes, a huge knobkerrie brandished rather pathetically. Constance looked behind her. The street lights arced away from them towards Piccadilly Circus. It was gone three in the morning and the traffic had finally stilled. It was now or never.

'Give it here,' Constance said.

CRASH!

Abernathy smashed a window further up the road. Dinah squealed.

Constance lifted the knobkerrie above her head. Suddenly, out of the night to her left, Nobbs screamed, 'Peelers!' She ran full pelt past them.

A policeman's whistle pierced the air. Then a second, and a third. Constance froze.

It was a long way from Lyons' Corner House. And that was part of the problem.

As soon as she'd returned from Germany, Constance had tried to get in touch with Dinah, never the easiest thing to do. Dinah rarely answered her telephone, and going to the place she shared with Abernathy, out in Barons Court, always felt like too much of a chore, except in Queen's Week.

She'd gone back to the Hampstead Society for Women's Suffrage. For once, the meeting contained some positive news – a march planned for Hyde Park and the Conciliation Bill, which proposed a vote for older, property-owning women, to go before Parliament. Two years previously, such a development would have put Constance in a good mood for weeks. Yet she failed to feel the excitement, the thrill, that those teas at the Lyons' Corner House had given her. That Dinah had given her.

Dinah had agreed to come to a meeting in Hampstead again,

to accompany Constance on her own, but the trip to Germany had scotched all that. Worst of all, though, Constance hadn't been able to get hold of Dinah beforehand and had stood her up. A week or two had gone by with the telephone still unanswered, and nothing to be seen of Dinah or the rest of the girls at Golden Square. Constance was on the verge of swallowing her embarrassment and heading out to Barons Court one morning when the telephone rang.

'Constance!' Dinah bawled down the line. 'Where have you been?'

'Where've I been? I—'

'Never mind. I'm so bricked you're still alive. Abernathy spoke darkly.'

'Of course I am alive. Why—'

'Lyons'. Four,' Dinah went on breathlessly. 'Do say you'll come.'

'I . . . well—'

'Bonzo,' she said, and rang off.

Dinah hallooed her over to the usual spot in the Corner House. 'At last,' she said, excitedly kissing Constance on both cheeks.

'Lost your cold feet?' Abernathy drawled.

'I beg your pardon,' Constance said as she sat down. 'I've been more than—'

Nobbs broke in. 'You know, I really think Tansy's on to something.'

'Not now,' Abernathy hissed. 'Pass those cheroots. I feel like a decent smoke.'

Constance had squeezed next to Dinah and turned to her while the others chattered on. 'I am so very sorry about the meeting up in Hampstead.'

'What's that?'

'I was called away unexpectedly,' she whispered.

Dinah tossed her head. 'Don't be a silly goose. I didn't go, of course. I don't want to listen to a roomful of old ladies.'

'Oh.' Constance puffed her cheeks out, blinked and tried to smile. Dinah reached for a scone. She tapped it on the table with a thud.

Abernathy funnelled cigar smoke above the round table and glared at Constance. 'Where did you go?'

'I beg your pardon?'

'You said you were called away unexpectedly. Where?'

A waitress slapped down a plate of grey sandwiches and four more raisin-studded grenades. 'Butter's extra,' she said. 'Pay at the till.'

Dinah groaned. Constance picked up one of the limp sandwiches, ignoring Abernathy's dagger eyes. 'Why don't we go to Rumpelmayer's for a change? I know we're campaigning for suffrage, but that doesn't mean we have to suffer.'

Nobbs's cup clattered into its saucer. She put a hand to her mouth. No one said a word. Constance knew it wasn't that funny, but she wasn't expecting this.

Finally, Dinah coughed. 'Nobbs's cousin is being held in Holloway.'

'And . . . ?'

'She's on hunger strike.'

'Oh.'

Nobbs sniffed. 'And they've started to force-feed her, the beasts.'

'Ah.'

Abernathy stubbed out her cigar violently into one of the sandwiches. 'She's got the stomach for the fight. Have you?'

'What do you know about this?' Constance cried, as soon as Kell came in the door.

'About what?'

'They are force-feeding women in Holloway – again!' She took a step towards him.

'Ah, I see.'

'Well?' She'd been waiting in the drawing room for him to come home, yet her anger had not abated. If anything, his appearance – top hat, Whitehall pinstripes, cane, the very epitome of male power – enraged her even more.

'Really, this is not my department.'

'It is *your* government.' She threw her hands up in the air. 'The government I so stupidly helped save from embarrassment. Why?'

'Why? Surely, that is a question for you.'

'Not that. I have no idea why I helped the British Government, a government that does such terrible things. Why are you force-feeding them again?'

'I'm not the governor of Holloway!' he snapped, then took a breath. 'It is for the prisoners' good. Otherwise they would die,' he said more carefully. The gentle rapprochement that their shared mission to Germany had effected seemed to be disintegrating. 'The prison authorities have a duty of care to all their inmates, however unhinged. They simply cannot be allowed to die. It's for their own good. This is what government is,' he said finally. 'It's civilisation.'

'It's barbarism!' She headed to the door. 'I'm going out,' she cried.

He shot out his hand and caught her arm. She glared at him and he let go, as if scalded. 'Are you involved?' he asked. 'In any of this illegality, vandalism?'

She glared at him. 'What do you mean?'

'Are you?'

'No,' she said. Then she shrugged on her overcoat and left him there, staring into the empty room.

And so it was that Constance found herself, heavy wooden club in hand, at three in the morning, contemplating in a split second whether to break the window, to run with Dinah, Nobbs and Abernathy, or to take her chances with the burly constables of B Division bearing down upon her.

14

'You've got nothing?'

'Nuffin' worth a spit.'

'Very pleasant, I'm sure,' Kell said. 'But it won't do. Report, military style – we are military intelligence, after all.'

Wiggins arched his eyebrow. 'Bethell at the Admiralty. I think he's clean but it's hard to confirm it. His habits are regular, from what I can see he don't have any hobbies that would put him in the red, and he ain't got any German connections. Clean as an RSM's backside, in other words.'

'Must everything be obscene?'

Wiggins relented. 'I can't watch 'em all on my tod, all of the time. And I can't say what they get up to behind closed doors. None of their gaffs would let in the likes of me.'

Kell looked at him. It was true. Wiggins wouldn't get past the door of any club in Pall Mall. 'No,' he said.

'I didn't say nuffin'.'

'But you thought it. I will not let you burgle these people's houses.'

'I wouldn't take anything.'

'What if they're innocent? We would have been breaking and entering the most powerful households in the land. We would go to prison.'

Wiggins shrugged. Kell glanced down at the list in front of him. 'Twelve names. It must be one of these twelve men. And you're saying we can't eliminate any of them?'

'Not yet.'

Kell threw his hands up in exasperation. He thought of Constance and their horrible argument of the night before. He would never forgive himself for grabbing her arm. She hadn't come back in the morning – or else she'd slept in the guest room and got up early – and he wondered for a moment if she ever would. What he really needed to do was put Wiggins on her, see where that ball of thread unravelled to, but that was part of the problem – and it was the reason for his agitation, he realised now, his aggression.

He'd come back home late in the evening, directly from a meeting with Churchill, who had summoned him angrily on the telephone.

'Why do you not return my messages?' he'd demanded as soon as Kell came through the door of his office.

'The service, sir, is stretched. We are under—'

'—resourced. It is all we ever hear. You do realise I am the only thing keeping the thing afloat. Whenever it comes up, the rest of the Cabinet is all for folding you into Special Branch. Is your heart not in it, man?'

Kell stood in the doorway still, unable even to take a seat. Churchill glowered through a plume of swirling smoke. 'My heart's in it, sir,' Kell said through gritted teeth.

'Capital. Now, I'll have whisky.' He jabbed his cigar at the drinks cabinet, and rounded his desk to sit down. 'I read your man's report on the situation in Wales – can't say I wholeheartedly agree with him. You are sure he is reliable?'

'Agent W is the best man I have.'

'He's the only man, isn't he?' Churchill snapped. 'Never mind. You'll have heard, I'm sure, about the growing unrest in Nottingham? The shipbuilders in Belfast. The boilermakers. And the dockers – the dockers everywhere are revolting.'

Kell nodded as Churchill lectured on. Industrial problems were breaking out all over the country. Whisper it quietly – as Soapy sometimes did – but one of the reasons for the mooted general election was to distract people from their current concerns. If people thought that an election was coming, that an election might usher in change, then they might leave off. Of course, this wasn't even mentioned as a reason in the press. To them, the election might be necessary to stop the Liberals' reliance on the Irish in the coalition and ultimately to overcome the Lords on the question of the Budget.

Kell listened to this political lesson from Churchill in silence. 'Kell?'

'Yes, sir.'

'I said, send him in. Agent W.'

'Where?'

'The docks this time. We have no reliable informants inside the unions – at least, Special Branch don't in London – and I need to know who the ringleaders are, why they are striking and what they plan to do.'

'But surely . . .' Kell hesitated. He could almost hear Wiggins's reply in the room. *They's striking cos their job's shite and they're paid shite.*

A sharp rap at the door saved Kell from actually uttering this thought. 'Enter,' Churchill cried. He grinned crookedly and Kell turned to see Sir Patrick Quinn, head of Special Branch.

'Quinn,' Churchill said. 'Good of you to join us. You know Captain Kell, of course.'

'That I do, sir, that I do.' Quinn looked down his long nose and nodded, infuriating as ever.

'Good day,' Kell said. It was a nasty shock to see him, but judging from the look on Quinn's face, he'd had no idea about the meeting either.

'I wonder, Quinn, if you could update us on the unrest out at West India Docks?'

For once discomforted, Quinn glanced at Kell, then back at Churchill. 'It's the usual stuff,' he said at last. 'Mild discontent, whipped up by a few troublemakers. Nothing serious.'

'Which troublemakers?'

'I am wondering, if I may, sir,' Quinn said slowly, recovering from the initial surprise, 'what such information has to do with the Secret Service Bureau?'

Churchill exhaled. 'Well wonder on, till truth makes all things plain.'

'Just so,' Quinn nodded. 'We haven't yet identified the exact identity of the troublemakers, sir, but we will do, we will do.'

'You'll forgive me if I don't have much confidence in your record so far,' Churchill said, taking a gulp of his drink.

Quinn hesitated and then, to Kell's surprise (and grudging respect), answered back. 'We only have so many bodies, sir, and there's much trouble being made just now, so there is.' He paused, looked over at Kell, then went on. 'There's a deal of prioritising going on, sir, if I may say. The suffragettes, for example, they are getting ever more militant. I wouldn't be surprised if there's a death at their hands soon.'

As he spoke this last sentence, Quinn looked hard at Kell. Kell felt in his pocket for a smoke and glanced up at Churchill, only to see that the Home Secretary was also looking hard at him. 'Indeed,' Churchill said at last. 'Thank you, Captain Kell, that will be all.'

Kell held the cigarette to his mouth unlit, nodded and got up. 'Sir,' he said. It took all his resolve to keep his walk steady, to pull open the door without shaking, and to walk away without trying to listen in. Churchill had engineered Quinn's appearance at the meeting, that was for certain. He was playing them off against each other, clearly, but to what end? Almost overnight, Kell had found himself in the middle of some political game that he didn't understand.

One thing he did understand, though, was that both Quinn and Churchill knew more about his wife's activities than he did.

'Sir!'

Kell snapped out of his reverie and looked up across his desk at Wiggins. 'What was that?'

Wiggins clicked his fingers. 'Who should I tap up next? I ain't hit anyone from the FO since Carter.'

'I need you down at West India Docks first,' Kell said, his mind still on Churchill. 'There's growing unrest and we have no idea who's instigating it, or why.'

'Not hard to guess why. You ever worked a shift on the dock? It'd break your back. And your wrists. And your fingers.'

'Yes, thank you for the poetry. I need you to go down there. Blend in. Find out who the troublemakers are – not the official union leaders, the real ringleaders. Get what you can on them. Their names, where they live, who they associate with, you know the drill.'

'They's all German spies, are they?' Wiggins sneered. 'We gonna find Van Bork hauling bananas off the quay?'

Kell paused. 'You will find out what I tell you to find out. Or it's over.'

Back at his digs, Wiggins dodged the side door and went into the pub proper for a drink. The £10 Cumming had paid him wasn't going to last for ever, especially since he'd started paying Jax to scout out the East End, but there was always change for a livener. Even the down-and-outs knew that.

She sat alone, facing away from the door, but Wiggins recognised her immediately. Shoulders square, back so straight it didn't even touch the chair. She didn't flinch when he came in, nor when he ordered his drink, not even when he walked over towards her and stood for a moment. But he knew she waited for him.

'You're a sharp 'un,' he said as he slid into the seat opposite.

Martha blinked. 'Never underestimate a whore.'

'You said that with pride.'

'I am proud. Look at me. My mother was born on a slaver, my daddy worked the fields – rice fields too, and if you don't know how hard that is, then you're a lucky man – and yet here I am, promenading the streets of Belgravia, drinking sherry wine and keeping a most attractive gentleman's rapt attention.'

'Sorry about that.' Wiggins blushed and looked away. It was the way she held herself, or her dress or he didn't know what, but it was hard not to look.

She laughed, sweet and light, not the deep, throaty laugh he expected. 'Big T's not so bad,' she said after a moment. 'What did you do to him?'

'What did I do to 'im?' He drained the last of his pint, shook his head, then called out to the barman, ''Ere, Ralph. Another half-and-half and . . . ?' He looked at Martha. 'Sherry, large.'

She raised an eyebrow, but didn't say anything. Instead, she looked him over with a faintly amused air, unashamed, undaunted by his stare. Wiggins shifted his eyes down to her chest, then quickly away. Her dress was made from a fine purple material, with embroidered flowers around the collar and frills on the hem. She wore long lace gloves, with a red ribbon poking out from one cuff. He guessed she was the same age as him, but somehow she seemed younger and yet older at the same time. Her skin shone like a youth's, but the way her eyes sparkled, the way her mouth turned up at the ends, told Wiggins that she knew more than him about a lot. Most importantly, she'd found him. Did that mean Tommy had found him too?

The barman slapped down the drinks. Wiggins pulled long at his pint, then looked at Martha once more. 'We knew each other once, as little 'uns. Street kids. But Tommy never cottoned to me. Or my boss, anyways.'

'You always do what the boss says?'

'No,' Wiggins rapped back. 'I just . . . Me and Tommy, chalk and cheese.'

She sipped her sherry.

'He send you?' he said.

Martha looked surprised. 'He's not my master.'

'Does he know?'

She drummed her gloved hands on the table in a rare show of impatience. 'I didn't take you for a dummy,' she said.

The double doors crashed open and a knot of transport workers came in – a driver and a couple of conductors, Wiggins saw from a glance. He took another swig and ran his hand through his hair.

Martha twirled the glass by its stem. 'What do people do for amusement round these parts?'

He looked up, surprised. 'Other than head to your gaff?'

'You don't approve of prostitution?'

'It's not that, it's . . . I don't know.' He clammed up. He didn't know quite what to say to Martha, or what she even meant half the time.

'It's an escape for some people. All they want is an escape. You ever want that?'

He shrugged. 'I'm London, me.'

'So you can tell me. What do courting couples in London do?'

'Ya want me to say?'

'In public. Where do they go out?'

'Ain't my scene,' Wiggins said. 'The boozer?' He swilled the beer in his glass, and looked down. She arched her back, slow and languid, then sighed.

'Not used to this, are you?'

He shook his head, unsure. She smiled suddenly, bunching up her cheeks. 'What do you do, then?'

'What do I do?'

'For money. You have the advantage on me – you know what *I* do, don't you?'

He felt the heat in his cheeks once more, and flicked his eyes to the window. She laughed lightly. For some reason, everything she said embarrassed him. He'd known streetwalkers his whole life, running around Soho and Marylebone. They'd call out to him as he ran past, their jokes getting bluer as he got older. It was all good-natured, and he looked on them like aunties rather than whores. But when Martha opened her mouth, he didn't know what to say or where to look.

She put down her glass with a heavy clunk. 'Poppy ain't your fault,' she said.

Wiggins nodded. 'What happened?'

'It happens all the time. It's a hard life, specially at the start. Some of the young girls can't see no other way.'

'And you can?'

She wiped a stray fleck from her lips. 'Maybe. We's all waiting for the shining white knight.'

Wiggins eyed his near empty glass, glanced up at the bar, then back at Martha. But rather than offering her another, he said, 'Have you told Tommy where I am?'

'What do you take me for?'

He looked at her. 'Once of Sierra Leone, spent time down

Haymarket in the old days. Eye trouble. Smoke with an 'older, but not often. Interest in needlepoint. And you're a senior whore at the plushest knocking shop in London. That's what I take you for. I need to know what you told Tommy.'

She shook her head. 'Thank you for the drink, Mr Wiggins.' She got up with the same grace and languor as all her movements, but her face was set.

'I didn't mean . . .' Wiggins reached towards her helplessly as she gathered her bag from the floor.

'I know exactly what you mean,' she said into her shoulder. Then she walked across the bar, turning the head of each and every man as she did so, pushed out of the pub doors and was gone.

'I've been rumbled.'

'Wot?' Jax said through a mouth stuffed with bacon sandwich.

'Tommy's got the gen on me and all. Had to move out of the pub, sharpish. And don't talk with your mouth full, you might drop some of it.' He took a bite of his own sandwich and began to chew carefully.

They sat at one end of Sal's cabby hut during a lull in business, sharing an enormous bacon sandwich. 'Ow!' Jax put her cup down hurriedly. 'Ma,' she screamed. 'This char is bloody scalding. Near ripped my lip off.'

'Chance would be a fine thing.' Sal ambled over and sat next to her, looking at Wiggins. 'How's my Holmes and Watson of the gutter getting on? Out of leads?'

'That place is dark, Sal, I'm telling you.'

'Leave it then.'

Wiggins shook his head slowly and glanced at Jax. Sal put her hands on the table and said, 'All right. What would Mr Holmes do? If he wanted round-the-clock gen on an whorehouse, the comings and goings and whatnot?'

'He'd ask us,' Wiggins said.

'Cos we could go everywhere, see everything and not be seen.'

'Zackly.'

'Well,' Sal said with a smile.

'Well what?'

She gestured at the cab drivers' paraphernalia littered around the cabin, the whip above the door, the lanterns hanging at each end of the long trestle table, and a stuffed tiger's head in pride of place, winner of the weirdest left-item prize since for ever. 'I got the best network in London, ain't I?'

Wiggins grinned. 'Can't send a cabby to an whorehouse,' he said. 'They'd only start competing for a fare. Putting it on the meter.'

'You really have gone soft,' she said.

Jax scraped back her chair. 'I'm going for a slash.'

'I'm so glad I shelled out for charm school,' Sal said.

'Can't teach class.'

They watched her crash out of the back door of the hut. Sal held her eyes away from Wiggins for a moment. She pushed a ginger curl out of her face. 'I'll put the word out. It'll take time, but I reckon we'll get an addy for every sad sod that visits the place. In the end.'

'Could work. Better than sod all.'

'You're not gonna get in there anytime soon, not if Tommy's on the watch. And before you say anything, I ain't having Jax sent in.'

'She's busy on something else.'

'I noticed – you paying her proper?'

'I'm paying her. It's safe, she's just taking a look-see, keeping an ear to the old horseshit.'

Sal pursed her lips. Wiggins could still see the child she used to be, around the mouth and cheeks, and her bright sparklers. But her back was bent, the skin on her hands red raw and she couldn't shake her frown no more. 'What's wrong?' she said suddenly.

'Nothing. Just thinking about the old days.'

'Wot for? You miss living in the streets, do ya? Miss scrabbling around, dodging beatings, eating scraps, picking up fag ends on Baker Street?'

'I miss the old you,' he said. 'You used to be all right.'

'Shut up.'

'I gotta get down the docks yesterday.'

She looked at him carefully. 'You all right?'

Wiggins felt the wooden table under his hands, bent his fingers, realised they'd been drumming. 'I got a lot on.' And then, while Sal still stared at him, 'I've got to find the Painter. That's what Jax is helping wiv, till my blunt runs out. And that's dark stuff going on at the Embassy. Tommy tried to have me killed, sure as eggs.'

'The rozzers?'

Wiggins raised an eyebrow at that. 'Yeah, right.'

Sal's spoon tinkled in her teacup. 'You don't have to stay, you know.'

'Leave London?'

'You could find her?'

Wiggins shook his head. 'No, no. That ship's sailed. Any roads, I can't leave. I've got a debt to pay. Two debts. Bill and the girl, Poppy. I won't let Tommy get away with that. And I need a job – and time – to pay 'em off. Even if it takes me until nineteen bloody thirty, I'll pay me debts.'

'Be a hero, what do I care?' Sal said.

'You owes me a tanner.' Jax burst back through the door and pointed at Wiggins. 'Expenses. Bus fares.'

'You ain't paid a fare in your life.' He flicked her the coin nevertheless.

She pulled a huge cap over her eyes. 'See ya,' she said, and was gone.

They both looked after her. 'No word of a lie, she's your spit,' Wiggins said, almost to himself.

'You think so? She always reminds me of her dad.'

Wiggins gathered up his coat and hat and appeared not to hear.

'I'll let you know how we get on with those addies. Pass the word. Free cup of cha for each. You might not get inside that bloody place, but you'll know who else does.'

'That's jam that is, Sal. Always the brains of the operation.'

'And you was the face. Where you get those strides, by the way? You look like a docker on the skids.'

'Master of disguise, like the Great Old Detective.'

'You never did see the old man straight.'

Wiggins left then, and it wasn't until later that he thought about Sal's parting comment, and what it might mean.

Kell watched from his bedroom window as Constance strode purposefully towards Hampstead Underground station. He'd given up trying to follow her; she was too fly. Any thaw that the trip to Germany had effected between them had been shot to pieces by those blasted women in Holloway refusing to eat. He couldn't see what was wrong with trying to feed them, even if they didn't want to be fed. Were the authorities really to sit by and do nothing while women in their care died? What else could they do? Either way, the government's response had led to a string of furious rows, and now Constance was barely speaking to him at all.

He looked out of the window once more. A figure in a flat cap and baggy trousers stood at the corner around which his wife had just disappeared. He crouched down, his back to Kell, and peeked after her. Then he, too, went around the corner.

Kell rushed down the stairs and out into the hallway. He thought of the man he'd found following him outside the house months earlier. Kell had assumed at the time that the man was tailing him – indeed, had suspected that the man might be in the pay of the government mole. But was it in fact Constance, not he, who had the tail? Who would be following her? And why?

He stepped out of his front door, only to realise he didn't have his shoes on. He hadn't breakfasted either. And when he came to think of it, what would he do if he did catch up with the suspicious man? He hadn't been able to follow his wife success-fully, and he felt damn sure that she'd lose the man on the corner soon enough. He gave it up and went back inside.

'Cook!' he shouted. 'I shall take a rack of toast, and a kipper. Make that two kippers.'

He padded barefoot into the breakfast room and tried to organise his thoughts about something other than his wife. Wiggins had turned up some useful information on the Cabinet, but as yet no smoking gun as far as the Committee meeting was concerned. None of the twelve men on the list had been definitively ruled in or out. His Foreign Office source, Moseby-Brown, had been supplying him with all sorts of Foreign Office gossip. A shifty chap beneath the sleek exterior, but he was prepared to give Kell an inside scoop.

There had been no breakthrough, though, and it was now October.

'Mrs Kell has gone out already?' the cook said, bustling through the door with a tray.

'An excellent observation. Thank you, Cook.' He snapped open the newspaper.

Dr Crippen was all over the front page. His trial had just begun. A man so sick of his wife, he'd poisoned her and then buried what was left of the body under his house before setting up home with another woman. Was the unfortunate Mrs Crippen a suffragette? Kell wondered idly as he bit into a corner of lightly buttered toast.

'Let's get nearer the front,' Nobbs said. 'My cousin Clarrie is to speak.'

Constance followed the four women – Nobbs, Abernathy, Dinah and Tansy – as they filed through a mass of demonstrators on the eastern edge of Hyde Park.

She thought of the King's funeral, her first day out with these young women, when Wiggins had stepped in. But this time, it was all women. This time, no one would look askance at their banners; this time, they were getting somewhere, for all Abernathy's grumbles.

'Keep up,' Dinah grinned. 'We don't want to lose you.'

They were the same words she'd used the month before when Constance had jumped into the cab at Oxford Circus, with Dinah, Abernathy and Nobbs.

Constance had run from the police. She'd thrown down the club in front of Boots, grabbed her skirts and run. Run like she hadn't done since she was seven, so that her heart hammered, her hat flew off and her feet sang with pain. But she'd also felt the power surging in her legs, and by the time they got to the cab, idling at the corner of Great Marlborough Street, she'd almost caught up with Dinah.

'Go,' Abernathy yelled at the driver.

The gears ground as the cab leapt away from the kerb towards Soho. 'North,' Constance called, and Abernathy leaned towards the driver, knife in hand.

Five minutes later, Constance called again. 'Out!'

'Now?' Abernathy said. 'Why?'

The taxi screeched to a halt. Abernathy waited on the pavement as the others got out. The cabby drove off, mouthing obscenities out of the window.

Constance shepherded them round the corner of Euston Square and out by Euston Station, which was still abuzz with business. The trains had ceased for the night, but the milk train would be going soon, late-night buses stopped by and the post was being hauled through the station. They could also see the odd cab scouting for early trade.

'Brilliant,' said Nobbs.

Abernathy nodded at Constance. 'Good idea, Euston.'

'A triumph,' Dinah trilled.

The moment of triumph hadn't lasted long, Constance reflected as she followed the girls to the front of the crowd, at least not for Abernathy. But she felt hopeful for the cause, despite the horrors of Holloway. A bill was to go before Parliament, offering limited voting rights for women. And once it started, she knew, it would not stop until they all got the vote. It felt closer, it felt real, and the thrill of being with these young women as they pushed it forward, whether it was acid-bombing post boxes or smashing windows, was something she'd been waiting for her whole life. It was real, it was progress.

They reached the front of the demonstration without too much difficulty. Purple, green and white banners ruffled in the breeze and a gentle burble of conversation and laughter carried over the throng. Next to their little group stood a delegation from India, dressed in thick saris with furs slung over their shoulders against the October cold.

A row of speakers stood on a raised platform, taking turns to rally the crowd. 'There's Clarrie,' Nobbs called.

'My, that is a pretty sari,' Constance said to a tall, thin woman in Indian dress with a red dot on her forehead. She leaned forward and fingered the material. 'Thank you for supporting us, in our struggle,' Constance said eventually. 'Do you know Princess Sophia Duleep Singh?' The Indian woman looked at her oddly, but nodded and smiled.

'Constance,' Dinah hissed. 'Over here. It's Clarrie's turn to speak.'

She smiled again at the Indian woman, who looked back, bemused. Up on the stage, Nobbs's cousin Clarrie belted out her diatribe at a good volume. 'The Conciliation Bill will go to Parliament next month. We have high hopes that enough MPs will see reason to grant this small, first step in getting women the vote. Consequently, we are formally announcing a cease in all hostilities until the bill gets to Parliament, as a sign of our good faith, and our reason.'

A big cheer went up, and some scattered clapping. After that, a small band readied themselves and the women on the podium held hands. 'I still say Fairyland's the place,' Tansy muttered. 'I still say it.'

'We must certainly be ready,' Abernathy growled. 'When they skewer the bill at Westminster. I second Tansy.'

'Second her about what?' Constance finally asked. 'What on earth are you talking about? What is Fairyland?'

'Is it safe?' Nobbs looked at Abernathy.

Suddenly, the stage and then the whole crowd burst into song.

Shout, shout up with your song!
Cry with the wind for the dawn is breaking.

'We need to know what the police know about us,' Abernathy said as the singing continued around them. The four women, Dinah, Nobbs, Abernathy and Tansy, had formed a tight knot, leaving Constance hanging off the edge.

March, march, swing you along,
Wide blows our banner, and hope is waking.

Dinah frowned back at Constance. 'Can you help?' she said at last.

'Help how?' Constance replied, cupping her ears.

'*Song with its story, dreams with their glory.*'

'The police.'

'*Lo! They call, and glad is their word.*'

Constance searched Dinah's face, the bright pink cheeks shining against the cold, her eyes hopeful but wandering. Dinah started to turn away.

'*Loud and louder it swells.*'

Constance caught hold of Dinah's hand, made her turn. 'I think I know a way,' she said.

15

Wiggins eyed the huge dome above him. The British Museum Reading Room. He'd had a reader's card for years, but he didn't go often. Great glass windows striped the lower half of the roof, like inverted petals. The glass at the very top of the dome let in the last of the afternoon light. He straightened his collar and walked round the perimeter of the huge circular room. Books lined the walls in dark leather colours. A further gantry above held thousands more volumes. But Wiggins wasn't looking at the books.

He circled the entire room, then chose one of the spindles that led to the centre. Each of these spokes, fanning out from the returns desk, was lined with desks. Readers stooped over books. Each spoke had a letter, and each desk a number. Wiggins walked down aisle G. As he walked towards the central hub, where three or four of the librarians busied themselves, Wiggins slowed.

Symes's billiard-ball head caught the light when he moved. Wiggins went up to him at the returns desk and handed him a book. They exchanged a nod. Wiggins glanced the way he'd come, then left the room.

The concourse in front of the museum teemed with late-afternoon visitors. Pigeons swooped and pecked, fluttering aside as he strode out of the building and across Great Russell Street. He went into the Museum Tavern, ordered a pint of half-and-half, settled himself beside the window with a view of the museum entrance, and waited.

Two hours later, as the museum closed, the man who had been sitting at desk G7 hurried across the concourse. He wore a long overcoat and a peaked worker's cap, in a Continental style, and he held a raft of papers under his arm. Wiggins finished the last of his latest pint, waved a hand at the barman, and went after the man.

Ivan, for that's how Wiggins thought of him, cut through the traffic at Theobald's Road. He looked around often. Wiggins dipped behind a bus, then reappeared on the other side of the road from Ivan and up ahead. For Wiggins knew this stretch of the road; there wasn't a turning for a quarter-mile at least. Ivan would catch up and pass him. It was always the best move to tail someone from in front.

Wiggins kept his pace even. This was the most promising Ivan he'd seen, a ferrety man with sharp features and bad teeth. Wiggins had no difficulty following him to the Crown Tavern, a lively corner boozer by Clerkenwell Green. The Ivan went in, and Wiggins risked going in after him – after all, if there was one place in London Wiggins could blend in, it was a pub.

He called all the men who sat at desk G7 'Ivan' because that's what Symes called them. It was the desk at which Karl Marx had written *Das Kapital* and *The Communist Manifesto*. Wiggins had been too busy watching Constance at the King's funeral to listen to what Symes was telling him at the time, but he'd realised it later on.

According to Symes, Marx was a hero to many of the revolutionaries. When he returned from Germany, Wiggins had gone back to Symes to see what he'd meant when he'd talked about the Ivans. And sure enough, desk G7 was a magnet for young immigrant scholars vying for a spot at or near the famous desk.

When he could, Wiggins followed an Ivan after the Reading Room had closed. Most of them behaved like real scholars, despite their wild hair and uncut beards. They returned to sober if cheap boarding houses, or ate moderate meals in coffee houses – not one Ivan had led him anywhere near a criminal gang.

That evening, though, as Wiggins regarded his latest Ivan in the Crown Tavern, he knew this was different. Or rather, that the Ivan's friends were.

Two men sat opposite the little Ivan, in an alcove. Empty beer glasses cluttered the table. Cigarettes buzzed between them. It was dark, but Wiggins could make out their muscular frames, the hang of their coats. One of them, a yellow scarf stuffed at his throat, cast glances around the pub at regular intervals. His eyes lingered on Wiggins for an instant, then flicked away. Wiggins didn't look out of place in a pub like this. He never looked out of place in a pub.

The pub was busy, but nevertheless Wiggins could hear the three men talking – though he couldn't understand what they said. Russian, he guessed, the way they barked out the vowels like they had their mouths full. The little Ivan was trying to make a point, but Yellow Scarf and his heavily bearded mate never let him get a word in. They spoke with great passion, and Wiggins might have thought they were having an argument, had he not seen Peter and Yakov and the rest speak like that. He didn't know whether it was a quality of the Russian language, or anarchists in general, but for all they spoke of unity and equality, he couldn't listen to a conversation without thinking it would end in either a pistol or a knife.

'Drowning 'em?'

'Eh?'

'Your sorrows.' The barmaid gestured at the near empty glass.

Wiggins picked it up. 'They're clinging to the wreckage.' He knocked back the last of the beer and handed her the glass. She smiled but Wiggins looked away sharply, his eye caught by movement in the mirror behind the bar.

The little Ivan was leaving. He gathered up his papers, nodding at Yellow Scarf and the Beard. Wiggins checked himself. Another pint on the way; too odd to scarper without drinking it. But more to the point, the Ivan wasn't made of the right stuff. He wouldn't put a bullet in anyone and he certainly wouldn't run with the likes of Peter and Yakov, at least not unless they had him in a headlock. Wiggins put a coin on the bar, and waited for the pint. The Ivan wasn't going anywhere interesting.

Yellow Scarf and the Beard continued drinking. Wiggins – in

the mirror – even saw them add a couple of shots to their beer glasses. They laughed. They argued. They got drunker. But they looked like the kind of men who would sober up in an instant. The instant it took to kill you. Wiggins nursed his beer.

Eventually the two men got up. Wiggins finished his drink and kept watch as the Russians bumbled through the late drinkers and out onto the street. He stood up and glanced at the clock. Gone midnight.

'I'll be done here in half an hour,' the barmaid said lightly, almost under her breath.

Wiggins hesitated, out of politeness more than anything else. 'Night.' He saluted with one finger, averted his eyes and was gone.

On the way out, he stole a small hunting cap from the hooks by the door and thrust his own flat cap into his pocket. He made out the two Russians as they headed east. The yellow scarf flashed in the gaslight, then he saw their forms by the windows of the Kodak HQ on Clerkenwell Road, lit up like a gunnery.

The two men kept up a good pace. Wiggins could hear them breaking out into song as they went first right, then left, then right again, down ever tightening alleyways. They skated north of Smithfield and into the poorer areas. The street lights grew sparser, and the noises less pronounced. It was deep into the night by this time. It was never truly dark in London, the centre of the world, but it was dark enough to die.

Wiggins found it easier and easier to keep to the shadows, to know that he hadn't been seen. Following two people was far easier than one, for a pal acts as reassurance. There's nothing like a friend to make you feel safe.

But he was alone. And all of a sudden, it felt like a trap. The ever-darkening twists and turns, the seeming oblivion of the two men ahead, falling back into the hellhole of the East End. But it was too late now. If he was ever going to find Peter, then this was the walk he had to take.

Suddenly, Yellow Scarf cried out in satisfaction. Wiggins crouched down behind a pile of rubbish. The bearded man slapped Yellow Scarf on the back as they pushed open the door of a terraced house on the corner. A pale light fanned onto the street for a second, and then they were gone. Wiggins let out his breath. They hadn't been doubling back at all. They'd been lost.

He pushed himself deep into the rubbish, and wished he was two pints lighter. They were in one of the poor streets near Bethnal Green. The front windows of the house were dark, but Wiggins knew these houses had back rooms, and small yards behind. They were normally multiple occupancy, with a family to each room on all three floors.

A rotten-egg smell caught in his nostrils and wouldn't let go. Wherever the two men had gone, it hadn't been the front rooms. Wiggins held a hand over his nose and considered his options. He couldn't stay in the street. There was no cover. The rubbish worked in the dark, but come dawn he'd be there for all to see – and not just the Russians across the road. Everyone would be out. He could go back to his digs, but there was no guarantee the Russians would still be there come tomorrow. He could hardly go in. Last time he gatecrashed a dive like this, he'd ended up near dead and in prison.

Wiggins stood up. He carefully scraped eggshells from his trousers, keeping his eyes on the door of the house. Nothing moved. Faint light spilled from a gas lamp on the far corner. Far off, a dog barked once. He stumbled across the road, like a drunk, and fell on the pavement near the house. He cursed, hauled himself up using the wall, and carried on his way. At the door to the house, he tripped again, cursed drunkenly, and rose onto one knee.

People were inside and awake, and not just the two Russians he'd followed from the Crown. Wiggins could feel the movement, he could sense it. He put the palm of his hand to the door. It fluttered and creaked. A distant murmur of conversation. Not a murmur, Wiggins realised, but a muffled roar. There were people in there, in a back room, and there were a lot of them.

He carried on stumbling. At the corner, he turned, straightened and felt the side of the end-of-terrace house. It was darker than the pit on this side street, with only the faint memory of a light spilling from the main street's far-off lamp.

But Wiggins couldn't wait for the moon. He cracked his shoulders, pulled his cap tight and reached up. In one fast movement, he was astride the wall that ran alongside the pavement. He crawled until he reached what he was looking for. Another wall, perpendicular to the one he was on, that ran along the back of the terrace. He turned along it, so that he was looming above the house's backyard.

That was when he heard them.

Three voices, Russian again, barking at each other in the yard behind the house. Wiggins, teetering high above them, didn't move. If he even crouched down, the movement would betray him. Not that the men seemed intent on anything other than themselves and their cocks. Wiggins felt the steam in the air, the hot stench, the splatter, as all three relieved themselves against the wall beneath him.

He could only make out the tops of their heads. None of them spoke while they pissed, but the bulky one on the left finished first, stepped back and pushed the other two against the wall. They exclaimed angrily. The bulky form laughed and turned back to the house. Wiggins began to let out his breath as the other two turned to follow him.

A lantern appeared at the door, casting a sudden golden glow. Wiggins dropped from view before he could see who carried it, holding on with arms stretched above him, on the other side of the wall. He daren't drop down to the ground, for fear of alerting them.

The man with the lantern barked at the pissers. His voice had an air of authority, of sophistication, superiority. It had the ring of power, lightly worn.

And to Wiggins, it had the ring of familiarity.

His body strained against the wall. He listened as the men grumbled their way back inside. The lantern's buttery glow did not move. Over the death-cold air, Wiggins heard the rustle of a sweet being unwrapped, the paper tossed aside.

Wiggins shook with the strain. Not only his fingers, his wrists and his arms, but now even his chest protested. His heart beat rapid and raw. For he knew the owner of the voice, the man who stood not five feet away, sucking on a sweet.

Finally, the lantern light flared above him and swung away into the house.

Wiggins clambered back onto the wall, legs astride. He rested his head flat on the bricks, breathing hard, realisation, relief and terror breaking over him like a wave off the Cape.

The relief didn't last long. He could barely make out the back of the house, but he knew now it contained at least four men, probably more.

And one of those men was Peter the Painter.

He'd waited more than a year for this moment but now his mind was flooded with indecision and fatigue. He was tired, oh so tired. He kept his head on the brickwork, let his hands hang either side, and tried to think. Going in there now would be suicide, even if he wasn't spent. He realised he'd been up since six, he hadn't eaten since for ever, and he was at least six pints down. The thought crossed his mind that he should wait, or find a lookout post further up the road, or go to the police. As these options flitted through his mind, he closed his eyes at last.

'Oww!'

Wiggins's eyes popped open with a start. Someone had fallen into the yard beneath him.

'For Christ's sake!'

'Jax, is that you?' Wiggins hissed into the darkness.

'My ankle's bust.'

'Shh . . .'

But the warning came too late. The back door of the house swung open. '*Privet?*' someone barked.

The lantern swung into view. 'Quick.' Wiggins reached down towards Jax. The light caught for a second in her startled eyes. She put her hand upwards.

The first man came thumping towards them. Wiggins sensed others at the door. Dressed, awake, alive, angry. 'Fack sake,' Jax screamed.

'Now!' Wiggins pulled at her arm.

'*Moy pistolet,*' someone shouted.

Wiggins pulled Jax up just as the first man lunged for her legs. They scuttled along the wall, Blondin style.

A brick skimmed his shoulder. Another burst of angry Russian.

Wiggins dropped Jax to the pavement, then jumped down after her.

'My ankle.'

Wiggins swung her onto his back and sprinted, the shouts of the Russians ringing in their ears.

They pushed west, then a left and a right. Wiggins's breathing grew louder and more laboured. Yet still they heard faint cries in the distance. He couldn't carry her much longer. They turned into an open artillery ground. Black as hell's teeth. He hustled her deep into the darkness.

'Where are we?' Jax whispered.

'Lie down, next to me. Flat, quiet.'

They both lay on their chests in the dust. Wiggins took great gulps of air.

'Is it him?'

'Shh.'

They were in a small artillery ground in the City. It was like a square, with a barracks building at one end and buildings lining each side. Wiggins knew the place long since, and he hoped the street lamps didn't penetrate this far into the space. Certainly, he could see almost nothing around him.

But he could hear all right. '*Razbros!*' More hushed Russian followed; he guessed at least five, maybe six men.

'Wiggins,' Jax whispered. Her voice quivered. Wiggins put his hand on her back, soft. He could outrun them alone. Not with Jax. And he couldn't fight either. They were sure to have guns.

He felt Jax's heart beating with his hand on her back, too fast. The Russians had gone quiet. Nothing stirred. Maybe they'd skirted around the square, maybe they'd—

BANG! BANG!

Jax cried out. Another Russian shout, more.

'Go, go, go.' He grabbed her and ran.

More shots. One two three, a barrage.

Mausers, Wiggins knew. Semi-automatic. But knock-offs, fake, inaccurate.

He pulled Jax through the gate at the far end of the square. She cried out in pain, but carried on. More guts than half the army he knew. 'Smithfield,' he urged her.

'What?' she gasped.

They heard their pursuers shouting now, scrabbling over the ground behind them. The gunshots would've woken half of Clerkenwell. But still they were pursued. These men meant business.

Jax limped badly. Wiggins thrust his arm under her shoulder. 'You go,' she said.

'Smithfield.'

He slung her over his shoulders, fireman style, and careened around the corner into Smithfield Market.

At last, people! It wasn't long past four in the morning, but London's biggest meat market was already open. Wiggins, Jax still on his shoulders – this time like a cow's carcass, carried up from the cold storage – jogged into the brightly lit east entrance.

'Fack me, we selling scrote now?' a butcher called out.

'A penny on the pound,' someone else said, and they laughed.

Wiggins shrugged Jax to her feet. 'Keep walking,' he said, glancing around.

They moved through the market, under its great roof, as natural as they could. Pink carcasses swinging on long hooks, legs of lamb racked up like shells, a stall selling pig's heads. Jax stopped in front of them. 'Let's stick here, till it's light.' She winced.

Wiggins looked back. Two bobbing heads, thick black hair on end, unhatted. They weren't going anywhere. Up ahead, another shape. He pointed. 'They've got us covered.'

Jax's eyes widened. They began again, slowly. Off to their left, through the hanging meat, she gestured. 'They wouldn't—'

Two more men barrelled towards them along a line of beef carcasses. Wiggins swung his feet at the beef, cannoning it into the men. 'Run,' he shouted.

They hustled down a side alley. Up ahead, another shadow, two, three, closing. Jax skidded to a halt. 'What—?'

A man with a moustache and thick black hair came towards them with a gun. Jax froze. Wiggins looked up. The man stopped, steadied himself and pulled up the weapon with a straight right arm.

'No!' Jax cried.

Wiggins shoulder-charged her through a doorway off to their left. He helped her onto a ladder that led downwards into the darkness. 'Slide,' he said.

They gripped the side rails one on top of the other and disappeared into the black.

A clanking, groaning roar rose up the ladder. Jax exclaimed as she fell to the ground, and Wiggins dropped down next to her onto gravel.

From above, Wiggins could hear the Russians arguing. And then the ladder began to wobble and bend in his hand.

He looked around, peering into the night. Out of the blackness, two lights suddenly appeared, coming towards them at pace. A train, cranking up the speed.

'Now!' He half hauled, half threw Jax into one of the cargo carriages as it accelerated past. He jumped in after her. The train picked up speed.

'Ugh!' Jax cried out in disgust.

They were both covered in blood and bones. The cargo car stank of death, but not their own. Wiggins bent out of the side and looked back. Their pursuers, moving shadows in the darkness, dropped down too late to get the train. He slumped back among the butchers' waste.

'Market has its own trains,' he said at last. 'Brings the beasts in, takes the rubbish out.' He breathed, heavy and deep, and didn't care a stuff about the smell. They were alive.

'What the hell were you doing there?' he said eventually, as the train clunked and clicked south.

'What was I doing there? What you asked me to, you nonce. Looking for Peter.'

'You should've come straight to me,' he gasped.

'I heard rumours, is all. What you want with him anyway?'

'I told ya. He killed my best mate. I'm doing it for Bill.'

Jax winced. The train swung left out of the tunnel and into the dawn, towards Blackfriars Bridge. 'Yeah, but he's dead.'

'It's not like that.'

'Wot, he ain't dead?'

Wiggins said nothing. The train rocked over the bridge.

'Do I get me fiver then?'

He stood up. 'Come on, this is us.' The train had slowed to the set of points between Waterloo and London Bridge. Wiggins clambered over the end of the cart. He pulled Jax to a stand next to him, on the running board. She clung to his waist, squeezed against him, stinking of blood and death and all, but still, it moved him, the physical contact. 'Easy,' he said into her ear, then together they jumped and rolled onto the gravel verge.

Jax's ankle obviously stung something rotten. She could hardly walk. 'Let's go to Sal's,' Wiggins said. They scrambled through the bush, over the wall and out onto the road.

Sal's hut appeared through the grey mist. Wiggins heard the *clack clack clack* as she pulled open the shutters. Jax's breath was fast and heavy, its plumes streaming out in front of them as she limped beside him. Sal turned. She waved first, then hustled towards them.

'What the bleedin' hell . . . ?'

'Shut up, Ma.'

Sal hugged her tight, glaring at Wiggins.

Once inside, with hot tea and toast, and a compress on Jax's ankle, Wiggins helped Sal with the doorsteps while Jax sat by the stove. He'd sponged down his jacket as best as he could, but his trousers were still streaked with blood, and he smelled of death and offal.

'Ain't you had enough of them bleedin' anarchists?'

'Sorry, Sal. I won't ask her again.'

'What about the coppers?'

He looked at her for a moment.

Sal sawed at the bread with venom. She turned to the cups and clattered them in rows by the urn, ready for the morning rush. 'What's she gonna do for brass? She can't run.'

'I'll see her right.'

'Yeah, you do that. And leave her out of it, whatever it is.'

'I'm not sure myself,' Wiggins muttered.

He'd found Peter. And whatever gang he was a part of now, they meant business. There must have been at least ten in that house, and they were obviously planning something. To risk running after them, to shoot, too, even in Smithfield, meant they were either desperate or on the verge of doing something desperate. They were certainly tooled up.

Another thing intrigued him. Although Peter had the charm and the brains, Wiggins guessed that the leader was the man with the gun in the market, handsome, with his moustache and thick black hair. Peter preferred to defer to, or lay the blame on, more like, someone else. That's what he'd tried with Arlekin last year, and now the same again. He wasn't the figurehead, but Wiggins would lay money that Peter was manipulating the direction of the gang.

He couldn't help but feel a surge of grim satisfaction, though, despite the near miss. For Peter was in London. He was preparing to show his face again. And Wiggins would be there when he did.

Sal's mention of the coppers got him thinking. They wouldn't listen to him, but they might listen to Kell. He dusted down his hands, determined to get to him at once. If he could persuade Kell to talk to Special Branch, they might raid the house. Kell hated Wiggins talking to him about anything other than German spies, but at least this was a concrete tip-off. If nothing else, the cops might recover some guns. It would probably be too late anyway, but it was worth a shot.

'Where now?' Sal said.

'I've gotta get to work.'

'I thought you was working down the docks?' Sal said, absently. She moved over to Jax and examined her ankle once more. 'Put it up, girl. Rub some mother's ruin in.' She measured out a glass of gin and handed it to her.

'Take her to the bones,' Wiggins said.

'You think I don't want to?' She rounded on him angrily. 'Think we can afford the doc? Where do you think we're living? We ain't all got toffs looking out for us now, we ain't yours to do what you like wiv, just cos you've got a shilling in your pocket.'

Wiggins stepped back. 'I'm just . . .' He shook his head, not quite sure what he was doing.

She gestured at the door, pointing him on his way. Jax looked up at him, forlorn and pained. He turned to go.

'Wiggins.' Sal called him back. Her face was hot and red, and she was still angry. She handed him a torn piece of paper. 'I near forgot, what wiv you being a selfish arsehole and all. Here's that list, from the drivers, 'bout the Embassy. Them's some regulars.'

'Ta,' he nodded. He glanced at the list. Then he looked more closely and counted them off: one, two, three, four at least. 'I don't bloody believe it!'

16

'Impossible,' Kell said, aghast.

'Could be a coincidence. Then again, I could be the King of Siam,' Wiggins replied. 'I don't believe in 'em. Mr Holmes didn't believe in 'em neither.'

'Show me again.'

The two men bent over Kell's desk and compared the lists. On one side, in elegant copperplate writing, Kell's list of Committee attendees – prime suspects in the case of the Whitehall leak of information. On the other side, in Sal's rough pencil markings, the return addresses of a number of Embassy 'clients'. Those 'regulars' used to taking cabs to and from the bawdy house of choice.

Kell pointed at Sal's list. 'I recognise most of the names on here,' he said to himself in disgust. 'It's pitiful.'

He'd put his key in the door that morning to yet again find out that his agent had somehow entered the office before him, although this time Wiggins had announced his arrival by smell alone. He stank. Kell had primed himself to upbraid Wiggins in the strongest possible terms, but the bedraggled, exhausted-looking man had leapt up from his desk and shown him the two lists almost immediately.

Now, as Kell looked over them a third time, he could hear Wiggins pacing the room behind him, obviously agitated. 'Another thing,' Wiggins said. 'You've got to get on to Special Branch sharpish.'

'Oh?'

'Nasty gang. Wiv shooters.'

The telephone buzzed into life on the desk. Kell ignored it. 'Not now, Simpkins,' he shouted. The bell stopped.

'I'll see what I can do.'

'Now,' Wiggins said. 'Or it'll be too late.'

'Look here, Wiggins.' Kell moved behind his desk and adopted as stern a tone as possible. 'I will not be lectured to by you, of all people. Why are you so anxious?'

Wiggins stopped his pacing and glared at him. 'There ain't much time.'

Kell held up the Embassy list. 'What are we going to do about this?'

Before Wiggins could reply, someone opened the door without knocking. Wiggins swung around. Kell looked up, startled.

'Hello, Mr Wiggins,' Constance said.

'My dear? What are you doing here?'

'Ma'am.' Wiggins nodded, and tried to brush down his filthy trousers.

'Are you quite all right, Wiggins?' she said.

The telephone burst into startling life once more. 'Simpkins,' Kell bellowed. 'Not now.'

'How do you know where I work?' Kell said, once the phone had stopped ringing. He held up his hand in what he realised might be an aggressive way. Wiggins glanced at him, then at Constance.

She broke the silence, unfazed. 'I *am* your wife, if you remember. It's natural I know where you work. I am curious.'

Kell shook his head. His wife still surprised him. Not only could she evade a tail, now, it seemed, she could tail him. It was most irritating, and unsettling. She rarely did things without reason. 'Wiggins is debriefing me.' Kell looked at him. 'On the docks. If you could give us a moment.'

The phone started once more.

'Oh, don't mind me. I popped in to say hello. I'm off to the Army and Navy Stores. Thought I'd pay my regards, though I didn't expect quite such a warm welcome. Is someone going to answer that telephone?'

'Simpkins!'

Constance began an idle turn around the room, looking at the maps on the wall. She made absolutely no attempt to leave. The telephone finally stopped.

'Go on.' Kell nodded at Wiggins. 'What news of West India Docks?'

Wiggins hesitated. 'Don't mind me,' Constance said airily.

Kell flopped his hands by his side helplessly. He trusted Wiggins had read him well enough to know that he didn't want to talk about the other matters in front of her.

'All they want is a pay rise. I told you.'

'Is that all? I hear the last meeting with the management was quite fraught.'

'What you expect?' Wiggins said. 'They's gone piecemeal, costs 'em a tanner a day, lest they break a back. And no guarantee of any work, yet they can't work elsewhere neither.'

Kell sighed. 'Spare me the soapbox speech. Just tell me – this being your job – is there any unrest planned? Any exceptional action?'

'Is this your work now?' Constance interjected. 'I thought you were about fighting dastardly Teutons, stopping world war, that sort of thing.'

Kell looked at her. She held in her hand a small stuffed bird, a piece of dusty decoration that came with the rooms. She examined it a moment longer, popped it back on a side table, and smiled at him. 'Isn't domestic insurrection the business of Special Branch?'

Yes, and your photograph is pinned to their wall, Kell did not say. *Who are you seeing? What are you planning? Why are you here?* He stared at her, almost reached out his hand . . . His mother on the platform at Paddington . . . Instead, he said, 'There is an intricate web, my dear, stretching countrywide. Many mysteries that defy simple understanding. Much like the mysteries of the human heart.'

She held his eye for a moment, searching.

Wiggins coughed.

'Well?' Kell turned to him. 'I'm waiting.'

'They's just a bunch of lads who want to be paid.'

'Anything planned? I repeat, this is your job, for which you are well paid.'

Wiggins hesitated. 'Wednesday,' he said. 'A protest, down the offices.'

'And the ringleaders?'

'I didn't catch a name.'

'Well invent one, for heaven's sake.' Kell let out a sigh of exasperation.

'Is this the Hidden Hand at work? The magic of spy-catching?'

'Yes, thank you, dear. That is most helpful.'

The telephone began to ring again. Kell looked down at it, then back at his wife. 'As you can see, I am rather busy. Simpkins!'

She raised an eyebrow and picked up her umbrella. The phone stopped ringing. 'I wondered if you would like to have luncheon, in the Army and Navy, once I'm done. But I see that perhaps Mr Wiggins needs you more urgently.'

'I need to speak to Special Branch, as it happens,' he said, glancing at Wiggins. 'Was there anything else?'

She hesitated at the door. Once again, Kell regretted his tone. Much as he'd like her to be his employee, she was not. He tried to smile, but she didn't respond. Instead, she nodded at Wiggins. 'Good day, Mr Wiggins. And please, don't take it amiss if I say that you need a change of clothes. Perhaps you should come with me.'

'Ta for the offer,' he said. 'But the boss is driving me something awful.'

'Yes, I can see that. Finding spies wherever he can.' She pulled open the door, stopped, and then delivered her final salvo. 'Oh, by the way, Vernon, I've invited Lady Quinn and her husband to dinner next month.'

'Lady Quinn?' Kell said, his heart dropping. He knew exactly who she was, who she was married to, and what Constance was going to say.

'Sir Patrick's wife. I met her the other day at a coffee morning. Absolutely delightful woman. We quite struck up a friendship. I hope that won't embarrass you, dear?' she added, needlessly.

She swept from the room, leaving Wiggins looking down in

dismay at his clothes, while Kell looked to the future dinner date with Sir Patrick Quinn with equal discomfort.

'Right.' Kell rapped his knuckles on the desk. 'Get down to the docks on Wednesday. Give me names and details of the ringleaders – real or imagined, it doesn't matter. Just make the report look genuine.'

'You talking to Special Branch about them shooters out east? I've written the address down and everything,' he said, handing the paper to Kell, though even as he did so he knew in his heart that Peter would already be gone. The East End was a warren, and Peter's mob knew every one of its holes.

'I said I'd deal with it,' Kell replied icily. He couldn't boss around his wife, but he'd have a good go at controlling Wiggins. He was the only person left who listened to him, and even then only when it suited. 'Most importantly, we need to act on this blasted whorehouse.'

'Can't we raid it? Send the rozzers in.'

'Why?'

'Well . . .' Wiggins hesitated. His face coloured. 'It ain't right.'

'You seem to think that because you work for me, the Metropolitan Police Force is at your own private disposal. They simply won't do as I say without good reason.'

'What then?'

The telephone began to ring again on the desk between them. Kell shouted, 'Simpkins!' But this time, the phone kept ringing.

Finally, Kell picked it up himself. 'I'm not here,' he said into the horn, and put it down. Then picked it up again and said, 'Get me Special Branch.'

~

Wiggins popped a sweet into his mouth as he walked through the plush back garden of number 14 Ranleigh Terrace. He opened the back door without knocking, then took the servants' staircase two at a time until he reached the very top of the house.

He came to a long, thin corridor and opened the first door. 'Anything?'

Simpkins, Kell's clerk, sat on an improvised stool at the window, looking down on the street with a Brownie in his hand. He turned to Wiggins, grinned, and put the camera down. 'Nothing particularly suspicious,' he said. 'Glad to see you. I'm famished.'

Wiggins looked at the logbook. 'Three cabs, a car and a couple of walk-ups?'

'That's about the size of it,' Simpkins said, gathering up his hat, scarf and coat. 'I say, you haven't seen my gloves, have you? It's freezers. Haven't been this cold since Fourth Form.'

'You've got them on,' Wiggins said, not taking his eyes from the log.

'Ha ha, look at me. Well, well, I better get back to the office. Have a good night of it.'

Wiggins grunted, and picked up the camera.

Simpkins opened the door, hesitated, and then said in a soft tone, 'I say, old man, if the chief does show, I'd pop another of those mints if I were you. Feel a bit squiffy myself, ha ha!'

Wiggins glared at him for a moment, then nodded. Simpkins was your typical public-school oaf – Wiggins had seen enough of them in the army – but he meant well. He certainly wouldn't grass him up for being one or two over the odds. 'Mind them stairs,' he said, and turned to the window.

They hadn't got anywhere in weeks. Kell had ordered him, along with Simpkins, to mount a surveillance operation on the Embassy. They'd set up in one of the servants' rooms in a house almost opposite. The family were away, and Kell had pulled a few strings to get them in there. Simpkins and Wiggins were left undisturbed. They had a high vantage point, but limited resources. They would take photographs with the Eastman Brownie, and make notes of the registrations of the private cars and the licence numbers of the hansom cabs. Simpkins would try to follow these up with names and addresses, but it was slow going.

When he'd first confronted Kell, Wiggins was outraged that they couldn't just raid the place. Kell had warned against it, especially given the social standing of some of the customers.

He'd been pleased with the bank of information he was growing. It was the place to be for the highest slice of London society. Tommy had really entered the top drawer. From lifting clicks off two-a-penny shoppers down Chapel Street Market and dipping the drunks at pitch-out, to the highest in the land. He'd risen, with the scum.

A motorised cab pulled up. *Click, whirr*, got the number. A tall, thin man in top hat and tails flitted across the pavement like a ghost. It was already beginning to get dark. He couldn't get a view of the faces of the customers as they waited at the door, even when it swung open, spilling warmth and faint music and jollity onto the streets. It wasn't so jolly for Millicent or Poppy, though, was it? Wiggins reminded himself. For all that Kell wanted to find out secrets and who had spilled them, Wiggins owed Poppy.

The man disappeared into the house, and Wiggins took the logbook in his hand once more. By the time they were done, Kell would have something on everyone in London. They had cabs delivering to American, French (course) and Austrian embassies, picking up from most of the gents' gaffes in club-land, the FO, Parliament. The Palace. They were a long way from Vere Street in Lambeth. Would any of 'em have given Millie a second look up that tenement building?

He thought again about Tommy, a mountain of anger and resentment, across the road. What was he going to do – march in there and fight him? Kill him? Go back to the Bloodied Axe? Wiggins couldn't bring himself to move against him without more proof. Tommy must have had him shanghaied, but he didn't know on whose orders, he didn't know who'd killed Poppy, and he didn't know where Millie was or what had happened to her. And brawling with Tommy weren't going to change that. They needed to arrest him.

Peter was a different matter. Special Branch had missed him, so Kell said. Wiggins knew they would; it was the longest of long shots. He and his gang had disappeared back into the East End.

But Wiggins wouldn't miss him again. Peter would show his face soon enough, or the gang would, anyway. You don't pack a house like that, with people like that, and guns like that, unless you mean to use them. And whatever happened, he'd go back to the Library, go back to following the Ivans: it'd worked once and it would work again. It would just take one Ivan at a time.

He set his sights back on the Embassy and waited. Waited for evidence of murder, of spying, of smuggling, of anything at all to give them an excuse to go in – but so far nothing but people had gone in, and nothing but people had come out. The whores, very occasionally, the boy to and from school, and Tommy to the pub. And the endless supply of Freds.

The street lights jagged and fizzed ever brighter in the night. Wiggins found himself waiting, hoping, wanting to see someone else come out of that door. He waited to see Martha.

'Now, why would you be wanting to sully yourself with all that dirty work, Captain Kell, when you come home to this every night?' Sir Patrick Quinn grinned ghastly at Constance.

A young footman lifted up a gleaming tureen from the table between them.

Kell tried not to stare at his wife in astonishment. She was actually smiling back at Quinn, seemingly charmed by his condescension, positively basking in his leers.

'Especially,' Quinn went on, glancing back at Kell, 'as it's not going so well, just now, is it?' He smirked. 'If you were my wife, dear, and if this were my table, I'm not sure I would ever want to work again.'

'No shop, Paddy,' Lady Quinn snapped at his elbow. 'Not in front of the ladies. And less of that Donegal charm too. You're old enough to be Mrs Kell's father, so you are.'

Kell bent to the last of his soup before it was almost lifted out of his hand. He cast a quick glance around the table. To his left, Soapy and his wife, Alice (known to Constance as 'silly, soppy Alice'), a nervous, angular woman with feather-light hair and an overbite. Soapy raised his eyebrows towards Kell and gestured at Quinn, who had somehow managed to seat himself at the head of the table.

A sumptuous array of plump white turbots appeared, with chilled Chablis glasses sparkling in the light of the electric chandelier.

That bastard Quinn, thought Kell with a bitter, Wiggins-accented pang. As soon as Wiggins had told him of the East End hideout of an anarchist gang, Kell had tried to get hold of Quinn on the telephone. They didn't like each other, of course, but Kell had hoped that such a tip might thaw relations between them – the capture of such an armed gang would be quite a coup for Quinn and Special Branch.

It had taken days. First, Quinn wouldn't take his call. Then he'd left him in the waiting room at Scotland Yard for three hours before leaving by the back way, claiming an emergency. Finally, Quinn had returned the telephone call and reluctantly agreed to send down some officers and an inspector to the address Wiggins had supplied. Kell went with them.

A large, multiple-occupancy house somewhere in the East End. Kell had rarely seen such dirt and filth. The beds were flea-ridden, human excrement caked the backyard and the stench was unbearable. Police constables barrelled through each of the rooms, shouting, while Kell took a look around. No wonder it was dirty, he thought. There was no running water. And now no people.

'Deserted,' said the inspector. 'False lead,' he added, in disgust.

'Can't you see who was here?' Kell asked. 'The neighbours, the landlord?'

'No one will tell us nothing,' the inspector spat. 'Unless we arrest 'em. And we ain't got proof of stuff all. If you'll pardon the phrase. The chief'll be livid. We're as busy as a knocking shop at Christmas. If you'll—'

'Yes, Constable, I understand.' It was embarrassing, Kell reflected, as he returned to the office. The news was all round Whitehall within hours, how Kell's specialised intelligence division had sent Special Branch on a wild goose chase.

Judging by the smile on his face now, as he devoured the turbot, perhaps anger wasn't the overriding emotion Quinn felt at Kell's humiliation.

'I am sorry, my dear, I truly am,' Quinn said to his wife. 'When you are a policeman it is very hard not to talk shop. When you are a policeman, everything is shop.' He burst out laughing at his own witticism.

Constance leaned forward. 'I don't think anyone minds hearing about *your* work, Sir Patrick.' She threw a withering glance at Kell, and went on. 'It's so interesting.'

'This toast is absolutely marvelloso,' Alice said. 'I was prattling away to Cook only the other day. You know, they've made a little machine which means you can make your own toast, *at the table.*'

Constance flicked her eyes away from Quinn for a moment. 'That, too, is interesting, Alice. Tremendously so. But it's not every day we're honoured by the presence of the head of Special Branch.'

'I wouldn't be saying honour, if I were you, Mrs Kell. You're buttering me.' He took a large gulp of wine.

'Excellent sauce, old boy,' Soapy said to Kell. 'Montrachet?'

'No butter, Sir Patrick. Just admiration. Tell me, how many officers do you have under you?'

He put his glass down. The footman hurried around, removing the fish dishes. 'Now, that's an interesting question in turn, Mrs Kell, so it is.'

Cook flitted between the diners, putting down the next course – a dial of perfectly grilled mutton cutlets. A bottle of claret appeared.

'It seems such a big job, that's all,' Constance purred. 'You have so many people to look after, and so many people to worry about. *The Times* is full of such ferment. Workers, the Irish, anarchists, the Indians . . .'

'Suffragettes,' he finished the sentence. He looked at her with level eyes over the rim of his crystal goblet.

'Pah!' Lady Quinn burst out. 'Those silly women will lose their airs and graces soon enough.'

'Isn't this politics?' Alice whispered to her husband.

'Why will they give up?' Kell asked. He tried not to look at Constance, who still seemed entranced by Quinn.

Lady Quinn shovelled a stack of finely cut fried potatoes onto her plate. 'Isn't this latest bill due to pass? Won't landowning women be getting the vote soon? And then it will all be over and we can go back to having babies, and tending home, like we should.'

'This is definitely politics.'

'Hush, my dear,' Soapy murmured. 'I say, old chap, is there another bottle of this stuff? It's quite reminded me why I like to drink.'

Constance scraped back her chair. 'I'm so sorry, Soapy. Wilkins! Another bottle of the '96,' she hollered. Lady Quinn looked up from her food in astonishment. Quinn grinned. Constance bent back to the table and pointed a fork at Soapy. 'You think the bill will pass?'

He licked his lips and offered a slow and lazy smile. 'Lady Quinn doesn't want us to talk shop. Alice here gets so upset when I talk politics. But what's a man to do when his business *is* politics?'

'Ah, at last,' Kell said quickly, as the cook re-entered the dining room.

She leaned in and placed in the middle of the table a glistening, smoking boulder of beef so big it cast a shadow. 'The remove.'

'We want meat! We want bread! We want fair pay for a fair day!'

Across town from Kell's sumptuous dinner party, Wiggins belted out a chant with the rest of the dockers. He was squeezed into the middle of a three-hundred-strong protest as they waited outside the warehouse headquarters of the Port Authority in Cutler Street. The protest had started earlier that day at West India Docks.

Wiggins had been to a couple of these strikes before, on Kell's orders, posing as a casual docker. He had the look, he had the lingo; it was easy enough. What was hard was being anything other than sympathetic. Most of the lads were casuals too, which meant if a ship didn't come in to West India that day, then no pay. Broke your ankle yesterday? No pay. In fact, *We might pay the lot of you less because we can* was the general drift. What was worse, the Port Authority had just taken over and cut the 'plus' money. There was now no overtime.

They'd marched westward earlier in the day and Wiggins had moved himself nearer the front, to the leaders. Policemen dotted their course but made no immediate move to stop them. As the light had faded, Wiggins noticed more coppers in attendance, and more of them out of uniform.

'Spotters,' he called softly to those around him.

'Wot?' someone said.

One of the men in the front, a lantern-jawed titan with bucket hands, glanced back sharply at him. 'Front, right, on the walls.' Wiggins gestured with his eyes. 'Cover your faces. They's Special Branch.'

Lantern Jaw pulled up a scarf over his face and many of the leaders did the same. 'Wot's a spotter?' a young scrap next to him asked.

Wiggins had looked up at the men peering over a high wall as the march wound into the City. 'Looking for trouble, stirrers. Making memories, pictures, so they know who to target.'

'All's we want is a fair wage,' the boy said. 'Ain't nuffin' wrong with that, is there?'

'You new?'

'And poor. I worked one day last week, for a shilling. I've got nippers.'

Peter would love this, Wiggins thought, as the march funnelled into the darkness around Cutler Street, torches bouncing and slicing in the wind. Real workers, taking on real bosses. Except maybe he wouldn't. This lot didn't care about a bollocks revolution. They didn't care about imperialism. They just wanted a job that paid enough to feed their family. He looked around at the dockers, poorly shod, thin jackets pinned around their necks with gloveless hands, breath wreaths twisting into the air above them. They didn't even want to fight; they just wanted to work.

Up ahead, the great warehouse loomed over them, the gates locked. Wiggins shivered and pulled his coat tighter. The crowd moved and whinnied like a dray horse pulling for the off; feet stamped, fag smoke plumed here and there; and the mass of men shifted and waited and cursed. Around them, it had gone quiet. Too quiet. The police so in evidence on the walk up had suddenly disappeared. Wiggins began to hustle forward to the leaders. 'This ain't right,' he hissed.

'Who *are* you?' Lantern Jaw turned to him. 'And what do you know?'

'Trust me,' Wiggins replied.

A surge in the crowd slung him sideways into the face of the boy he'd been talking to. 'Get out,' Wiggins said again. 'It ain't right.'

The boy looked up at him, before falling back into the crowd. Wiggins whipped his head round. First one whistle, then a second, and a third, until the blackness sang.

The warehouse gates swung open. Out of nowhere, a troop of police horses streamed into the crowd. Panic, fear, flight. A phalanx of police on foot appeared amid the crush.

Wiggins was pushed to the floor in the rush, the desperate scrabble for escape. Around him the whistles sang, but now they were drowned out by the shouts and cries of the men. Horses ten feet high, real, shod, deadly. Truncheons whirled, boots swung. Heads cracked. Dockers flailed arms helplessly. Outnumbered, out-armed, trapped.

A face screamed, silenced by a fist. More and more police came funnelling out of the warehouse behind the horses, a black tide. The torches jagged and fell. 'Run run run!' a voice cried above the din. The protest split apart. Wiggins was pushed and harried down a side alley and away. All around him, dockers fled, flitting into the side streets in desperation, despair and blood.

Constance couldn't wait long enough for the coffee to go cold. She spent an interminable twenty minutes in the drawing room with Lady Quinn and Alice, while the men smoked in the dining room.

'The pheasant was more than passable,' Lady Quinn said. 'And the ices were exquisite. I do wonder about the sardines, though. Does your cook buy them tinned, do you think, Mrs Kell? Constance?'

'Sorry, miles away. Gosh, is that the time?' She got up and moved to the door. 'I'm sure the gentlemen will be leaving soon.'

Sir Patrick Quinn liked her, she could tell, but she hadn't got far enough with her questioning. She'd told Dinah and the girls that she'd have some information for them soon, using her 'contacts', but she'd managed to unearth precious little. She didn't even know how many men Special Branch deployed against their cause; she didn't know whether they intended to scale up their operations; she didn't even know which of his detectives ran the surveillance against them.

'Perhaps you're right, Lady Quinn.' Alice sipped at her coffee absently. 'I am very suspicious of canning.'

'What are you *talking* about?' Constance couldn't contain herself any longer. She glared at the two women.

They looked up at her, surprised. Just then, she heard the dining-room door open and the raised, half-drunk voices of the men echoed across the tiles. 'Thank God,' she muttered, and threw open the door onto the hallway.

Her husband ushered Sir Patrick and Soapy out of the dining room. The former droned on in his excruciating Irish drawl. 'That's the view at the Yard, I'm thinking. It would be no dishonour, Captain, no dishonour at all.'

'To resign a command?' Kell hissed icily. Constance, even from across the room, could tell he shook with suppressed rage.

'Constance!' Soapy cried, alerting the two men to her presence. 'A triumph of an evening, if I may say so. The cellar, the food, the company. Now, where is Alice, we must be going.'

The hustle and bustle of coats and scarves and goodbyes and *see you soon*s began. Constance stood by Kell, an ice volcano, his antipathy to Quinn palpable.

'Sir Patrick,' she purred. 'I would so like to visit you at work. Perhaps with our eldest, Victor? I visited Vernon but his operation is so very dull.' She cast Kell what she hoped was a pitying glance. 'In comparison, at least, with the vital and energetic work that you run out of the Yard.' She rested a hand on his shoulder.

He leered at her once more, the port high in his cheeks. 'Five years ago, maybe, Mrs Kell, maybe you could have taken a gander. But we've become a very hard school now. I'm thinking it's no place for a woman such as yourself. Thank the Lord, we now have a Home Secretary who knows the importance of a firm hand. We are taking ever sterner measures to combat society's miscreants, so we are. It is manly work.'

'Victor will be so disappointed.' She squeezed his hand. 'He so wants to be a policeman one day.'

'Not army?' He shot a delighted glance at Kell.

Constance went on. 'I wanted him to see the best, in action, as it were.'

'Wasn't there enough butter with the parsnips?' Quinn teased.

'Patrick, are we away?' Lady Quinn glared.

The telephone rang. It leapt and jangled on the side table. They all looked at it, startled. 'That's our cue, what?' Soapy said, stepping to the door. 'Goodbye, old man . . . Constance.'

'I'll get that,' Kell said at last and stepped to the receiver.

Alice and Lady Quinn went out, and Soapy followed them. Quinn, the last to leave, turned on the doorstep and regarded Constance.

'*May* we visit?' she said, imploring him one final time.

He pulled his gloves on, slowly, then fixed her with a steady gaze. Suddenly, all the life and jollity and drunkenness drained from his face, and his eyes were clear and crisp as a winter's morning. 'I'm sure we at the Branch will be seeing you soon, Mrs Kell, to be sure. Goodnight now.'

17

'It's a fucking set-up!' he bawled into the telephone.

'Calm down.' Kell's voice was a reedy crackle. 'Not now. I have guests.'

'Not now, not fucking now! There's boys dying out there,' he cried as he stood at the bar. Heads turned, but Wiggins didn't care. 'Fucking rozzers!'

'Do not swear at me. I am in no mood for insubordination.'

'Insubord-a-fucking-nation? They's killing folk.' He took a breath and glanced around at the rest of the pub. As one, they turned back to their glasses, their conversation, their newspapers. Wiggins realised he must have looked a dreadful sight, shouting into the horn, clothes torn and trampled, hand shaking. He gripped the receiver hard and braced his foot against the wall. 'I ain't doing it,' he said in a hissed whisper. 'I ain't ratting anyone out, and I ain't telling you or any of your bloody mates nothing about no union. Ever.'

'Ratting people out?' It was Kell's turn to raise his voice. 'Who the hell do you think you are? What is it you think you *do*? Get back to Ranleigh Terrace, as planned. Get back to your job. And never, ever call me at home.' The line went dead.

Wiggins stretched his back and felt again the tender part above his hip. He looked back down onto Ranleigh Terrace, at the dark Embassy doors, and wondered whether anything would change. They'd kept watch round the clock on the whorehouse for over a month and the place was as tight as the proverbial.

He'd said as much to Kell the previous week, but the man wouldn't listen to sense. There was only one way to crack open the place as far as Wiggins could see, but Kell wasn't man enough for it. He wasn't man enough for the truth neither.

After the police charge at the warehouse, Wiggins had escaped. He'd copped a horseshoe in the back before scrambling into a side road that led down to the river. It was there, in the crush and panic and mauling, that he looked back for an instant and saw the young father trampled, then beaten. Wiggins tried to turn back, but was swept away by another mounted charge. By the time he looked up, the boy was gone.

He'd stumbled down an alleyway leading to the river, where friendly boatmen were ferrying fleeing dockworkers to safety. From there, Wiggins jumped a tram to the Elephant and Castle. He walked straight up to the barman, ordered two double gins, a pint of half-and-half and a counter for the telephone, which hung just to the right of the bar.

He and Kell hadn't spoken of it since that telephone call in the pub. Instead, the next night and the night after that and so on, Wiggins relieved Simpkins at six and waited, watching men enter and leave that house of ill repute. He still hadn't debriefed Kell about the docks; he would not do it. There'd been nothing in the papers about it – there rarely was – but he'd heard rumours, down the docks and around, about trouble all over the country. It was a battle. And whose side was he on?

All of a sudden, Tommy appeared on the street. His huge form cast shadows left and right, pinned by the two street lamps. He didn't move. Instead, he waited on the pavement, one arm stretched back towards the Embassy steps. Wiggins crouched forward. This wasn't his night for the Axe, and he wasn't going out alone.

A moment later, a woman tapped down the steps and took his arm, ever the lady to his hulking gent. She turned her face up to Tommy, in the lambent glow of the lights. Wiggins started in surprise. Martha. It was too dark for a photograph, but it was Tommy and Martha all right. They set off northwards, on foot, like a courting couple.

Wiggins hesitated. The Embassy still had another night of business ahead. More names to note, more licence numbers to take, another twelve hours of data. He took the backstairs two at a time. He pulled on his cap and ran down the garden, out into the mews. If Tommy and Martha were heading into town, they'd be on the road soon enough. He sprinted, slithering to a halt at the corner.

A small crowd gathered around a brazier, selling sweetmeats and roasted chestnuts, and Wiggins shrank into it, waiting for his turn. Sure enough, a minute or so later, making stately progress, his marks ambled by on the other side of the street, heading into Victoria. They looked for all the world like lovers, with Tommy's head bent down to catch Martha's words. Pantomime lovers, Wiggins hoped.

He pulled his scarf up around his face, shoved his hands into his pockets and set off after them. If they nipped a bus or tram, he wouldn't have a hope. Tommy might be interested in Martha, but he was still an ex-Irregular; he was still sharp enough to spot Wiggins in an enclosed space.

As they broke through Grosvenor Square and then into the hustle and bustle around Victoria Station, Wiggins moved closer. Taxis whizzed by, the trams clattered and sang, and the buses belched and groaned. Pedestrians zigzagged across the roads, streaming to the mainline station in the evening rush. But Tommy was too big to miss, even in such a crowd.

He shepherded Martha across the road. Wiggins realised where they were going, an almost impossible tail to pull off. ROYAL STANDARD MUSIC HALL blazed out in lights. Beneath, in black letters, *Last Night*.

Tommy shoved Martha through the crowded front of house. It took Wiggins a little longer. *Sold Out* signs criss-crossed all the posters. It was the last night before the place was due to be abolished and rebuilt. This meant he had to dip a ticket from a singleton. (No use stealing one ticket only to find yourself sitting next to his mate, or her husband, or some likely lad with half a bottle of gin in him and a Lonsdale Belt.)

The way Martha and Tommy were dressed, nines, suggested they'd be upstairs in the posh seats. He lost sight of them as they joined the throng funnelling through the main double doors.

Large posters were plastered on every available wall. Wiggins jostled in amongst the crowd, pretending to read as he looked for a mark.

The Queen of Comedy MARIE LLOYD
The 3 Laurels
The 4 Figaros
The 5 Hunters
THAT BRUTE SIMMONS

And slashed across each poster: SURPRISE GUEST STAR.

'It'll be that greasy dago Espinosa,' a large man bawled to no one in particular. He peered at the poster. 'Or else that skinny bitch Florrie Forde. Bet you.' He looked around, satisfied with his own ignorance. 'Any money?'

'I take that bet,' Wiggins said. 'A general?'

The big man twisted around, eyeing Wiggins warily. 'Make it two,' he said. 'Back here, after the show. I'll take my buck.'

'Good man.' Wiggins grinned and tapped him on the side in comradely fashion. Then he melted back into the crowd. There wasn't a chance the loudmouth would turn up if he lost the bet, of course, but that wasn't the point.

Two minutes later, Wiggins entered the hall using the big man's ticket – easily nipped from his inside pocket, like taking sweets from a child. The lobby teemed with excited theatregoers, a hodgepodge of classes, clothes and accents. Laughter, chattering, pulling and shoving and all sorts. A young girl was crying some-where, unseen. Jaunty lads broke into song. A glass broke. A cheer. The usual Saturday night out.

Wiggins looked up at the staircase in front of him, up to the circle, all top hats and dinner jackets. The Royal Standard was a mixed bag, not like the music halls he used to go to as a kid, which were full of trash, wall to wall. The Standard took in some quality, albeit quality looking to slum it for the night.

He joined the line filtering into the auditorium. The band had already struck up, and harassed waitresses toted drinks through the throng.

The house rocked. Wiggins squeezed into his seat six rows back. A warm-up man leapt onto the stage. He rapped out a few gags, and the audience roared with laughter and booze and a desire to be entertained by whatever appeared in the footlights.

Wiggins slumped back and circled the theatre with his eyes. Around him, everybody smoked and drank, except the women, who just drank. Great clouds of smoke hung over them. Behind him, the circle sagged down low over the back of the stalls. He could make out the faces of those in the first few rows. Boxes ran down either side of the house, the top seats. Wiggins scanned as the MC went on.

'Enough of this malarkey, no, please. Enough, I say.' The MC waved his hand at the audience. 'You've seen the posters, haven't you? Have you? Missus, please.' Another roar from the stalls. He went on, listing the forthcoming acts. 'Oh, I near forgot. Mr Memory will be on too.' More laughter. More drink.

'But first . . .' the great man up in the lights opened his hands stage right '. . . the Four Figaros!' On bounced four gussied-up male singers, yodelling for all they were worth. A few cheers went up as the band struck a tune, a few groans too.

Wiggins glanced up to his left and there in the second box sat Martha, caught for a moment in the upturned glow of the stage lights. Straight-backed, stately, her face impassive. Tommy appeared at her shoulder, standing, one hand pinned to the base of her neck. His eyes flitted across the crowd, around the circle, back into the pit – never at the stage. Wiggins followed his gaze.

One by the front exit, standing, pulling at his knuckles.

Another at the stalls bar, sipping a half.

A third, arm hanging over the balcony, like a great ape at London Zoo.

He's come tooled up, Wiggins realised with a thrill. This ain't no visit to the halls, Tommy ain't here to be entertained. He's here for business. Wiggins tensed. The next act was up onstage now, the crowd near hysteria, a cackling in his ear. He looked up at Martha, a rictus on her face – fear, pain? Tommy's hand pinned to her neck.

Then suddenly a movement in the back of their box, a flash of another dinner jacket, another man, though Wiggins didn't see a face. Tommy dipped out of the box.

'Where're the lavs?' Wiggins asked as he tried to push towards the aisle, amidst the catcalls and the banter.

'The lavs?' a woman burst out loudly.

'Here, hark at him and the lavs – I'm using me bottle!' the comic on the stage cried, setting up another great roar.

He shot a quick glance up to the box. Martha was staring down at him, shocked. Not the best time in the world to be pointed out as a heckler. But Tommy wasn't in sight. Wiggins dodged out of a side door beneath their box and took the stairs two at a time. It was his only chance before Tommy returned.

Wiggins pulled the heavy curtains aside.

'Get out of it,' Martha hissed, barely turning around. 'It's dangerous.'

'Come wiv me,' he urged. 'Tommy's bad medicine. Come.'

'You don't understand anything.' She swivelled around to stare at him. 'Get out, now, before he comes back.'

Another burst of laughter from the audience. Wiggins crouched down beside her, out of sight of Tommy's lookouts. 'It ain't safe there no more,' he said, pleading with her.

'What are you saying?'

'I can save you,' he said.

She turned her head away. A great barrage of applause from the crowd. Wiggins's eye snagged on a handkerchief on the floor, a flash of a monogram. 'You can't,' she said.

'Will you let me know you're safe at least?'

'You're watching the Embassy?' she said in surprise.

'Jacko!' Tommy shouted from somewhere down the corridor.

'Something bad's coming,' Wiggins said. He wanted to tell her more, to tell her that soon the whole place could be raided, that if Tommy got wind of it, he might do anything to anyone. But all he said was, 'Please.'

Martha looked around, then down at him. 'Top right window, look for the red ribbon. If it ain't there . . .'

He nodded and stood up.

Suddenly a short man in top hat and tails barrelled into him with a loud shout. Heads turned. The audience rippled. The comedian on the stage looked up at the box, and stumbled in his delivery. The short man grabbed Wiggins by the lapels. Clearly quality, judging by his evening wear, he was nine sheets to the wind, and then some. 'Excuse me,' he said. 'Doyouknowthewaytothebar?'

Wiggins just stared at him, pinned by surprise and indecision.

The drunk lurched, one way then the other, clinging on to Wiggins as he did so. Behind him, Tommy suddenly appeared at the curtain with a heavy in tow. He gave an involuntary yowl when he saw Wiggins.

Just then, the sozzled toff tumbled sideways towards the box's balcony. Wiggins caught hold of his collars, but the man flipped over anyway. Wiggins clung on. They fell the five feet to the running board that led to the stage, in full view.

The audience gasped.

The comedian onstage berated the drunk. Out of the corner of his eye, Wiggins saw one of Tommy's men hurry towards them. Tommy himself glared over the box at him in outrage. The drunk had somehow leapt to his feet before Wiggins could and had now stumbled onto the stage proper. He circled the comedian in a seemingly drunken daze. The audience were beginning to laugh.

Wiggins ran onto the stage and dived into the wings. As he did so, he saw Tommy drag Martha away.

The Five Hunters scattered as Wiggins tumbled backstage, casting around for the exit. Gusts of laughter cascaded down from the audience now, clearly in thrall to the Drunk's act.

Wiggins turned left down a corridor but a commotion at the far end put him off. Instead, he dodged right, behind the stage scenery itself. But before he could make good his escape, he caught sight of the heavy from the bar pushing backstage on the other side. *Pinned.*

At that moment the Drunk crashed through the paper backdrop just to his left, a perfectly executed pratfall met with hysteria. The Drunk looked at Wiggins with the brightest eyes he'd ever seen. They shone and danced beneath his craggy brows. And in the instant they met Wiggins's, the eyes flicked skywards, and then at a set of guy ropes gathered on their hook.

Wiggins leapt to the ropes and in one swift movement unspooled the heaviest one. He held on as it ascended to the rafters, while a heavy backdrop whistled down to the stage. The Drunk sprang to his feet just in time to avoid being bisected by the falling backdrop. The audience went wild.

As the act continued, Wiggins jammed his feet into a stanchion and hooked his arm around the rope. He looked down as first one of Tommy's men, then another appeared backstage, hustling fey performers aside in a futile search. Wiggins waited in the flies. It didn't take them long to conclude that he must have done a runner. They hurried off, no doubt out to the stage door.

The audience roared again and Wiggins saw the MC bounce back onstage. 'My lords, ladies, gents, please show your appreciation for the Inebriate – otherwise known as the one, the only, Charles Chaplin!'

Chaplin waved as he walked off to deafening cheers, which echoed and blasted all around Wiggins in his lair. He watched as the small drunk, now looking so lithe and youthful, reached the wings. As he did so, Chaplin looked up high into the flies at Wiggins, and winked.

He had to get inside the Embassy. Martha had death in her eyes. Tommy was deep in the darkness now, and she'd be dead if he didn't do anything. He wouldn't let that happen twice. Not after Poppy.

Forget Kell's secrets, forget the randy politicians, the perverted diplomats, the wizened old bishops limping up those steps. People were dying in that place; Martha could be next. They had to get inside.

'*No sun – no moon,* eh?'

　'*No morn – no noon –* '

　'*No dawn – no dusk – no proper time of day.*'

　'*No* – oh, dash it all, I've forgotten the rest.' Kell rapped the table with his knuckles.

Harry Moseby-Brown sat down opposite. 'I won't hold it against you, sir.'

'You can drop the sir,' Kell said, and whistled at the waiter.

'Nothing for me, thanks. Can't stop.'

They were in the Stranger's Room in Kell's club, on a dull November morning not long after Kell's disastrous dinner with Quinn and his wife. He hadn't even spoken to Wiggins since their row over the telephone, and he now had Churchill in his ear wanting a full report on the dock disturbance, a report that Wiggins had resolutely refused to supply. To cap it all, he hadn't got to the bottom of Constance's strange behaviour. First she turned up at the office – his secret office – unannounced, then she invited Quinn for dinner and then she had tried to charm the lecherous rogue.

As soon as the door closed on Quinn that night, though, the mask had dropped and she went back to the cold shoulder, or rather, she retreated once more into her own personal cocoon, which only the most banal of enquiries could penetrate. He said nothing to her, nothing of any importance, because he couldn't. Perhaps Lady Quinn was right, perhaps if the bill passed granting limited suffrage, then a thaw could begin.

'Sorry I haven't more for you, bit rushed actually,' Moseby-Brown continued. 'So if you don't mind . . .'

Kell shook his head. 'I beg your pardon, my mind drifted. Nothing more to report?'

'No.'

Kell looked out across the room. Browns and dark reds dominated – the leather wing chairs, the never-read books on the high shelves. It was November all right. 'Tell me,' he said suddenly. 'Are you married, Moseby-Brown?'

Moseby-Brown hesitated, and shook his head.

'Sweetheart? Is that the word they use nowadays?'

Moseby-Brown dropped his cigarette box. 'I, er . . .' He'd lost all his normal poise. His cheeks reddened slightly, and he tugged at his collar in a swift, nervous movement.

'I didn't mean to embarrass you, old man. Just seeking enlightenment, wherever I can. I'll let you get on. And thank you, once again. Your reporting may seem trivial, but it is vital to the nation's safety.'

Moseby-Brown nodded, and left. Kell watched him go, hurrying through the ancient chairs in his pristine suit of clothes sharply creased in all the right places, monogrammed. Since they'd met in the Committee, Kell had been using him as a source inside the Foreign Office, collecting any titbits that might help identify a leaker or – more usually – add to Kell's growing store of information on those in important positions. Moseby-Brown had been remarkably keen to help – as any good patriot should, thought Kell – and had provided interesting snippets on a number of people. The under-secretary who gambled, the chap with French family, the ambassador who liked young boys: all grist to his intelligence mill, names for a watch list, but nothing that had yet led to the breakthrough. Still, Kell reflected in the taxi back to the office, it was always nice to spend time with a Thomas Hood enthusiast.

Back at the office, Wiggins was waiting for him in the usual style, feet up on the desk.

'We gotta get inside,' Wiggins said as soon as Kell opened the door.

'Impossible,' he snapped. He wafted Wiggins's feet off the desk. 'How many times have I told you, the police won't do my bidding without evidence.'

'Don't talk to me about the cops.' Wiggins spat the last word out, as one would turned milk. 'They's damned near killed a boy out east. Maybe they did, I don't know.'

'Are we going to fight again?' Kell said, sitting down at his desk. 'I can't fight on every front.' *My wife is bad enough*, he did not say.

Wiggins glowered at him. 'I said my piece. I mean it – I'll go back in, if you pay me, but I'm never going to give you another name again. Ever. We's about protecting the country from the bloody Germans, not snitching on our own.'

Kell sucked in but said nothing. He wasn't going to force Wiggins back into the unions, it was Churchill's bugbear, after all. But he'd have to find a way to placate the Home Secretary, whether through lies, exaggeration or some version of the truth, he didn't know. Wiggins himself was almost certainly exaggerating. As was common with so many of his class, he held the law in utter contempt. Anything he said about police violence had to be treated with caution, if not flat disbelief.

What was certain, however, was that Churchill had ordered an escalation in the way such disturbances were handled. Quinn had said as much at dinner – a hard school, getting harder – and Kell hadn't picked up on it. He'd been so angry at the suggestion of his own resignation, the insinuations that he was out of his depth, over the hill, that he'd missed the suggestion of a change in policy.

The West India dockers weren't the only workers in the firing line. Rumours were bouncing around government circles about trouble brewing in the Rhondda Valley. There was even talk of sending in the army against the miners. Kell hoped his false report, in Wiggins's name, wouldn't come back to bite him.

'Very well.' He gave Wiggins a hard stare. 'I thought you had more backbone than that, I must confess.' He let that hang in the air for a moment. Wiggins was busy enough at the Embassy, and Kell himself felt a certain distaste for Churchill's commands when it came to infiltration and political meddling, but he wanted to let Wiggins stew a little. It did no harm to make your under-lings feel indebted to you.

Wiggins tilted his head in disdain.

Kell tsked. 'Now, the Embassy – I hate calling it that. This house of ill repute. We still have nothing definite? No link to Germany, say?'

'Germans are about the only mob who don't go there,' Wiggins said. 'We need to get in there, I keep telling you.'

'But how?'

Wiggins nodded at him, and waited. And waited.

'Well, speak up, man. What?' Kell felt the heat rising in his face. 'You don't mean . . . No, I . . . well, I couldn't possibly do . . . It's impossible. In no way . . . never.'

And so it was that, on the evening of the 17th of November 1910, as Welsh miners fought running battles with the army, as cavalry soldiers charged on their own countrymen in the Rhondda Valley, and as Wiggins looked on from his vantage point high above Ranleigh Terrace, Captain Vernon Kell, late of the South Staffordshire Regiment and the Staff, veteran of campaigns in China and South Africa, now head of the Secret Service Bureau, found himself staring up at the door of the Embassy of Olifa, knocking shop to the quality.

He hesitated, hand at the doorbell, even at this stage unable to go through with it. What the hell was he doing? He was on the verge of turning back, to hell with Wiggins, when the door sprang open.

'Good evening, sir.' A woman had opened the door. She had tight black curls bound up on her head and a darkness to her skin. She smiled. 'Would you like to come in?'

'Er, I . . .'

'This is your first time, I see,' she went on kindly. She wore a long golden dress that shimmered when she moved. Kell shifted his eyes from her décolletage, and looked beyond her into the room. 'Come this way. There is nothing to fear.'

'I was recommended by . . .' He tailed off. The woman sashayed away from him across the large hallway, her heeled shoes tapping ever so gently against the chessboard tiles. She turned, and beckoned him on. Her walk was most disconcerting, and Kell could do nothing but follow.

Get a grip, man! He tried to take in the room. Doorways left, right and centre, as well as a grand staircase up to the first floor. Immaculate decoration, he noted, gilt-framed portraits, the lot. The black woman reached a door at the far corner of the hall and gestured him over.

As she did so, a great Atlas of a man picked his way down the stairs. He glanced at Kell, in a way that suggested he'd been watching him all along – certainly from the time he entered, but even before that, too. He had the same kind of penetration in his look that flashed across Wiggins's face every now and then, like he was reading your secrets. Kell nodded at him and hurried over to the woman, who held open the door.

Inside, an older lady sat at a quaint little writing desk. 'Good evening. Please, take a seat,' she said. 'My name is Delphy.'

Kell sat down. The room was much like a respectable lady's small sitting room, with clumpy pot plants and a compact suite of easy chairs complete with heavy antimacassars. He placed his cane on the floor and tried to concentrate.

'How did you hear about us?' She peered at him over her glasses. He thought of his prep-school matron, asking him how often he went to the lavatory.

'Er, Middleman, at the Admiralty,' Kell said, as he'd prepared with Wiggins. Using one of the names from the list supplied by the cabbies. 'He's a member of my club. Said this place is just the ticket, for, um . . . a chap like me?'

Delphy clicked her tongue and made a note in a large leather-bound ledger. 'First-timers need to place a deposit.'

'Will five pounds do?'

She nodded. 'And the name of your banker? For the future, we try to deal with cash as little as possible.' Kell wrote down the name on the paper supplied. 'And your signature,' Delphy pointed, then slipped the paper into the ledger.

'And your work? What is your position?'

'Civil service,' Kell muttered. 'Former staff captain.'

'Ah, yes, life can be so dull in the service. We'll mark you down as an attaché.'

When going through his cover story with Wiggins, his agent had advised him to stay as close to the truth as possible. Constructing cover was all about making yourself credible – and nothing was as credible as the truth.

'Just so,' Delphy said and looked up from the ledger, her pen poised. 'And what do you like?'

'Er, claret?'

She tsked with impatience. 'Your predilections? Peccadillos? Types? Oh for heaven's sake. We offer new guests a parade of the girls . . .'

'Yes, I see,' Kell croaked at last. His collar pinched, his breath was short and his fingers tingled. He wondered if he was having a stroke.

'Or Martha here.' Delphy gestured to the black woman in the gold dress, who stood at the door.

Something inside Kell died. Or at least, that was the sound that emanated from deep within him. 'Martha?' he said, in a high-pitched, reedy voice that he didn't recognise as his own.

'That will do for the moment. We can set you up an account if the service is satisfactory. There will be more conditions then.'

Kell tried to collect his thoughts, tried to resort to Wiggins's methods, tried to see around the furniture, Delphy's school-matron act, for clues.

'Off you run then, chop chop,' Delphy said.

Kell stood up, shaken. The black woman, Martha, smiled and sauntered towards the stairs. Kell could only follow, mute.

'Boy, get out of it,' the huge man cried as a small boy sped past him. Kell turned back to Martha, who was already swaying up the stairs. He gulped.

'Oh, I forgot my cane,' he said and strode back to Delphy's room. He pushed open the door and crouched to retrieve it from the floor.

Delphy swivelled around and straightened, surprised. In her hand, she held the leather ledger and behind her, in what Kell had previously thought a standard living-room armoire, the open door of a safe.

'I beg your pardon,' Kell said. 'My cane.'

Delphy slammed closed the heavy safe door and glared at him. 'Back to your room,' she rasped. He nodded and fled. It hadn't escaped his notice that along with the ledgers and a pile of bank-notes, Delphy's safe also contained a revolver.

Martha waited for him at the top of the first flight of stairs. 'Naughty,' she said.

Kell coughed and followed her as they rounded the landing and took the next flight. He stared at the heels of her feet. Any higher was too disconcerting. She led him down a plush corridor, with doors off it either side.

He tried to shut out the sound of groaning, the squeals of ecstasy, the fake laughter, a strangulated scream that ended with a high-pitched 'Hallelujah!'

Martha glanced at him. 'Don't mind the Bishop,' she said, as she opened a door. He kept his eyes down as he followed her in. It wasn't just her sheer physicality that was so disconcerting, or her beauty. It was her manner, her air of sophistication and poise. He'd expected the whole experience to be sordid, dirty even, but this was very different. She was very different. The air smelled good – lavender, musk and something else, something heady. It reminded him of somewhere that he couldn't place.

'Let me take those for you,' she said.

He stood stock-still, unable to move, beguiled.

'Your hat, coat and cane?' she went on.

'Oh, of course,' he fumbled.

The room was large, with a big sash window and framed paintings on the wall. A red velvet curtain hung over one wall, but all Kell could really see, and feel, was the bed, which domi-nated the space. He turned away in embarrassment and pretended to study the apparently bland watercolour on the near wall.

He looked closer. Japanese, he guessed, with a man and a . . . It was actually an erotic print depicting the most unnatural human act, something he thought physically impossible. He averted his eyes hurriedly, only to see Martha leisurely shrugging off her dress from the shoulders. 'Interesting, don't you think?' she said.

'The Japanese exhibition has brought us all sorts of curios. You can wash there,' she said, nodding her head at a basin and jug on a small side table.

'Righty-ho,' he said. He rolled up his sleeves and lathered away with a will, relieved to have something to do with his hands, something to concentrate on. When he'd finished, he turned around to Martha and shook his hands. 'You don't happen to have a towel, do you?'

She looked at him in astonishment for a moment, then burst out laughing, all façade of sophistication gone in an instant. 'I didn't mean your hands, dear.'

'I . . . ?'

18

Constance waited for her husband. Waited for no other reason than to confirm her worst fears, so she could report back to the Hampstead ladies, and to Dinah and the girls. She waited, dressed and ready to go.

'Apparently Asquith's going to kill the Conciliation Bill.' The chairwoman of the Hampstead branch (and confidante of Emmeline Pankhurst herself) rang that afternoon and told her the news, or the rumour. 'Do you know anything?'

Constance hung up. She called Dinah, out in Barons Court, only to find out they already suspected. She called every campaigner she knew. The telephone line crackled with rumour, outrage and suppressed hope. No one had confirmed with any certainty what Prime Minister Asquith was actually planning to do the following day in Parliament, but the mood was black and angry. It appeared the ruling Liberals were about to call another general election, thereby consigning their half-hearted suffrage bill to the scrapheap. All those she spoke to, Dinah, Hampstead and the rest, urged her to find out more.

And so she waited for her husband. She would wait all night if she had to.

Her detective work on behalf of the others hadn't come to what she'd hoped. The first thing she'd realised in trying to ascertain the movements of Special Branch, what the police did and did not know, was the extent of her husband's influence. It had proved to be surprisingly, and disappointingly, meagre. At the rounds of social gatherings she usually eschewed – charity shindigs, coffee mornings for army wives – it was clear that Kell was a star descending. No one spoke in such crude terms, no one mentioned details, no one even referred to her husband. But the way they treated her was enough. In government and army circles, the professional standing of one's husband bore a direct relationship to the social standing of his wife. And she was washing up the coffee cups.

These suspicions were confirmed when she'd surprised Kell at his office. It was a paltry set-up, without much activity. A clerk, some dusty furniture and the ubiquitous Wiggins hardly made for the pulsating centre of a web of spies.

If anything were needed to further add to her disappointment, the dinner party with the odious Sir Patrick Quinn and that snake-in-the-grass Soapy was the final straw. Quinn was clearly deep in the midst of a scheme to oust Kell completely from the government security apparatus, whilst Soapy looked on. To make matters worse, it was obvious that whatever co-operation Quinn might offer Kell, it would not involve information on the suffragettes. The dinner party at least confirmed this: not only was Special Branch closely involved in monitoring the movement, it seemed that Quinn suspected (or knew of) her own commitment to the cause. He'd implied as much as they had parted – he would never trust Kell with any intelligence bearing on his wife.

No, Kell wasn't the inside man she'd hoped. Nevertheless, he was still on good terms with Soapy – who *was* Asquith for all intents and purposes, certainly when it came to parliamentary business – and so she waited, waited on for a man diminished.

She stood up when she heard his key in the front door and went to the drawing-room window. He swept in and made straight for the drinks cabinet, at first unaware of her presence.

'Vernon!'

'Good God,' he started. 'You near frightened the life out of me.' Sweat streaked his brow despite the November cold, and he wore full evening wear, right down to the top hat and tails.

'Tell me it isn't true.'

He took a step back. 'I don't know what you mean.' He looked away, then downed his drink in one swift movement. 'Shouldn't you be at a meeting?'

'I was waiting for you.'

He poured himself another drink, and held the cabinet with his free hand. 'So I see.'

'Well?' she went on, annoyed. 'Stop being so shifty. Tell me what you know, Vernon. It's unpardonable that you won't admit it.'

He looked at her strangely, a mixture of awe and fear in his face. 'I really don't, I couldn't . . .'

She strode right up close to him in her anger. 'Is Asquith really withdrawing the bill tomorrow? Is he ditching suffrage?'

'Oh.' Kell stared blankly back at her.

'What do you know? What's the point if you won't tell me anything? What's the point?' she repeated.

He blinked. 'He's going to dissolve Parliament tomorrow. They are calling a general election.'

'And the bill will go to blazes,' she cried. She pushed his shoulder in frustration and anger, then stormed out into the hallway. He didn't go after her. She bustled with her umbrella, bag and scarf, and wiped away the first prickle of tears.

She put her hand to the front door and then hesitated. Something snagged, something not quite right.

'Where have you been?' she said as she strode back into the drawing room. It wasn't just his shifty manner that didn't ring true, it was his smell. 'I can smell you from here.' She had to go. She had to know.

His hand shot to his neck suddenly. 'It's not what you think,' he said.

'My God,' she cried. 'You've been with a woman!'

As she said this, Kell opened out his hand in a reflex movement. It was smudged with rouge. He looked up at her, lies spread across his face like a rash.

'Who is she?' Constance asked, pulling her coat tightly. The tears came to her eyes at last, tears of frustration and anger. She dashed them away.

'No, honestly, I can explain,' Kell pleaded. 'It really isn't what you think.' He took a step towards her, clearly fumbling for the right thing to say. 'I was in a brothel.'

'We may have to go in hard. It's regrettable, but necessary.'

'Quite right too, this kind of illegality needs to be crushed.'

'Hear hear! They are inhuman.'

Kell glanced around the room and kept quiet. The grey beards of the Committee for Imperial Defence were bending yet again to the police. Sir Edward Henry, the Met's head man, had been briefing them about the demonstration massing outside Parliament. 'Sir Patrick Quinn here informs me that the crowd could reach as much as a thousand.'

'That's an outside number, sir,' Quinn said. 'What we are thinking, though, is that there will be many – ' he glanced up at Kell ' – *radical* elements in play.'

'What the devil do these women want anyway? How dare they intimidate Parliament – have they no respect for democracy?' an old buffer from the Home Office blurted out angrily.

'I rather think they want to take part,' Soapy drawled. 'But these women must not be allowed to sabotage the PM's announcement. Sir Edward, Sir Patrick, I trust you'll ensure the disturbances are policed with all due force and attention. I quite understand the need to make the state's position clear on this kind of violent intimidation. As to the rest of us, it goes without saying that this should not appear in the newspapers. Any suggestion that the police are in any way concerned with anything other than the safety of Parliament and the public is utterly absurd. Understood?'

Kell left without saying a word. He hurried back through the park to his office. He was due to meet Wiggins. They needed to go over the disaster of the night before at the Embassy. Just his luck that Constance had been at home when he got back. She had stormed out of the house and he hadn't seen her since. At least he knew where she was going to be that day. She, along with hundreds of other extremist suffragettes, would be outside the Houses of Parliament. According to the briefing, as laid out by Quinn and Sir Edward Henry, they were turning up in order to institute a People's Parliament, in protest at the general election that Asquith was going to call that day – an election that automatically quashed the proposed suffrage bill.

'How's tricks?' Wiggins said as Kell burst through the office door, more than an hour late.

'What in heaven's name does that mean?'

'A joke.'

'I'm not in the mood for jokes. Simpkins is due back to report any minute. What have you to say?'

'You were the one who went in.'

'I employ you, don't forget that.'

Wiggins looked at his watch theatrically, then stretched. 'No one followed you out.'

'Which suggests they didn't suspect me.'

Wiggins waited. 'Have a nice time, did you?'

'How dare you?' Kell snapped. 'I will not answer such, such . . .'

'Easy on,' Wiggins said. 'I only wanna know what you found out.'

Kell glared at him as he pulled off his gloves. 'We either need to break in—'

'Last time I nosed round there someone died. And someone else almost did – which was me.'

'—or else concoct a pretext for the police,' Kell went on. 'I have an idea. It will take time to organise, but I think I can manufacture some bait.'

'You sure they're bent?'

'It's a brothel.'

'I meant, are we sure they've got anything to do with your leaks?'

'But the coincidence! You said so yourself – the lists match. There must be something going on there. What better way to extract information than in the bedroom? That brothel could be a hive of international spies, insinuated into the very heart of the British Establishment.'

'Or it could just be a whorehouse for the quality.'

Kell looked at him steadily. '*You* urged this course of action. *You* sent me into that horrible place, *you*—' He suddenly stopped, took a breath and began again. 'I need results, desperately. And it's the best lead we've got.'

Wiggins nodded. 'Something ain't right there, it's true.'

'Now, as to the question of bait, my chap at the Foreign Office could help. His name's Harry Mo—'

The office door crashed open. Simpkins stood in the doorway, loose-lipped, wide-eyed, agitated. 'Sir,' he said.

'Not now, Simpkins.'

'But, sir, I really think . . . There's a frightful row going on in Westminster.'

'Yes, I know. The suffragettes are protesting. What of it?'

Simpkins looked between him and Wiggins. 'I came through Parliament Square. Chaps, women, bloodied . . . It's awful, sir – running battles, women beaten.'

'Constance,' Kell said.

Wiggins was already following him to the door. 'Stay here, Simpkins,' Kell cried, ramming on his top hat as Wiggins and he skittered across the landing to the stairs.

Kell hesitated at the roadside, looking for a cab, but Wiggins ran past. Kell went after him. In less than ten minutes, breathing hard, they came into Parliament Square.

A dark swell of women massed outside the gates to the House of Commons. Wiggins and Kell stopped running, but hurried across the square towards the commotion. Men of all classes jeered and shouted, enjoying the spectacle. It reminded Kell of a day out at the Derby – except this wasn't the sport of kings, this was the sport of the gutter.

From afar they saw a woman knocked down by a police truncheon. Blood burst from her forehead. Kell shouted, 'You there, Constable! Stop that at once.' But no one heard. They got closer.

'I'll go round the back,' Wiggins muttered and melted into the crowds. Kell scanned faces, hats – anything – in the crush for Constance. Another woman ran past him, hatless, holding her face.

Huge policemen, helmets pulled low, suddenly ran into the crowd of women once more. A great howl went up. Kell stood stock-still, astonished. All around him, police pushed and jostled the protesters, squeezed their breasts, grabbing, tripping, jeering. Two suffragettes suddenly managed to reach the railings at the front of the building, but they had barely got to the top before they were hauled down with sickening thuds.

Time and again the women surged at the gates, only to be repelled by truncheon and fist. Kell swivelled around as a woman came careering out of the crush and sprawled in front of him, screaming. Two giant policemen, one of whom had obviously pulled her from the crowd and onto the pavement, stood over her with truncheons drawn.

Kell, shaken into action, tried to insert himself between her and the police. 'What are you doing?' he cried. 'Can't you see the lady is injured?'

One of the policemen stared at him with incomprehension, veering into contempt. 'Stand back, sir. You could get hurt.'

'I?' Kell said, amazed.

He turned back. The lady had scrambled away, past a photographer with a huge press camera. The photographer stepped aside from the camera for the moment, and looked right at Kell. Another great wail went up from the main crowd.

Kell was all ears and eyes once more. He had to find Constance. Some madness had overcome the police, he had to save her. He pushed through the onlookers – mostly men, mostly cheering on the police when they landed their blows. A couple even pitched in with kicks and swipes of their own.

And then he saw her.

She was at the front of another wave coming across the road, with three young women, linked arm in arm. Faces set, cheeks pink against the cold, they looked magnificent. She looked magnificent. Kell gasped at the courage. He stepped forward. A surge of black obscured his view – the police charged at the suffragette line, and he lost her once more.

Enraged, he pushed through more bystanders, men and women, leering passers-by. 'Out of my way, barbarians.'

He grabbed at the arm of a policeman hauling a young woman to the floor. Without looking, the policeman swung his arm around, backhanded, and caught Kell flush in the face. He fell to the floor.

Pain seered across his skull at another blow. His head cracked the pavement. He looked up, through a thicket of legs, to see the huge policeman of earlier bearing down on him, club in hand.

Out of nowhere, Constance appeared between the two of them. Hat gone, hair wildly astray, she stepped into the policeman's path, half turned away from him, thrust her hip out, and then in one swift movement threw him to the ground. He landed on his back, and his weapon skittered away among the rushing feet.

Kell blinked, then his eyes closed, his skull raging. Constance crouched at his side, hands on his head, Wiggins at the other side. And then nothing.

'You!' Abernathy took one look at Constance and turned away in disgust.

She left the front door open, however, and Constance followed her in. It was more of a studio than a conventional house, on an eccentric little terrace out by Barons Court.

Abernathy strode through one of the doors off the hallway, cigarette smoke trailing from a hanging hand. Bright light suffused the large room, with a huge painting studio off to one side. She went after Abernathy and found her in a small sitting room.

'Constance!' Dinah cried, getting up from a divan. 'I'm so glad you are well.'

Nobbs reclined on a chaise longue, while Abernathy sat cross-legged on an old bentwood chair and smoked. Tansy was nowhere to be seen. 'I can't stay long. My husband—'

'Cut out to be with hubby, did you?' Abernathy sneered. Constance noticed a large bump on her forehead.

Dinah grimaced at Abernathy, then turned to Constance. 'Beastly, wasn't it?'

'I wanted to make sure you were all right.'

'All bones intact. Abernathy's got another bump on the head.'

Abernathy snorted.

'Is this your house?' Constance asked.

'God, no.'

'Friend of my sister's,' Nobbs drawled from the chaise longue. 'Let's us bed down every now and then.'

Dinah went on. 'She just paints and paints and paints. It's such a terrible bore.'

'Did everyone escape? Where's Tansy?'

Nobbs muttered, 'Practising, I shouldn't wonder.'

Constance didn't quite hear but before she could push the point, Abernathy picked up a newspaper and flung it at her. 'Did you see *The Times*? I imagine your precious *husband* takes the wretched rag. Have you read its report? Have you?' She stood up and began walking around the room. 'I've been saying this for months – they'll never bow unless we make them.'

'Are you all right?' Constance held Dinah's hands in both of hers. 'Please tell me you won't do anything stupid.'

'Stupid!' Abernathy cried. 'Did you see those bloody policemen? Did you see the power of the state? What, please tell me, would constitute stupid?'

'My cousin says Mary Clarke was badly beaten – she still hasn't woken up yet.'

'And *The Times* reports that two policemen had their helmets knocked off!' Abernathy grasped the paper back. 'Oh yes, and here – another got kicked in the ankle. There is nothing of the truth, nothing.'

Nobbs straightened up, shuffling through the newspapers. 'Except the *Mirror*. Bertie's sister, Flea, says they've been buying up all the copies they can. It's a photograph of Ada Wright, on the ground.'

'It's true,' Dinah said, handing Constance the paper.

Constance held Dinah's hand again. 'Please, Dinah, don't do anything rash.' She searched Dinah's saucer eyes, tried to hold them steady. What had happened outside Parliament would be enough to shake anyone. Dinah stared back like the child she was. They were all children, Constance realised with a horrible, shocking stab of guilt. Draped around the room still in their night things, playing at adulthood. And the game had just got nasty. 'Please,' she said again.

Dinah squeezed her hands and gave a hesitant smile. 'Would you like tea? I'm sure we can rustle some up.'

'I must go,' Constance said.

'Back to your lord and master? The ever-pathetic hubby?'

Constance ignored her and spoke directly to Dinah. 'Let us meet again in a day or two. Don't do anything without me. Please?'

Dinah nodded absently, looking about her.

'I'll have that paper back, if you please, Mrs Wifey,' Abernathy said.

Constance glanced down at the photograph on the front of the *Mirror*. It did indeed show Ada Wright on the floor, with two huge police constables bending over her in a threatening manner. It also showed a passer-by, a gentleman in a top hat and overcoat, trying to insert himself between the policemen and Ada. A man clearly remonstrating against her treatment. A man she recognised. A man not so pathetic after all. Her husband.

While Constance hurried away from bohemian Barons Court, a mile or so south Wiggins made enquiries with the well-to-do traders down the North End Road. He took a pint with the delivery boys outside the Wounded Hart. He posed, convincingly, as a collection agent for a furniture store out Putney way. His previous trade as a debt collector made this particular deception easy enough.

He took a turn down the Fulham Road and then off one of its side streets to the address he'd found among Kell's notes in the office. It was a small cottage, in a row that ran from the main road down towards Walham Green, in a quaint little dead end. A plaque to the left of the door read *Whitefields*. An elaborate birdbath and weathervane stood in the front garden, the metal vane a silvery flash even in the low light. Wiggins had confirmed, earlier that morning, that the owner was at work in far-off Whitehall. Reports from the pub differed as to whether he lived alone or with a maid.

Wiggins stood looking at the cottage for a moment, noted that all the curtains were drawn, despite the misty November light. No smoke from the chimney, no carriage or car by the gate, no milk bottles left uncollected. He squatted to the ground and shuffled through some detritus by the rubbish bins. The collectors must have just been, but there was enough strewn about to be useful. He put two things in his pocket, then entered the gate and rang the bell. Nothing. He rang again. If there was a maid, she was either too scared to answer the door or she wasn't at home. Or else she was just used to avoiding the debts – the debts that every trader on the North End Road (bar the laundry and the chemist) was more than happy to tell him about.

He walked back down the path to the gate. He didn't hesitate when, in the reflection of the weathervane, he saw the downstairs curtains twitch open for an instant.

'I've woken up.'

'So I see.'

'No, no, you don't see.'

Kell tried to push himself out of bed. A pain shot through his left temple and he slumped back into the pillows. 'Lie down.' Constance put her hand on his head, stroking his arm with the other. 'You may have woken up, but you need to rest. You've been in and out of consciousness for most of the weekend.'

'I didn't mean . . .' Kell said, breathing hard. 'What I meant is, I am sorry. No, I shall say this now. What you had to put up with – you were amazing. The police, the authorities, despicable. I will ask questions. It is unconscionable. Barbarism. How did you learn to – with the policeman . . .? You saved me. You were like Vulcana herself.'

Constance laughed. 'Ju-jitsu,' she said. 'It is a martial art of self-defence. I am Miss Edith's star pupil. It comes in handy, does it not?'

Kell gazed up at her. 'The brothel – it wasn't, I didn't, I . . .'

'I know,' she said quietly.

'But I was so glad when you were angry. I thought, I hoped, it meant you still cared.' He grasped her hand in his. 'That it mattered to you.'

She disentangled her hand from his. 'Of course!' She held his face in her hands gently, gently, and they kissed.

Kell recovered himself. 'I had to go into that horrible place. It was a mission, on a case, I—'

She stopped his lips with her finger. 'Wiggins told me.'

'Wiggins? He is here? What happened after I . . . ?'

'He helped me get you to your office, then we took a cab back here with the doctor. Wiggins is a good man in a crisis, I must say. We thought, in the circumstances, that you'd rather your involvement in a public-order incident be kept from the authorities.'

'I see, thank you. Is the scandal all over the press? Whitehall, Fleet Street, must be in uproar. I've never seen such an outrage.'

'There was one report,' Constance said. 'Would you like to see Saturday's *Times*?' She handed it to him. The doorbell, a new electric one, buzzed loudly. 'I'll see who it is. I told Agnes not to let anyone in without my strict permission.' She left the bedroom.

Kell read the report on what *The Times* called the 'disturbance' with mounting disgust. The police actions were entirely defensive, he read, and many of them had lost their helmets. Their actions – which Kell had witnessed as oversized and out of control, as beatings, battery and various degrees of assault – were described by the anonymous reporter as lacking 'nothing in vigour', although they also kept their 'tempers well'. That was it. No mention of the bloodshed, the injuries, the humiliating attacks on the women. There was even a snide remark about a woman scaling the railings who was 'unused to mountaineering'.

When Constance opened the door again, he said, 'You were right, my dear. I am so sorry.'

'It's Wiggins. Shall I bring him up?'

But Kell needed to speak and he knew it must be now. He'd had enough of keeping things to himself, of second-guessing her every move, wondering if the pangs in his heart matched hers. 'He can wait. There are things I need to tell you. Please, don't interrupt.'

'I was just going to say – oh, well, carry on then,' she said as she saw his look.

'What the police did in Parliament Square was unpardonable. That *The Times* is so brazen in misreporting it confirms my suspicions, however painful it is to admit. They planned to be severe on you ladies. Churchill's been wanting to get tough for months.'

'I know all this, Vernon, I have been in the movement for years.'

'Yes, yes, but I didn't know. Or rather, I didn't know the depths that some would plumb to defeat your cause.'

'This is all very touching – no, really it is – but a man in your position can't very well go around supporting votes for women, can you? You'd lose your job, your career, the lot.'

Every time she spoke, Kell fell more in love with his wife.

'I would still have you,' he said.

'You'll always have me. You idiot.'

'There's one more thing. I will never inform on the movement, I will never lift a finger to help the police against the cause, and I will never let you be taken. You have my word.'

She looked down on him for a moment, careful, appraising, but softly too, like she used to. 'Thank you,' she said at last.

'And did you know, Special Branch may be after you and your friends? There is a photograph pinned to the wall at Scotland Yard in which you appear – although I'm not sure if they can identify you yet.'

To his surprise, she smiled. 'I thought as much,' she said. 'Shall I get Wiggins?' She bent down and picked up another newspaper from the side table. 'Funnily enough, there's another photograph doing the rounds which I think most people won't be able to identify.' She handed him the *Daily Mirror*, and stepped out onto the landing. 'Wiggins!' she hollered, as Kell stared agape at the paper.

'It's a good likeness,' Wiggins said, nodding.

'It is not!' Kell said, and then, 'You really think it looks like me?'

'You'd have to be looking,' Wiggins said, soothing. 'No one will know.'

'Simpkins, perhaps. But he'll say nothing.'

Wiggins stood awkwardly by the window. Kell lay propped up against a mountain of brilliant white pillows, a nightshirt open at the collar. Two electric lamps shed extra light onto the bed, though the last of the afternoon sun filtered in from the high windows. Wiggins held his cap in front of him and looked down. It was one thing to deduce things about Kell at the office or out on the streets, his public front, but this was the man's bedroom. It made him uncomfortable; not just Kell's appearance, his private world, but Constance's too. A small pile of books by one side of the bed, reading glasses, handkerchiefs – he tried desperately not to look closer. He could smell her scent.

He looked out of the window and fiddled with the lock on the sash. 'How's the noggin?' he said.

'I beg your pardon.'

'Ya bonce. Ya head.' He tapped his own.

'I'll live. And thank you, for helping me, for helping Constance.'

Wiggins nodded. They held a silence for a moment, as Kell smoothed the covers over himself. Perhaps it was the mention of her name, her presence so immediate in the room even though she had now removed downstairs, that made them both self-conscious. Either that or, Wiggins thought, the last time they'd talked he'd been trying to get out of Kell what had happened at the Embassy. Not the easiest question in the world, asking your boss how his visit to a whorehouse went.

For once, it was as if Kell read his mind. 'Wiggins, can you ask Constance to come back in,' he said at last, taking a deep breath. 'I will explain to you both what happened at the Embassy. We are the Secret Service, the Hidden Hand, at least until Christmas. Once the election is over a new government could ditch us, or this one for that matter, if they get back in. That's our timetable. If we've cracked this leak by then, we survive; if not, who knows. Until that time, however, that is who we are: the Secret Service.

'And now the time for secrets is over. I must tell Constance everything. God willing, we will find out enough to keep the nation's secrets safe a little longer, and to keep our own jobs into the bargain.'

Wiggins breathed out, relieved. 'It ain't just that, chief, you'll wanna know what I just found out in Fulham.'

19

From London to Ladysmith via Pretoria by Winston S. Churchill.

'Liar,' Wiggins muttered to himself. He'd picked up the discarded book from an empty desk at the British Library Reading Room, and skimmed a few pages.

Ladysmith was death all right, but there weren't many heroes, and it weren't blood and glory. It was disease and dirt and hunger and thirst; folk coughed up their own blood more often than they shed another's. Poor Knightly bleeding out. He and Bill all bones and eyeballs with the hunger, waiting for relief. What if Bill had died at the hands of the Boer, out there in the heat and dust? Would Wiggins have pursued the killers of his best friend across that pitiless veldt?

He'd been coming back to the Library ever since the near miss at Smithfield, watching the Ivans sit at 'Marx's desk', following them home when he could, sniffing around what Symes called the 'blasted revolutionaries'. But he'd come up blank. And now, with Churchill's account of the Boer War once more flooding his mind with memories of his dead best friend, he wondered whether his thirst for revenge would ever be quenched. Should he let it go, this burning sore in his soul, and turn his eyes to the future? Bill was never coming back.

Wiggins put the book down, and began a final turn of the Reading Room's outer ring. He thought of Martha, holed up still in the Embassy, under the malign command of Tommy. Wiggins had been there each night since, and each night she'd tied a red ribbon in the top right window. She was still alive, at least, but for how much longer? He was plagued by a sense of foreboding – Tommy's hand pinned to her shoulder in that box, Poppy's pale, dead face. But he tried to shake the feeling away. Sherlock Holmes would have told him he had too little evidence to suggest Martha, or anyone else, was in imminent danger. Cold hard reason suggested she was safe enough. But cold hard reason was all very well for the likes of Holmes and the Doctor, tucked up in their comfortable rooms, with a housekeeper and a roaring fire.

If you'd grown up on the streets, you needed more than cold hard reason to survive; you needed your instincts, you needed to act with no time to think, you needed to feel. And experience had taught him to trust his instinct for danger. He wouldn't be alive without it, for all the cold hard reasoning in all the books in all the world.

Kell had turned his full attention to the Embassy as the best lead in uncovering the Whitehall leak, but had ordered Wiggins to wait, and to watch in the evenings. Hence he found himself again at the Reading Room during the day, in the fruitless search for Peter.

He turned for home. No Ivans there today. But as he did so, he knew he'd be back. Bill was long dead. Revenge was a pointless emotion, a sore that could never be salved. But then what were you, if you weren't a friend to someone? And did it matter if they were alive or dead? He would have pursued Bill's killer across the veldt, had he died in the Boer War. He would pursue Bill's killers across the world if necessary; pursue them to their death, or his own.

As he drifted towards the exit, Wiggins caught sight of a reader stooped over a pile of books at a side desk all of its own. He would recognise that stoop anywhere.

'Mr Holmes!' he whispered.

The great detective hurriedly pushed a book aside. 'Ah, Wiggins, I was wondering how long it would take for you to see me.'

'Sir.' Wiggins grinned.

'You have a reader's card?'

'The under-librarian Symes, sir. If you remember, we helped him out.'

'Ah, yes. A trivial matter if I recall.'

'Not for him,' Wiggins muttered under his breath, then nodded at the pile of books visible on Holmes's desk. 'Still on them bees, sir?'

'I am writing my own text on the subject,' Holmes said. 'I may be retired, but my mind rebels at stagnation. And I've promised the Doctor never to return to those other, darker pursuits.' Wiggins glanced away in embarrassment. He'd seen the little bottles, the syringes, even remembered Holmes in his younger days, red-eyed, pale-faced and half cut on some skank or other, back in the early 90s.

He turned back to see Holmes giving him a long, hard stare. His eyes burned as bright as ever, but Wiggins noted the lines around them crackled deep and dark. Holmes shook his head sadly. 'You've been away this year, at sea – and in Germany, with Kell, I trust? But it is regrettable that you're still hell-bent on this foolhardy mission of revenge.'

'It's one man, guv'nor, one man and I'm done.'

'It's a shame you don't have your younger self to call on.' Holmes gave a weak smile. 'He would find the man in a trice, would he not?'

'It ain't that simple, these Rooskis are a different breed.' Wiggins explained, in hushed tones, what he'd been doing on and off at the Reading Room for weeks. Holmes tented his fingers as he listened, then shook his head again as Wiggins finished.

'Wiggins, the drink has addled your mind.'

'What you mean?'

'Ask Symes. To acquire a reader's pass here at the Reading Room, you must provide a residential address. Symes will be able to provide you with the names and addresses of all these miserable republican scribblers. He will even be able to give you a list of the books they've been reading, I shouldn't wonder.'

'Why didn't he say?'

'He's a librarian!' Holmes exclaimed. 'You have to ask.'

Wiggins stared at the detective and nodded slowly.

'Now, off you go, young Wiggins. I have work to do. The queen is one of nature's most humbling enigmas. She needs my full attention.'

As he went in search of Symes at the main returns desk, Wiggins couldn't suppress a smile to himself. For when he'd initially approached Holmes at his work, he'd seen him reading a quite different book from those academic tomes on beekeeping. The Great Detective, the Pure Thinking Machine, the font of Cold, Hard Reason, had instead been reading that most instructive of volumes: *The Adventures of Sherlock Holmes*, by Dr John H. Watson.

Wiggins strode out into the late-afternoon gloom of Great Russell Street. The electric lights fizzed, buses clogged the road, and the clerks of the nearby publishing houses and bookshops, manuscripts stuffed under their arms, chopped their way through the museum tourists, fighting the long fight to get home after work. He set his sights south-west to Belgravia and the Embassy, as he had done every day that month – to keep up the watch and to make sure Martha's ribbon appeared. Poppy's death hung heavy on his heart and he wouldn't be responsible for another.

He thought of getting the 24 straight to Victoria, but just then, and downwind of him as he stood on the corner of Tottenham Court Road, the gates of Meux's Horseshoe Brewery swung open. Brewers spilled out onto the street smelling of yeast and hops, of fermentation and sweat and, most of all, beer. There's always time for a swift one, he thought, as he ducked across the road. Symes had agreed to compile a list of the Ivans – 'Why didn't you ask, lad?' he'd said, bemused – and there was nothing to be done on that front. Martha wasn't due to make a signal until six at least. And besides, something Holmes had said was jangling around his mind but he couldn't quite grasp the meaning. He needed beer to help him think.

It wasn't until he reached the corner of Oxford Street, and the nearest pub, that he heard a hollering newsboy.

'Murder in Houndsditch. Policemen shot dead. Murder in Houndsditch. Anarchist gang at large.'

It had all started with a policeman shot dead on the streets.

His policeman, his Bill. And now it had happened again, somehow. Wiggins felt it with ice-cold certainty.

Peter was back.

As Wiggins hurried southwards, through Soho and towards Trafalgar Square, he hoped he would find Kell in his office. But he wouldn't be there. No one with any official position in the security apparatus of Whitehall was in their office.

They were all in a large Cabinet briefing room waiting for the police to report on events at number 3 Exchange Buildings, Houndsditch, in the City of London. Kell picked his usual position, standing at the back, and waited. Members of the Cabinet ringed the large table – Asquith, the Prime Minister himself! – Haldane, the Secretary of State for War, and, of course, Churchill, always Churchill, though for once the Home Secretary was indeed needed at such a gathering.

The story had broken in the papers already, but the panic had spread across Whitehall well before that. Kell had been at an early lunch with Soapy when a minion came running across the club dining room and whispered urgently in Soapy's ear. He'd been with Soapy ever since as he tried to corral the dramatic evidence as it came in. Finally, Soapy had called a full meeting of the Committee.

Kell had never seen any of the ministers looking quite as peeky as they did now, their faces creased with worry. A fevered anxiety crackled through the air, rippling out from the large table through the various ranks of assistants, who either sat or stood behind their chiefs in a clear demonstration of rank.

Sir Edward Henry, Commissioner of Police, stood up at the far end of the table, flanked by Quinn on one side and on the other by a uniformed officer who, it turned out, was the head of the City of London Police. The bigwigs leaned forward intently. Kell bit his tongue. He couldn't help it. The last time the Committee had been so outraged was over the problem in Tottenham the year before – when Wiggins's constable friend Bill Tyler was slain by anarchists.

Now, the atmosphere was even more charged, the anxiety

palpable – and all because, Kell realised with a dull pang of despair, the country was midway through a general election. The polls had opened two weeks before, and still had days to run. The murder of policemen on the streets of London, under their watch, was therefore causing the Prime Minister and his senior men rather a deal of anxiety that had nothing to do with public safety.

The chief of police began his briefing. 'In the early hours of this morning, a City of London policeman noticed some unusual goings-on at Exchange Buildings in the City. He knocked on the door and found two or three foreigners, who did not answer his questions convincingly. He returned with colleagues, and a gun battle ensued. I say gun battle, but none of the constables were armed with revolvers or guns of any kind. Two of our men are dead already, another three lie gravely ill.'

'Outrageous!'

'Who are they?'

'Have you made an arrest?'

Sir Edward drew up to his full height. 'Both the Metropolitan Police and the City of London force have dropped everything, My Lord. We will find the gang who did this. It will not stand.' He gestured at Quinn, who continued.

'My investigators are of a mind that the constables interrupted a robbery in progress. These men, this gang you might say, were tunnelling into a jeweller's. The paraphernalia . . .'

He savoured the word, damn him, thought Kell.

' . . . the accoutrements you might say, of such a crime have already been recovered from the scene. We have witnesses that saw at least three men fleeing the scene and going into the East End – one of these men appeared to be injured quite badly. Shot in the act, of course, by one of his – are we saying "colleagues"? Such an injury will not remain secret for long, I'm thinking.'

A murmur broke out in the room. 'Is it normal for burglars to carry firearms?' Asquith said, silencing everyone. The Prime Minister rarely spoke at such events, in Kell's experience. He was wise enough to know that most of the time speaking made him look foolish.

'Ah, no, sir, it is not normal. But these men are not normal. They are revolutionaries, we believe, certainly Jews, foreigners – Russians or Latvians, we think. Anarchos.'

'Good God,' Asquith muttered. And then, in a loud voice across the table, 'Churchill, have you given the police everything they need?'

'And more, Prime Minister, and more. We will cancel all leave, every available officer will be pressed into the investigation, Special Branch will be accorded all necessary funds. It will be the greatest manhunt in history.'

'We don't want this blowing up in our faces. Apprehend these men, sirs, and whatever you do, make sure you effect an arrest before the polls close.'

Sir Patrick grinned. 'Sure we will too, sir,' he said. 'These are the wanted posters going up all over town. Please circulate them in your departments. I'm not thinking you will be bumping into any of these men, but it doesn't do any harm to know the devil's face, now does it?'

The meeting broke up. Kell edged around the side of the table towards the doors.

Houndsditch had already taken everything else off the front of the evening papers – the rest would follow tomorrow, and it would continue to dominate until the gang was rounded up. He cursed inwardly. He had spent the last three weeks setting a trap, a trap to be sprung on the eve of the election results, for maximum effect and to save his bacon when the new government formed. If the strategy worked, and his hopes were proved correct, then he would take out the foremost mole inside the British Government and destroy a nexus of foreign intelligence-gathering at the heart of the diplomatic community. The Embassy, the brothel, would be done in. If he was right, of course, and if the plan worked. If not, he would fall into an embarrassing heap all of his own making, be sacked without appeal and spend the rest of his days signing requisition forms for the catering corps.

But now the police would as likely rob the Bank of England as jump to Kell's request for a speculative raid on a house of ill repute, at least until Houndsditch was solved. The plan against the Embassy would have to wait a little longer.

'You look as if you're thinking deep, Captain Kell, if I may say so.' Quinn broke in on his thoughts as he drifted to the door.

'Sir Patrick.'

'Sorry for interrupting. There must be some grand strategies working their way around that fine mind of yours, if you don't mind my saying.'

'I don't mind,' Kell said shortly.

'Ah, good. I'm thinking they'll have to be mighty grand to save the Service, though, all the same. I'll be getting more resources after all the shenanigans, what with the militant suffragettes and all – shocking they've become, don't you think?'

'Look, I thought we were here to catch some revolutionaries.'

'Right you are, always onto the point,' Quinn said, as he scanned the room. 'We'll get back to the case, and leave you to the Germans so we will. I'm thinking whoever solves Houndsditch will be in a grand spot, so he will.'

Quinn said it to gloat, Kell knew, to show that he was the man with the chance to catch the devil. But it was the reverse thought that gripped Kell: what if he (or, more honestly, Wiggins) tracked them down beforehand? Wouldn't that be a coup worthy of saving any Secret Service Bureau?

'Oh, Kell,' Quinn said absently, grabbing something from the table. 'Don't forget your wanted posters. If you could, ah, well, show your assistant, that would be grand.'

Kell took the three posters and glanced at them. The first one, a photograph of a nasty-looking man with dark eyes, too much hair and a large moustache; the second, much the same, although this fellow also looked filthy, with a tatty scarf at the neck. The third poster was an artist's impression, done with charcoal or something similar, with WANTED printed across the top: the man had longish hair, piercing eyes and a strong, clean-shaven jaw. The face looked familiar. Kell squinted and then, with a thrill of horror, realised why.

It was a picture of Wiggins.

Part 3

20

Great, dead geese hung in bunches over Leadenhall Market; the carts of Covent Garden teetered and sagged with horse chestnuts, Brussel sprouts and sacks upon sacks of potatoes; the pubs over-flowed with beer and port and Christmas cheer; the streets of the West End bristled with shoppers, harried, burdened, scowling; the stores of Regent Street were festooned with spruce and holly; and the air hung heavy with the scent of burning nuts, hot cider and cloves. And carol singers at every corner.

Bloody carol singers, Constance thought as she pushed past another knot of depressingly jolly warblers. She'd lost the knack of Christmas shopping, and Oxford Street made her melancholic. It was the department stores, Selfridges and John Lewis – the idea of a shop that had everything, she found unutterably sad. She turned down Regent Street and stopped for a moment outside the window of Boots the Chemist. The same window she'd almost put a knobkerrie through.

She'd not seen Dinah since the conversation in Barons Court in the aftermath of the protest in Westminster, a month or so earlier. Many in the movement were already calling it Black Friday, and it was common knowledge that at least one woman had died, probably as a result of a beating. The government and courts had done nothing. A publicity battle raged. The Pankhursts were trying everything to get the real story in the papers; the government was trying everything to kill it. Radicalism gripped even the Hampstead ladies. Dinah's remarks would be more than welcome now. If only she could find her.

There'd been no answer for weeks on the Barons Court

telephone number. When Constance had finally gone round there, a woman in her thirties with a paint-flecked face and bare feet answered the door. She said something vague and distracted about young people coming and going. Dinah, Abernathy and Nobbs had gone. Constance didn't even know Dinah's full name, and she had no way to trace any of them.

She drifted back onto Oxford Street. A newsboy raced past. 'Funeral of dead police set for St Paul's. Alien gang at large.' She worried for Dinah, worried what the girls might think it necessary to do. There were a slew of women already starving themselves in Holloway, and Abernathy's talk would be wilder than ever. Black Friday might have realigned the priorities of most suffragists into more active protest, but it would surely send Abernathy and Nobbs into a whole different order of militancy.

Black Friday had had a rather different effect on her, Constance mused, as she wandered towards Tottenham Court Road, all thoughts of shopping gone. For one thing, it had saved her marriage. To see her husband intercede on her behalf – and not just hers, but Ada Wright's too – against the police deeply moved her. For him to act against the state's representatives in such a way showed that to do the right thing, he was prepared to over-turn all that he thought and had previously believed in.

Kell had also given her a job. She'd had to sign the Official Secrets Act, and she could never be referred to by her real name in any of the correspondence, but he'd recruited her in the role of an 'adviser' or 'analyst'. After his bang on the head, he'd told her she was the cleverest person he'd ever met. And at that very moment, he was doing the first thing she'd suggested.

She looked down at the shopping list in her hand, not one item crossed off. Then she tossed it into the air and hailed a cab. She was a liberated woman. She would empower the nanny to buy presents.

The taxi took her down the rest of the street, then north up Tottenham Court Road. 'Stop!' she screamed.

'Wot the hell?' The driver slammed on the brakes.

'Wait here!' she cried as she tumbled out onto the pavement and back ten yards to what had caught her eye.

She'd finally found Fairyland.

While Constance shopped, Kell went to his club. Harry Moseby-Brown startled when he saw Kell come through the big double doors.

'I can't stop, Kell. I can't stop. Italy is revolting.'

'This won't take long.' Kell pointed Moseby-Brown to a line of wing chairs that dotted the lobby. The young man from the FO looked as immaculate as ever, with a high polish to his shoes, a perfectly knotted scarf at his neck, and a top hat you could see your reflection in.

They sat. 'You know, I'm not sure how much longer I can—'

'This is very important,' Kell said, pulling an envelope from his inside pocket. 'I have been impressed with your work, Moseby-Brown. You are a patriot and a brick. What I have here is explosive and highly confidential. This is the only copy. It's too dangerous to reproduce. You understand?'

'Well, I—'

'Good. I am trusting you with a national secret. Because I need your help.' Kell leaned in and gestured for Moseby-Brown to do the same. 'We in the Bureau,' Kell whispered, 'may be forced to act on the information contained in this letter. We've been waiting for the results of the general election. If the opposition had won, then of course this wouldn't be necessary.'

'I don't follow, sir.'

'Read that letter. It is damning, if true. I need to confirm its truth, I need you to do that.'

'But – ' Moseby-Brown unbent his body ' – what has this to do with me?'

'It's not you,' Kell said with a smile. 'It's Grey. We suspect him. If what we've found out, as contained there, is true, then it seriously weakens his position in the Cabinet. You'll see for yourself. If this gets out, it will massively weaken our position in the world, whatever happens.'

Moseby-Brown gulped. 'Gosh, sir.'

'Gosh indeed. Take that letter. Guard it with your life. Cross-check its contents against your boss's movements, what you know of him.'

'I'm not sure how comfortable—'

'This isn't about your comfort, Moseby-Brown, it's about the Empire. Grey poses a potential threat to that. Understand?'

'Yes, sir.'

'Give that back to me after Christmas, once it's confirmed. Now, off you go. Stop Italy revolting.'

Kell left the club, stopped in at a grocery on Victoria Street, then went to the office.

'Any beer?' Wiggins said as he rooted through the bag.

'You ask that every day, and the answer's always the same.'

'I'm a believer,' Wiggins said as he ripped open a packet of biscuits, 'that one day you will discover your heart.'

'Tsk.' Kell sat down at the desk. 'It's done.'

'So we wait,' Wiggins said, snapping a custard cream in two. 'Again.'

'Look, I can hardly have you running around town in the middle of the day, can I? You don't think I like you living here, do you?'

Wiggins scowled, but said nothing. Ever since Kell had come back into the office with that wanted poster, he'd insisted Wiggins stay in the office during daylight. Wiggins had been heading over to the Embassy once it got dark, to check that Martha's red ribbon was still hanging in the window (it was), and to carry on with the surveillance. At least, that's what Kell thought he'd been doing each night. 'What news from the Embassy?'

'You do know they's tooled up proper?' Security had increased tenfold at the Embassy. The door had been reinforced, and Wiggins had noted at least two extra guards and a new gun placement covering the front porch. Tommy wasn't taking any chances.

Kell nodded slowly. 'I've set the hare running now. We wait and watch.'

Wiggins picked up a tin of Fray Bentos corned beef. He weighed it in his fist. 'Any news? Nothin' in the rags this morning.'

'The police are still looking. Nothing since Gardstein.'

Wiggins picked up an old newspaper, with a photograph of the dead Gardstein on the front page. The press called him the leader of the gang. He was the man Wiggins had seen that night with Jax, the one who had pulled a gun on them in Smithfield.

The papers were full of the Houndsditch murders still, more than a week later. One of the injured policemen had died in hospital, taking the police dead to three. And now Gardstein had followed. He'd been one of the men in the robbery and had taken a bullet from one of his own. The police had arrested him the next day, after a doctor got cold feet and led them to the dying man. But the rest of the gang were still at large, including Peter.

'You gave 'em the addresses?' Wiggins said.

'Every last one!' Kell snapped. 'I've told you already. The police have raided half of Stepney looking for your bloody librarians.'

Wiggins grunted. 'Ain't no good raiding 'em.' He knew the police would bungle it. But when Kell had barrelled into the office with that wanted poster in his hand, Wiggins couldn't think of a better way. He told Kell about the Ivans, and when Symes came up with the addresses of the suspicious readers, Kell had passed them straight on to Scotland Yard.

'Yes, well,' Kell said. 'I'll pass on your concerns to the Commissioner of Police.'

'They ain't found much, have they?'

Kell tutted. 'The leader of the gang is dead. They've made a number of arrests. But you're right, they do believe the murderers are still at large. The entire police force is concentrating on finding those men. Let's leave it to them, shall we?'

'I could get out there, help.'

'And have Special Branch pick you up for murder?'

'Ain't never heard of disguise?'

'No,' Kell said. 'Our job, as you well know, is to prove the whereabouts of the diplomatic leak and to safeguard our own future. I'm sure you know the result of the general election.'

'I don't do politics.'

'The Liberals won again, which means if we don't rustle something up by the time Parliament sits, you'll be back on the streets.'

Wiggins scowled at him. 'I've always been on the streets.'

'Don't be so melodramatic.' He paused. 'We're clear, though, yes? Your job is to concentrate on the Embassy at night, rest here by day and keep out of sight until we can work out why you're on that blasted poster.'

Wiggins grunted.

'And whatever you do, don't go east of Aldgate.'

'*For auld lang syne, my dear, for auld lang syne . . .*'

'Shut the fack up, Jock scum!' The publican of the Rising Sun took the drunkard by the collar and drove him from the bar. None of the daytime drinkers jumped to his aid. He clattered through the pub doors, out into the snow-slicked street. 'You're too facking late! That was yesterday.'

The drunkard turned to the pub and shouted obscenities at the frosted-glass windows. Then he whirled on one leg, and collapsed against the wall. He was wrapped up like a bundle of rags, with a loose balaclava around his head, thick wadding around his hands, and ripped boots.

Great fat snowflakes drifted down Sidney Street. It would take time to soak you, take time to settle. But it could be a foot deep by morning, enough to bury a drunkard dead.

Wiggins scratched at his head under the rough balaclava. Being a drunk was one cover story he could play blindfold. The cold gripped his insides as he settled his attention momentarily on a row of houses further down the street.

He was in Sidney Street, a long cobbled road that ran between Bethnal Green Road and Commercial Road in Stepney, just east of the 'Chapel, and certainly east of Aldgate.

Wiggins had not kept his promise to Kell to stay out of the East End. Kell hadn't come into the office on Christmas Day. Wiggins went east. He found nothing. Kell didn't come on Boxing Day either. Wiggins went east again, looking for Peter. On those days when Kell did come in, Wiggins would go from the Embassy – always checking that the red ribbon hung in the window – out east. Scoping the Ivans' addresses, following Ivans, hoping for a break. It was all Christmas trees and mince pies in the West End. Out east, they were too scared for Christmas.

It hadn't been like that since the Ripper. But this fear stretched even further east. Half the people in Stepney and Bethnal Green were scared of the police. Many didn't speak English, Wiggins knew, and came from countries where the coppers could drag you away for sod all. They was keeping shtum. The other half were scared of the gangs. A body was found in Victoria Park, another on Clapham Common – supposedly the feller who grassed up Gardstein.

No one was talking. No one would ever talk. Which was why Wiggins was now slumped against the Rising Sun and got up in the worst kind of tramp's gear, freezing his bollocks off.

The police had drawn a blank with Symes's list of Ivans. But, as Wiggins repeatedly told Kell, that was because they'd just raided the addresses rather than waiting to see where the Ivans went, and who they spoke to. As soon as the cops came banging, anyone inside just clammed up.

He shifted and chattered to himself. Someone went in the pub and Wiggins shouted at him. 'Facking nuts.' Then he flicked his eyes back to the row of houses opposite.

The locals knew this stretch of terrace as Charley Martin's Mansions. A terrace of ten houses between two side streets, they were much bigger than the rest of the street – four storeys high. Wiggins kept coming back to them. One of Symes's Ivans had given 102 as his address for his reading ticket, and Kell told him the cops had duly raided the whole row. They found nothing. But that was more than a week ago and Wiggins knew Peter and his gang would be changing rooms as much as possible. And Charley Martin's Mansions was the perfect place.

Each house would have at least four families in it, he guessed. Most of them inside wouldn't speak much English, all of them would be scared – of either Peter, or the cops, or their own shadows. It was the perfect place to hide out, an urban fortress. The huge dosshouses of the 'Chapel would be too obvious, and the police were keeping tabs. These Sidney Street houses, on the other hand, had families in. Too many comings and goings for anything to be suspicious, too many people to raise an eyebrow with the neighbours. And Peter was the kind of fly chancer who would choose to stay in places that had already been raided.

He bashed his hands together against the cold and wondered how long he'd last outside. When he was a kid, the streets were littered with old dead down-and-outs come January, finished off by the weather and the Christmas booze and the bloody do-gooders doling out dinner for one night of the year.

Just then, a man walked past on the other side of the road carrying what looked like a camera and tripod under his arm. It was wrapped in a white sheet. The man strode quickly along the pavement, then stopped and knocked on the door of 100.

Wiggins slunk down deeper into his ragged coat.

A woman answered the door and gesticulated. The man stepped halfway inside, and seemed to shout upwards, talking to someone at the top of the stairs. An argument ensued, and then he went inside. Wiggins waited. It was the camera that snagged in his mind, something in one of the reports from the week before. He needed to check with Kell.

Fifteen minutes later, the man with the camera came out and strode quickly away.

'Any word from the Embassy?' Constance said, as she passed her husband a glass of whisky.

'Nothing. But it's only a matter of time.'

They stood together, staring into the fire. Nanny had just taken the children to bed, and Kell rested his drink on the mantelpiece and thrust a poker at the blaze.

'Happy New Year,' she said, raising her sherry.

He looked at her and smiled. 'Out with it.'

'It's about the Bureau.'

'Oh Lord, you don't want a pay rise already, do you?'

She laughed. 'To get a *rise*, I'd need to be paid.' She twirled her glass and sat down on the chesterfield. 'Are you – we – allowed to act in a preventative capacity?'

He opened his mouth to answer with a question, to ask her what she knew, why and what she was planning, to pin the matter down. But then he stopped himself. The rapprochement with his wife was the happiest thing to happen to him in a long time, and such delicate blessings should not be risked lightly.

'Yes,' he said, simply. 'This is what Wiggins was doing in the provinces. He was trying to identify people who *might be* spies in the event of war. Do you need my help?'

She shook her head. 'Not yet,' she said, and held her hand out towards him.

The telephone rang. 'That blasted Bell,' Kell said. 'I'm sure he was the devil.'

He strode into the hallway and ripped the receiver from the wall. 'Hampstead 202.'

'Hundred Sidney Street. They're there.'

'Wiggins?'

'The landlord at the Gardstein place was a photographer, right, working out of Cable Street? I sees it in the police report you had in the office.'

'What on earth? Er, yes, I think you're right. What of it?'

'Tell the cops 100 Sidney Street. I'm going back to check, but the rozzers have got to be quick.'

'I told you to stay in Victoria. Where the hell are you?'

But the line had gone dead.

Wiggins limped down Sidney Street, playing the drunk once more. He'd followed the photographer back to the gaff in Cable Street and that's when it rang a bell in his mind. Perelman, or some such, was his name and he'd briefly been in the frame because he'd rented Gardstein a room – the room he'd been found dead in.

Before the police murders in Houndsditch, Gardstein hadn't been a name on anybody's lips, no one cared. But by now, more than two weeks later, he and his gang were the most famous people in London. Gardstein had bled out in a small room in the East End, grassed up by the doctor, but his accomplices – at least four of them, according to the press and police reports – had escaped. A week later, the police had arrested Yakov Peters. When Wiggins knew him, Yakov had been Peter's right-hand man, a stinking, violent bomb-maker. It confirmed Peter's involvement, though by now the City of London Police were after him by name – along with two other named gang members, Fritz Svaars and Joseph Sokolov.

Fine snow wafted through the pools of light cast by the gas lamps. It would have been beautiful, Wiggins thought, if it weren't colder than death. He began to sing. '*Hoorah, up she rises, hoorah, up she rises.*' His voice echoed down the empty street. Even the Rising Sun looked dead. No one out on such a night now, not with the police and the gangs and the snow all over the East End like a pall. And still Wiggins sang at the top of his voice. He reeked of the gin he'd doused his scarf with, and he swung the half-empty bottle by his side as he walked.

He stumbled along Charley Martin's Mansions, battering at the windows, shouting inanities and continuing to sing. 'More booze,' he shouted, as he reached the door of number 100. He hesitated for a second. He couldn't be sure Peter and the remaining gang members were inside.

When he'd rung Kell, he'd made sure he sounded convincing. But he was far from certain. It was based on evidence – the design of the houses, the photographer/landlord – but it was still only a hunch, the kind of hunch that would have disgusted Sherlock Holmes. But this wasn't a nice little problem about a missing jewel, or the recovery of a compromising letter – this was a gang of heavily armed, volatile men on the run, who'd killed three coppers and would kill more if they had to. Peter had already almost killed Wiggins once. He had to make sure.

Number 100's front door stood one down from a doctor's surgery. The ground-floor windows were black. All he could hear was the hiss of the gas-lamp globe that hung on the corner of the street. He could just make out the lettering on the surgery window: DR KRESTIN, LONDON. The street was still empty, the snow still fell. It was as dark as hell and twice as cold. He knew he should walk away, wait for Kell and the cops. But he also knew he had to make sure, if only for a moment. The last time, the cops had been too late.

He slammed the front door with his fist. 'Doctor Krestin,' he shouted, 'I needs a doctor! Help, please.' Nothing moved. He tried again, rapping the glass in the door and screaming.

Suddenly, the door sprang open. Wiggins stumbled headlong into a tight, dark hallway. He fell flat on his face, arms out in front of him.

When he twisted around, he saw a woman standing over him, holding a candle. She'd opened the door to him, and she now gestured next door. 'Doktor,' she muttered, urgently. She pointed again, eyes wide with fear. 'Sorry, love,' Wiggins slurred. 'I'm looking for the bones.' He tried to stand up, then pretended to stumble into the open doorway off the hall, the front room.

A small child said softly in the dark, '*Bagrisn fremder.*' The woman – probably the child's mother – called out softly, '*Shtl, Rosa.*' Then she stepped towards Wiggins. 'No Anglish,' she implored.

Wiggins righted himself and turned to her, suddenly ashamed. He put his hands up in apology. 'I'm going, I'm going. No fear.'

'*ZAKROY DVER!*' someone unseen shouted from the top of the stairs.

The woman looked up, beyond Wiggins, startled. She stepped back, and shut the front door. Wiggins arched his neck, trying to see up the stairs into the darkness.

A pair of rough boots came into view. The stairs creaked. Wiggins peered into the gloom; too late to run. 'Sorry,' he said again, keeping in character. 'Looking for the bones, is all. The doctor.'

'If you said you were looking for drink, then maybe I believe you.'

Peter the Painter stepped down the stairs and into the candlelight. 'Come upstairs, old friend, join us. A long time.' He pointed an ugly pistol at Wiggins.

Wiggins shrugged. 'Do I have a choice?' he said.

Peter weighed the Mauser in his hand. 'Today, I don't think so. Sometimes bear must do what master says. And sometimes bear eats master. Up.'

21

Kell took a cab to Leman Street police station in Stepney.

It was a foul night. Rain and snow and wind lashed the windscreen and he could see almost nothing. On receiving Wiggins's call, Kell's first thought had been to telephone Special Branch, to give Quinn the news.

'No,' Constance said. 'You must go to the local police in person. Involve yourself. Only then do you inform Quinn and Churchill. That way the Bureau will be guaranteed the credit.'

'Or the blame,' he said.

He got to Leman Street at about eleven in the evening. 'I need to speak to an inspector,' he said at the charge desk, waving his credentials.

The inspector came out shortly after, and took him into his office. 'You're the Secret Service Bureau, you say? That would explain why I've never heard of you. And you know they are there? How sure are you?'

'Sure,' Kell said. 'At least that one of them is there.' He wasn't sure, but Wiggins was in the field. If in doubt, trust Wiggins.

The inspector considered for a moment. 'We must wake up the division commander, Superintendent Mulvaney. He lives on Commercial Road. I will make a telephone call to Arbour Square station, then you will join me, if you please.' He picked up the telephone on his desk.

Then they walked to the divisional commander's house to wake him up.

'And you're sure?' Mulvaney asked Kell. The three men stood in the hallway under a bare electric bulb.

'I'm sure,' he said.

Mulvaney turned to the inspector. 'You've told Arbour Street? Good.' He looked back at Kell. 'We will need as many men as possible, if it's who you think it is. Of course, that means if you're wrong we will be the laughing stock of London.' He tugged at his overcoat. 'Very well, let's get back to the station.'

Back at Leman Street, gone midnight, Kell stood as a silent observer while Mulvaney corralled his various commanding officers.

'We have a hundred men from the City force to match our own hundred. The first thing we must do is seal off the house.'

'Why do we need so many?' someone asked. 'Aren't there only two or three of them left?'

Mulvaney glanced at Kell, as if looking for confirmation of the numbers, but then went on briskly. 'They are heavily armed. Remember what we found at Gardstein's. Mausers. Semi-automatics. Bomb-making materials. Enough rounds to take on Aldershot. And I know these houses. The passage and stairway is very narrow. If we storm the house, they will have a clear shot at anyone coming up the staircase. It's so narrow that it would become blocked with bodies. It will be a bloodbath.

'So, we surround the area and wait. Do we know who else is in the house?'

An inspector coughed. 'One of my constables knows it, sir. A tailor named Fleshman, or some such, lives in the ground-floor front room with his family. Another older couple in the back room. Then he rents out the first and second floor to all sorts, and has his workshop in the attic.'

'Thank you, Inspector. I think it's safe to assume if they are in there – ' he glanced at Kell ' – then they'll be on the upper floors.'

'*If,* sir?' the inspector said. 'You mean we ain't sure?'

'I'm sure,' Kell said.

Mulvaney looked at him carefully for a moment and nodded. He pulled a pipe from his pocket and addressed the men once more. 'It's almost twelve thirty now. First job is to secure the exits out the back and along the street. I believe there's a sawmill opposite. Commandeer that. We have rifles? Good.'

He stuffed his thumb into the bowl of his pipe in an irritable gesture and went on. 'Now, I don't want any married men on this detail, clear?'

The ring of inspectors nodded gravely and shuffled their feet. Everyone knew what this meant, including the constables. Mulvaney never liked risking a married man if he could help it. An improvised map of Sidney Street and the surrounds was laid out on a table. Mulvaney gathered them all round. Their heads dipped into the light.

'You see your sections. Now you . . .' he pointed to the inspector who'd given the details about number 100 '. . . lead the evacuation of the neighbouring houses. And try to get the family out from the bottom of the house. If we do this quickly and quietly, we can get them out before the anarchos are any the wiser. Understood?'

The inspectors nodded and retreated through the door to their men in the call room. Mulvaney finally lit his pipe and took a long drag before turning to Kell.

'It's a nightmare. We can't shoot at them until they shoot first.'

'The law,' Kell nodded.

'And that staircase is a deathtrap. These men couldn't have chosen anywhere more like a fortress if they tried.' He tapped his pipe out on the table in annoyance, refilled it and then looked at Kell once more. 'You have informed Scotland Yard?'

'Not yet.'

Mulvaney's gigantic eyebrows raised in unison. Kell went on. 'I will, when I return to the office. We don't always get on so well with Sir Patrick.'

Mulvaney hesitated, then barked, 'Ha! I can see that.'

'I'll go now. Do you mind if I come back, to follow the operation?'

'No, so long as you don't get in the way. You'll have to take your share of the blame, mind, if your information is flawed.'

'I understand.' Kell put on his top hat and strode to the door.

'You're absolutely sure of your source – he's good?'

Kell thought for a moment. 'He's the best.'

Kell's cab sped across the dark city. He'd hired the car for the night, at ruinous expense to the department, but he reasoned that if the night went badly, there probably wouldn't be a department in the morning anyway.

He stopped at the GPO and sent long telegrams to Scotland Yard and the Home Office. No one would be in any doubt where the information came from when they arrived for work in the morning, in the event that Wiggins was right (or wrong).

There was no sign of Wiggins in the office in Victoria Street. He dashed off a couple of telephone calls to follow up his telegrams, then took the cab out to Belgravia, and Ranleigh Terrace.

Kell burst in to find Simpkins slumped over the box Brownie at the window of the surveillance post.

'Where's Wiggins?' Kell shook him awake.

'Sorry, sir,' Simpkins spluttered. 'He didn't come by as usual to relieve me. I thought I should stay in position until he did.'

Kell looked out of the window, down at the dark Embassy. He shuddered. 'Anything to report?'

'Nothing, sir.'

'And did Wiggins tell you where he was going? Did he leave any clue?'

'No.'

Kell almost stamped his foot in frustration. 'Go home, Simpkins. Come back in the morning as planned. There's nothing more to be done here.'

'Thank you, sir.' He gathered up his coat and gloves, and dropped the camera. 'Oh, there is one thing, sir, about Wiggins.'

'What is it?'

'He told me to watch out for a red ribbon in that window yonder, and to let him know if and when it appears in the evening. He's usually here to see it himself, of course, and it's been put there every day. But he did mention it.'

'I don't know what this has to do with me?'

'Well, the thing is, sir, it hasn't appeared this evening. The red ribbon is gone.'

'You don't give up, mad Anglish.'

'Why, do you?'

'Maybe you should.' Peter sucked hard on a sweet.

They were in a small, candle-lit attic. A large tailor's table took up most of the room. Rolls of material shot from cupboards about the walls and tape hung down from every nail. Wiggins tried uneasily to shift his weight. His arms and body were bound to the back of an upright chair. The thick curtain cord stung his wrists as he moved. Peter watched on, unmoved.

'If you try escape, I kill you,' he said calmly. He stood by the doorway, twiddling a ribbon in his hand. He didn't have to pull the gun out of his pocket. Wiggins knew it was there.

'Why don't you kill me anyway?' he said. 'You tried it once already.'

Peter puffed out his cheeks. He still had the good looks Wiggins remembered – the thick shock of hair with the grey streak, the deep, dark eyes, the swagger – but he looked on the edge now. His soiled shirt was ripped at the collar, his left cheek was bruised, and his once immaculate fingernails were black and split. 'You think that's who I am, a killer?'

'That I know of? Bill Tyler up in Tottenham. Three coppers in Houndsditch. Yeah, you're a killer.'

'These people.' Peter gestured to the door vaguely. 'They don't know when to stop. They want to kill *you*.'

Wiggins snorted. When Peter had appeared on the stairs, he'd gestured him up at gunpoint to the landing, then up the stairs again. Two men in the front room of the first floor came to the door and glared at him. He recognised one of them from Clerkenwell, the one with the yellow scarf. The two men followed them into the attic and bound him tight, before Peter ordered them out.

Peter popped another sweet into his mouth. Then he grasped a handful of coloured cloths from the table and slumped onto

the floor. He leaned against the door, opposite Wiggins. 'Why
are you here?'

'I told you, I'm here to pay my debts.'

Peter shook his head sadly.

'I won't give it up,' Wiggins went on. 'I'll see you in prison or
the grave. Either way, you'll have to kill me if you want me to
stop.'

'Or leave London?' Peter said.

Wiggins laughed at that.

Peter wove a red ribbon around his hard felt hat as he talked.
'You see, they arrested Yakov. Your friend!' he chuckled. 'Gardstein
is dead. Joseph and Fritz downstairs and I, we are only ones left.'

'I'm sorry. Sorry Yakov didn't find a bullet.' Wiggins grunted.
His wrists chafed and his back was beginning to ache. If ever a
man deserved a violent, lonely end, it was Yakov.

'But he was right,' Peter said. 'You are not to be trusted.'

'And you are?'

Peter held his newly decorated hat up to the candlelight. A
broad red band now covered most of the hat above the rim.
'When will they come for you?' he said.

'I work alone.'

Peter put his hat down carefully on the floor beside him. He
got up and began making himself a bed, using material pulled
from the tailor's stock. 'I am not so sure of this,' he said. 'But I
do not know. We go in morning.'

Wiggins grunted again. 'Not sleeping downstairs?'

'Fritz and Joseph can have room to themselves. They not smell
so good. I stay here so you don't escape and tell police.'

Wiggins glanced down at the ropes. 'At least tie me to the
table or something.'

'Ha!' Peter said, and blew out the candle. He lay down on the
improvised bed across the door. A manhole-sized skylight above
them offered the faintest glow, and a draught.

Wiggins slumped forward, his chest sagging against the ropes.
Despite the aches in his back and the cold, he felt his eyelids
drooping. He hadn't slept in over twenty hours, what with the

surveillance on the Embassy and being out chasing shadows. 'I thought you was a believer,' he muttered into the darkness. 'I've got nothing to lose but me chains.'

'I could untie you. But you would still be in chains. Chains in your mind. Even now, when they make you most-wanted man, you still do their work for them. You still a hunting dog, happy to catch prey for master. In return, pat on head.'

Wiggins grunted. Tommy had said the same thing, near enough. *Why are you working for the posh bastards in charge, why aren't you working for yourself and your own?* Shouldn't he be running with those lads in the docks, or the miners, against Kell and Churchill and their bloody Empire? What had the Empire ever done for him? What had Sherlock Holmes ever done for him, for that matter? Had his whole life been working for the boss man? Was that all he was?

'Why don't you kill me now?' he mumbled, as much to himself as to Peter. He drifted into near sleep.

'I will exploit you. Just like they exploit you. You are my capital, in case. Capitalists call it insurance.'

Wiggins had a sudden memory of Archibald Carter, the clerk, and his brother, who had invited him in for cards. The bonhomie of the family table, the easy way they asked him about himself, and how he'd had to be evasive, to keep with his cover. But they'd lulled him with their kindness, and he'd told them about the war and before, his life on the streets, and it was all right, and no one had to die and the fire was warm, and the cards straight and the smiles real. But that wasn't real, and it wasn't his family, or his table, or his life.

'No one cares about me,' he said before he fell asleep.

'Captain Kell, welcome back.' Superintendent Mulvaney waved his pipe at Kell. 'The man himself.'

'Oh?' Kell pulled off his gloves. He'd gone directly back to the police station and was shown into Mulvaney's busy office in moments. A large clock behind Mulvaney showed the time as half-past two.

The station bristled with action. Inspectors ran to and fro, issuing barked commands whenever they saw a constable. The telephone rang constantly. Doors opened and closed. But Mulvaney stood in his office, still amid the hurly-burly, and smiled grimly. 'Your information appears to be correct,' he said. 'Your source impeccable. This is it. We've run the gang to ground, thanks to you.'

'Thanks to my source. But how do you know?'

'Come with me. I'm about to take up a position opposite the house. I'll brief you on the way.'

The two men, plus an inspector and a constable, walked back through the station and out into the snow-flecked night. Sidney Street was only a short walk away. Mulvaney pulled on his pipe as they walked, and spoke after every puff.

'You were right. There are at least two men holed up on the first and second floors of the house. We have evacuated those living on the ground floor – two families – and a woman who lived on the first floor. She claims some ignorance of the exact details, but she is a friend of one of the gang, Fritz Svaars. We tricked her into coming into the hallway, and now we have her in custody. She says Fritz and another gang member, Joseph Sokolov, are in the front rooms.'

'There is no mention of anyone else?'

'You're thinking of Peter the Painter, the last member of the gang? We're not sure. We're waiting for a Yiddish interpreter. He may be in the attic, which is a tailor's workshop. Ah, here we are.'

They'd turned down a tiny alleyway. Kell assumed they were passing down the back of one side of Sidney Street. Mulvaney turned to him. 'We have the whole block completely surrounded. No one is getting in or out without us knowing. Whispers now. This is directly opposite number 100. We've got the family out, and have set up a viewing post on the first floor. No noise, no sudden movements.'

Kell followed Mulvaney as they soft-footed it through a back door, then up a carpeted staircase lit by a lantern turned down low. Mulvaney took a seat at the back of what appeared to be a small drawing room and gestured Kell next to him. He could just make out the form of two constables at the far window, crouched over long, thin guns.

'Morris tube rifles,' Mulvaney muttered. 'We reckon they are armed to the teeth in there.'

Kell shifted in his seat and for once hoped Wiggins was asleep dead drunk in a pub. 'What do we do now?' he said.

'We wait.'

22

Wiggins dreamed of Bill. Big bluff Bill who took him under his wing in the Gunners; who showed him how to stand tall, how to drink a pint, then two; who belted out 'God Save the Queen' and belched: big broad Bill, smiling into your face, like he meant it. 'God Save the Queen'. But she's dead, like dear, dead Bill. 'God Save the—'

He flicked open his eyes. Thin morning light pooled down from the window. Peter stirred in front of him, a jumble of loose material. And over the morning mist, as clear as any Big Ben, came the sounds of a brass band, thumping out 'God Save the King' as if their lives depended on it.

'What the—?' Wiggins shook life back into his neck. He guessed the band were playing out the back of the house, in the next street, but he couldn't be sure.

Peter got up. 'Anglish,' he said. He looked at his watch. 'It's seven o'clock. What is this?'

Wiggins shook his head. 'It's the East End,' he said. The band stopped, then struck up another, jauntier number. 'I need a piss.'

'Huh? Oh. I get bucket.'

He tossed the bedding aside and went out. Wiggins tried to stretch and bend his neck as best he could. He looked down at Peter's hat, adorned with the red ribbons. His own hat must be out on the street. It had fallen off in his drunkard routine and he had nothing now.

Peter came back in. 'Here it is. Now piss.' He put the bucket down.

Wiggins looked up at him. 'You gonna take my cock out then, or what?'

Peter glowered. Then he placed the bucket in the corner,

shunted Wiggins to face it. He was still attached to the chair. 'Feel that?' Peter asked, as he pressed the cold wet muzzle of his pistol to the back of Wiggins's neck. 'I will untie. You piss. I tie. If this does not happen, I shoot you. Good, yes? I am keeper, you are caged bear.'

'I just need a slash, not a lesson in Russian poetry.'

Peter loosened the rope and stepped back. Wiggins stood and pissed. 'This give you a thrill, does it? Bit of the old nip and tuck. You can watch if you want.'

Peter shuffled around. The band switched to a marching song as Wiggins pissed on. 'What's wiv that red ribbon on your hat?'

'Red is colour of revolution.'

'That right?' He'd barely finished when he felt the gun on his neck once more. 'Easy, I'm done.' He sat back down and waited as Peter tied the ropes again. Then he shunted the chair around.

'I can save you,' Peter said. 'We can save each other. But you must tell me truth.'

'What, that I've seen the bloody light? That I've been exploited all my life, that the revolution is nigh? Is that the bollocking truth you chatting on about?'

'No, not this foolishness,' Peter said. 'What I mean—'

Bang! Bang! Bang!

Rapid shots from inside the house. Then a faraway *pop, pop,* and then another, longer burst from downstairs.

Peter exclaimed in anguish, grasped his gun and rushed out of the room.

Kell was shocked by the devastation. The windows shattered. A screaming started up from outside. *Pop, pop,* the police rifles went.

Then another crescendo from the house. The wooden frames splintered. The bricks chipped. And the screaming went on.

Mulvaney gestured at him frantically, and they hurried down the stairs and out of the back door.

It had been a long, sleepless, deathly cold night up until that point. The dawn light had started to grey the horizon when

Mulvaney began to get impatient. 'Let's see where we're at, shall we? Send a sergeant down to knock on that window.'

They had watched as the sergeant hunkered along Sidney Street, back close to the wall, and smashed the ground-floor window with the butt of a revolver. Seconds later, the second-floor windows had lit up with gunfire.

Now, in the backyard, Kell shouted at Mulvaney, 'Are you sure they are only two?' Slates flew from a nearby house.

'It's Mausers. Semi-automatic.'

A wounded policeman was carried into the yard, screaming blue murder. 'I am dead, I am dead. Bury me in Putney.'

'Get this man out of here,' Mulvaney cried. 'And someone tell that blasted band to shut up. What are they at anyway?'

'A bakery advertising their opening, sir,' a constable said. 'They refuse to leave off.'

'Then arrest them.'

Suddenly, the firing stopped. Kell put his hand on Mulvaney's arm. 'You are outgunned, Superintendent. A Morris tube is no match.'

'But we have no others. A gunsmith in Cable Street has offered up his stock, but it's nothing like those things. And half my men can't fire a popgun, let alone anything useful.'

'You must call in the army.'

Kell went with Mulvaney through the backyard and down the alley. As they did so, another furious fuselage echoed off the cobbles. The occupants of number 100 Sidney Street would not go easily.

Back at the station, Mulvaney called Scotland Yard and then the Home Office. 'I need to talk to the Home Secretary apparently,' Mulvaney offered as an aside to Kell. 'But he is in the bath.'

Kell stepped back a discreet distance from the phone and looked about the station. All pretence of normal business had been dropped. Rows and rows of policemen left at regular intervals. More came into view on the street, as Kell stood outside to watch.

Mulvaney joined him on the stairs. 'Will you walk with me? We're to go to the Tower to get the Scots Guards. I'd value your advice as an infantry officer.'

'I'm off the active list.'

'You still know more than me.'

'Why so many more police?' Kell asked, as constables ranged about them, heading back to Sidney Street. 'I thought you had them surrounded already.'

'You'll see,' Mulvaney said.

And he did. As they walked past the south end of Sidney Street, they had to physically push through the crowds of onlookers. 'I've called up a thousand men,' Mulvaney shouted back at him. 'I reckon by the end of this there'll be thirty times that trying to watch.'

As Kell followed him, he thought exactly that – it was a sporting crowd. Men jostling against each other, angling for a better view, excitement etched on their faces, bright smiles, jokes, catcalls. As they walked on, they heard the burst of gunfire every now and then, countered by the weak popping of the police rifles.

At the Tower of London, Mulvaney was shown straight to the duty captain of the Scots Guards, who agreed to give him twenty men armed with Enfield rifles. At Kell's prompting, Mulvaney gave the men a short, sharp briefing in the forecourt outside the barracks. Just as the superintendent was finishing, the platoon captain by his side and Kell behind him, Sir Patrick Quinn hurried up with a fleet of Special Branch detectives in tow.

'What is this?' he cried, marching up to Mulvaney.

'Sir Patrick, I believe?'

The detectives and the army captain slunk back, sensing an argument between superiors. Kell stood his ground.

'You have them surrounded?' Quinn said, clearly agitated. He glared at Kell.

'There is no way out,' Mulvaney said. 'We are to return with more firepower.'

For once, Quinn looked at a loss. He glanced again at Kell, at the platoon of soldiers, then back to Mulvaney. 'Do you mind if I speak with the men?' he said at last.

'If you insist, but be quick. I must get back to Sidney Street. Captain,' he called to the Scots Guardsman commanding the troop. 'You know what to do. I shall see you at Sidney Street in twenty minutes.'

The army captain saluted. Kell left with Mulvaney, but he glanced back to see Quinn huddling close with the soldiers. A number of them, in their heavy grey coats and distinctive diced cap bands, bent towards Quinn, nodding.

Kell did not go back to the house opposite number 100. Instead, he left Mulvaney at the northern end of Sidney Street. The police cordon strained against the crush. Hundreds more had joined to see the spectacle, or at least hear it, and still the bullets popped and banged. He entered the side entrance of the Rising Sun pub. The enterprising publican had opened the roof up to the press and Kell joined them, for a small fee.

If one of the anarchists had been so disposed, he could have slaughtered half the reporters of Fleet Street with one well-directed barrage. But alas, thought Kell, all the gentlemen of the press were intact. As always, they had the best view.

Across the street and to the left, stood number 100. The windowpanes were shattered, the brickwork chipped. Every now and then a gun appeared, twitching at the window in a deadly dance before retreating once more.

'Got the bloody arsenal in there,' one of the reporters joked. 'They've been firing for two hours straight.'

'Three,' muttered Kell. 'I was here at eight.'

Further down the street, he could see four soldiers take position on the ground, rifles poised. Past them, stretching right down to Commercial Road and beyond, a river of humanity, as Mulvaney had predicted. It was the same looking to his right. Outside the pub, three more soldiers lay on the ground. Behind them, up to Bethnal Green, another vast swathe of people, listening for the gunfire, straining for a view. It was the most exciting thing to happen in Stepney since for ever.

In every doorway and archway down the street, policemen crouched. He saw two more soldiers on the brewery roof at the far end of the street; plain-clothes men had heavy revolvers drawn; policemen with rifles stood atop ladders, or poked them out of windows. Beyond the street, the rooftops were dotted black with heads: spectators, onlookers, thrill seekers. It was as if half of London had come to watch the show. But it wasn't a show, thought Kell, it was a public execution.

The soldiers on the roof opened fire. The police followed. The house shook. The tiles jumped and shattered, the air roared.

The firing stopped. Silence. Even the crowds were still, ears upturned, waiting. Smoke hung in the air, tinged with cordite. Kell could hear a man to his left scribbling hurriedly in his note-book. Was it over? He looked at his watch.

A burst of gunfire came back from the house. More windows shattered. Someone was still alive in there, still armed.

The reporters reset themselves, and began talking again. 'Here, look at that!' one of them cried, pointing down into the street on the right. 'Is that who I think it is?'

Kell peered over the side of the pub. Churchill had arrived. He had an entourage, of course, and Kell picked out Mulvaney next to him, pointing. On the other side of the street, Kell even saw a film crew setting up. Blast the man, he thought, he even brings his own publicity machine. Is no event too tragic to make into political capital?

He looked back at number 100, then out across the road and the rooftops, the hundreds of armed men bristling to bag an anarchist cop killer, covering every angle. He hoped to God Wiggins wasn't in there, a hope he knew to be forlorn. It was a charnel house.

No one was getting out alive.

'Let me go parley,' Wiggins said.

'You can't even get out of door.' Peter squatted down opposite.

As soon as the firing started, Wiggins had shunted the chair up against the chimney breast.

'What about those two?' he gestured downstairs.

'They have gone mad.'

'Tell 'em to throw a white flag out the bloody window.'

Peter had been running back and forth throughout the morning, giving Wiggins a commentary on what was happening. It seemed that his companions Fritz and Joseph had reached for the heavy artillery and there was no going back. Wiggins could hear they had serious weaponry.

'If only,' Peter muttered to himself. He looked up at the skylight. 'If they know who I am, I won't be killed.'

Wiggins was about to scoff at this suggestion, that Peter had fallen in love with his own fame, when the truth suddenly hit him full in the face, like Tommy's right hook. 'Of course,' he cried.

CRASH!

The attic exploded in an inferno of bullet fire. The skylight shattered. Bullets pinged through the roof. Peter collapsed to the floor. Wiggins upended his chair.

They huddled against the barrage. Then all of a sudden, it stopped. 'That's army,' Wiggins hissed. 'Enfields.'

From beneath them, the crackle of gunfire resumed. Fritz and Joseph, still defiant. Wiggins shook his head and locked eyes with Peter. 'Do something.'

'I will try. One last time,' Peter said. He crept towards the door and was gone.

Wiggins lay on his side in the broken glass, still strapped to the chair.

He had got his revenge. Peter was a dead man. But so was he. Was the revenge worth it, he wondered, as he lay amongst the shattered remains of the window and listened to the guns: was this how it was always going to end?

'I wish they'd hurry up, I've got to file by two to make the West End Final.'

'Boohoo, you should work for a daily.'

'Call that a newspaper?'

The pressmen bantered on, or else buried themselves in their notebooks. Kell kept up his vigil, looking down on that house of death. He'd gone downstairs at noon and forcibly removed one of the journalists from the telephone, whereupon he'd raised Simpkins on the line, and then Constance. Still no word from Wiggins.

Now, back on that roof, he wondered whether he could intercede in any way. Speak to Mulvaney, Churchill even. For with each passing hour, his suspicions were hardening into conviction. Wiggins, alive or dead, was in that house.

He turned to go back inside: it was worth telling Mulvaney, if no one else.

'There she blows!' a reporter cried in excitement. Kell rushed back to the edge. The house was on fire.

A torrent of flame shot out of the top-floor window. 'That's the gas!' Streams of thick black smoke began funnelling first out of one window, then a second, then a third.

The place was an inferno within minutes, sparks flying, great crashes of falling masonry, tongues of flame shooting into the sky, and thick black smoke rolling along the terrace rooftops.

Kell stood and stared, like the reporters. The police and soldiers, too, fell silent for a moment. The fascination of watching men die. 'It's an oven,' someone said quietly. Smoke obscured the whole upper portion of the house until it was lit up like a beacon.

Suddenly, as if by silent command, the soldiers started firing, followed immediately by the armed police. Every man within three hundred yards let go with everything they had.

Kell flinched as the besiegers poured hot lead into the inferno, a lethal hail of bullets. Finally, the shouts and cries of the commanding officers halted the senseless waste of ammunition. You didn't need to kill a dead man twice.

The fire burned on, spreading to the ground floor. No one moved, inside or out. The vast crowds beneath stood still, watching as a fatal black pall ribboned into the sky.

'Fools!' Peter cried as he crashed through the door. 'Scum.'

Wiggins was still pinned to the chair, lying on his side on the floor. His hands were red raw and bleeding. He'd been shuffling about in the glass for the last hour, gnawing away at the rope as best he could.

Peter scrabbled around the room, pulling up bits of material, a fistful of newspaper, almost in a panic.

'What you doing?' Wiggins gasped.

He stopped and looked at Wiggins for a moment, his deep, dark eyes wild. 'Making hell,' he said and left again, just as another burst of gunfire strafed the roof.

Wiggins gave one final wrench and pulled his left arm clear. He began to wriggle out of the bonds. As he did so, he heard shouts from below. The floor grew warmer. A plume of smoke passed the skylight. Gas hissed.

He got to his feet just as Peter came back in. They stared at each other for a moment. Peter didn't pull a gun. 'Don't go downstairs,' he said, and rammed his ribboned hat on his head. 'Fire and death.'

Smoke crept under the door. Peter glanced up at the skylight, weighing something in his mind. Wiggins followed his glance. 'They'll pick you off clean,' he said.

'Not in smoke,' Peter said. He leapt onto the table and put his hands either side of the broken window and disappeared upwards.

Wiggins shot a glance backwards. Flames licked the door. Smoke billowed in from every crevice. He grabbed a ribbon from the table and sprang up to the skylight.

It was as black as the pit, in the smoke, but he heard Peter skittering along the slates.

Wiggins went after him, bent low, using his hands to keep his balance. From behind him, he heard a great burst of gunfire. It reverberated and redoubled. The troops were giving it everything.

Peter flashed into view, nearing the end of the terrace. Wiggins closed. He was surer on his feet than Peter on the snow-slicked tiles. As they reached a clear stretch of roof, Wiggins glanced left. Across the road, on a rooftop opposite, he saw through a break in the smoke a soldier standing, gun raised, staring at them, shocked. Wiggins held up the ribbon, and ran on.

The soldier did not shoot.

Peter looked back quickly at Wiggins, then slithered down the roof. He caught the guttering at the last gasp, then swung out of view.

Wiggins slid down after him, catching on to the gutter and then shinning down the drainpipe. Peter dropped into the alleyway at the back of Sidney Street. He rushed out into the side street. His hat tumbled aside as he did so.

Wiggins crashed down the last few feet of the drainpipe and went after him.

The street was rammed with people, streaming around the corner, all abuzz. Wiggins was momentarily taken aback. It was like a demonstration, or chucking-out time at the test match down the Oval. A seething mass of people chattering, laughing, as if on a day out. Nothing the East End liked more than the smell of blood. A sudden surge in the crowd allowed him to push through out into the crush, eyes fixed on the dark shock of Peter's head.

Wiggins didn't turn to look for a copper. He assumed he was still on the wanted list, and he knew if he let Peter out of his sight for a second, he'd be dust.

He reached the other side of the road just as Peter ducked down another alley and ran. 'It's over,' Wiggins cried. Peter had run into a dead end, a high wooden fence cutting off the street between two warehouses.

But Peter, spurred on by fear, vaulted onto the fence and over.

Wiggins, neck and arms straining with the pain of being strapped up overnight, creaked over it too. He landed heavily and glanced up.

They'd come into an industrial area crammed behind the small terraces that ran up to Whitechapel. A large brick factory tapered away from them.

Peter dodged to the right of it, but he swerved again, put off by traffic further down the building. He ran to a metal staircase on the side of the factory and began to climb.

Wiggins followed. At each floor, he could see Peter try the door. All locked. He shot a glance at Wiggins, but went on, up the towering staircase.

Wiggins could barely breathe. His throat was dry, his neck raged with pain, and his legs were about to give way. But still they rose.

Peter tried the last door, failed to open it, then pulled himself up onto the roof of the factory, just as Wiggins reached him.

Wiggins roared, but Peter ran out of view. With one final effort, Wiggins hauled himself up onto the roof.

The factory was long and high. A thin spike of brick and iron ran along the centre of the roof. Glass panels tapered away from either side. At the far end, a Union flag jumped and jagged in the wind. Halfway along the middle, limping now, was Peter.

Wiggins gulped in a couple of deep breaths, braced himself against the gusting wind and went after him.

Peter reached the far end, and stopped. He put his hand to the flagpole, looked down, then turned back to Wiggins.

'You're Special Branch, ain't ya?' Wiggins shouted. He walked slowly towards him along the thin walkway. 'That's what the ribbon was for, a signal. To let you go.'

Peter shrugged. 'Special Branch, Okhrana, it is all same to me.'

'You put me on the wanted list, and all.' Wiggins edged forwards and went on. 'You take the money to stir the pot, that it? You and Bela both.'

Peter looked surprised at that.

'Yeah, that's right,' Wiggins went on. 'She took it from the Germans, you take it from the British and the Russians.'

'It is normal,' he said. 'Secret police live to fight trouble. When there is no trouble, they pay, we make it.'

'It's all bollocks then, is it?' Wiggins cried. 'All this power to the people, revolution shite? Are you all just in it for the money?'

Peter glared at him. 'We are little people. You, me, boys on street, everybody. We do what we can. We get used. We use. Maybe Yakov is pure. But the rest of them . . . it is not simple.'

'Christ,' Wiggins cursed. 'The fucking bomb-maker believes.'

A gust of wind rocked them both, and Peter stepped back towards the edge. He glanced down. 'You work for police too, I think. I see you at Grove Street. We almost get you in market. Police come. Here again, police come. You are lapdog, like rest.'

Wiggins steadied himself and stepped forward again.

Peter went on. 'You want kill me, for them? This is not you. Give it up. We could go together. Come to Paris. Meet girls. Make money. Drink. I have good plan.' Peter crept forward as he said these words. Then he sprang towards Wiggins.

He went to dodge past, but Wiggins caught him by the waist. They fell to the walkway. Peter fumbled in his pocket for a knife, and Wiggins leapt back.

They stood again, both glaring at the knife. 'Out of my way,' Peter said.

Wiggins charged. He batted the knife away with his heavy cuff. The two men barrelled towards the edge. The knife skittled down the glass roof.

They grappled and strained, wrestling for supremacy, face to face. 'You push me, we both die,' Peter grunted.

Wiggins suddenly pulled back. 'Not for them, for Bill,' he said.

Peter looked at him, breathing hard, puzzled.

'I wouldn't kill you for them. For Bill. But you ain't even worth that. You ain't even worth his spit,' Wiggins said. He turned back to the fire escape. He'd come all this way, over a year, looking for Peter, seeking revenge. Bill had died in the gutter, Peter's gang behind that bullet, for no good reason. But Bill weren't coming back and Bill hadn't saved his life, out there in the dust and heat of Ladysmith, to see him throw it away on scum.

Revenge was a dead man's game, and he didn't want to die.

Peter roared. He leapt on Wiggins's back and drew the flag line around his neck. He throttled him, dragging him back to the edge. 'You think you know all,' Peter hissed in his ear. 'But you won't take me. You will die.'

Wiggins struggled for air. His hand scrabbled at the line, trying to get his fingers under the rope before he choked. His eyes swam, his muscles raged.

Then he relaxed his body. Peter's grip slipped, and Wiggins got his hand on the rope. He forced Peter backwards.

They tottered and tipped towards the edge, Peter still with a hand on Wiggins's coat. His feet slipped, and with a horrible scream, he toppled over the side.

He took Wiggins with him.

23

'Wiggins is dead.'

'Oh no,' Constance cried.

Kell held the receiver to his chest for a moment. He looked at his empty office chair, then put the horn to his mouth once more. He explained what had happened earlier that day at Sidney Street, the persistent hail of gunfire, the inferno that eventually engulfed the house, all seen from amid the reporters on top of the pub.

'But are you sure about Wiggins?' Constance asked again.

'I had a brief look afterwards with Mulvaney. Some of it's probably still burning now. They've found the remains of two men already. No one could have survived such a scene.'

'And you are sure he was there?'

'The last time I spoke to him, he was going back to the house. He can only have been there.'

'Come home,' Constance said, finally.

'I must go to the empty house in Ranleigh Terrace first, to relieve Simpkins, at least for an hour or so.'

Kell dismissed the cab driver and let himself in by the back entrance at Ranleigh Terrace. He ascended the staircase wearily. The adrenaline and thrill of the siege were wearing off, and he realised he'd been up all night – most of it outside in the cold and wet. He pulled one heavy leg after the other. Without Wiggins, could he even go on? Did he want to?

'Afternoon, Simpkins.'

'Sir?' Simpkins stepped back from his post at the window. 'No Wiggins?'

Kell shook his head, and glanced down at the logbook. 'Something's up?'

'Trunks delivered, sir. As if someone is packing.'

Kell peered out of the window. It wasn't yet five in the afternoon, but it was as dark as midnight now. The street lamps fizzed and jumped. Stray snowflakes drifted in the air. The pavement glistened. And the Embassy lights blazed on, open for business as usual. Kell flicked his eyes to the high window on the right. No red ribbon.

He would never know its significance, not now his agent was dead. He dropped his head for a moment. Wiggins was the best man he'd ever known, and probably the wisest too.

'What now?' Simpkins said.

The door crashed open. A figure stood there staring at them: hatless, bedraggled, wild-eyed, and very much alive.

Wiggins.

'Beer,' he croaked and fell to the floor in front of them.

They sat Wiggins up against the wall, and Simpkins rummaged around for a bottle of beer. He shrugged at Kell's look – how on earth did they have a store of beer? – and put the bottle to Wiggins's lips.

Wiggins gasped. His eyes popped open. 'Here.' He took the bottle from Simpkins and downed it in one. 'Again,' he said, holding out his hand.

Simpkins thrust another bottle at him. Wiggins took a more measured sip, then sighed. 'Christ alive, I needed that. Even if it is Bass.'

Kell noticed Wiggins's torn clothes, and the burn marks on the sleeves and legs. 'How did you get out?' he said.

'That ain't the half of it.'

'Where were you?' Simpkins said, ripping open a packet of biscuits and handing one to Wiggins.

Kell noticed the easy rapport between the two men. Simpkins' reservations about working with a lower-class man had clearly evaporated. 'Wiggins,' Simpkins said as Wiggins munched on the biscuits. 'The red ribbon is gone.'

He looked up at Kell sharply. 'We gotta go in,' he said. 'Now.'
'I don't think—'
'It's all set up, right?'
'Yes,' Kell said slowly. 'But the police are not ready. More than half the force were drafted out east until a couple of hours ago. In any case, do you really think they'd be prepared to mount another siege? The last one didn't go particularly well.'
'They's all dead, ain't they?'
'We are not in the business of killing people for the sake of it.'
Wiggins cursed. He took another gulp of beer and handed the empty bottle to Simpkins with a nod. Then he looked up at his boss once more. 'It's down to us.'

'Well, I must say, Mr Wiggins, for a dead man you look the absolute cat's whiskers.'
He regarded himself in the mirror. Constance Kell picked a piece of lint from his shoulders. 'Ta,' he said.
'Vernon struggles to get in this one nowadays.'
Wiggins had on the finest suit of clothes he'd ever touched, let alone worn. Reassuringly heavy dinner jacket, tails, silk shirt, Savile Row style. He even had on a pair of patent leather shoes that felt as if they'd never been worn.
He and Kell had raced back to Hampstead from Ranleigh Terrace. They'd rehearsed their plan in the cab, and now Wiggins was completing his disguise. Constance had ransacked Kell's wardrobe, and Wiggins looked like any well-heeled toff out on the tiles – specifically, out at a place like the Embassy.
'Vernon has a further disguise for you downstairs,' she said.
'And a drink?'
She nodded. 'I need your advice,' she said. 'No, don't worry, I'm not deceiving anyone. I want to find someone.'
Wiggins took the hat and cane, and they turned to the door. 'Know their haunts?'
'I suspect one place,' she said as she led him back down the stairs.

'Time. You just got to wait it out. And money, if you've got it. Someone there you can pay?'

They entered the drawing room. 'At last,' Kell cried, before Constance could answer. 'We must get going.'

'You've made the arrangements with the Foreign Office?'

'Yes, they're briefed. I have two cabs waiting. Are you ready, my dear?'

'I am,' Constance said. She tied her hat under her chin. 'I have Wiggins's note. If Jax is not at the cab hut, I am to leave word with Sally and head straight to Whitefields without her.'

'Bang on,' Wiggins said. 'Tell 'em I'd trust you with me next drink. They'll know I sent you.'

Kell handed Wiggins a false beard and the tinted spectacles he'd so unsuccessfully used when trying to follow Constance. He also gave him a canary-yellow silk scarf. 'Will you take a firearm?' Kell asked. 'I have a spare revolver.'

'I don't like guns. They kill people.'

People just like Peter.

Wiggins got into the cab with Kell. He said nothing as they turned south to the Embassy. He didn't tell Kell what had happened on that factory roof, probably never would. He would tell him about Peter, but not how he died.

'I'm glad you're alive,' Kell said into the darkness of the compartment as they hurtled through the night.

'Me and all.'

Peter had fallen back off the roof, screaming horribly as he did so. But he'd managed to pull Wiggins with him.

They fell, locked together in a gruesome, final embrace.

But only one of them was holding on to the flag line.

Wiggins twisted his arm around the cord. It whiplashed him against the factory wall. Peter screamed out as he dropped.

Wiggins heard the crunch.

Way below, a parked-up fleet of dustcarts, ready to take away the factory waste. In one of them, staring up dead-eyed, Peter, spreadeagled in a rising halo of ash.

Wiggins pulled himself up the flag rope, which frayed with every heave. Finally, as the rope almost came down, he clambered onto the roof.

He lay on his back, gasping for air, as the Union Jack fluttered down the pole and caught on his legs, flapping uselessly in the wind.

'We go in nine sheets, yeah?' Wiggins took a gulp from Kell's flask.

'Just so,' Kell replied.

'And you're sure she'll remember you?' Wiggins asked for the third time.

'How many of her customers walk out without, er, executing the deed?'

Wiggins nodded grimly. Dark thoughts crowded his mind. Martha didn't start at shadows. If she'd failed to put the ribbon up in the window, then something bad had either already happened or was about to happen. Poppy's face rose before him again. Tommy's victim. He'd never forgive himself if Martha was next.

The cab turned into Ranleigh Terrace. Kell checked the action on his revolver for the umpteenth time. 'Here's fine,' he said to the driver.

They got out a few doors from the Embassy and looked each other up and down in the uneven light. 'Ah.' Kell raised his hand just as they were about to go in. 'What should I call you?'

'What a perfectly spiffing question,' Wiggins said in his best twerp accent. 'Why don't you call me Jonny, old bean?'

Wiggins slung his arm around Kell's shoulder as they waited at the door. Kell tried not to shrink back. He glanced left and right, saw the fixed muzzle gun poking out of the brickwork, covering the entrance. Wiggins leaned hard against the door with his other hand.

The door opened and Wiggins tumbled into the hall. He lost his grip on Kell and fell to the floor.

'Wot the bleeding . . . ?' A young woman stared down at Wiggins, then looked at Kell.

'Good evening, dear. I do very much apologise for my friend here. He has very slippery shoes,' Kell slurred.

The young woman stared at him with saucer eyes. Then she smiled. 'You cut?'

Kell smiled back.

'You're over the odds, gents,' a voice boomed. Kell looked up to see an enormous man tapping down the stairs. The man Wiggins said was Tommy. 'Come again another day.'

Wiggins wobbled to his feet, straightened his dark spectacles and stretched his arms out wide. With the long false beard and bright scarf, he looked like one of the fast young men who frequented the gambling dens of Haymarket.

'Do excuse Jonny boy,' Kell said, looking up at Tommy. 'Just a dash of New Year cheer.'

Tommy reached the hallway and scowled. 'No drunks,' he said.

'Let me introduce him to . . . Delphy, is it? So we may come back another day?'

'There's no harm in it.' Delphy stood across the hallway at the door to her room. 'I remember this one.' She nodded at Kell. 'He's harmless,' she said, with the smallest of smirks.

Tommy shrugged, but he took up a position on the stairs and waited. 'Top-hole!' Kell exclaimed. Wiggins tipped the rim of his silk top hat, and they tottered across the hallway towards Delphy.

As they did so, a small boy appeared from under the stairs. He watched them walk past. Suddenly the boy gasped at the sight of Wiggins and held his mouth open wide. Kell saw Wiggins tense. 'What-ho, young shaver,' Wiggins said, and twirled his cane in the lad's direction.

The boy said nothing, and they entered Delphy's sitting room. Wiggins slapped Kell on the back as they did so. He grinned drunkenly. They'd sketched out a plan in the cab, but Kell could barely suppress his anxiety. It was one thing to discuss theoretical strategies, but now they were in the lion's den.

He was to introduce Wiggins – Jonny – as a new customer,

then ask for Martha again. Once in the hallway or on the staircase, Kell was to create a disturbance such that Delphy would
leave the sitting room long enough for Wiggins to filch the ledger
from the safe. The hope was that they'd also find the incendiary
false letter Kell had planted in the heart of the FO.

Kell had made the mistake of telling Wiggins about the time
he had faked an epileptic fit at Eton. That was to be the distrac-
tion. 'The old dear used to be a nurse, I reckon,' Wiggins said.
'Medical emergency will do dandy.'

Delphy pulled the ledger out of the safe and opened it. 'My man
outside there is a little concerned about your state of inebriation,
gentlemen. Can you assure me that you'll not do anything
brutish?'

'I'll say.' Wiggins grinned.

'Apologies, Madame Delphy,' Kell said. 'Jonny here is cele-
brating a promotion. He's just been made an undersecretary at
the Admiralty.'

'Ahoy there!' Wiggins said.

Delphy looked up carefully, nodded and went on. 'I have your
details. But Mister . . . Jonny must give up his own.'

'Of course,' Kell said, helping Wiggins into a chair. 'In the
meantime, madam, I was wondering about . . .'

'You would like to see Martha again? Are you up to it tonight?'

Wiggins laughed. 'Bit of trouble with the hydraulics, Bloater?'

'I will be fine,' Kell said to Delphy, ignoring Wiggins's cackle.

'Boy!' Delphy cried. The young boy appeared instantly at the
door. 'Run up and knock for Martha. She has a gentleman caller.'

The boy dashed off, and Kell turned slowly to follow him. He
waited at the door for a moment, and heard as Wiggins – still in
perfect character – began slurring his way through his details.
What an actor he'd have been, thought Kell, as he prepared for
his own performance.

He stepped out into the hallway, heels clicking. A black-haired
man with a heavy moustache now stood by the front door,
checking the locks. Kell glanced up. He could hear the little boy's

feet on the stairs above, probably bringing Martha back down
with him. No sign of Tommy.

Curtain up.

CRASH!

The boy screamed out. Wiggins flinched in his chair. Kell had
gone down like a thunderclap. He looked around.

'Delphy! Delphy!' the boy cried.

She swiped the ledger into the safe behind her. 'I knew he was
drunk.' She got up just as Boy reached the door.

'He's gone loopy,' the boy cried. Wiggins could hear Martha
crying out now from the hallway, and doors opening and closing.

Delphy ran out, muttering. 'No deaths. If he dies, Thomas, get
him to the river.'

Wiggins leapt to the safe. It was a simple enough combination
lock, but it still took time. Someone else was screaming in the
hall now. 'A wooden spoon,' Delphy shouted.

'Keep it up,' Wiggins muttered to himself as he put his ear to
the drum and twirled. *Click* went the lock.

'Where's the other one?' he heard Tommy say.

Click.

'Hold him down!'

Click.

'That's it,' Tommy cried and flung open the door.

Wiggins sat slumped drunkenly in the chair. 'Oi!' Tommy
grabbed him by the shoulder.

'What's that you say?' Wiggins said. 'Is everything all right?'

Tommy glared around the room, but let Wiggins get up and
move past him into the hallway.

Kell lay stretched out at the foot of the stairs, stock-still, eyes
shut. Delphy and Martha knelt next to him, the former holding
a wooden spoon in his mouth, the latter cradling his head. Boy
sat on the stairs, teary-eyed. At the door, Wiggins clocked one
of Tommy's heavies. He stood with his arms crossed, glowering
over his moustache. One of the other girls – a pale slip of a thing
– stood halfway up the stairs and whimpered.

And behind him, Tommy.

Delphy looked up sharply. 'Oh do shut up, Matilda! Get back to His Excellency at once. He'll be awake soon.'

The girl turned and went up the stairs.

Kell's eyes fluttered open. 'Thomas, get this man a glass of water,' Delphy went on.

'Boy,' Tommy grunted.

Kell pushed himself up on one arm. 'I'm terribly sorry, madam, miss. I must have had a fit.'

'And some,' Wiggins joked. 'You look an absolute fright, old bean. I say, can that little lad get me a highball?'

Kell looked up at him questioningly. 'I am not myself. Maybe we should leave?'

'I feel like the man who broke the bank at Monte Carlo,' Wiggins twinkled. 'Why don't you toddle off home, while I can enjoy the attentions of this lovely young filly here. What's your name, dear?'

Martha stared at him evenly. 'Martha,' she said.

'Jolly good.'

Kell clambered gingerly to his feet as Boy came back in with a glass of water. The boy dodged past Wiggins. He rested a steadying hand on Wiggins's leg as he did so.

'Perhaps, then,' Kell said after draining the glass, 'I could, er, watch?'

The man on the door laughed. Tommy cursed and turned away. 'Knew it. It's always the limp ones.'

Delphy, standing by this time, looked between her two new customers and then at Martha. 'You will have to pay double. And no rough stuff.'

'I thought you might come back, after last time. Bit of Dutch courage.'

'Look, I'm perfectly capable of—'

'Shush!' Wiggins grabbed Kell by the arm and put a finger to his lips.

Martha gasped in surprise. 'You!'

She'd taken Wiggins and Kell up to her room following Kell's suggestion. Tommy had glared at them all the way up the stairs but didn't follow. Now the three of them stood in her room, in front of the erotic Japanese print.

Martha stared at the two men in alarm. 'Wiggins, T'll kill you.'

'Where's the letter,' Kell hissed at Wiggins.

'It weren't there.'

'But you have the ledger? We must go while we still can.'

Wiggins turned to Martha and whispered urgently, 'Why no ribbon? What's wrong?'

'Big T's locked us all up, even me. Something's up, something big.'

'He must have the letter somewhere,' Kell said.

'Who the hell are you, anyway?'

Wiggins shook his head quickly. 'No time. Come wiv us. We can save you.' He stared into her eyes, urging.

She shook her head. 'I can't. It's not what you think.'

'What's he got on you?' Wiggins hissed. Then a scratching sound caught his ear and he bent to the wall beneath the print.

'Do you know where Tommy and Delphy keep the most important documents?' Kell asked nervously.

'The safe? But, sir, you really shouldn't—'

Wiggins leapt across the room, pulling Martha and Kell to the floor as—

BANG! BANG! BANG!

The Japanese print shredded in an explosion of gunfire.

'The peepholes,' Martha cried.

Still on the floor, Kell drew his revolver and Wiggins pulled open the door. The corridor was in uproar. Whores screaming. Men in shirt tails cowering at the doorways opposite, a tumult.

The print exploded again in another round of gunfire. The barrage ended in a sudden click, and then a foul burst of swearing.

Wiggins dragged Martha out into the hallway and onto her feet. She screamed out, and Wiggins turned to see the moustachioed thug at the top of the stairs.

The thug raised a revolver in his hand. Wiggins tensed.

BLAST!

The thug toppled backwards, blood pumping from his neck. Kell stood beside Wiggins, and withdrew his gun. 'I think we've outstayed our welcome,' he said.

'There's a man on the front door with a Maxim,' Wiggins said. 'Take him. I'm going after Tommy.'

Kell nodded and ran at a crouch, skipping past the body of the thug without a second look. It had all taken a few seconds, but Wiggins was thinking clearly now, at last. 'Get the boy. And his schoolbag,' he whispered to Martha, and crept back down the passage.

It had been less than a minute since the firing had first started from the peep room. The screaming was still going on, but after Kell's shot all the doors along the corridors had closed, and it was once again deserted.

Wiggins reached across and rattled what he supposed was the door to the peep room. 'Tommy, it's over,' he shouted.

Bang! Another round of fire splintered the door. *Bang! Bang!*

Wiggins screamed and threw himself to the floor with a great crash. Bullet holes pockmarked the wall opposite. He cried out with as much agony as he could, while simultaneously getting up into an attack position and gripping his cosh. He whimpered and wailed again.

The door pushed open slowly.

Wiggins brought the cosh hard down on Tommy's gun hand. The gun clattered wide. Tommy grunted, but dodged left as Wiggins swung again.

They closed. Tommy heaved Wiggins against the far wall. He snarled and reached for the pistol.

Wiggins swivelled on the floor and kicked it away down the corridor.

Tommy drove a fist into his chin. *On the inside, son, on the inside . . .* Wiggins heard Bulldog's words in his ears. But this wasn't a boxing ring now, this was kill or be killed. Wiggins flinched and caught Tommy an uppercut to the bollocks.

He turned to go for the gun, but suddenly Tommy had him

by the throat. A tight cord whipped around his windpipe. This time, he had his hand underneath it, but it was all he could do to stop himself being throttled.

Tommy dragged him down the hallway, roaring, 'Any whore who helps these cants is dead!' He kicked the moustache man's body out of the way, and pulled Wiggins on. 'That facking toff your bumboy, is he? Always puckering up for the quality.'

Wiggins kicked and squirmed, but he felt empty. The siege, the last-ditch fight with Peter. He could barely hold the cord around his neck much longer.

Tommy jeered at him. 'Since you was a kid, you've been bending over for 'em.'

He suddenly let go of the cord, and flung Wiggins against the bannisters on the landing. Wiggins gasped for air. He ripped off the false beard and looked up. Tommy had the gun.

'Boy don't touch no one he don't know,' Tommy said, pointing the gun at Wiggins, breathing hard. 'But he knew you. I was slow, cos I couldn't think what that limp-dick toff had to do with it. Then I remembered. You's always been a lapdog, taking it from the top.'

Wiggins sat slumped against the bannister, spent. He glared at Tommy but he had nothing left, not even a cheap quip. 'Why didn't you kill me, outside the Axe?'

Tommy hesitated, as if perplexed by his own actions. 'You gave me a chance once,' he said. 'I owed you one.' Then he aimed the gun and said, 'Not any more.'

A door behind Tommy opened, and Martha stepped out. Tommy hesitated, flicked his head – and in that moment, she plunged a metal syringe deep into the side of his neck.

He clutched at it, stunned. The gun dropped to the floor.

Martha stepped back, kicking the gun away as she did so. Tommy stared at her, hand pinned to his throat. He opened his mouth, uselessly. Then he stumbled and fell backwards against the wall. His face twisted into a horrible rictus.

Wiggins hauled himself to his feet and scrambled for the gun. He glanced back at Tommy. The huge man went into convulsions, his great body bucking and twisting. A white foam bubbled at his lips.

'What is it?' Wiggins asked, fascinated and appalled.

Martha stared down at Tommy, unmoved. She nodded her head slightly. A door opened down the corridor and a man in a nightshirt poked his head out. 'Is it safe?' he said.

Wiggins looked back at him. 'Who are you?'

The head disappeared.

Tommy stopped writhing and choking. His body heaved one last breath, and then he breathed no more. He lay there, like a tree trunk felled in a storm. The worst of the Irregulars.

'Is that what happened to Poppy?' Wiggins said.

Martha stared at the body still. 'I think so. Too much of a good thing.' She snorted at her own dark joke. 'Sometimes it happens by mistake. Tommy weren't happy she met you, so he probably killed her that way. Triple dose. They dumped her in the river.'

'What's in it?'

'Wiggins!' Kell's voice echoed up the staircase. 'Wiggins!'

He ran down the stairs, Tommy's gun tucked in his cummerbund. Kell stood by the front door, revolver in one hand, while the other rested on the Maxim gun, pulled clear from its emplacement. Boy stood by, looking out of the window into the street.

'All clear?' Wiggins asked.

'I think so. Thanks to the boy.' Kell nodded. 'He jammed the gun while we were upstairs. And Tommy?'

Wiggins nodded slightly.

Boy ran over to him. 'Sorry, mister,' he said. 'Big T knew's I clocked ya. I didn't want no one hurt, see.'

Wiggins put a hand on the boy's shoulder lightly and crouched down. 'Where're his soldiers?'

Boy pointed. 'One out the front run off when the gun don't work. Scared of the gent's shooter. Fat Harry's normally out the back, but he's yella – I fink he's escaped. They's all scared of Big T.'

'And Delphy?'

The boy shrugged.

'Go get your schoolbag, would ya?' The boy ran off to the door under the stairs.

Kell looked a quick question at Wiggins, who waved it away. He walked over to Delphy's room. He kicked open the door, gun drawn. A cold wind blew towards him: the French windows at the far end hung open onto the back garden. 'Gone,' he shouted to Kell. The safe, too, was empty, apart from a medical kit, a red ribbon and a syringe. He strode back into the hall.

His boss was on the telephone, revolver hanging carelessly by his side, every inch a gentleman assassin. He put down the horn. 'The police are on their way. Inspector Carlton from F Division, if you remember. I trust him.'

He picked up the receiver again. 'Get me Whitehall 100. The Foreign Office.' As he waited, he looked over at Wiggins. 'Did you find the letter?'

Wiggins pulled out the ledger that had been stuffed down the back of his waistband and dropped it on the side table in front of Kell. 'It's coming,' he said.

From above, they heard the sounds of the Embassy's customers and hostesses coming back to life. Doors opening and closing, a shriek. Wiggins looked up to see Martha coming down the stairs towards them.

Kell turned towards the telephone quietly.

Boy came running back into the hall with his bag, which he held up to Wiggins. He gave the boy a weary smile and pulled open the heavy leather satchel. He took out the schoolbooks carefully, laying them on the side table. Martha, Boy and Kell watched as he felt the inside lining, then ripped it clean away.

In his hand, a clutch of close-up photographs. Kell peered in. They quite clearly showed a copy of an incendiary letter, supposedly written by the Foreign Secretary Sir Edward Grey, but actually dictated by Kell himself and handed over to Harry Moseby-Brown just before Christmas.

They had their leak. They had their proof.

24

'Who ran the operation?' Kell asked.

He sat at Delphy's desk, triumphant. About and above him, on the four floors of the Embassy, police took down names and details, scoured the building and locked the place down. He heard Inspector Carlton's barked orders at every turn. In Kell's hand, he had both Delphy's ledger – a treasure trove in itself of the Embassy's clients – and the photographs of his fake letter, proof that Moseby-Brown was the leak in the Foreign Office and the Committee.

In front of him, Martha stood without saying a word.

'The only way this works for you is if you talk. There's a dead man upstairs. A murder charge isn't too far away.' She looked up at that.

'I'll speak to Wiggins,' she said, finally.

He examined her for a moment, heavy shawl around her shoulders, make-up smudged, not the temptress of an hour ago. 'Wiggins!' he shouted.

His agent limped in, holding an envelope in his hand. He tossed it to Kell, then slumped down on the small settee.

'I get that yous was using the joint to pick up information,' Wiggins said before Kell could continue. He didn't look at Martha as he spoke. Instead, he sipped from a flask and stared up at the ceiling. 'Nuffin' makes the tongue looser than the pillow, right? You work for the highest bidder, or just the Germans?'

'Germany!' Kell exclaimed in excitement. 'Do you have proof?'

'You mean other than the fact that the German Embassy was the only diplo gaff in town that sent no clients here?' Wiggins gestured to the letter he'd found. 'There's that. Sewn into the waistband of Tommy's trousers,' he said. 'Martha?'

'Big T, Tommy. He dealt with all that. But yes, I think, Germany . . .'

Kell pulled open the letter and began reading it as Wiggins went on.

'So, yous was all in on it. Treason. What hold did they have on you? You's the jammest of the jam. Could go on your back anywhere.'

Martha looked daggers at him. But then she went into the safe and pulled out the medical kit, complete with syringe, a small bowl and pot of a powdery white substance. 'Heroin, I think it's called. Delphy said they make it from laudanum or something. She cooks it up, and injects each and every one of us, three times a day.'

Kell left off from reading the letter and looked up at Martha. 'Is it addictive?'

'Like you wouldn't believe, mister. Those girls upstairs will be screaming mad if they don't get a dose soon.'

'How . . . ?' he asked.

Martha rolled up her sleeve. She took a red ribbon from the safe and wound it around her arm, pulling it into a tourniquet. Then she tapped her wrist. 'There's the vein, see?'

'This is what you just pumped into Tommy?' Wiggins asked. She nodded.

'And this is what killed the young girl?' Kell interjected.

'I already told him.'

'And why didn't you place the red ribbon yesterday? What happened?' Kell said.

She glanced over at Wiggins, who now had his eyes closed. 'Yesterday, something big came in. Tommy jumped at shadows. He locked us all up, I think he was planning to clear out.'

'Must have been the letter,' Kell said.

Martha looked at Wiggins. 'I don't know what happened to Millie, honest.'

'Yeah, you do,' Wiggins said, and sighed.

She fiddled with the ribbon on her arm. 'You found her?'

Wiggins shifted in his seat. He leaned forward and looked at her, tiredness hanging off him like a shroud. 'Spill it, else we can't help you.'

'She had a Fred, a sweet one. I don't know his real name. Fallen real hard, so she said. Big T, Tommy, he sold her to the Fred.'

'He *sold* her? For information?' Kell asked, appalled.

Martha nodded. 'And once he sold her, what was the Fred to do? Tommy had him then. Could blackmail him in spades, couldn't he? I know posh folk don't give two stuffs about a young whore, but buying one as your slave is probably going a bit too far – even for the likes of you.' She gestured at Kell.

'Tommy kept going back to the well,' she went on. 'We met him at the Standard, night you showed.' She nodded towards Wiggins. 'In the box.'

Kell reread the letter in his hand. Addressed *To Whom it May Concern* in the most perfect German, it instructed whoever read it to afford the bearer – one Thomas Clay – every assistance, on behalf of the German Government. It was signed, in a flourish of red ink, *Van Bork*. Kell moved to the door and then nodded at Wiggins. 'It's time,' he said.

Wiggins stood up slowly and limped after him. Kell went out, calling for the inspector. Wiggins turned back to Martha. 'The name of the Fred, in case you're wondering, like, is Harold Moseby-Brown.'

They left then, Wiggins and Kell. They left the Embassy, Martha and all the pale young women in police custody. They did not speak much in the cab. The name on Tommy's letter, Van Bork, hung between them. They had thwarted yet another of his infor-mation-gathering networks, they had rooted out another spy – and yet still the kingpin remained unfound.

It was almost seven in the morning by the time they arrived at Kell's house in Hampstead. A baby's cries greeted them when they came into the hallway. Constance opened the drawing-room door at their approach. 'Don't worry, Vernon,' she said. 'It doesn't happen that quickly. Did you succeed?'

'We did.'

She ushered them into the room. Jax sat next to a young woman who held in her arms the baby, her child. It had stopped crying and now offered up a milky smile. 'There you go, girl, ain't too bad, am I?' She offered a finger, then looked up at Wiggins. 'This is Millie, but I fink you know that.'

Wiggins nodded.

Millie glanced up, distracted and red-eyed. 'Don't blame Harry, sirs. He did all he did for me.'

Constance nudged the two men back into the hall. 'I had no trouble bringing them back here. But she is a little addled.'

'She's a drug addict,' Wiggins said. 'Moseby-Brown's had her there for months, on the drip drip.'

'Is he in custody?'

'Yes,' said Kell. 'Grey detained him at the Foreign Office last night while you went for the girl, and now the police have him.'

'I need to go to bed,' Wiggins said. He hung up Kell's silk top hat on the hat stand. 'You got anything more my style?'

Kell handed him a flat cap. 'Take this. It belonged to someone who was following me. Working for Moseby-Brown, I thought.'

'Nah.' Wiggins looked at the cap carefully for a moment, then put it on his head. 'It's Special Branch, sure as.'

'But—'

'Doing a tail in an hat like this, the hair oil, the grease, the close-cut hair. Fair 'nuff, but the maker's name is the tell – it's next to the Special Branch training HQ, out Battersea. Simple, if you look.'

Kell was about to make some objection, but a sadness had come over his agent while he made this speech. He delivered his deduction without the usual sass, and his shoulders shrank into his jacket. 'Get some rest,' Kell said. 'Come back when you're ready.'

Wiggins nodded to Constance, then Kell. He limped to the front door, opened it slowly and stood looking out into the dawn.

'You've done your King and country proud,' Kell called out.

His agent seemed not to hear. He stood still, head bowed,

waiting. Finally, he lifted one hand in the air in a solitary salute, and was gone.

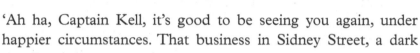

'Ah ha, Captain Kell, it's good to be seeing you again, under happier circumstances. That business in Sidney Street, a dark day. But it is over now.'

'Indeed,' Kell said, eyeing Sir Patrick Quinn carefully.

They were in the corridor outside Briefing Room A in the Cabinet offices, waiting for the Committee for Imperial Defence to reconvene. Kell, for once, was early.

Quinn smiled. 'I hear it was one of your men who found the hideout.'

'It was.'

'And congratulations on uncovering the Whitehall mole. I am thinking this is a triumph, of sorts. A triumph that took almost a year. I was half hoping you would fail in that task, I must admit it to you.'

'Good of you,' Kell said, and nodded at a couple of men who went past into the committee room.

Quinn stepped closer, so that only Kell could hear. 'Nevertheless, Kell, I am thinking it best if you stepped aside. I am not sure what our superiors would say about a man with a militant, potentially criminal suffragette wife running the Secret Service Bureau, eh? We wouldn't want to be embarrassing anyone, now would we?' He let the words, the threat, hang there for a second. More men pushed past them into the room. 'My recommendation is for Special Branch to take over, so it is. I'm sure you won't demur. Mr Pears is entirely behind me on this one, so you know.' He grinned at the last.

Soapy's entirely behind you, is he? Kell thought, but did not say. Instead, he nodded slowly and then leaned right into Quinn's face. 'I am much obliged, Sir Patrick. I would say only this. While you may think my wife's perfectly *legal* activities are embarrassing, I rather think they are not quite as dangerous – or as publically damaging – as the head of Special Branch employing a police-murdering anarchist as an informant. Peter sends his regards.'

The colour drained from Quinn's face.

'Nor are they as damaging as taking the word of this said murdering anarchist to put a perfectly innocent individual on a wanted poster. It was Peter who gave you the final description, was it not?'

Quinn nodded mute.

'As I thought,' Kell went on. 'So, I'll be thinking that we can all get along just fine as we are, to be sure, to be sure.'

'That's blackmail,' Quinn whispered.

'It's secret intelligence,' Kell said finally. 'I have my own Bureau. And by the way, I'd take that last wanted poster out of circulation if I were you. Good chap.'

Kell turned into the committee room. Soapy stood at the head of the large table, shuffling papers, checking that everyone was in their right position. Kell walked straight up to him, and pulled him aside.

'What's troubling you? We're about to start. Just waiting for Haldane, I think.'

'Is the Bureau's future on the agenda?'

'Sorry, old man, Quinn's been making quite the case to take you over.'

'I'm not so sure about that.'

'Oh, really?' Soapy scoped the room with his eyes. He raised an idle hand as Haldane entered the room.

'And I wouldn't be if I were you, either.'

'Why?'

Kell whispered into his ear. 'I have the Embassy of Olifa's client list. Interesting reading.'

Soapy straightened. He smiled around at the room, then put his hand on the small of Kell's back. 'Why don't you take a seat today, Captain Kell,' he said loudly, and then under his breath, 'You know, on reflection, I think I'll recommend an expansion.'

'Just so.'

And that was that. The meeting passed off in triumphant fashion. Kell announced the uncovering of Moseby-Brown, with thanks to the Foreign Secretary for confecting the false letter; he went on to mention the exclusive 'establishment' he'd uncovered in Belgravia, and its links to spying. In the same breath, he also happened to mention that he had a ledger listing the names of all that establishment's many customers. He glanced around the table when he made this last point, and noted with satisfaction that few of the men met his eye.

The rest was a formality. He was praised for providing the information that led to the siege at Sidney Street; the police were commended on their bravery and told to buy better guns; and Churchill was mildly rebuked for turning up at the scene himself. The news that Brandon and Trench had been sentenced to four years apiece was to be regretted, but as Soapy remarked, this was a failure of naval intelligence, not the Secret Service.

The meeting closed with a renewed commitment from all to the Secret Service Bureau. Quinn said nothing at any point, while Soapy was particularly voluble in his support.

Kell skipped out onto Whitehall, whistling. *Rule Britannia, Britannia rules the waves, I shall never never never be a slave.*

Later that same day, Wiggins drank. He stood outside the same pub where he'd tailed Bernie and Viv so many months ago, and waited. From his position on the corner, he could just see the entrance to Kell's building on Victoria Street.

Finally, she came out. 'Over here,' he called, waving.

She hesitated, then crossed the road towards him.

'Sherry, right?' he said.

They sat in the saloon bar. Wiggins stared at his beer. 'I'm sorry I said you'd get on your back for anyone. That was out of order.'

She waved it away.

'What you gonna do?' he said.

'They didn't tell you?' She glanced behind her, as if a minder stood at the door. 'Captain Kell got me a job with your Mister C.'

'Doing what?' Wiggins said, surprised.

She looked at him as if he was a fool. 'Brussels, I think, first.

I speak French and German, and the Belgians have a particular taste for the exotic.'

Wiggins shook his head. 'I don't get it.'

She held his gaze questioning, then she took a sip of her drink, set the glass down and spoke very slowly. 'C wants me to set up an Embassy of my own, run along the same lines, do Delphy's job, keep the girls sweet. Not on my back at least. We're to collect military and diplomatic secrets.'

'Fuck sake,' Wiggins said, disgusted. 'You can't do that.'

'What else am I meant to do?'

He shook his head. 'The others?'

'Boy's coming with me, a couple of the girls.'

'But we freed you,' he said at last.

'Freed us to do what? We're whores. If we had choices, you think any of us would be?' She set down her glass in exasperation.

Wiggins looked away, embarrassed, ashamed again. 'I thought . . .' he stuttered.

She went on more softly. 'Look, mister, you're not interested in me. You're a little bit interested in what I look like, sure, but your heart's elsewhere. What's she called, by the way?'

'Bela,' Wiggins muttered.

'Where is she?'

'I don't know. New York, maybe.'

Martha pulled at her hands gently. 'Even if you do like how I look, I won't look like this for much longer. And then where would we be? I've got to think of the future, for me and Boy.'

Wiggins swilled the beer in his glass but did not drink. He could barely breathe.

'It's what there is for people like us, Wiggins. We get used, and we try to make the best of it. I thought you'd be pleased. At least now I'm on your side.'

'My side?' Wiggins said, appalled.

'You know, King and country.'

Across town, at a corner table in the first-floor tearoom of Heal's furniture store on Tottenham Court Road, another watcher waited.

Constance sipped her third cup of tea and gazed out of the window, as she had done for a number of days and hours that week. The building she looked at stood across the road at an angle. Picked out in large, sparkly letters above the frontage, one word: FAIRYLAND. It was an amusement arcade, with a wide, open doorway and various carnival-style games, like a miniature fairground in the middle of London. Constance had been in a number of times since she'd first discovered it, and the only way in or out was through this front door.

The arcade's chief attraction was its firing range, which provided shooting practice for any member of the public at the back of the building. Constance had never been in Fairyland without hearing the continual *pop pop pop* of rifle fire.

She put her cup down and checked her watch in irritation. She thought of the poor girl she'd rescued from Fulham, with Wiggins's young friend Jax. A tiny baby, a drug addict and a man who'd bought her. Jax had told her something of Millie's life before the brothel, the poverty, the mother drunk, and for a moment Constance understood – or understood, at least, that living in hiding, in squalor even, with a man who could not marry her was still better than that.

Millie had stayed the night, but soon after, using Constance's charitable contacts, they'd found her space in a home for fallen women. Although how she would get up, Constance did not know.

The tea tasted suddenly bitter in her mouth. There was only so much lapsang souchong she could endure.

Then she saw them. Swaddled in thick overcoats and fur hats, it was Dinah's red hair that gave them away: Dinah and Nobbs, entering the arcade.

By the time Constance got to them, Nobbs was already in position on the range, firing wildly at a wax dummy. Dinah waited her turn.

Constance tapped her on the shoulder. She jumped round, startled. 'Oh, hello,' she said.

Pop! Pop! Pop!

'Can we talk somewhere?' Constance cried, her hands over her ears against the noise.

Dinah shook her head slightly. 'It's my turn in a mo.'

'Where have you been? I've been trying to find you.'

Dinah shook her head again, almost annoyed.

'This isn't the way,' Constance went on.

'What?'

'You saw at Parliament how ugly violence is – don't give in to it. That's *their* way.'

Dinah looked over at Nobbs, firing at the target. 'Abernathy hasn't been the same since that day. She's had a headache for weeks. It's not fair.' A tear began to form in her eye.

Constance searched her face. *Pop! Pop! Pop!* 'Are you lovers?' she asked, suddenly.

Dinah stared at her but did not reply. She did not need to.

'Look, you must do something else, not this.' Constance gestured at the guns and the range. 'You're young. Don't do anything stupid.'

'Oh bother you, Constance. You've had your fun with us dippy girls. Now it's all got too serious, you can leave us alone. You've seen how we live, you've had your holiday.'

'No, no, not that,' Constance said loudly, above the gunfire.

'We are real people. We are adults too.'

Nobbs stepped back from the range, and glared at Constance. She leaned over towards Dinah without a word.

'Goodbye,' Dinah said and took the gun.

Constance left then. Dinah put the rifle to her shoulder and pinged the target repeatedly, dead centre every time.

'Why so glum?' Kell asked. 'You look as if you found a penny and lost a pound, as Granny would say.'

He sat at his desk, smiling, while Wiggins paced to and fro in the office, a face like thunder. He'd marched straight up there after his meeting in the pub with Martha, steaming inside.

Kell, on the other hand, couldn't contain his good mood. 'We've got everything we ever wanted,' he went on, unperturbed. 'The future of the Service is guaranteed, we are to be expanded even. Your friend Peter the Painter is dead. Our Foreign Office leak is discovered. How did you cotton on to Moseby-Brown in the end, by the way?'

Wiggins stopped pacing. 'Lover boy? He offered to be your spy, that was the clincher. Never trust a man who's willing to sneak on his mates, *for nothing*. He reckoned it would be the perfect cover. And it was.'

'Yes, I see that.'

'And I found his hankie at the music hall. When you let on his name, I took a look-see down Fulham way.'

'That poor girl, with child too.' Kell shook his head sadly.

'She sorted now?'

Kell nodded absently.

'What about him?'

'Moseby-Brown? Oh, he'll never work in the Foreign Office again. I think the plan is to send him to somewhere in Africa, in the Colonial Service.'

'He ain't going in stir?'

Kell shook his head. 'If we put him in prison, we'd have to make it public and the Foreign Office simply can't countenance such a disgrace.'

Typical, Wiggins thought, as he scuffed at the floor with his feet. Typical, but not surprising: the same thing had happened last year. They'd never nail a toff unless they really, really had to.

'But none of this explains why you're so angry.'

Wiggins sat down. 'I just spoke to Martha.'

'Ah.'

'Was you gonna tell me?'

Kell pulled out a cigarette from the case in front of him. 'You must admit, it's a good idea for intelligence-gathering. Van Bork was definitely on to something there. But it's nothing to do with us now. That is C's department.'

Wiggins scowled. 'It ain't right. You's pimping out girls.' He leaned forward in his seat, heat rising to his face. It wasn't just the three pints of Watneys talking. He thought of those Embassy girls and where they'd come from; he thought of the ragged dockers being beaten up by the police; he thought of Millie's sister, little Els, piss-poor and no one lifting a finger to help; he thought of Sal, hard at work her whole life long, and still nothing more than a shilling to show for it. He even thought of himself, his younger self, scraping a living from the age of seven on the streets, trawling Paddington Station for scraps, watching as the rich kids boarded trains for Eton with more luggage, more stuff, at *fourteen* than he'd own in his entire life.

'What we doing here?' he said. 'Nothing's bloody changed. Them girls is still whores, Millie's still on the dope, Moseby-Bollock's not inside. It don't make a blind bit of difference.'

'That's what we want!' Kell cried, triumphant. 'That's our job. To protect what we have, to conserve, to secure. That's what security means.'

They stared at each other across the desk. Finally, Wiggins shook his head. 'I need to be somewhere else. This ain't for me no more.'

'Don't be so dramatic. Next you'll be telling me you're skipping town on this new unsinkable ship. Maybe I should buy you a packet.' His laughter died on his lips. 'You're serious?'

Wiggins nodded.

'Think it through. It's been very difficult lately. Take some time.'

'I think pretty quick.'

'But I need you,' Kell said. 'Van Bork is still at large. And the Empire needs you.'

'The Empire, eh?' Wiggins scraped back his chair and stood up. He'd had enough talk of the Empire in the army; he'd fought for the bloody Empire against a ragtag army of Afrikaner farmers, and he hadn't much liked it then.

He felt a sudden pang of disappointment. It surprised him, and it had nothing to do with any plan to set up a whorehouse. Peter being in the pay of Special Branch, he realised with a lurch.

If it hadn't been for that, he could have railed at Kell, at the Empire, at the state; he could have used all those highfalutin revolutionary terms, and maybe even meant them a little. But Peter was bent, just like Bela before him, as bent as the Empire itself.

Were Peter and Tommy right all along about him? he suddenly thought bitterly. Was he nothing more than a rich man's hunting dog: running around picking up sticks, first for Sherlock Holmes, then the army and now Captain Vernon Kell and the bloody government itself?

But no, even if there was some truth in that, he was damned if he was going to take anything from those murdering bastards. Even if they were right, they were wrong. They'd always be wrong.

He would listen to Sal. She was right, just as Martha was. He needed to find Bela, or forget about her. One or the other.

Kell strode around the desk towards him. He realised he'd made a mistake mentioning the Empire. 'Look, I'll lend you the money for a passage, if that's what you really want. On condition you come back if we're in real trouble.'

'You mean war?'

'I'll buy you a passage on this Eighth Wonder of the World. In return, you cable me where to reach you, so I can recall you if necessary.'

Wiggins stood by the door and shook his head. 'I'm done with having debts.' He shot his hand out suddenly, surprising Kell.

They shook hands for the first time, and probably the last.

Wiggins closed the office door behind him, even got halfway across the hall. Then he remembered how much money he had in his pocket; he thought about what he might have to do to earn a passage to New York.

He poked his head back into the office. 'What did you say that wonder ship was called?'

Kell beamed at him. 'The *Titanic*.'

HISTORICAL NOTES

Some of the events and many of the characters depicted in the novel have a basis in historical fact. In particular, the mission of Bernard Trench and Vivien Brandon to Germany, the events outside Parliament at the suffragette demonstration known as Black Friday, and the Siege of Sidney Street.

Trench and Brandon

Royal Marines Captain Bernard Trench and Lieutenant Vivian Brandon undertook a spying mission to northern Germany in the summer of 1910, sponsored to the tune of £10 by Mansfield Cumming. The circumstances of their capture in Borkum are related in the novel accurately. The use of flash photography at night did indeed prove their downfall. They were tried and convicted later that year, and spent three years in prison. There is no mention in official records of anyone else in attendance, be it Cumming, Kell or Wiggins. This is unsurprising, however, as the whole episode was a distinct embarrassment to the British Government in general and the intelligence community in particular.

Black Friday

On 18 November 1910, more than 300 suffragettes and suffragists gathered outside Parliament to constitute their own 'parliament', in protest at the decision to ditch the Conciliation Bill granting limited suffrage to women. Eyewitness accounts, as well as photographic evidence, attest to the incredibly rough and violent handling of the protestors by the police. The subsequent police report whitewashes this brutality, as does the report in *The Times* the following day. The authorities also did everything they could to suppress the photograph of Ada Wright that appeared in the *Daily Mirror*. The picture shows her slumped on the pavement, with two policemen looming over her, and rather gives the lie to any notion that the police behaved proportionally.

The Siege of Sidney Street

Contemporary accounts of the events at Sidney Street on the evening of the 2nd and the day of the 3rd of January 1911 are very similar to the account in the novel. Superintendent Mulvaney organised the preparations for the siege, much as described, and the siege turned into a gruesome gunfight that ended in the fire. Huge crowds, Winston Churchill among them, came to watch. The bodies of Fritz Svaars and Joseph Sokolov were found in the wreckage of the house. There is no note in the official records as to the identity of the informant who placed Svaars and Sokolov at 100 Sidney Street. We now know this was Wiggins. Similarly, although the police expected to find Peter the Painter at the same address, his body was never found – indeed, Peter disappeared from any official accounts and was never heard of again. This is another mystery that has now been cleared up.

The Baker Street Irregulars

In his own accounts of Sherlock Holmes's work, Dr Watson briefly acknowledges the role of the Irregulars on three occasions. Young Wiggins is cited as the leader of the gang working on two cases – *A Study in Scarlet* and *The Sign of the Four* – while in a third case, Wiggins is mistakenly identified as 'Simpson'. Dr Watson's accounts are notoriously hazy on dates and names, however, and most historical sources are convinced that the Irregulars, and Wiggins in particular, played a far more substantial role in Holmes's work than Watson credits. This would be in keeping with the mores of the time, where it was rare for lower-class people – and street 'Arabs' or urchins in particular – to be given prominence. There is no mention of Tommy, Big T, in any of Dr Watson's accounts. It may also be that after the cases referenced above, Holmes himself wanted Wiggins's name taken out of any accounts so as to maintain the effectiveness of the child agents.

ACKNOWLEDGEMENTS

I must thank my editor, Nick Sayers, for patience, insight, and steak; my agent Jemima Hunt; everyone at Hodder, especially Eleni Lawrence and Cicely Aspinall. The beautiful cover was designed by Ben Summers, and the exceptional copy edit was again performed by Caroline Johnson. Any mistakes are most definitely mine.

Thanks too, to all the team at Quercus USA, especially Amelia Ayrelan Iuvino, Nathanial Marunas and Amanda Harkness.

Thanks to: Saul Dibb, Stephen Guise and Tom Lyle.

Thanks also to the staff of the British Library, where much of this book was researched. I drew on too many historical sources to name them all here, but I must mention the following: *The Defence of the Realm* by Christopher Andrews, *The Security Service 1908-1945* by John Curry, *MI6:The History of the Secret Intelligence Service 1909-1949* by Keith Jeffery, *The Quest for C* by Alan Judd, and especially *The Houndsditch Murders and the Siege of Sidney Street* by Donald Rumbelow.

Most of all, I want to thank my family: the wondrous R and E, and my partner Annalise Davis, for her sharp wit, innate wisdom and inspirational energy.